The Mother of All Problems

Nancy Peach is a writer of women's fiction, a mother of three, and an owner of various ridiculous-looking pets. She is also a practicing doctor working for the NHS and a national cancer charity, and has been writing (in a terribly British, embarrassed, secretive way) for as long as she can remember. Nancy's debut, *Love Life* was published in 2021.

the mother of all problems

NANCY PEACH

San Diego, California

Canelo US
An imprint of Printers Row Publishing Group
9717 Pacific Heights Blvd, San Diego, CA 92121
www.canelobooksus.com

This edition originally published in the United Kingdom in 2023 by Hera Books.

Published in partnership with Canelo.

Correspondence regarding the content of this book should be sent to Canelo US, Editorial Department, at the above address. Author inquiries should be sent to Canelo, Unit 9, 5th Floor, Cargo Works, 1–2 Hatfields, London SE1 9PG, United Kingdom, www.canelo.co.

Publisher: Peter Norton • Associate Publisher: Ana Parker
Art Director: Charles McStravick
Editorial Director: April Graham
Editor: Julie Chapa
Production Team: Beno Chan, Julie Greene

Library of Congress Control Number: 2023949697

ISBN: 978-1-6672-0733-9

Printed in India

28 27 26 25 24   1 2 3 4 5

For my mum.

Thank you – for everything.

Winter

Chapter One

Morning

I was in the middle of downward dog when my father called. Bendy Lydia hates it when somebody's mobile goes off in yoga class and, despite being contorted into a particularly improbable configuration, she managed to convey her displeasure through nostril flaring and deep exhalations alone. She is an immensely talented woman in this regard – if I ever tried to demonstrate how annoyed I was by snorting and sighing, I'd probably sound like a pantomime horse.

My phone had been switched to silent mode at the start of the lesson – as instructed, in no uncertain terms, by the bendy goddess herself – but, nonetheless, it was now rattling against my keys in a manner that suggested I had a large and active vibrator in my handbag. Given that this was a mixed yoga class of relative strangers and not an Ann Summers party, I went to great lengths to ensure they could see the offending article was, in fact, a simple iPhone, pointedly holding it aloft while hissing, 'Sorry, sorry, it's my phone,' in the loud whisper I usually save for pushing past people when arriving late at the cinema due to one, or all three, of my children having needed an

3

urgent toilet stop, snack, or tantrum during the opening credits.

Once outside, I realised that in my rush to leave the ambient warmth of the community centre I had forgotten to bring anything weatherproof with me. As a result, the only barrier between me and the arctic wind was a thin layer of 'activewear' – a Lycra-polyester mix not known for its insulating properties. Undeterred, I pressed my phone to my ear in the hope that the radiant heatwaves might prevent frostbite rather than giving me actual face cancer.

'Penelope? It's Dad,' my father announced unnecessarily, given that his name and face were showing up on my screen. 'Sorry to be a bother. Bit of a problem. Taken a little tumble and seems I may have cracked the old hip bone. No need to worry. Just, the small issue of your mother. What to do and such like.' He paused.

'Shit, Dad! Are you OK?' I forgot that my father can't abide sweary women. But luckily, he had other things on his mind.

'Yes, yes.' His voice was strained. 'As I say, all fine, little trip down the stairs. Fell over a pair of your mother's drawers on the way to the bog. Never mind about me. Thing is, I'm in the QEH at the moment and, well… Your mother… She's a bit confused by it all. You know…'

I gave a long exhalation that Bendy Lydia would have been proud of and there was a pause while we both processed the implications of his last comments. It was clear that, broken hip or not, Mum's dementia made this more of an emergency scenario than would otherwise be the case. Dad's voice was as cheerful and efficient as always, but even he was having trouble disguising the edge of panic. I was as reassuring as it is possible to be while freezing your arse off and contemplating, at best, a complete overhaul of my day's meticulously planned timetable. I told him I would be there as soon as possible and then tiptoed back into the hall, blue and mottled as a large wedge of Stilton, to make my excuses to Lydia. She managed to be simultaneously zen and fuming, especially when I dropped my water bottle and it rolled across the floor to nestle against Marjorie's buttocks, just as she went into happy baby pose. It is hard to discreetly remove an item from between the splayed legs of a retired geography teacher, but I think I managed not to disrupt her chakras too much.

I then retrieved the remainder of my belongings as follows:

- Water bottle. Comedy slogan on the side confusing 'gin' with 'gym' or some other hilarious wordplay dreamed up by marketing executives to appeal to a generation of Prosecco Mummies. (So patronising, yet so effective.)
- Coat. (Weatherproof but still passably fashionable, novelty poodle print, seemed a good idea at the time of purchase.)
- Keys to the house and temperamental family wagon.
- Purse. (Crammed full of receipts, broken zip, empty of change save for an old pound coin – now obsolete.)
- Yoga mat. (Chewed extensively by dog and very unwieldy when held under armpit with coat and all the above.)
- Foam block. (Seems to serve no purpose but is brought religiously to each yoga session in the vain

hope it may one day reveal the mysteries of the East
when I press my forehead into it.)

Once everything was securely stashed about my person, I
vacated the building calmly and efficiently – if not quietly.
Double fire doors tend to slam loudly and my phone, now
no longer on silent vibrating sex-toy mode, was ringing
again with *The Muppets* theme tune that had been so
amusing when the children downloaded it, but was less
entertaining now that I wanted to slip away unnoticed.

I would love to be one of those braying women who
feel no shame in answering their phones loudly, barking
instructions to Tamara or Hermione to '*Tell the delivery
driver to take the ruddy thing straight back to the supplier*' or
arranging a casual supper at the '*Gorgeous little place on the
High Street*'. But sadly, I am not. I do not stride unapolo-
getically out of a room, confident that my absence will be
keenly felt. I am more of an embarrassed scuttler than a
strider, aware that the remaining women will have barely
noticed me, other than to regard my uncharacteristically
noisy departure as a minor inconvenience – but there we
are.

My immediate concern on the drive down was to sort
out childcare, so I called Zahara and explained about Dad's
accident.

'Do you want me to collect Maisie?' she said, like the
wonderful friend she is. 'I'd been thinking of taking Darcy
to Swift Farm, but it'll be easy to take both of them.'

'Really? Oh, Zahara, that would be great, thanks so
much. Are you sure?'

'No problem. And don't worry, we'll stay away from
the llamas. After last time…'

'Oh, yes, of course. Although, that wasn't really
Maisie's fault.'

There was a brief pause and I did wonder if the connection had failed, but Zahara's voice came through again. 'Right, so are you OK to let preschool know I'm picking up? And then I'll just keep hold of her until you're back.'

'Yes, absolutely. I'll be as quick as I can. Five at the latest?'

'I haven't got any of those special fish fingers she likes, would she have sausages?'

Oh, Christ. I was too embarrassed to say that there are only certain types of sausage she'll tolerate. 'Umm, actually, look, don't worry about food, I'll be back in time for tea, so…'

'No, I'll tell you what, we'll eat at the farm. That's easy.'

'Great. She likes the pizza there. Only the cheese one though. And she might lose her mind if they put any salad garnish on. She'll have a slice of tomato, if they put it on a separate plate. But not touching the pizza.'

'Yep. Don't worry. I remember.'

'Thanks so much, Zahara. You're a legend. I know she's not the easiest and after last time, with the hair straighteners and the superglue and everything… I'd totally understand if you said no…'

'It's not a problem, really. Are you sorted for the others?'

'I'm just going to try Caz now, see if she can collect Tom from football when she picks up Alex. Grace'll be fine on her own. In fact, an empty house is probably preferable to one with me in it. I'll text to remind her to let the dog out, otherwise she'll probably just lie there morosely while Colin pisses in the laundry basket again.'

I rang off feeling guilty, but had to remind myself that I don't often call in favours from friends. In fact, as one of the only stay-at-home mums in my little group, and especially one with a reputation for being unable to say no, it's much more common for me to be called upon to assist with looking after other people's offspring. This is a role the other mums seem to assume I will automatically embrace – I obviously have little else to keep myself occupied. Still, Maisie is a law unto herself and the most challenging of all my children, which is saying something.

The arrangements regarding Tom were significantly easier to organise, what with him being ten and completely unfazed about who collects him, where he's going, or when he'll be back. Like the dog, as long as he's fed and exercised, he's happy. So, once I'd ensured that Caz could pick him up, I was finally able to call my husband, Sam, who was, predictably, very busy.

'I'm in a meeting, Penny. Can't really talk.'

'OK. Sorry. It's just that Dad's broken his hip and…'

'Christ! Sorry, Brian, can I just duck out for a moment? Family crisis.'

There was a pause as Sam left the boardroom. 'God, Penny, is he all right?'

'I don't know. I'm driving down to the hospital now, so I'll have a better idea once I see him. I've sorted out the kids, but I wondered if there was any chance you might be able to leave work early? I'm not sure I can get back in time for Grace's dance class.'

'Oh, right, yeah. Thing is, love, I've got meetings back-to-back until seven and then it's all dependent on whether I can get the earlier train. I'm sure it will be all right. Grace'll be fine.'

I pulled a face at the phone. Sam was still labouring under the impression that our eldest daughter was the sweet pre-teen of yesteryear rather than the surly hellcat who had replaced her.

8

'I'm not sure she'll be *fine* but, anyway. Just see what you can do.'

'Of course, yeah. I will. Sounds like you've got it all under control. Love to the Old Man... I'd better get back—'

'Sam,' I interrupted him. 'I might have to bring Mum home with me.' There was a pause. 'Sam? You still there?'

'Yeah, it's fine. Don't worry, love. We'll manage. Oh, does this mean you won't be able to do ribs for dinner?'

-

I turned the car radio up to full volume for the remainder of the journey and sang along to every song that came on. This is my preferred method of managing a stressful situation, although it does draw some curious glances when I pull up at traffic lights. Parking at the hospital was a bloody nightmare. After twenty minutes of desperately circling the multi-storey, I ended up choosing the spot that everyone with a normal-sized car was avoiding because it was a space designed for a motorbike. Reversing under pressure while the sensors of a gargantuan Renault Espace beep at you in increasingly shrill and frantic tones is not my idea of a good time. If my car could have spoken it would have been bellowing in my ear that the space I was entering was *too bloody small, you foolish woman* (I am certain my car's voice would be that of a patrician headmaster of a large public school).

Once my ears had stopped bleeding, I managed to bruise the majority of my internal organs exiting the vehicle in the manner of toothpaste extruded through a two-inch gap between door and concrete wall. I also ripped my leggings thus helpfully exposing a significant portion of upper thigh. Hobbling to the main entrance on what felt like a dislocated knee, while vaguely prodding my abdomen to check I'd not ruptured my spleen, I was redirected to the A&E department via an extremely draughty corridor that smelled like a chemical toilet. Finally, I arrived – broken, frozen and disproportionately harassed – at what I assumed was the correct place.

The waiting room was relatively quiet, other than a background chorus of coughs and sneezes from an assortment of mucousy-looking individuals and a teenager rifling through a bin. Thankfully the meth-heads, violent psychopaths and plague victims of my imaginings had not yet materialised and a friendly nurse called Charlie helped me locate my father through a scientific process of shouting his name loudly across the unit until he responded.

Dad was sitting up in bed looking relatively chipper, all things considered. Beside him, Mum sat reading a copy of *Woman and Home* upside down, clutching a polystyrene cup of milky tea. I leaned in to give her a kiss and turned the magazine the right way up.

'Hello, Mum. Nice trousers,' I said, pointing to the mail-order monstrosities being advertised on the now correctly positioned page. She nodded vaguely, pushing her cup towards me in an incongruous 'Cheers!' gesture.

'Dad,' I said. 'How *are* you? Are you in any pain?'

'Nope,' he replied cheerily. 'Morphine. Marvellous stuff. Can see what all those druggies are banging on about now. Might take up a heroin habit once I'm out of this little spot of bother.'

'An excellent plan. We'll ask them to give you the contact details of a good local dealer when you're discharged shall we?'

'You may joke, Penelope, but Larry from the golf club swears by the wacky baccy he gets from young Sidney Finnigan. It's worked wonders for his arthritis.'

I was dying to hear exactly where Sid Finnigan conducted his deals with this illustrious branch of the golf club membership – presumably not the gentleman's bar overlooking the eighteenth hole. Perhaps instead Larry was sneaking down to the Hope and Anchor on a regular basis and chillin' with his bitches, blending in unobtrusively in his Pringle jumper. The mind boggled. However, intriguing though this conversation was, I was starting to suspect that my father was a little disinhibited by the medication so chose not to probe any further. Instead, I announced my decision to have Mum come to stay with us. I mean, there really was no other option. She's my mum. She looked after me. Therefore, I am fully intending to look after her.

For a few days.

In what I hope will be a fairly limited capacity.

Because being noble and selfless sounds good, but in practice it's a bloody nightmare.

–

For a start, getting Mum into the car was clearly going to be nigh-on impossible. The space I had parked in was so narrow that I had ripped my leisurewear and likely my innards whilst exiting the vehicle myself, and, while I'm no Bendy Lydia, my mother is even less flexible than me. Faced with the prospect of leading her up three flights of stairs and shoehorning her through a gap barely big enough for an emaciated child, I did what any sensible, self-respecting daughter of a woman with dementia would do. I left her completely alone, standing by the pay-station, while I legged it as fast as my pelvic floor would allow up three levels of industrial concrete and vaulted into the driver's seat via the passenger door.

However, as anybody who can pick up on the subtlest of clues could have told you, Mum was NOT WHERE I HAD LEFT HER when I pulled up two minutes later.

I was, I'll admit, marginally frantic at this point. I screeched to a dramatic, car-chase stop but then remembered myself and sensibly put on my hazard lights, pulled into the side and waved on the vehicles queuing behind me. This was a mistake because there was absolutely no room for those cars to get past and my waving them generously on seemed only to aggravate the situation. I exited the Renault and avoided making eye contact with the driver immediately behind me, who looked as though he may be about to have an aneurysm at my incompetence.

'You're supposed to pay before you get in the car!' someone shouted helpfully as I scanned the horizon of car roofs for my mother's head, feeling the sensation of escalating panic tighten my throat. I couldn't see her anywhere. There was now a queue of approximately twelve vehicles behind me and two of them started beeping furiously. Which obviously improved things no end.

'Excuse me, miss. Are you looking for this young woman?' The voice came from behind me and I turned to see a heavily tattooed man with his arm around my smiling mother. For a moment I thought she was being mugged, but quickly realised that a criminal would be unlikely to appeal for witnesses. He also appeared to be in some kind of tabard-based uniform – always reassuring. Relief washed over me like a cliché.

'Yes. Oh, my God, thank you. I mean, thank you so bloody much!' I was cool and collected.

'No problem. We were just chatting about the pigeons, weren't we, Mary?' The tattooed saviour reached out a hand and introduced himself. 'Ben. I'm one of the physios.'

'Penny,' I said. 'I'm one of the… visitors.' I held his hand for slightly too long, such was the enormity of my gratitude. It became awkward after about two minutes, and I dropped his hand and turned to my mother.

'Mum,' I tried not to sound exasperated. 'I said to wait, I was only gone a moment…'

'I've been here for hours, Penelope.' Mum's arms were crossed in front of her chest. 'Goodness knows where your father's got to. If it hadn't been for this lovely gentleman here, well, I don't know what I'd have done. You be sure to tip him handsomely.' She started to make her way towards the exit until I grabbed her and steered her towards the car instead.

'He's not, like, a *doorman*, Mum. Christ.' I mouthed a 'sorry' to Ben over her shoulder and he shrugged, amused. 'No problem. Safe journey.'

Chapter Two

Friday 10 January

Evening

Zahara had a pained expression on her face when I arrived at hers an hour later and Maisie's dulcet tones could be heard wailing in the background. My heart sank. I followed Zahara through into the kitchen and was confronted with a scene of relative devastation. Had it been my house, I would have thought little of the hummus smeared on the walls, the dry pasta scattered across the polished parquet floor, or the jug of mud, leaves and Ribena suggesting one of Maisie's 'potions'. But this was not my house. This was Zahara's house. And Zahara's house was pristine. Always pristine. Her children appeared to have no desire to trash their surroundings and on the rare occasion that a mess was made, her husband Hugh was on hand to help her tidy up. Yes, you heard me right. Her *husband* was one of those extraordinary creatures who would take one look at this scene of carnage and say to Zahara, 'Off you pop, darling, into the sitting room. Me and the kids will clean this up in no time. It'll be fun, won't it, gang? And I'll bring you a glass of wine through in a moment.' I have witnessed it. I had to scrape my jaw up off the carpet, yes, but I saw it with my own eyes. Anyway.

'I'm so sorry.' There was no need to explain what I was sorry for. The evidence was clear; this was the work of *my* four-year-old, not hers, who was currently sat cowering under the kitchen table.

'Nooooo problem!' Zahara's voice was over-bright, bordering on shrill. 'Maisie! Mummy's here.'

Maisie emerged from a cupboard with a face like thunder and threw a handful of rigatoni at me.

'Did you go to the farm?' I crouched to pick up the pasta. Maisie nodded, a surly expression just visible through the smudged poster paint on her cheeks and forehead. I fished a wet wipe out of my bag and rubbed her face a little harder than required before making a frankly ineffectual attempt to clear some of the hummus from the kitchen floor.

Zahara stopped me. 'Really, Penny. There's no need. I was just about to give the place a spring clean anyway. How was your dad?'

I abandoned the futile wafting. 'Not so good. It's definitely a fracture. He's being operated on tomorrow, hopefully. Mum's in the car.'

'She going to be staying with you for a while?'

'Ye-es. Just for a few days. It's obviously great to have her but…' I hesitated.

'…it's not going to be easy.' Zahara finished for me.

'No. She's quite confused about what's going on and we're going to need to pop back down to visit Dad tomorrow. The kids have still got all their usual weekend things that need sorting out, *like, now, at this very moment, Mummy!* and Sam's working late tonight… You know how it is.'

'I do, but... give yourself a bit of a break, yeah?' She squeezed my shoulder. 'You don't need to be superwoman.'

'Says superwoman.'

She snorted. 'Hardly. Anyway, I hope everything works out OK. Let me know if there's anything I can do.'

We moved towards the door, Zahara gathering Maisie's belongings into a carrier bag. 'Maisie, do you want your collage in here or would you like to show it to Granny?'

Maisie made an indeterminate noise. She had a doll clutched under her arm that looked suspiciously like Darcy's Baby Annabell.

'Maisie, that's not your dolly, is it?' My voice was weary. I just wanted to get home. 'Give it back to Darcy, and what do you say to Zahara for having you over today, and taking you to the farm?'

She looked mutinous and squeezed the doll tighter. I tried again to do the capable parent routine, the one that requires phenomenal amounts of self-discipline when you feel like having a tantrum yourself. 'Maisie. I'm going to count to five and I want you to have given Darcy her dolly back. OK?'

No response.

'One... Two... Three... Otherwise there will be no *Peppa Pig*. Four... Five...'

The number hung in the air and, of course, Maisie held fast to Baby bloody Annabell.

'Maybe she can just take her for tonight?' Zahara was studiously ignoring the crumpling face of her own daughter, who was evidently less sanguine about the prospect of Baby Annabell's abduction.

'No. Honestly, Zahara, it's Darcy's doll. It wouldn't be fair. Maisie, if you don't give it back there will be no *Peppa*

16

all weekend.' I was really trying not to spit with venom as I hissed out those words. *Peppa* was my trump card, but now I had played her.

Maisie looked down at the doll and decided the trade was worth it. I spotted her expression just before she had a chance to verbalise this and made a lunge for Baby Annabell. But she had the measure of me, as she often does, and ran back to the cupboard, shrieking. I felt that familiar sense of despair; the one when you're sure everyone is looking at you, thinking, *She's just given up, that mother. She can't handle those kids / that child / her own miserable life.* It doesn't seem to matter so much if your children behave like utter bastards when there's no audience, but add one capable mummy and her impeccably behaved daughter, seat them in a previously immaculate kitchen that has recently been redecorated in the newest Farrow & Ball shade of Moroccan Hummus by your own child's fair hand, and launch into a wrestling match over a plastic doll who can *cry real tears*, and you have the ingredients for an overwhelming sense of judgement and failure. Even when the impeccable mummy in question is a lovely friend. Even when she has just done you a *huge favour* – in fact, especially when she has done you a *huge favour* – the guilt layers up nicely on top of the general sense of being a crap human being. It really is the cherry on the cake.

I just didn't have the energy for a fight and my daughter knew it. Zahara, too, seemed to sense that I was now incapable of basic parenting, if I ever had been in the first place.

'Just take the doll today,' she said gently. 'Bring it back tomorrow maybe? Bye Maisie, it's been lovely having you.' She nudged us towards the door.

'I'm so sorry,' I said, slightly broken. 'I think she's just tired. Maybe unsettled by not having me collect her?' I was obviously aware this was complete bollocks. Maisie would behave in this fashion if she had slept like the living dead and been escorted from preschool strapped to my maternal bosom. I know, because she has done exactly that in the past.

'I'm sure you're right,' Zahara said with a sympathetic smile. 'It was no bother having her, honestly.'

I bleated a weak expression of gratitude, took hold of Maisie's hand and pulled her towards the car.

'I am *so* disappointed in you, Maisie,' I said, trying to use my stern voice which, as we have already established, is completely ineffectual. 'We are taking that dolly back first thing tomorrow and you are going to say sorry for behaving like that, do you hear me? Mummy is very, very cross. Poor Darcy.'

Maisie looked down at Baby Annabell as my words drifted uselessly over her head and into the January evening. 'Hello Granny,' she said, clambering into the car. She reached into the front and offered her grandmother a dollop of glitter Play-Doh by way of a gift. Mum treated it with the reverence it deserved.

'Very twinkly,' she said, peering at it closely. 'Like a firework.'

'Zactly, Granny.' Maisie folded her arms, fully vindicated.

Excellent.

–

Collecting Tom from Caz's house was less fraught, mainly because I promised he could continue his Xbox *Fortnite* battle with Alex once he got home, the advantages of remote interaction being that they no longer need to be in the same room to enjoy shooting the crap out of each other. I realised, as I squeezed the car past the wheelie bins on our narrow drive, that I'd left his football kit behind, but that was the least of my problems.

'Here we are then, Mum,' I said, letting myself in through the front door using the patented method of complex alternating half-turns of the rusty key and a firm kick to the base where the wood is warped. Our house is old. I like it that way – indeed, we paid what seemed like an eye-watering sum to have 'character features' when we first bought it in those heady days of only having a cute pre-schooler and baby to worry about. 'Look at the gorgeous beams!' we exclaimed as we were shown around by the estate agent, Tom gurgling adorably on my shoulder, Grace holding hands with Daddy and pointing at the crooked staircase, the hidden cupboards, the wonky floors. 'Brammly Edge,' she'd said, referring to her favourite story where tiny mice live in cosy, if architecturally improbable, hedgerow nests. Sam and I were sold. I'd always wanted to live in a *Brambly Hedge* house.

However, nine years on and an extra child in the mix had taken the shine off these period features, some of them quite literally. The wonky staircase was not easy to navigate balancing a loaded basket of washing on one hip and an equally loaded toddler on the other. The plumbing and electrics were temperamental to say the least and at any given moment the toilet would block, a bathroom tap would come off in your hand, or the lights would go out and you'd be plunged into darkness. The Wi-Fi seemed incapable of travelling reliably through the corridor or penetrating the stone walls and there was a perpetual issue with damp, not helped by the mountains of washing draped over every available surface.

If one had the time to keep it in mint condition – repairing the crumbling plaster, attending to the frankly alarming cobwebs and sweeping up the general detritus created by a family of five and a boisterous dog – it would be a beautiful home, the kind of thing estate agents would describe as 'charming', 'quaint', and 'chocolate box'. Unfortunately, I *didn't* have the time, and as a result the only chocolate box our house could be compared to was the kind a neighbour might have picked up on holiday with their last remaining Euros to thank you for feeding their goldfish, the one you kept in the back of the cupboard 'for emergencies' until you found it fourteen years later, the cardboard carton soft and mouldering, the original cover design faded beyond all recognition and the chocolates completely inedible. This house was just one more thing that I wasn't really 'on top of'. I tried not to take it personally, and most days, I loved the comfy squalor of it all, but sometimes, when friends came around or when Sam could barely see out of the smeary, warped window-panes, or Tom sneezed twelve times in a row from the dust, or indeed when I tripped over yet another pair of sodding shoes someone had left in the corridor, it felt like another rebuke.

Having ushered Mum, Tom, Maisie and Baby bloody Annabell inside, I found Grace sulking in a darkened corner of the kitchen. I was absolutely determined not to rise to it and brought forth the cheery voice I'd been diligently manufacturing all day.

'Hello, darling. Granny's come to stay. Isn't that nice?'

'I. Missed. Dance. Class.' The monosyllables were barely audible.

'Sorry, darling, what was that? I can't hear if you're mumbling, particularly when the dog's barking. Have you let him out by the way? Clearly not, judging by that puddle on the floor. I take it that *is* urine? Excellent.'

'I missed dance practice. That's all.' Grace stomped off upstairs and my attention was caught by the sight of my mother frozen with panic while Colin raced in small circles in front of her, keen to show off his prowess in that particular exercise.

'Mum,' I said, pulling out one of the kitchen chairs. 'Come here, let's get you sat down. I'll do us some burgers. Tom, can you go and run yourself a bath? Get some of that mud off. And let Colin out…'

My voice disappeared into the freezer as I shovelled through the available food options. 'Or… perhaps a combination of burgers and…' I turned an unrecognisable box over in my hand '…and vegetable escalopes?'

'I am *not* eating those.' Tom's voice was withering. He started making retching noises as he ran upstairs, until Grace threw a heavy-sounding object at him and shouted, 'Shut up, you disgusting individual. You are *SO GROSS*.'

–

Later, after Maisie had face-planted into her Angel Delight with exhaustion and I had seriously contemplated following suit, I managed to get both the youngest kids into bed. Luckily Maisie's appalling behaviour at Zahara's seemed to have tired her out – I mean this in a good 'tired' way, in that she went to bed with little complaint. Note that this is not the same as when people say, 'Oh, she's

21

a little over-tired isn't she?' and they actually mean 'She's completely fucking wired. You haven't got a hope in hell of getting her to sleep for another forty years.'

Grace had materialised briefly to complain about dinner and push a portion of vegetable escalope around her plate while muttering about how people could 'still be vegetarian and not like every single vegetable'. I maintained a dignified air, squirted a liberal helping of tomato sauce over my own escalopes and tucked in, determined not to reveal that I too found them completely devoid of gastronomic merit.

'Mmmm. Delicious!' I forced myself to swallow, a beatific smile on my face. She rolled her eyes in response, turned down the offer of Angel Delight with a look that implied I'd suggested a bowl of offal, and retreated back to her room, presumably to stick pins into a voodoo doll, scowl at the wall or lie very still doing absolutely bollock all.

By the time Sam came home, I had regained a modicum of control. Mum and I were enjoying a glass of wine watching *Coronation Street* and I left her sitting comfortably in front of the fire, pondering the latest goings-on at the Rovers Return, while I went to have illuminating and stimulating conversation with my husband.

Sam dropped his bag onto the floor and thumped heavily into one of the kitchen chairs, resting his elbows down on the table as I triumphantly brandished a plate of dried-out burgers and oven chips.

'Oh.' His face fell.

'Sorry. I wasn't sure what time you'd be back and I had to feed the kids. I just shoved everything I could find on a baking tray and...' I looked at the plate. 'Admittedly it's not the most appealing meal I've ever dished up but at least you got away without having the vegetable escalopes.'

'The what?'

'That was your son's reaction. And Grace's too, despite her vegetarianism being the only reason for having them in the house.'

'Ah, yes. The vegetarianism that precludes eating most vegetables.' He smiled.

'The very same.' I pulled up the chair opposite and poured him a glass of wine. 'That should help wash it down.' I got back up again. 'I'll get you the ketchup. How was your day?'

'Yeah, OK I s'pose. Brian's got an arse on about the Bradford contract. We're over budget…' He stopped mid-sentence to chew on a particularly tough bit of meat. 'How's your dad?'

I filled him in. 'He's hopefully being operated on tomorrow. He was still in Casualty when I left, on morphine, but you know what he's like.'

'Oh, I can imagine: "Lot of damn fuss about nothing. Buck up, Penelope, old girl." That sort of thing?'

'Exactly. He's not remotely worried about himself. It's Mum.'

Sam wiped the ketchup from his mouth with the back of his hand and lowered his voice. 'Yes. How's she coping with it all?'

'I'm not really sure,' I said. 'It's obviously all a bit unsettling but she seems better since we came home. Maybe it was the hospital that confused her. Anyway, I'll take her to see Dad tomorrow and pick up some of her stuff. Are you OK to keep an eye on the kids while I'm gone – I'll probably head off mid-morning?'

Sam paled. 'You don't want to take them with you to see Grandad? Might cheer him up?'

I eyed him sceptically. 'I don't think so, do you? I can't think of anything less likely to aid recovery. Anyway, it'll be nice for you to spend a bit of time with them.' I laughed. 'It *will*. They haven't seen you all week. Just don't let them have too much screen time and maybe see if you can get Grace to walk Colin, that would be a real help. Or you could all go for a nice dog walk together? OK, maybe not.' I registered his expression. 'You'll be fine.'

'Hmmm.' He picked up a piece of bread and butter, wiping it around his plate. 'Anything for pud?'

'Umm. There's the rest of that sticky ginger cake in the tin. Yes? I'll just heat up some of the custard to go with it and then, d'you mind if I head off to bed, once I've got Mum sorted? I'm really knackered.'

Sam looked wounded. 'I've only just got back. I thought maybe we could catch up on *Succession*.'

I leaned in and kissed him on the forehead. 'Sounds like a delight that will have to wait. It's been a bit like *Succession* here at points this evening anyway.'

'What, in terms of feuding siblings, or coke-fuelled orgies and million-dollar deals?'

'Sadly, only the former.'

'Maisie?'

I nodded. 'She's just so bloody *exhausting*.'

'Really looking forward to having them all day tomorrow…'

I patted him fondly on the arm. 'Enjoy.'

–

Mum was still glued to the television, despite the fact that her favourite soap had been replaced by footage of minor

24

celebrities writhing in Perspex boxes along with a variety of hideous-looking insects.

'Gosh,' I said. 'The standard of living on *Coronation Street* has deteriorated a bit.'

She dragged her gaze from the television to my face. She looked vaguely troubled. 'Sorry, dear?'

'Nothing. Never mind. I'm heading up to bed. Shall I leave some things out for you or are you ready to come up too?'

'I'll just wait until your father's back, dear.'

I crossed to the sofa. 'Mum. Dad's in hospital, remember.'

There was a pause and her brows knitted together in consternation. Her expression reminded me of Maisie's face when I'd tried to explain that Colin couldn't actually speak to her, like on TV, and this wasn't because he was stupid (although he was) but because animals couldn't really talk to humans. It was a mind-blowing concept and Maisie remained unconvinced. I still often found her chatting happily to the dog as they cuddled up on the sofa, taking Colin's resigned expression and occasional farts as signs of communication on a higher level.

'He had a fall,' I tried again. 'He's broken his hip.'

Mum looked horrified. 'How did he do that, silly old fool?'

This went on for about an hour, but eventually I persuaded her upstairs and into the spare bed, which I had hastily divested of suitcases, sports kits and piles of laundry. I was still awake when Sam got to bed and I reassured him that Mum would only be with us for a couple of nights, but it was hard to ignore her presence when she kept wandering into our bedroom inexplicably looking for the Hoover. Past midnight this became an unacceptable scenario, so I got into bed with her – a situation conducive to neither sleep nor marital relations.

Chapter Three

Saturday, 11 January

I was woken by the sound of Mum's gentle snoring and a sudden realisation that Tom had an away match with an early kick-off and his football kit remained at Caz's house. I went downstairs to phone Caz but realised that seven o'clock on a Saturday morning is not an acceptable time to call anyone. Besides, the kit would be stinking and damp from yesterday. Sam, who was already up, took one look at my sleep-deprived face and scarecrow hair, thrust a large mug of tea under my nose and offered to help with the sourcing of football attire for our son while I contemplated what an excellent man I had married.

However, despite Sam's best intentions, he was distracted by something amusing on his phone and it ended up being my responsibility to cobble together a football kit of sorts while also blearily supervising the boys' bacon sandwiches. Tom tried not to look too devastated as I spread out the slim pickings on the kitchen chair, which included Grace's old gym shorts and last season's too-small shirt. In desperation, I suggested that Sam swing by Caz's house to collect the rotting kit from yesterday as a back-up option, should Tom find himself unable to face the shame of playing football in what was essentially a crop-top and hot pants.

Mum and Grace were still sleeping when Sam left the house accompanied by his son and heir, who looked like an angry lap-dancer, so I snuggled up under a blanket with Maisie watching *Peppa Pig* on my phone, the threats from yesterday to veto Peppa for the weekend forgotten (deliberately erased from my memory) in order to facilitate peace and order in the household. I'm always aware how important it is to be consistent with my children. Following through with sanctions helps them establish clear boundaries and it's lucky I'm so good at it.

Unfortunately, I managed to fall asleep and when I woke from my power nap I found that Maisie had commandeered the phone and was now watching an extremely unpleasant video called 'Peppa Goes to The Abattoir' on YouTube. Wrestling a device away from a determined four-year-old is not easy, but she was suitably mollified with the promise of Coco Pops and we came to a mutual agreement that two hours of screen time was probably sufficient for a Saturday morning. There was no noise from upstairs and I decided it was better to feed Maisie before waking either the confused mother or the furious teenage daughter.

Sadly, Maisie had decided between the sitting room and the kitchen that she no longer liked Coco Pops. In fact, nothing could be more contemptible and disgusting to her. She would only consent to Cheerios and, needless to say, there were no Cheerios in the house. I resorted to more Peppa while I went to investigate the sleepers. As I said, consistency is the key to good parenting.

Discontent and resentment were radiating from Grace's doorway so I bravely avoided it and ventured back into the spare room where I caught sight of myself in the mirror. My face was as saggy and puckered as an unhappy scrotum

– not a look I'd usually go for, but there you are. There was a familiar nappy-ish aroma coming from what was evidently a recently wet bed and Mum was perched on the edge of the mattress looking anxious; her expression almost exactly the same as Maisie's the time that she poked plasticine into the TV aerial socket and Sam went ballistic at her. My heart broke a tiny bit.

'Mum,' I said, trying to disguise my shock at this abrupt role reversal. 'Shall we get you up and have a nice shower?'

I managed to get her to the bathroom without drawing attention to the wet patch on the bed and planned to get myself dressed while she was occupied in the shower, but then remembered that Maisie was still downstairs, unattended and likely watching Peppa being eviscerated, set upon by hounds, or sent to war. My nerves were somewhat frayed as I shouted to Grace to go and keep an eye on her sister while I *Sorted Granny Out*. Mum was clearly hurt by the implication that she needed 'sorting out' in the manner of a broken appliance. Grace was outraged by the call to action and the suggestion that she should mobilise beyond her bedroom. I needed more tea and possibly a bottle of tequila while I contemplated this recent development in proceedings. Dealing with Mum's confusion and poor short-term memory was one thing; loss of control of bodily functions was entirely another.

An hour later and Mum was showered. This was not quite as straightforward as it sounds. Initially I had pointed her in the general direction of the bathroom with a towel and bottle of shampoo, assuming, perhaps unwisely, that she remembered how our shower operated. I stripped the spare room bed and left it to air by opening the windows to let in the bracing cold and sleet, which really added to the homely atmosphere. I then retrieved a pile of clean bedding from the airing cupboard and took the damp load down to the washing machine, which was already full of yesterday's wash that I'd forgotten to take out and now smelled like a neglected cellar. Great.

I went to check on both girls in the kitchen, hopeful that they were consuming an appropriate breakfast. Sadly not. Grace was sitting in the corner with a glazed expression as she swiped her thumb absently across her phone, with no clear evidence of having consumed or prepared food of any description. Maisie's cereal bowl contained Frosties, liberally topped with golden syrup and ice-cream sauce that she had located while supervised (completely ignored) by her elder sister. She also appeared to have redecorated the kitchen with the combined foodstuffs in a manner not dissimilar to the hummus Jackson Pollock painting at Zahara's yesterday. Perhaps my youngest child is, in fact, an artistic genius?

The floor was particularly crunchy and Colin was over-joyed, bounding about with several Frosties around his muzzle and stuck to his paws. My attempts to persuade Maisie that a bowl of granola or slice of wholemeal toast would be just as tasty as her current choice were met with a look of complete derision followed by a wobbling lip indicating a tantrum may be on the way. I capitulated massively and left her wolfing down spoonfuls of the aforementioned refined carbs faster than you could say 'poor parenting leads to tooth decay'.

Back upstairs, the bathroom door was ajar and I noticed Mum stood shivering in puddle of water, with a tiny hand towel gathered ineffectually around her middle.

'Mum?' I pushed the door open and touched her on the shoulder. She was freezing; tiny droplets gathered on her goose-pimples. The shower was still on and the cubicle was wide open. Water was pouring out onto the floor where two towels had exceeded maximum absorbency and rivulets were trickling into the corners of bathroom, which presumably meant that it would be a matter of moments before they filtered their way into our already dodgy electrics and started pouring out of the sockets downstairs (this had happened before, when Sam left the bath running after a rugby match – on Mother's Day – while I was pregnant. It was not his finest hour). I reached in to turn it off, having to step directly into the blast in order to do so. The water was absolutely stone cold and both of us were now sopping wet and borderline hypothermic.

It seemed that Mum had inadvertently set the shower dial to a glacial run-off level. With our dodgy plumbing, finding the right temperature is akin to cracking a safe so this could have happened to anyone, but God knows how long she stood under it – her skin was starting to turn blue and I realised we needed to warm her up as a matter of some urgency. I reset the thermostat to a level more compatible with human life and nudged her back into the cubicle. She was now evidently confused beyond belief by the whole showering concept so I ended up basically getting in with her and washing her hair myself. By the time I finished, my pyjamas were pasted to my skin and I was reminded of Grace's swimming lesson where the trainee lifeguards have to jump into the pool fully clothed and save a large plastic float from drowning.

An hour later and we were both dry and dressed. The process had been completely exhausting and I felt I may be on the edge of having a small nervous breakdown. The bathroom looked as though an entire rugby team had dropped in for a water fight, but Mum seemed to be happy just to be in warm, dry clothes, so we had a little sit down with a cup of tea and contemplated our good fortune until the boys returned from football. Tom was back in the minging kit from yesterday's practice session, which was now so filthy it could have stood up and walked into the house itself, but he was happy with having set up a goal for Alex. Or at least, this was his perception – Sam informed me over his head that Tom's assistance had been minimal, bordering on obstruction. Having swept up the mud from Tom's football boots, given strict instructions about lunch and made Sam promise to walk the dog, Mum and I left for the hospital.

- Husband and three children all safely at home – check
- Mum in car – check
- Mountain of change for extortionate hospital car parking – check
- Mobile phone in handbag – check
- Handbag still in heap by front door – Oops, back to house.

On my arrival at the QEH I found a normal-sized parking space. I then located the A&E department with ease. I am now a complete legend at this hospital-visiting lark. Nurse Charlie (perhaps he never leaves?) was dealing with a vomiting patient who was clearly hammered and screaming obscenities at staff and visitors between puking bouts. It smelt so strongly of cider that I was momentarily transported back to my youth, but I shook the memory from my head and steered Mum away. I am, after all, a forty-two-year-old, responsible woman, mother of three and official carer for a parent with dementia. I assumed a serene and capable expression.

Sadly, being forty-two and responsible does not automatically equip one with the skills to deal with hospital navigation. Because, of course, Dad was no longer in his A&E bed. A small, frightened-looking woman was there instead. I fell once more on the mercy of Charlie, who had managed to wrestle the drunken vomiter into a cubicle where his swearing was marginally less disturbing. He explained that Dad was 'no longer with us'. Momentary panic took hold as I misunderstand and thought perhaps Charlie was telling me, in an extremely casual fashion, that my father had died, but thankfully no. It appeared that he was still alive and, having exceeded his four-hour wait by some margin, had been transferred during the night.

To where? Nobody seemed to have a bloody clue.

–

I finally located Dad on Ward Two, which appeared to be a sort of surgical purgatory where broken people go to await their fate. He looked exhausted. Mum was overjoyed to see him and patted him for a lengthy period, seemingly less to console and more to confirm his presence. I felt quite moved by this moment of tenderness, until I realised that four minutes of face-patting is probably quite annoying if you are tired and in pain and have a broken hip, so I gently encouraged her into a chair.

Dad appeared to be on today's operating list but had no idea when he might be 'taken down' (which apparently was not as ominous as it sounded) and was, as a result, nil by mouth. He looked enviously on as Mum and I tucked into the cups of tea and digestive biscuits offered by a lovely lady with a trolley, and I realised, halfway through a mouthful, that my father had no provisions with him at all;

33

no book, no clothing, no toothbrush. He was untroubled by this fact, being an army man and used to coping on low rations, but I was wracked with guilt and suspected that the nursing staff may have already reported me to social services for neglect of a vulnerable elderly person.

I knew that gathering up both parents' belongings would be a far easier job if done alone, but I couldn't leave Mum at the hospital in case Dad was called down to theatre (thus prompting further calls to social services as Mum, left unattended, wandered into either the high-dependency unit, the doctors' mess or the main road) so we finished our tea and got back to the car park as speedily as was feasible. I parted with fourteen pounds for the privilege of visiting my incapacitated father and resented every coin that clinked into the machine as I muttered about daylight robbery – I really hope that someone is spending this fortune on a new bloody ward or transplant centre but I suspect not. Anyway, at least this time I didn't lose my mother betwixt ward and car. In the way of all good impromptu carers, I am learning on the job.

–

I took Mum back to their house. The place was a bomb site and it wasn't particularly clear whether this was evidence of actual burglary or just a general deterioration in standards of cleanliness all round, so I left Mum watching television and went to investigate the source of various unpleasant aromas. The cat litter tray was unemptied, and Mr Tibbs had clearly been availing himself of the facilities for some time; thus I discovered the cause of Unsavoury Smell Number One (number ones and number twos, actually).

The carpets were thick with dust and cobwebs and the windowsills were sprinkled liberally with dead insects. There were encrusted plates in the kitchen, slugs of toothpaste and grey hair clogging up the bathroom sink and toilets too grim to describe, which is really saying something, given the regular state of our downstairs loo at home. I realised that Mum was no longer in charge of domestic duties as she had been for most of my life. Now, evidently, the dementia had taken over the running of the house like a self-appointed ship's captain after a mutiny and it appeared that this pirate was both drunk and blind with scurvy.

The pleasure to be had from taking that analogy, making it walk the plank and watching it drown, did little to compensate for my distress at finding the house in such a state. I tried to remember the last time I had seen my parents in their own home; it must have been at least six months ago and during that last memorable visit I'd been so mortified by Grace's sulky behaviour and lavishly applied eyeshadow that I hadn't really paid much attention to my surroundings. Truth be told, I'd been desperate to get back home, what with Grace looking like a homicidal prostitute, Tom embarking on a burping competition with himself and Maisie demanding more cake, knocking her apple juice onto the best rug and then screaming when Granny didn't have the right sort of crayons. It made me squirm. It's not that my parents don't love their grandchildren and it wasn't that the kids were particularly badly behaved, but like all children they can sense weakness. Knowing I wanted them to acquit themselves well is as good a reason as any to do the exact opposite. As a result, visits to Mum and Dad's house have dwindled in the past couple of years and the times that they come to visit me are limited to Christmas and Easter, when frankly a grenade could go off in the kitchen and I'd be less stressed. So, perhaps I had been too distracted by the kids last time, but surely it hadn't been as bad as this? The combination of this morning's wet bed and this afternoon's scene of domestic carnage was causing me to question how far Mum's dementia had progressed and how much Dad had been covering up for her. I genuinely had no inkling of the level of squalor they were residing in, blithely assuming that my mother remained the perfect housewife.

My parents have always had a very conventional marriage, with Dad going off to work and Mum looking after the children and keeping the homestead spick and span. She had prided herself on her housekeeping skills – her home was an extension of her own person in the same way that middle-aged men seemed to view their cars, just without the phallic symbolism. This is not something I have inherited from her, as previously mentioned. In fact, it used to really get on my tits that we had to pretend we didn't actually live in our home – instead it was as if our house was in a perpetual state of readiness for a photo shoot or a state visit; primped, preened and hoovered to within an inch of its life. The presence of mud on the carpet or dust on the surfaces would be met with the same level of horror as the vicar being served a used condom with his cup of tea. So, the vista that greeted me proved to be quite a shock.

Regardless, I ploughed on, gathering belongings like a whirling dervish of packing expertise. I waved a damp cloth in the general direction of the kitchen surfaces and vacuumed most of downstairs, including the windowsill insect burial sites. I dropped a note round to Agnes next door asking her to keep an eye on Mr Tibbs for a couple of days. I put some fresh food out for said feline and emptied the overflowing litter tray, generally feeling quite proud of my demonstration of practical skill and my calm, unflappable state. I also managed to maintain the jolliest of voices while performing a running commentary for Mum, although she was fully absorbed by *Bargain Hunt* and didn't look up once to note the cheerfulness of her daughter in the face of adversity.

Frankly, I was pretty disappointed that nobody else was present to witness my superior coping skills. I mentioned it to Sam when I returned home, but clearly he felt that being left with the children all day was the short straw and just gave me a non-committal shrug – not really the response I was after. He then immediately disappeared upstairs, claiming he needed a lie down while I prepared dinner, emptied the washing machine, put another wash on, made up the spare room bed with clean linen, virtually re-plastered the bathroom ceiling and unpacked Mum's meagre belongings.

Chapter Four

I woke at six and lay staring at the ceiling for an hour or so before being called downstairs to arbitrate in a fight between Tom and Grace, who had fallen out about Marmite – the result being that Grace had felt it necessary to smack Tom in the face with a piece of buttered toast. Tom retaliated by thumping Grace in the shoulder, Grace pushed him off his chair, Tom rolled over ostentatiously a couple of times like a badly tackled footballer before laying prone and apparently incapacitated, staring up at the ceiling and appealing to me in the loudest possible terms to intervene – i.e. shout at Grace and send her to her room, while tenderly checking him for signs of mortal wounds and agreeing that he was the more maligned party. Maisie, self-appointed video assistant referee, clapped her hands in delight and started lobbing toast at all and sundry, including a cheerful Colin, who, to be fair, gets a lot of his nutrition this way.

I made myself a cup of tea with my back to the table, studiously ignoring them all and hoping that they would somehow sort it out between themselves. Sam was nowhere to be seen. We had stumbled into each other on the landing half an hour earlier and he had been heading for the toilet with a newspaper under his arm. Nobody with anything resembling normal bodily functions needs to be in the bathroom for that long, so he was now essentially hiding from his family. We've all been there. Many's the time I've hidden in the loo when I wanted some peace – unfortunately the children always know this and continue to seek me out with inane questions.

'*Where are you, Mummy?*'

'*Mummmmmmmeeeeeeeee!!!!*'

'*Are you in the loo, Mummy?*'

'*Why are you taking such a long time, Mummy?*'

'*Are you doing a poo or a wee, Mummy?*'

'*Can I come in as well?*'

'*Can you read me a story/get the lid off these crayons/find my rugby boots/look at my sore finger, Mummy?*'

'*But I need you, Mummy!*'

'*Mummmmmeeeeeeee!!!*' et cetera, et cetera, ad infinitum, until you are sobbing into a fistful of toilet roll.

Tom gave a plaintive yelp from flagstones that were still sticky from yesterday's syrup coating, courtesy of Maisie, and I turned slowly towards the tableau of sibling bliss.

'Grace!' I said calmly, or perhaps shouted maniacally, 'Why did you push your brother onto the floor?'

'Because I hate him!'

'OK, marvellous.' I took some deep breaths. 'Tom, are you all right? I think you can probably get up off the floor now?' I poked him gently with my toe and he rolled around in agony, telling me he was extremely worried he might have a brain haemorrhage. I suggested that this was unlikely and asked if he could please just get back up to the breakfast table? Yes, the other end of the table from his pig-troll of a sister would be fine. Could Grace at least ask if her brother is OK and apologise for hurting him?

No, obviously not, because he punched her, didn't he? Well, yes, she had a point. Could Tom apologise to Grace, please? No? Excellent. Could Maisie stop throwing toast now, please? No? Excellent.

I muttered something quietly to myself, as I do on occasions such as these, and Maisie asked 'What are Little Fuckers, Mummy?' just as Sam sauntered in, fresh from his extended bathroom vacation. The room went quiet. Grace looked at Tom, they both pursed their lips together to stifle a giggle as Maisie, pleased with the reaction, made up a glorious song entitled 'Little Fuckers' and, lo, sibling harmony was restored. The liberal use of swear words is obviously an excellent parenting strategy and I made a mental note to use it more often.

Sam told me that my brother Rory had called yesterday evening while I was still at Mum and Dad's cleaning, tidying, collecting and generally being an exemplary offspring. I steeled myself for a return call to Australia and had to look up the time differences online; not remembering whether he was in Perth or Brisbane – an important distinction, it seems – so I chickened out and texted him instead. My hope was to convey via said text that everything was under control. I also hoped to convey that the reason for this state of control was because I am managing all eventualities like a complete hero. I briefly imagined that he would appreciate this. He won't.

Rory is a doctor. He is also a parent's dream come true, having breezed through medical school, part-funded by the army, to then be recruited by the SAS and travel the world as a forces medic. His story is the stuff of dinner-party legend. The bragging rights afforded to the progenitors of such a pillar of the community are extensive and my parents' friends, I am sure, have tolerated many hours of poorly concealed pride and smugness.

'*What, Rory? Oh yes, the medal ceremony was lovely but you know him, doesn't like to make a fuss about his achievements!*'

'*Hmm, he was involved in that thing in Kabul. Of course, it was top secret and we were worried sick, but, you know, his country needed him.*'

'*Yes. It does make me very proud. But no, I'm not surprised, he always was so focused, that boy. And so bright! And, yes, you're right, such an excellent sportsman – a real all-rounder!*' (allowing themselves one small, self-deprecating smile). '*No idea where he gets it from!*' (little laugh, move on, repeat conversation ad nauseum).

A slight variation occurs whenever anyone enquires about me. I suspect the response then is along the lines of:

'*Penelope? Yes, she finished her degree course. Didn't really achieve her full potential though.*'

'*Hmm, the music thing never really took off. You can't make a career out of it, can you? She still plays the piano a bit, makes up those songs of hers, I think.*'

'*Yes, the kids are lovely, bit of a handful though – parenting seems totally different to how it was in our day!*'

'*No, we don't see them that much. She's very busy. School activities and whatnot. Yes! The things they do now! If it's not karate or Mandarin, it's kid-friendly Pilates! Don't know what's wrong with reading a good old-fashioned book or kicking a ball about! I remember when…*' (Cue lengthy segue into reminiscing about their own childhoods where they had to make do with a tin can and a piece of string, or playing in the road and '*nothing much wrong with how I turned out!*', et cetera, et cetera.)

A few moments after my text the phone rang and t'was he, the legendary Captain Doctor Rory Andrews himself.

'Penny?' He was brusque. Clearly, he was busy as well as being very important.

'Hi, Rory.' I quickly apologised for texting rather than calling, I also apologised for not knowing the correct medical terminology and generally apologised for everything that was wrong with life. I then discovered that Rory had already phoned the QEH and spoken to the consultant looking after Dad. But of course he had. 'Chap I knew at med school. Jenner. Top bloke.' (Rory picked up this type of chat when he was at Sandhurst – it is unspeakably irritating).

'Uh-hum,' I murmured non-committally.

Rory told me all about Dad's procedure and how it was definitely scheduled for today, thanks to his intervention. 'How's Mum?' he asked at the end, but when I started to list my concerns, particularly about the state of our parents' house, he cut me off.

'Well, Penny, you'll need to make sure the old boy has a decent rehab environment when he gets out, significant effect on post-op mortality rates, you know, anyway, got to push on, search and rescue mission at oh-eight-hundred. I'll call when I'm back.' He hung up and I stared at the phone for a few long minutes.

Sam raised his eyebrows when I returned to the kitchen. 'How is the old devil?' he asked in a 'Captain Rory' voice.

Grace giggled, letting her guard down for a rare moment. 'Ruddy good show, Old Bean!' she added.

'Yes. Quite. About as helpful as one would expect.' I felt I was being a little ungracious so explained that although my brother may be a bit of an arse, he could also

42

be quite useful, having managed to gather information (or 'intel') about Dad and hopefully bumping him up the operating list due to the surgeon being a 'personal friend'.

'Of course he is,' said Sam, delighted. 'Is he a chum from rugger perhaps? Or the club? I bet he's a cracking bloke, to boot.'

There was nothing for it but to let them take the piss out of Uncle Rory in his absence, so I wandered through to the sitting room where Mum was perched uncomfortably on the coffee table. I steered her towards the more appropriate seating of the armchair. She looked more like her old self today; her clothes were clean and I had helped her brush her hair and put a bit of make-up on (mainly as a means to escape the children). It was dawning on me that having Mum to stay has a few perks, not least being able to shut myself in the spare room for an hour under the guise of 'helping Granny', which is a much more justifiable course of action than, for example, Sam's hiding in the toilet.

'That was Rory on the phone,' I said.

'Rory!' Her face brightened. 'Oh! My Rory?' She nodded to herself, beaming. Amazing what Golden Boy can do even from afar, his name alone inspiring such joy. I was fleetingly jealous, but I've had forty-odd years of being in his shadow and it is no longer painful. Well, not excruciating, anyway.

'Could I speak to him?' she asked hopefully, and I felt the crush of her imminent disappointment.

'Oh, Mum, it was a really quick call – I'm so sorry, I know he'd have loved to talk to you but he was very busy. He did manage to speak to the hospital though.'

She looked confused.

'About Dad?'

43

Mum screwed her eyebrows together in concentration and mumbled something under her breath. I realised that she didn't know where Dad was, so we went through the now familiar routine of me reminding her of the events of the past seventy-two hours and her responding with shock and astonishment.

'Broken hip?' she muttered. 'Well. Silly bugger!' She was evidently furious with him and I knew I'd have to have the same conversation tomorrow and again the day after, so I omitted most of the detail this time and instead persuaded her to come into the kitchen, bask in the warmth of the family home and generally share in the joyous companionship of her beloved grandchildren while I prepared a lavish yet wholesome Sunday roast (chicken from Aldi, instant gravy and a few squishy potatoes I was hoping to transform to golden crispiness by immersing them in hot fat). She agreed and we made our way through to this promised nirvana, just as Grace ran past us shrieking and flailing her arms, closely followed by Tom, who was puce in the face and yelling like an extra from *Braveheart* as he threw his football boot at her head. At least, I assumed he was aiming for her head and not the hall lamp, despite that being where the boot actually landed, smashing the bulb. This prompted hysterical laughter from his sister, accompanied by shouts of 'You are such a dick! You throw like a total nob-head!' and other such joys.

Maisie was cackling and swinging from the kitchen door like a baboon. She had resumed singing her 'Little Fuckers' song and Colin was circling frantically underneath her, barking loudly. Sam, when we finally got into the room, was sat innocently reading the sports section of the Sunday papers, apparently oblivious to the unruly

44

behaviour of the fruit of his loins and acting as if nothing out of the ordinary had occurred. Which, I suppose, it hadn't.

Chapter Five

It seems that even Captain Doctor Rory Andrews can't manipulate the grinding cogs of the NHS from Brisbane or Perth, or wherever. His great mate Mr Jenner was occupied with other emergencies, so Dad's surgery was delayed until today. Mum and I drove down to visit but managed to miss him entirely as he was in theatre until late in the afternoon, so I paid the obligatory kidney in the car park for the trip to *not* see my father and we came home just in time to pick Maisie up from preschool in a car-to-entrance dash that an Olympic sprinter would have been proud of.

I left Mum in the Renault (having parked perilously close to the preschool doors so I could see her) and found Maisie clutching the hand of Miss Janice, who looked pointedly at her watch. I have never previously been late at pick-up so felt that this wordless judgement was most unfair, but explained breathlessly that I was terribly sorry for almost being late (I was not late) and that the reason I'd parked so close was due to fears about my mother's safety. Miss Janice glanced across to the car where Mum was waving cheerfully to Maisie and appearing not in the least frail, confused or in need of emergency parking access. Miss Janice smiled thinly and handed Maisie over just as

46

High-powered Joy clipped around the corner to collect her daughter.

I couldn't face a discussion with the immaculate Joy. She has an enviable reputation in the world of passive-aggression and is so highly skilled at bullying people into submission without them even realising it that one enters into a conversation with her entirely at one's own risk, knowing that the likely result of a brief exchange is signing yourself up to a lifetime of indentured servitude in the form of childcare provision for her daughter, The Terrible Evangeline.

'Penny!' High-powered Joy called imperiously from the gate. But I was too quick for her and in a squeal of tyres had left the preschool entrance before she could hunt me down.

–

By the time we were home, I had started to feel a bit guilty for abandoning Joy though. It was all well and good championing working mothers but the progression of the sisterhood relied on people like me to help out from time to time. Usually this was a role I was happy to take on. In lieu of my own interesting and fulfilling career, which stalled years ago, I occasionally gained some vicarious pleasure through the work of others, providing childcare and support to their offspring while they went out into the wild world of commerce and industry. I do sometimes wish they wouldn't be so bloody patronising about the help us 'stay-at-home mums' provide though, as if they have a God-given right to back out of community life and responsibility just because they have spent the day in the boardroom rather than the hell of a soft-play centre. Maybe we *homemakers* (such a menial descriptor) would like to be back in the boardroom? If the prospect of returning wasn't quite so terrifying, obviously.

I had once nurtured dreams of a high-powered career. Well, perhaps not 'high-powered' exactly, but a career of sorts. Well, perhaps not a 'career' as such – a part-time job would do. Zahara has a job. She works from home during child-friendly hours, for a high-end furnishings company. Hence the glorious house. It's not the glittering legal career she's qualified for but it gives her a sense of purpose. And her own money. Not that she needs it – Hugh earns a fortune and is more than happy to share all of his worldly goods with the woman he loves, often surprising her with little unexpected gifts: flowers, perfume, designer handbags, trips to Paris, etc. But there is a certain satisfaction in the way that she pays for a new outfit herself or (goodness) a 'facial treatment' that inspires respect and possibly envy in those like me who are reduced to a humiliating existence of justifying the basic household expenses of school uniforms or putting food on the table. This is before we would even dream of asking our husbands for money to spend on ourselves, like, for example, seven pounds per week for a yoga class (which is an indulgence, don't get me wrong, but Sam did make me feel as though it was a weekly trip to the Hamptons).

I know how middle-class this all sounds and I know how lucky I am. I don't need to go out to work. Sam brings in enough money for us to manage and we sacrifice extra income for the security of knowing I'm bringing up the children. We tell ourselves this is 'best for the kids'. And most of the time I'm happy with this particular life choice. For a start, I'd have to earn a hell of a lot for it to make financial sense to pay someone else to look after my three. But I see those mummies who say smugly, 'My children are my life. I couldn't possibly need anything else', and I think, *really?*

–

Later that evening, I called the ward while I was dishing up Sam's dinner.

'Everything all right?' he asked as he sat down. 'Did he have the op?'

'I think so.' I attempted a shrug with the phone wedged under my chin. 'We didn't see him at all while we were there so I'm hoping he was in theatre.' I was trying to keep my voice light but I was exhausted. The fruitless journey to and from the hospital had been a bit demoralising, and the repeated explanations to Mum had further chipped away at my energy levels. I was now desperate to go to bed, yet again aware of the fact that I have given my husband zero attention on his return from work. Still, hopefully Dad wouldn't be in hospital for much longer and once he was mobile I would be free of the daily car journeys and, much as it pained me to admit it, free of the burden of constantly reassuring Mum and attending to her needs on top of those of the children. Maybe once both my parents had returned home with some sort of care package arranged by the hospital, Sam and I could get a babysitter and go out for the evening. I began to scroll through the diary in my head as I waited for the ward clerk to find someone who knew what was going on with Dad. After what felt like an eternity, a Dr Fernandez came on the phone and I verified that I was indeed Gordon Andrews's next of kin.

'I'm afraid there were some complications when your dad was in theatre…' he said, his voice trailing away ominously.

'What? Oh my God, is he alive?' There was a sudden tightness in my throat, making it hard to breathe, and I leant against the wall, feeling the cool paintwork against my cheek as Sam rushed to my side.

Dr Fernandez paused for a beat. 'Yes, he is. But he's had a blood clot on his brain. A stroke.'

Chapter Six

Tuesday, 14 January

Nobody slept last night. Well, obviously the children did, to varying degrees. Grace in that comatose teenage state, Tom in an untroubled, tired puppy way and Maisie in an unpredictable fidget until around five a.m., when she apparently charged into our room and jumped on Sam. He had spent the previous four hours trying to persuade Mum that the landing did not need hoovering, but had eventually admitted defeat and given her the unplugged vacuum cleaner. She then spent the two hours before dawn wandering wide-eyed up and down the corridor, pushing the silent Hoover in front of her and looking as much like a wraith as it is possible for a slightly overweight woman in a Tom and Jerry nightie to look.

After getting off the phone yesterday, I had rapidly concluded that taking Mum back to the hospital was a mug's game, so I went alone. The doctor had been hesitant about allowing me to visit in the middle of the night but once I'd burst into tears he said he would clear it with the ward staff and entreated me to drive carefully on the icy roads. Which was thoughtful, given the fact that the rest of my life seemed to be turning to shit.

I did try and heed his advice though – the last thing anyone needed was me sliding off the road and into a ditch – but I was starting to feel as if I was functioning on autopilot. My face was numb and tingling around the eyes in the way it used to when the kids were babies and woke up for night feeds, except this time I had to concentrate on traffic and navigation rather than nipple shields and Lansinoh. I'm not sure I had fully absorbed the implications of the scenario as I drove. My attention was on the immediate task of getting to the hospital and making sure my father was still alive.

My overwhelming thought on seeing him was that he looked so old. Such a frail, elderly man. I'd never seen him like that before. The stroke seemed to have shrunk him somehow and he no longer looked like the robust no-nonsense military chap that was my father. I sat with him through the quiet, dark hours on the ward, holding his heavy hand in mine, and I began to feel a tight knot in my stomach as I contemplated the immediate future.

If Dad was incapacitated for a long period of time, which seemed increasingly inevitable, then I was going to have to sort out a plan for Mum. I had genuinely no idea where to start so I simply let the thoughts spin through my head like so many hamsters on wheels. There was the *Oh my God, my dad is now terribly unwell and he might die* hamster – he was a cheerful little soul. Then there was the *What am I going to do about Mum?* hamster – she was a wide-eyed ball of fluff, distracted by the sunflower seeds. And then there were the *What's Sam going to do about work today? / Was it this week I booked the car in for a service? / What will the kids eat?* hamsters, who all considered themselves to be of equal importance. The *What happened to my life?* hamster was in the latrine corner struggling to get back on her feet having fallen off her wheel. You get the idea.

By the time the nurse brought the early morning drugs trolley round (which sounds a lot more fun than it actually is) Dad still hadn't opened his eyes and I wasn't certain that he even knew I was there. I'd been holding his hand for so long that my arm had gone to sleep and I briefly wondered if I'd had a stroke of my own. My eyes and mouth were sandpaper dry, my bladder felt as though it may explode and my buttocks were regretting the decision to choose a hard plastic chair to rest upon for six hours. I hadn't dared leave his side in case something terrible happened but with the nurse in the general vicinity I felt it was probably OK to dash into the ward toilet – OK in the loosest sense, given the actual state of that particular toilet.

When I returned, Dad appeared to be awake. At least, one eye was open and half of his mouth turned up in a smile as I approached the bed.

'Oh, Dad.' I hoped that my voice sounded steady but he looked so frail that it was all I could do not to burst into tears. He went to try and speak but the only sound he could make was a sort of wet *phffut* noise and he lifted his good hand in frustration, whacking it down on the bed beside him.

'You've had a stroke, Dad,' I said, knowing that he would want the facts immediately. 'That's why you can't speak.' I was determined not to cry so I foraged in my handbag for a piece of paper and a pen for him to write on while the fizzing sensation in my nose settled down. One of the singular advantages of having small children is the Mary Poppins nature of my handbag. It contains enough tissues, snacks and methods of entertainment to sustain an entire preschool for a week. I managed to come up with:

- A partially completed picture of a rabbit

- Two blue crayons
- Seven-and-a-half fruit chews
- A wrinkled apple
- Four dog biscuits
- A tin of Dobble cards (the greatest game in the universe according to Caz and she's not wrong)
- Two sanitary towels
- Three packs of wet-wipes (I know – the oceans. I know)
- A broken umbrella
- A plastic giraffe
- And a copy of *Mr Nosy* with the cover missing.

I pulled the table across the bed and placed the rabbit picture face down so he could use the blank side.

'Can you write, d'you think?' I held up the crayons enticingly.

He shrugged with one shoulder and made another indeterminate grunting noise before a shaky *yes* appeared on the paper.

Via this method, we established that he was comfortable, and he was able to ask after Mum with a painstaking 'M' that took him an eternity to complete.

'She's fine,' I said. 'She's been listening to Maisie read and singing songs with Tom.' (Tom had been most amused yesterday to introduce Granny to Skepta and Aitch's back catalogues, explicit lyrics and all.)

'I haven't told her about the stroke yet but really, don't worry. We're looking after her. She's perfectly happy.'

He pointed to me.

'Am I OK? Yes. Absolutely. Tickety-boo.' I smiled. 'I'm worried about you, obviously, but I'm sure you'll be fighting fit in a day or two. Up and about, ordering the nurses around.'

Maybe he couldn't hear the wobble in my voice or maybe he was just exhausted by the communication, but he closed his eyes and looked fairly satisfied. Although, it's hard to assess satisfaction levels from a facial expression when one half of the face isn't working properly.

I went to call Sam, who was struggling to marshal the children into some semblance of order. I could hear the television on in the background and he kept breaking off the conversation to answer queries regarding clothes, homework and sports kit with an, 'I dunno, just find something'. I fully expected them to be turning up at school mid-morning in jeans and T-shirts having spent four hours playing *Resident Evil* on the Xbox. That was if they made it to school at all. Still, this was as close as our family had ever come to a proper crisis and I expected the various educational establishments to cut us some slack.

'Were work OK about you missing today?' I said, hopping from one foot to the other in an effort to keep warm. Despite being more appropriately attired for this emergency hospital trip, it was still bitterly cold outside A&E, where I had gone to use my phone. I was sheltering next to a couple of smokers and the smell of their cigarettes combined with the sleep deprivation was making me feel as though I'd been up all night partying, a sensation made all the more unfair by the fact that it had been years since I'd even managed to stay out past midnight, and that occasion had been a Jamie Oliver homewares party where the highpoint had been my winning a nutmeg grater.

'Yeah, they said fine for me to take the morning off. I said I'd try and make it in for the meeting this afternoon. Do you think you'll be back by then?' He sounded hopeful but my heart sank. I had been banking on him taking the whole day and therefore being able to sort out the practicalities of preschool pick-up and hockey club while I made a leisurely return journey, locked myself in my room and sobbed ostentatiously for a few hours.

I looked at my watch. 'Yeah, I should be. I'll see if I can speak to the doctors and then I'll head home. How're the kids? How's Mum?'

'Umm… It's all a bit feral but we'll manage. How's your dad? And how are you, love?'

I turned towards the wall because my face was starting to crumple. I told Sam about the limited communication my father and I had managed via the medium of crayons. 'It's really hard. You can see how frustrated he is. And exhausted. But I guess he's medically stable – he's conscious and on a normal ward, not, like, in intensive care or anything.'

'Well, that's something, I suppose. In fact, it's probably a really good sign.'

I knew he was trying to sound upbeat for my benefit but suddenly I needed him there beside me rather than on the end of a phone. I wanted to crawl into bed and feel his strong arms wrapped round me until I woke up and discovered the whole thing had been a bad dream, but instead of sharing this insight I gulped back a sob and put my big girl pants on.

'So, I guess I'll see you later tonight then.'

'Yeah, make sure you drive carefully on your way back, you must be exhausted too. D'you want to speak to the kids?'

I had a quick chat with an excitable Maisie ('Daddy said it was OK to eat whatever the hell I want as long as I got my arse in gear') and Tom, who asked what I'd done with his rugby socks. Grace clearly felt she could get through the day without speaking to me and instead shouted 'TELL GRANDAD TO GET WELL SOON,' after forceful prompting from her father.

I ended the call and leant up against the hospital wall suddenly overwhelmed with fatigue and emotion and just the total shit-ness of life. My breathing was unsteady and my nose had started to run. It was only a matter of time before my entire face dissolved into a puddle.

'Are you OK?' A male voice startled me out of my... I want to say *reverie* but I don't think that deeply depressing thoughts constitute a reverie, so let's say melancholy and be done with it. My eyes creaked open, red and piggy as they probably were.

'Yes, all fine, thanks. Bit of hayfever.' I wiped my nose on the back of my hand attractively and looked a little closer at the friendly stranger. It was the same tattooed hero who had rescued my abandoned mother from the multi-storey. 'Oh! Ben, isn't it?' I extended my hand and then realised there was probably snot all over it so retracted it hastily. He gave me an uncertain smile.

'Ye-es. That's me.'

'Sorry. You looked after my mum in the car park the other day. That's how I knew your name. I'm not, like, a stalker or anything. I'm Penny.'

'Of course.' He smiled. 'Are you sure you're all right? You look a little...' He gestured to the scene of devastation that was my face and I returned his smile with a wobbly one of my own.

'Dishevelled? Horrific?'

He smiled again, 'No. Distressed was what I was going to say.'

I stepped back to avoid a man with a plaster cast and crutches. 'It's my dad. He broke his hip and now he's had a stroke.'

Ben grimaced. 'Ah. Yep, that's pretty rough.'

'And my mum has dementia, you may recall.'

He nodded.

'And so, she's staying with us for a while. Well, I thought it would just be a week or so while Dad recovered from his surgery but clearly, a stroke puts a different perspective on things.'

He nodded slowly. 'It does. I work on the stroke rehab unit for part of the week. It's a slow process. Was it recent, your dad?'

'Last night.'

'OK. Well he might not be on the rehab ward yet but I'll look out for him. What's his name?'

I gave Ben the scant information I had regarding Dad's current situation and he said he'd pop and see him later today. I almost hugged him, completely overwhelmed as I was with gratitude for the second time in a week, but managed to restrain myself to a profuse verbal outpouring of appreciation instead. He probably regretted having extended the offer but to know that someone – anyone – would be keeping an eye out for my father in my absence was so reassuring. I think he realised that I was over-tired, overwrought and generally more of an emotional shambles than a normal person would be. Maybe NHS staff just assume that everyone behaves like this all the time?

Chapter Seven

Monday, 20 January

We managed to cobble together an existence of sorts over the latter part of last week. I took Mum to visit Dad every other day. He seemed to be making progress, but following a discussion with the stroke team on Friday it became apparent that we were likely looking at several months before he would be fully fit to return home. Armed with that news and having discussed it with Sam over the weekend, I have decided to start looking at options regarding Mum. I say 'options' as a euphemism for residential care or a nursing home because I can't bring myself to use those words, but it is increasingly obvious that she cannot stay with us indefinitely. She is bewildered by not having Dad around and I'm not sure that a busy family home with noisy young children is really the best place to care for someone in a fragile state of mind. There is no chance of peace and quiet, the days are hectic and if I'm honest I don't think I can cope with having another person to look after. In the past four days Mum has tried to plug the hairdryer into the boiler, wandered out of the front door and halfway down the village in her nightclothes, buttered the dog and offered the contents of her purse to the milkman. I am deeply ashamed to admit it, but this is my diary, so bollocks to it all. I can't do it. I am being stretched so thin that I am in danger of disappearing entirely.

So, I've looked into the finances. My parents fall into that limbo of having enough money in savings to disqualify them from state help, but not having enough to pay for the kind of luxurious residential home that one sees advertised from time to time – those pensioner paradises of golf and tea dances where mid-afternoon cocktails are brought directly to your mobility scooter. Instead what we have is a modest sum that will cover your basic, entry-level residential home for about six months. After that, who knows? Do they get the bailiffs round to take the television or physically throw geriatrics out onto the street? I don't even want to think about it.

We began our 'Tour of the Great Houses of Hertford-shire' today. This is what I have optimistically entitled our search for a care home, hoping that it's sufficiently misleading to avoid distress and confrontation. I have learnt to my cost that even the most seemingly inattentive person can be surprisingly astute when you least want them to be. Witness the tired toddler who appears to be falling asleep in the car but develops the sonar hearing of a bat when you discreetly reach into the bag of boiled sweets by your side, or the ten-year-old boy with a psychic ability to sense that a borderline porn scene has flashed up in the middle of your post-watershed television viewing and chooses exactly that moment to come downstairs to say goodnight. Also, witness the seventy-year-old woman with dementia who hears the words 'Residential Care' mentioned in a discussion about politics and out of nowhere launches a shoe at your head and stomps out of the room. I was going to have to be very careful indeed. And remove all potential footwear missiles.

After school drop-off we went to visit Dad, where Mum went through her soothing ritual of patting him on the face. Luckily, I have managed to steer her towards the left side of his body, which he is currently neglecting. Rory told me over the phone that this was quite normal; apparently after a stroke one almost forgets about the existence of the affected side. My brother seems to find it fascinating; this combination of Mum having full mobility but limited awareness and Dad having the exact reverse. I suggested that it was a real shame he couldn't be here to observe it directly, but he didn't appear to notice my stinging retort or, if he did, it merely glanced off him as he proceeded to rattle off statistics regarding differing brain injuries.

More usefully, Ben has been giving me updates on Dad's progress with exercises to restore his mobility. It seems a positive attitude is critical and luckily determination is something my father has in spades. I told Ben this and he smiled.

'He's ex-military, isn't he?' He gestured to Dad, who had fallen asleep.

I nodded.

'I've worked with a few amputees in the past, army blokes, legs blown off by IEDs. He's got the same look in his eye. You watch. He'll get through this.'

'Not sure I will though!' I laughed, perhaps a little too shrilly, as I reached out to stop Mum applying Dad's strawberry yoghurt to her face.

–

The first stop on our Tour of Great Houses was 'Orchard Meadows' – something of a misnomer, given its proximity to the industrial estate. The rain was torrential, drubbing down on the glass as we entered the conservatory reception area and I had to shout loudly to make it understood that we had an appointment with the 'hotel manager'. The girl on the desk nodded slowly at my exaggerated 'nod, nod, wink, wink' expression and picked up the phone. A few moments later a Mr Henry O'Brian appeared and in a booming voice asked my mother how she felt about coming to look round a care home. Cover well and truly blown, I persuaded a reluctant Mum to accompany me and Mr O'Brian on a tour of the facilities, pointing out such highlights as the bingo room, the disabled-access toilets and the 'quiet area' for jigsaws.

I found myself using the artificially bright voice I had employed when showing Maisie round preschool: 'See, darling? Look at the children over there having fun! Watch them paint! See them play! Behold their unbridled joy at being in such a glorious establishment!'

That was me today, but more along the lines of: 'See, Mum? Look at the very elderly gentleman nodding in the corner over there. Doesn't he look cosy and well cared for? And just look at those ladies playing a card game? Yes, they do all appear to be in their nineties but aren't they enjoying themselves? Yes, I know you don't like card games.'

We made our way through to the central corridor and I continued with my horribly patronising children's television presenter voice. 'Oh look! A lift! *And* a laundry room. That'll certainly be useful! All mod-cons here.'

And up the stairs to the first floor. Mum looking increasingly mutinous.

'What's that around the corner, Mr O'Brian? One of the bedrooms! Mum look at this, such nice furnishings in a very practical wipe-down fabric. I wouldn't have imagined that a polyester twill could come in this interesting shade or pattern. And an en suite, how luxurious, with one of those delightful ballerina loo-roll covers, and presumably these are the previous resident's dentures?'

On and on I rattled, aided and abetted by a deafening Mr O'Brian, proudly listing the activities available on a weekly timetable. These consisted of Morris Bingley and his Banjo on a Monday, Recipes from the Great War with Noreen Pinkerton on Tuesday, Gardening with Gary Fontaine on a Wednesday and a visit from Jazz the Hairdresser on alternate Fridays. Thursday was clearly designated for 'Free Time', as was the weekend. This time could be spent in a variety of ways, but judging by the other residents, most of it was taken up with staring into the near distance for an indefinite period.

I wasn't sure we needed to see any more. My carefully constructed fabrication that Orchard Meadows was in fact some kind of country club had fallen apart and I thanked Mr O'Brian warmly and took Mum to a proper National Trust tea room for a muffin. The lingering institutional aroma seeped out of our clothes as the heat from the cast iron radiators gently steamed us. We sat in companionable silence, Mum continuing to look suspiciously around her as if a band of geriatrics were about to pop out from behind the cake counter and wrestle her into a straight-jacket.

I had two other care homes on my list but Chiswell House looked so gothic and foreboding standing grey in the drizzle that we didn't even cross the threshold, and Moreton Springfields, while sounding like a Norwegian popstar, was even less appealing a prospect; the sight of two orderlies depositing a blood-stained mattress into an industrial waste bin as we pulled into the car park not being the best start. The manager of Moreton Springfields, a Ms Wendy Cavern, had an unfortunate squint which caused both me and Mum to be perpetually looking over our shoulder whenever she addressed us. When she then began to limp down the corridor, veering haphazardly from left to right, I wondered if I had walked into a Victoria Wood sketch. Mum caught my eye as we followed Ms Cavern and started to giggle, which was unexpected, but not as surprising as when she started to mimic both the limp and the squint with quite considerable comedic flair. I hadn't seen this performative side of Mum's personality for some time and a snigger escaped from my mouth, causing Wendy to shoot round, one eye fixed on her impersonator while the other went rogue.

'Just clearing my throat – tickly cough,' I said, smiling innocently, but as soon as her back was turned Mum started again, not stopping until I was clutching my sides helpless with laughter.

Wendy's mood was not improved by discovering that a phantom crapper had deposited their load in one of the display bedrooms. She caught sight of the steaming pile perched jauntily atop the vinyl-covered armchair and limped back into the corridor to holler 'Barbara! He's been at it again. Bring the decontamination kit!' Whereupon a large woman appeared with a carrier bag and a pack of wet-wipes. The visit was brought to a hasty conclusion with a trip to the Relaxation Lounge, where most of the residents were asleep although one woman reached her hand out imploringly. 'Don't leave me here, Lavinia,' she called as I left, which I have to say was pretty disconcerting. I really hope I don't look like a Lavinia.

Chapter Eight

I have abandoned the search for a care home. Mum spent most of Monday night in tears and when we went to visit Dad today she kept talking about turds in armchairs and strange men taking her into bedrooms. One half of Dad's face looked concerned about what exactly was going on in our household, until I explained to him that Mum and I had been visiting places where she might be able to stay while he got better. He nodded in a lopsided fashion and tried to articulate some reassuring words to his wife, but was barely intelligible so resorted to the notepad.

Mary, he wrote, *P making sure you OK until I'm better. Won't be long.* He added a smiley face. *Like a holiday!* Mum's eyes filled with tears and she grabbed his hand. 'I want to go home,' she said.

Soon, he wrote, and they held each other's gaze for a long time. Seeing the two of them together like that, united against the world, made me feel a bit emotional and I wondered if perhaps they wanted a moment alone. I also really needed the loo, it having been four hours since I'd had sufficient time for the luxury of emptying my bladder. However, by the time I returned to the bay, Mum had gone. Dad was gesticulating wildly with his good hand and making odd groaning noises, which appeared to be

65

cries for help. I could see that he had pressed his patient alarm and a light was flashing above his bed but it seemed that nobody had so far responded.

'Where's Mum?' I tried not to reveal my escalating panic, hoping that she would appear from behind the curtain, or that my dad would calmly write that she was with one of the nurses, but his manner was more one of frantic agitation.

Gone, he wrote in an unsteady hand.

A whey-faced nurse (*Hello, my name is Dani*) who looked about thirteen stuck her head round the curtain. 'I'll just turn your buzzer off, my love,' she said in a kindly but strained voice. 'Seems you've set it off by accident?'

'It wasn't an accident.' My voice may have been a little louder than I had intended. 'He needed help. We need help. It's urgent.'

She gave a sigh and smiled tightly at me. 'What's the problem?' she said, in a tone that really meant *Why the fuck are you wasting my time?*

'My mum has gone missing.' I said and she looked at me, confused.

'Your mum?'

'She's not here. I don't know where she is. Have you seen her?'

Dani looked doubtful. 'Dunno. What's she look like?'

'Grey hair, pink cardigan. About my height, old-ish.' I said, gesturing to various parts of my body in case Dani was unaware that grey hair would be located on your head or how a cardigan might be worn. 'She's got dementia, not that you'd be able to tell from looking at her, but she sometimes wanders off, and she was a bit upset anyway, we were talking about care homes you see and…' I trailed off and she nodded thoughtfully.

66

'OK, OK. I'll call one of my seniors. I haven't done the Missing Persons Training Day yet. Don't you fret, we'll see what we can do.' She proceeded to amble back to the nurses' station with all the urgency of a clump of frogspawn.

I had absolutely zero confidence that Dani would be able to locate her own shoes, let alone my mother, but an hour of frantically pacing the length and breadth of the QEH later I returned to the ward to learn that Mum had indeed been found and was currently being detained by the security guards on the ground floor. It appeared that she had been distracted by the provisions on offer in the hospital shop and had strolled in, picked up a copy of *The Economist*, four boxes of corn plasters and a two-litre bottle of Cherry Tango, then left without paying.

I spent the remainder of the morning reassuring a sceptical security team that my mother was not a master criminal and that her shoplifting was entirely accidental. I paid for said items in triplicate and left a hefty donation in the League of Friends box and finally they let me take Mum away with just a caution and the advice that *The first step is admitting you have a problem*.

I took her back to Ward Seventeen to reassure Dad that she had been found and then left the hospital before she could commit any further acts of theft, vandalism or general misdemeanour.

–

Later, I made myself a cup of tea and phoned my brother to update him on recent events, including the failure to find a care home and our recent brush with the long arm of the law.

'Well, we've obviously got no choice now,' he said. (I loved the 'we' – like *we* were both making equal filial contribution to the situation). 'She's going to have to go into a home. You simply won't be able to manage.'

I bristled at the tone. Something in his phrasing implied that if he, Captain Rory, were in the same situation, he *would* be able to manage (natch) but clearly it wouldn't be feasible for his inept little sister to tackle such a challenge.

'I don't know if it's that clear cut, Rory,' I said. 'She's so upset by even the suggestion of a home. The thought of going to one of the places we saw this week and actually leaving her there – I don't think I could do it. She's struggling enough to understand not being with Dad. If I took away everything familiar, maybe she'd get worse?'

'I know it's hard, Pen, but you're going to have to man up. It's for the best. I mean, being at your place is hardly relaxing for Mum, I'd have thought a care home where the staff is trained to deal with the kind of difficult behaviour she's exhibiting would be better all round.'

'It's not really "difficult behaviour", Rory. She's just upset about her husband being critically ill in hospital.' His attitude about the whole situation was really pissing me off. 'And what d'you mean about my place not being relaxing?'

He gave a short bark of a laugh. They must teach you to do that in the military. 'Well, no offense but it's a mad house most of the time, isn't it? Not wanting to tell tales out of school and all, but Dad said those kids run rings around you.'

My throat went tight. It wasn't that what he said was wrong exactly, I do let my kids get away with a lot more than I was allowed to, but that's just because I want them to be happy. And it's all well and good Rory making comments on my parenting when he has no offspring of his own, but there is also the small matter of him running rings around Mum when *he* was a child. The hypocrisy and level of sneery judgement were breathtaking, even for him. I was hoping for righteous indignation but what came out was unfortunately a lot more squeaky.

'Well, that's charming, isn't it?' I said. 'I guess if it's a mad house then Mum will fit right in. Thanks for your input, Rory. Really fucking helpful.' And I slammed the phone down (what I mean is that I jabbed the end-call button as hard as I could and threw my phone at the cushion but granted, it's not the same as an old-school slam).

At about the same time Mum came wandering into the sitting room carrying a box of lightbulbs. She handed them to me. 'Can you make sure you pack these for me, darling. We always run out at the most unfortunate moments.' She rolled her eyes to the heavens.

I took the lightbulbs off her. 'Will do.'

She looked at the phone on the sofa cushion. 'Rory?' she said hopefully, reaching out to pick it up and put it to her ear. She held it there long enough for me to wonder if I had actually disconnected the call, but once it became obvious that there was no voice on the other end of the line I gently took it off her. 'No, Mum. He had to go. He sends his love though and can't wait to see you. He's really pleased about how well you're coping with everything.'

She smiled, tears in her eyes. 'Always such a good boy,' she murmured, easing herself down onto the coffee table. 'Now, did I tell you about bumping into Elsie McGovern's daughter today? She's been having it off with the man from PC World. He likes to do it doggy-style apparently.'

Chapter Nine

I ended up having a bit of a row with Sam last night. With hindsight, it wasn't his fault. He caught me at the end of a very long day, after what felt like a series of long and traumatic days. Mum's disappearing act had left me more shaken than I cared to admit and my conversation with Rory had not improved my mood. When I suggested to Sam that we stop looking for care homes and keep Mum here with us, he wasn't exactly overwhelmed with enthusiasm. What I really needed to hear was an unequivocal, 'Of course, I'll support any decision you make, my darling.' What I actually got was, 'Oh, shit, yeah, right. Hmm, not sure that it's the best... What about the kids? And what about this thing with the Hoover, and all the inappropriate comments and the wandering off? How are we going to manage?'

'It's me who is going to have to manage, Sam. As far as I can see, it should have minimal impact on you, but good to know you've got my back,' I said, my voice heavy with tired sarcasm.

He looked wounded. 'That's not fair. I'm doing my best. And I'm worried about you, Pen. It's a lot to take on. For you, for us as a family... it's not easy for anybody.

And if you think there's been *minimal impact* so far I'd hate to see what your version of a significant impact is.'

'Well, I *am* sorry, Sam. It's not my fault that my father's now disabled, my brother's a sanctimonious prick and my husband appears to want me to abandon my already confused and distressed mother, leaving her to the tender mercies of an institutional care facility where people shit in each other's rooms and call everyone Lavinia.' (Admittedly, this last bit didn't really make sense and Sam just looked bemused, but, you know, I was emotional.)

'I know it's not your fault,' he said gently. 'I know it's been really hard for you. I just don't understand why you'd want to make your life even harder. And I'm just trying to be honest: having your mum around does make life more difficult. For me, for the kids and especially for you.' He gave me a pat on the shoulder that was doubtless intended to soothe, but to me felt laden with condescension. 'There's no shame in admitting that it's too much and that you can't cope. You don't need to prove yourself to anyone. Least of all your brother.'

Well, that touched a nerve, as you can imagine. Of course, I needed to prove myself where Rory was concerned. I rolled over in bed to look at the wall, my face thunderous. 'Well, thanks for the vote of confidence. I'll tell you what, seeing as I'm so hopeless and inept why don't *you* take over the outsourcing of care for my mother? You can investigate residential homes until you find one you're happy with and then you can take the challenging burden of Mum off my hands to stop me worrying my pretty little head about it.'

Sam sighed. 'For Christ's sake, Penny.' He rolled away from me so we were both silently fuming at our respective walls. Eventually he fell asleep – emotional stress is no barrier to essential restorative processes if you're a man, it seems. His snoring did little to endear him to me as I lay awake next to him, muttering under my breath.

I *am* going to cope.

I'm going to be the best goddamn coper the world has ever seen.

Chapter Ten

I spent most of the weekend ignoring Sam, which is remarkably easy in a packed household with regular, timetabled commitments. Marriage with children is, after all, pretty similar to being board directors of a non-profit company and I know lots of people who simply immerse themselves in the day-to-day running of the business in order to avoid taking the long view.

There is scheduling, balancing of the books, workforce planning and goal setting. There is reimbursement of basic expenses (if lengthy administrative processes are undertaken). There are rotas (who is taking which child where), board meetings (can be conducted via text), action plans (to-do lists on the back of receipts) and long boozy lunches (wait, there aren't any of those). Working on this principle, Sam and I could probably run this business without ever actually having to speak to each other again and still come out at the end of it having at least broken even.

In an attempt to demonstrate my superior coping skills, I have been organising the shit out of everything, even stuff that doesn't *need* to be organised, like the airing cupboard. When Grace saw me elbow-deep in pillowcases at eleven o'clock at night, she sighed.

'You'd think it was enough that we already have *one* highly confused person in the house,' she muttered under her breath, but I smiled benignly and handed her a fitted sheet. I am going to need to think the bedding situation through if Mum is to stay with us for the foreseeable future. An online purchase of mattress protectors may be required, but I can do that sort of thing once the kids are asleep. Tonight, for example, I will be mainly sitting in front of the computer googling *mobility aids* and *incontinence pads.* In fact, I must have searched for these things so many times that they are now popping up as adverts whenever I'm on the internet looking for something else. Tom informs me that this is something to do with cookies – disappointingly the computer rather than the chocolate-chip variety.

So, there are a number of reasons why I no longer converse with my husband during the evening. These include:

- I am too busy making indiscriminate online purchases.
- I am sitting in front of the computer staring in baffled amusement at the plethora of medical equipment available online. I have seen websites dedicated to stoma bags, convenes, commodes, IV stands, portable ultrasound scanners and mechanical hoists. All extensively tested and some, it would appear, marketed for recreational use. Don't ask.
- I am too cross to do anything other than bark instructions regarding re-heating his supper, which he meekly accepts.
- I am too caffeinated to string a coherent sentence together.

I have consumed more tea, coffee and diet cola products in the past week than an army of nightshift workers. The only other time I needed this sort of synthetic energy boost was when the children were tiny and I was far too devoted a mummy to pollute my breast milk with caffeine back then. Instead, I existed in that semi-comatose state of oblivion that I still occasionally see zombie-stamped across the faces of some of the preschool mums. That level of tiredness where you memorise the words of a story so you can close your eyes as you read it to your child, or you invite them to play doctors and nurses using your own inert form as 'the patient', letting them hit you with plastic hammers and bandage your legs with old T-shirts while you snore like a warthog. It fades from the memory of course, like the pain of childbirth, otherwise who on earth would ever repeat the exercise, but sometimes I'll see one of those mums – baby strapped to her back, toddler tugging at her arm, a streak of vomit on her shoulder and the face of a hostage released briefly into the outside world – and it all comes flooding back.

The fatigue I am currently experiencing has subtle differences but the main one is the unfettered access to legal uppers and downers. I'll admit, the glass of wine I previously enjoyed while eating dinner with my husband each evening has now become two glasses, possibly three, thrown down my throat in the hour before I crawl into bed. It's possibly not a sustainable solution but I am very much dealing with the here and now, thank you for your concern and/or moral judgement.

As part of my organisational overdrive, I took Mum to the local GP practice to restock her supplies of medication as per Dad's written instructions. This was no small feat given that I was initially told the next available slot for routine appointments was March. I queried this and the receptionist confirmed what she had said in the weary tones of one who has repeated herself over and over again to more sweary and abusive customers than me, with my meek incredulity.

'It's March for a routine, love. Or I could book you a phone call with a nurse in three weeks' time?'

'But – what do people who need to be seen more quickly do?' I asked as politely as I could. 'I didn't have to wait that long last time when I called about my little girl's sore throat.'

'Nah. Kiddies and emergencies we do on the day, love. Is it an emergency?'

I wrestled with my conscience – Mum wasn't actually ill, other than the slowly progressive degeneration of her brain, obviously. There was no acute medical problem that needed to be sorted out today. It was a classic ethical dilemma of honesty versus necessity, and the receptionist couldn't help but give me a steer: 'Because if it *is* an emergency I can get you in with Dr Golding at ten-fifteen.' She paused.

'Today? Um. Yes. It's an emergency.' I heard her clacking away on the keyboard as she booked Mum in.

–

Two hours later, having explained the situation to the GP in as discreet a fashion as I could manage with my mother sitting in the chair next to me, we were driving back home from our appointment with a crisp, white paper bag of medication.

'You all right, Mum?' I asked as we crawled our way up the high street.

'No, Penelope. I am not all right.' There was a small pink spot of anger on her cheek. 'I'm ashamed of you, making all that fuss in there. Airing all our private business. What will that lovely doctor think of us?'

'Err. I assume she'll just think we were coming in to get your prescription,' I said slowly. 'Like most of her patients do?'

'But I don't need any medicine. There's nothing wrong with me.'

'I know.' I aimed for a casual tone, feeling the animosity radiating off her. It was like being with Grace – all that rage to vent but no clear direction for it. I assumed that this little parcel of anger would also be coming my way – if the past few months with my daughter have taught me anything, it's that I am an ideal target for toxic feelings.

'I think it's just your usual tablets,' I said carefully, wondering if this was sufficient explanation. 'Same as you have at home?'

'Oh!' Mum nodded. 'I see, my vitamin tablets, yes. Your father usually sorts those out.'

I breathed out a sigh of relief that there hadn't been more backlash but Mum's anger was almost instantaneously diffused and she began to chuckle.

'She was a bit hopeless, wasn't she really?' She plucked at her cardigan. 'But then, I've never had much confidence in her. Do you remember when Rory broke his arm and she sent him home? It's a wonder she's still in practice.'

'But you've never met her before, Mum.' My voice was gentle.

'Of course, I have, Penelope. Don't be so silly. She used to work with that other doctor, what was his name? Had the beard and the eyebrows, you know. The one who was

78

very insensitive when Marjorie Blackman had her troubles down below.'

I kept my eyes focused on the road as she drifted into this particular vignette. The trouble sometimes is that she speaks with so much conviction and sounds so plausible I end up wondering if it's me that's confused. She went quiet for a while and we were almost home when she started up the conversation again, mid-sentence, as if there had been no pause.

'Anyway,' she said. 'He had very little understanding of women's problems and was a bit over-familiar, if you know what I mean. She's best shot of him.'

Who was best shot of him? I didn't know. Marjorie Blackman and her gynaecological issues? Dr Golding? The doctor who Mum was confusing with Dr Golding? Or perhaps some other fictitious individual imbued with new life by Mum's increasingly overactive imagination. I took the easiest course. 'Certainly sounds like it. Now, shall we have some soup for lunch?'

Chapter Eleven

So, this afternoon was my turn to have The Terrible Evangeline to play. Evangeline, as her *nom de guerre* suggests, is not a favourite among the preschool mummies, but we are all seemingly incapable of saying no to High-powered Joy when she directs us to care for her child. Tuesday afternoons (in fact, many afternoons) are 'absolutely manic' for Joy and rather than book additional childcare, she is shameless about fobbing her unpleasant daughter off onto weaker women such as my good self; women who are often so surprised by the brazenness of the request that we immediately acquiesce and spend the rest of the day wandering round with the dazed expression of one who has been railroaded into an act of self-harm.

Nobody really likes Joy. Nobody is sure what she does for a living other than the fact that it is extremely high-powered and important and it seems that she has a memorised rota, or possibly an app, to alert her when it is, for example, Penny's turn to have Evangeline for a playdate. The approach is nothing short of military – and it is relentless. If one has the temerity to respond to her emails with an excuse as to why extra childcare duty will not be possible this week, e.g.:

Joy – Lovely to hear from you, hope all well!? Terribly sorry but this Tuesday we're going straight to Snape-hill Park to meet up with old friends who we haven't seen in years. Happy to have Evangeline another time though! She's such a poppet!

Penny XXXX

She will be right on it:

That's OK Penny, Evangeline loves Snapehill Park! *smiley emoji* She'll have a great time! I guess it will take you a while to get back so shall I collect her a little later? Say 6pm? 7pm absolute latest. Got to write these reports to present to the Board. Thanks, you're an absolute star!!! XXXXX

If one is feeling exceptionally brave, one might then respond again:

Joy – Reports sound like a nightmare! Obviously happy to help but we won't have space in the car once we pick up our friends on the way to the park. Jane (my dear friend who I haven't seen for AGES) has twins so it's going to be pretty cosy anyway! Sorry. Let me know if there is anything else I can do. Penny XXXXXXX

And then have it turned back on you again:

Penny – I thought you had one of those cars with fold-down seats in the boot? Perhaps one of your friend's kids could go in the back? I would say Evangeline could but you know how car sick she gets *sad emoji*

> Thanks so much – It makes a real difference when
> people help out. Happy to return the favour, just let
> me know when would be good for you. The next
> couple of weeks are ABSOLUTELY MENTAL!!! but
> any time after then! XXXXX

Needless to say, the favour is never returned, there is
no time in Joy's calendar that is not ABSOLUTELY
MENTAL.

The unreciprocated childcare would not be an
enormous issue if Evangeline was an easy child to look
after. In fact, she wouldn't even need to be an *easy* child,
anything short of a complete delinquent would be more
manageable. But sadly, Evangeline is a biter and a pincher,
a teller of tales, a stirrer of woes. Many's the time that
one of our children has come home with bruises, tearfully
reported to have been inflicted by the pinchy little fingers
of Joy's monster child. And while most of us would shy
away from saying it out loud, it is clear that we would all
be entirely unsurprised to learn twenty years hence that
Evangeline is a serial killer.

I am aware that there is an element of hypocrisy here.
I too have a small daughter capable of questionable behaviour. It's not impossible that friends of mine may refer to
my child as 'The Terrible Maisie', although they would
struggle to legitimately refer to me as High-powered
Penny unless it was regarding my caffeinated state. But
although I'll admit to my daughter being 'difficult' and
'challenging', she is *not* a biter. I'm sure she's not.
Preschool would have told me. They must have told
Joy, unless they are scared that *she* might bite them. The
thought of High-powered Joy leaning over the tiny paint-
speckled table to take a chunk out of Miss Janice is quite

entertaining, actually. Anyway – suffice to say that a play-date with The Terrible Evangeline often brings with it a serious risk of personal injury and I find this tends to impact on the cheeriness of the occasion.

Lo and behold. Not two hours into this afternoon's fun and games but there was a wailing and a commotion from the kitchen where the girls were briefly (*briefly*) unsuper-vised while colouring. Maisie blundered down the hall, hair stuck to her face with snotty tears, clutching an arm that was slowly turning purple, dappled with tiny finger-marks. I had just been helping Mum get herself out of the airing cupboard, where she had become inexplicably wedged while trying to reach for a beach towel. She has taken to gathering random items and collecting them in plastic bags under her bed and I am not clear as to whether she is stockpiling for a future nuclear apocalypse, preparing to run away or simply 'tidying'.

It was immediately clear from Maisie's gulping that she was in pain – hers is not the histrionic, shouty response to minor injuries inflicted by other children (see Tom for further details). Maisie's arm really hurt and she was shocked to have been thus assaulted. The fingerprints showed a clear, repeated and sustained pinching attack (I like to use forensic terminology when detailing Evan-geline's crimes – it may be useful in future if the police ever need to question witnesses) and suddenly I got the fury. I picked Maisie up to give her a cuddle and strode back through the hall with her clutched to my side, like an enraged baboon mother. I may even have bared my teeth as I turned the corner. Evangeline was quietly colouring, but her saccharine smile rapidly deteriorated into a trem-ulous display of waterworks, an immediate response to the telling-off she knew was coming. Even Maisie had stopped whimpering, knowing that this was the real deal – Angry Mummy.

'What have you done to Maisie's arm?' I wrestled my child from my hip and thrust the evidence of injury under Evangeline's nose. 'Is this playing nicely?'

Evangeline let out a wail and flung her head down upon her colouring. 'Wouldn't let me have… glitter pen…' came the muffled response.

'I did, Mummy!' Maisie was quick to interject, not wanting my wrath to deflect onto her. 'I did let her have the pen! But then I wanted a go… And I… took it back.' I looked at her sternly and she screwed her face up. 'I snatched it!' she announced, her relief at this admission of guilt palpable. 'I snatched it. And now *I'm* in trouble.' Even in pain and cast as the victim, Maisie couldn't quite bear to concede all of the limelight and drama to Evangeline. She wanted a piece of the action but I was too cross to take my focus off the master criminal.

'That was a mean thing to do, Evangeline,' I said, the anger plain in my voice. 'You shouldn't *ever* pinch. You shouldn't *ever* hurt people. Even if they don't share their glitter pens with you. It is *unkind* and it is *not right.*'

'Penelope!' My mother had appeared in the doorway, apparently unscathed by her recent brush with suffocation in the airing cupboard. 'Why are you shouting at this little girl?' She glared at me and instantly it was as if I was eight years old and caught wearing her high heels.

'She pinched Maisie…' I trailed off feebly as Mum crossed the room and put her arm around Evangeline, leaning down to the table to peer at her.

'Well, that's a sad little face, isn't it?' she said and pulled the piece of paper out from underneath Evangeline's arm. 'Shall we see if we can draw a nice smiley face instead? I'll go first, shall I?' Mum drew a shaky circle with two dots for eyes and a frowning mouth. 'Is that right?' She looked at Evangeline, who shook her head solemnly and took the crayon to draw a happy face. Mum nodded thoughtfully. 'Ah! Well, I can see that you're much better at this than me. Could you show me how you did that?' She pulled up a chair alongside Evangeline. Maisie and I exchanged a bemused glance before she detached herself from my side and went to join her grandmother and the vicious little witch who I could now see was actually just another four-year-old girl. The anger drained away.

'Right!' I said brightly. 'I'll get the kettle on.'

–

Mum kept both girls entertained with drawing for a full hour, which allowed me the luxury of putting yet another wash on, unloading the dishwasher, booking a vet's appointment for Colin and calling the ward to check on Dad. Then they all disappeared upstairs and were ominously quiet until, with the inducement of biscuits, they emerged, beaming and covered in blue eyeshadow and wonky cerise lipstick.

'We've done Granny's pretty face,' Maisie informed me importantly, gesturing to my mother's Technicolor visage with a flourish.

'It's for a shelfie,' Evangeline added, with an uncertain look at Maisie, who nodded clarification. 'Yes, Mummy, we need a group shelfie for the 'gram. Can you do one?' She struck a pouty pose and gestured to Evangeline and Mum to do the same. I duly recorded the image for posterity on my phone and promised that when they were old enough to have social media accounts I would upload it to their profiles.

They all piled into the car with me to collect Tom from football. He, to his eternal credit, managed to avoid rolling around in hysterics when he saw their ludicrously painted faces. I like to think that this was because he quickly assessed the appropriateness of making fun of his little sister, her friend and his grandmother and realised that to do so would be unkind and unnecessary. The reality is that he probably just didn't notice that he was being picked up by a car full of drag queens.

By the time we got home, Grace had returned and I made a colossal vegetable pasta bake. Initially Evangeline refused to eat any of it, sitting with her lips clamped shut and arms folded and telling me in no uncertain terms that she would not eat pasta 'with bits in'. I contemplated making a separate dish, it wouldn't be too hard, after all, to knock up a plain tomato sauce and I often had to do the same for Maisie. But there is nothing like seeing the actions that you tolerate in your own offspring reflected back at you in the form of someone else's child to make you realise that actually, it's bloody annoying and it's not on.

'Evangeline,' I said. 'In fact, all of you, listen up because this is how it's going to be from now on. This is the meal. OK? If you're not hungry then don't eat it. I won't be cross. But you won't be getting anything else. This is not a restaurant.'

There was silence for a moment and then everyone looked back down at their plates. Mum had taken advantage of the distraction provided by my declaration and started helping herself to Evangeline's pasta. Both the younger girls stared as Mum's arm snaked across the table and speared two or three fusilli with unerring accuracy, surprising given her inability to button her cardigan up

86

or hold a mug properly. At the prospect of sustenance vanishing in front of her eyes, Evangeline was left with little option than to scoop up a few pasta twirls herself. Maisie followed suit and soon there were clean plates all round. Nothing like the threat of imminent starvation to focus the mind.

High-powered Joy came to collect the slightly less terrible Evangeline later that evening. After dinner, both girls had gone to go and watch the bedtime hour on CBeebies with Mum in the sitting room and by the time the doorbell rang I was feeling relatively calm. In contrast, Joy's face was pinched and she gave me a mechanical smile when I opened the door. Colin started circling enthusiastically in front of her while I tried to gather up Evangeline's belongings and I heard a loud gasp of disapproval as his enthusiasm gave way to over-excitement, a puddle appearing underneath him.

'Oh. Gosh. Sorry.' I hauled Colin out through the back door, returning with a wodge of kitchen towel and disinfectant which I sprayed liberally over the floor tiles and Joy's three-inch suede heels. 'He's... um, not had a walk today.' I didn't add that the reason for my dog's lack of exercise was Evangeline's refusal to accompany us outside earlier in order to walk him. Joy still hadn't said a word but continued to stare down at her shoes, which were now splattered in a combination of dog piss and Pet Rescue spray.

'Um. I'll go and get her, shall I?' I made it halfway down the corridor but then backtracked. 'Joy... I, um. There was a little incident earlier.'

'Incident? With Evangeline?' She raised a single eyebrow.

'Yes. She… She pinched Maisie,' I gulped, trying to sound brave and matter of fact. 'Quite hard. Nothing to worry about and all OK now but I just thought you ought to know.'

'Oh!' Joy's face was a picture of incredulity. 'Really? That's quite unusual.' I felt myself wither under her gaze. 'She must have been provoked.'

'Provoked? Well, if you consider not sharing a glitter pen to be sufficient provocation then yes, I guess she was. But it was really quite a nasty pinch, or series of pinches judging by the bruising. Look…' I could see Joy's nostrils flaring. 'I'm not trying to sound judgy at all – God knows my kids do all sorts of things when they're a bit angry. It's just, if it was me, I'd want to know.'

'I see.'

'And… I did give her a proper telling-off.' I thought it best to get all my cards on the table now in case Evangeline brought out a woeful tale of the verbal abuse she had received while a guest in my house.

'Goodness.' The lips were pursed. 'I hope you didn't shout at her, Penny. She's a very sensitive child. She doesn't like raised voices at all. It really upsets her.'

I gave a tiny laugh to cover both my embarrassment and outrage – sensitive child, my arse. 'Well, seeing my daughter sustain a nasty injury upsets me. So there we are. I'll go and get her for you. They're watching TV.'

I rounded the corner of the sitting room with her hot on my heels and there we encountered a scene of domestic bliss rarely witnessed in my household. Both Maisie and Evangeline were curled up on the sofa, their heads in Mum's lap, thumbs in mouths and fast asleep. Mum had her head tilted back and was snoring gently, all three were still covered in make-up. I turned my head to Joy and raised my eyebrows. 'Sorry about the state of them,' I said. 'But I think they've enjoyed themselves. Do you want to wake her up or just carry her out to the car?'

Joy glanced at Evangeline's make-up smeared face and then down at her immaculate suit. 'She'll have to wake up and walk,' she said briskly. 'I've only just got this back from the dry cleaners.'

'I'll carry her out to the car for you,' I said, before I could stop myself. The sight of monstrous Evangeline snuggled up against my mother just like a regular sleepy pre-schooler was just too sweet to ruin with overtired tears and wailing. Even wild animals look cute when they are heavily sedated and she was much less likely to pinch, bite or otherwise assault me if she remained comatose.

Joy gave me a curious look, probably bemused as to why I would do this for someone else's child – as bemused as I should have been by my own overly indulgent behaviour no doubt. But she didn't say anything so I scooped Evangeline up into my arms and her sticky face lolled against my jumper, hair plastered to her warm forehead.

'Could you get the door?' I whispered to Joy, who was still looking peculiar. I inclined my head towards Evangeline's Smiggle satchel and she mutely picked it up along with her daughter's coat and wellingtons.

I managed to get Evangeline into the car seat without too much fuss – I've had a few years' experience of posting sleeping children into awkward gaps, a bit like that Saturday-night television show, *The Wall*, where people contort themselves into all sorts of odd shapes to fit through the space provided. I did end up with a smudge of lipstick and orange blusher on my jumper but I merely rubbed it into the dried pasta sauce and Play-Doh that I was already coated in.

'I'll probably get at least another day's wear out of this before it needs to go in the wash,' I exclaimed gaily to Joy as she slid gracefully into the driver's seat. I don't know whether I was trying to demonstrate how relaxed I was about my dishevelled appearance (which was already fairly obvious) or make a point about water wastage and carbon footprint. Most likely I was just feeling a bit awkward and filling the conversational gap with something inane.

I turned to go back inside and carry my own pre-schooler to bed, but caught a fleeting glimpse of Joy's expression as she reversed off the drive, and suddenly knew where I'd seen it before. It was the same covetous face that Evangeline had pulled when she wanted Maisie's glitter pen. It briefly crossed my mind that what I had mistaken for Joy's contempt at my lowly behaviour had actually been envy, but then I caught sight of my fat scarecrow reflection in the kitchen window. Perhaps not.

Chapter Twelve

I decided to celebrate the arrival of the half-term holidays with a delightful shopping trip, accompanied by my mother and eldest daughter. I say *delightful* when what I actually mean is *complete horror show*. Grace had announced earlier in the week that she needed an outfit for Milly's party and that she had ABSOLUTELY NOTHING TO WEAR that didn't make her look fat, stupid, ugly or all three. I know enough of my daughter's moods at present to understand that nothing short of a complete outfit overhaul would persuade her otherwise. She's been particularly out of sorts the past few weeks, snapping at me and Tom as standard, but also at Maisie. She'd even told Sam to shut up on Thursday and usually she tolerates his teasing with a forbearance reserved solely for him – and the dog. I do wonder whether something is going on at school or with her friends but it's difficult to know because any time I ask she rips my head off. There is a fine balance, it seems, between being 'there if she needs me' or 'completely in her face' and it's not a balance I appear to have struck.

We arrived at the shopping centre without incident and Grace immediately abandoned us lest she should be seen, and therefore associated with, a member of her actual family. The shame of shopping with one's mother and grandmother would have been UNBEARABLE. We agreed to meet in one hour on the ground floor of Marks & Spencer. All good.

I had asked Mum if there was anything she would particularly like to look at, shopping having been a big feature of her life when I was growing up. She had enjoyed being fashionable – as evidenced by the glorious photos of eighties jumpsuits, blazers, skirts and heels in exactly the same pastel shades – but she had also enjoyed buying clothes for other people and was always brilliant at purchasing gifts, particularly for me. Many was the Boxing Day that my female cousins would gaze in awe at my fashionable seasonal attire and lament the sensible woollens they had received from their own mothers. I, of course, had no idea how lucky I was and instead of the on-trend outfits gifted to me spent most of my teens wearing a Dutch airman's trench-coat from the charity shop teamed with a hideous purple tasselled skirt which smelt of incense and Marlboro Lights. But I always knew there would be an appropriate garment in the wardrobe if I had a party to go to.

However, over the past years of creeping dementia, Mum's interest in shopping, along with so many other things, has waned, as has the interest in buying for others. I thought that the trump card of this particular trip might be looking at clothes for her granddaughters, specifically Maisie – after all, what fashion-loving grandmother can resist the pull of a sparkly dress or pretty hair accessories for four-year-old girls? This grandmother, it seems. She was completely disinterested in the girls' clothing section and looked at me bemused as I held up rainbow this and unicorn that.

It's odd how this disease changes the little things, those preferences that make up our personality. I had been watching a documentary about Alzheimer's on television last week and the wife of a man with dementia had talked about how her husband used to enjoy motorsport but now prefers football; and how he used to like jazz and now can't bear it (so there are some benefits). Of course, tastes and interests change with age, but the sum of these myriad choices makes us who we are, and sometimes these are the hardest aspects of Mum's illness to deal with; the change in fundamental characteristics; the erosion of who she once was.

When she was first diagnosed, her symptoms were more conventional, things you would expect someone with dementia to experience – not that one considers dementia as a possibility in someone her age. She forgot we were coming around for dinner one Sunday; she would get stuck halfway through an anecdote, or started questioning arrangements that had been agreed in previous conversations. Dad admitted that she couldn't do the *Times* crossword anymore and eventually she agreed to see the doctor, but only because we were worried. A friend of hers had recently had a brain tumour, another friend had been diagnosed with clinical depression. Both made much more sense than considering dementia in a sixty-year-old woman. Alzheimer's was something old people got.

It's a common misconception of course, I know that now. Just like I know it's not all about forgetting where you put your glasses or who the prime minister is. Dementia doesn't just affect Mum's memory. It's had an impact on her speech, her mobility, her inhibitions, her social interactions and ultimately her whole personality.

I watched her stroking the mirrored panel at the end of a clothing rail, lost in her own world, and realised that dementia has unravelled her as a person.

However, we didn't have time for wallowing in self-pity. We had purchases to make. Undeterred, we proceeded to the women's clothing department where it transpired that Mum was after a pair of shorts.

'I'd like a nice pair of those blue ones. Like, um, like... the girl. You know?'

'Like Grace?' I asked. (Does Grace have blue shorts? Seems unlikely.) 'Like Maisie?'

'No.' She was getting frustrated. 'The girl on the telly. Singing the song.' I wracked my brains. We had watched an old *America's Got Talent* compilation show the night before last (against all better judgement – it was either that or *Mrs Brown's Boys* and, dementia or no dementia, I have to draw the line somewhere) but surely, she couldn't mean... 'Nicki Minaj?'

Mum nodded. 'Yes. The shouty one. Nice shorts. Diamonds on them.'

'They were very short though, weren't they, Mum? The ones with the diamante trim? Yes. I suspect she didn't get them in M&S, to be honest. And your legs might get a bit cold, what with the sleet we had yesterday?'

She considered this for a moment. 'Good for holidays, though.'

I sighed. I wasn't going to win this discussion. 'You're right. And there I was forgetting about the week's clubbing in Ibiza I'd booked for us all. Well, in that case, we'd best keep an eye out for some then.'

Round and round the trouser rails we plodded in search of the elusive, unseasonal and completely age-and-size-inappropriate garment on my mother's wish list. Skinny jeans, comfortable cords, boot-cut, high-waist, low-rise; we viewed and eschewed them all until I eventually managed to persuade Mum to try on a couple of pairs of leggings and led her to the changing rooms. We then had an awkward moment where Mum walked in on no less than four people in various states of undress before finding the cubicle that corresponded to her numbered piece of plastic. I hovered in the seating area reserved for bored-looking husbands reading copies of the Saturday papers and waited. And waited. And waited.

The husbands had all come and gone, replaced by new bored-looking ones with new papers. I asked the assistant if I could just go and check on my mother and found her leaning against the side of the cubicle with one leg stuck in the arm hole of her jacket and both pairs of leggings draped extravagantly over the mirrored lighting. I knew better than to draw attention to the fact that the trying on of clothes was not going according to plan. 'You OK?' I was non-committal. 'Have you tried the leggings on?'

She pulled her leg out of her jacket crossly. 'I haven't really had time, Penelope. What with one thing and another.'

I glanced at my watch. She'd been in there for twenty-seven minutes. 'Sure, of course. Shall I give you a hand?' Again, I kept my voice casual, as if needing assistance in differentiating between garments designed for upper and lower limbs was entirely normal. She grumbled a bit but eventually let me haul the Lycra up her body in a manner reminiscent of a sumo wrestling move. We both had a bit of a sweat on by the time we conceded that they were a touch snug and I couldn't face a repeat performance so I made a judgement that the next size up would probably be perfect and hurried her to the checkout.

Here we encountered yet another awkward scenario when Mum handed over her debit card to the cashier, only to look blankly at the chip and pin machine as it was held out to her. She stood there for a few moments, seemingly hoping that the girl would remove the offending gadget from under her nose and I could see the cashier becoming increasingly worried by the lack of response. In an effort to close at least one transaction and come away from the shopping ordeal with a single purchase, I barged through the queuing shoppers who all grumbled in a dissatisfied, British, 'I'm cross but I'm not going to do anything about it other than raise my eyebrows to my neighbour and tut mildly' way, and reached the cash desk as Mum was about to walk off and leave her leggings, her handbag and her debit card with the cashier.

'Mum,' I caught my breath. 'You've got to pay for the leggings. What's your PIN number?'

She turned to me bemused. 'My what?'

'Your PIN. Your number, the one that goes with the card. So that you can buy stuff?'

'Where's Gordon?' Her expression had changed from one of confusion to fear. 'What have you done with him?'

The queue of shoppers stared suspiciously and the cashier leaned in towards Mum, asking quietly, 'Do you know this woman?'.

I grabbed the card. 'Just put it back in your purse, Mum. I'll get these.' I handed my card to the cashier. 'Sorry about that.' She pursed her lips and I waited for my receipt.

I really wanted to add an explanation; just to say 'She's got dementia and I'm her daughter, as opposed to a predatory villain trying to steal money from pensioners in order to buy navy leggings.' But I didn't want to add to

Mum's mortification. It would have helped if Mum could have looked more obviously disabled, but I realised that this was a curious thing to wish for and, short of holding up a sign to announce her diagnosis, there was little I could do without making her cross and embarrassed.

I shepherded her through the bras and knickers to go and meet Grace, who was standing resentfully, if that's possible, in the foyer area of the ground floor. I waved cheerily as I caught her eye and stepped out onto the escalator and she responded with a minute shrug of her shoulder. Still, it looked as though her shopping trip had been more successful than ours because the tote bag on her shoulder was bulging with goodies, doubtless manufactured in sweatshops by tiny urchins who would infinitely prefer a square meal to a hundred party outfits. I was halfway down, about level with the tops of the mannequins' heads, when I realised that Mum was not with me. In a manner not dissimilar to horses faced with Becher's Brook in The Grand National, she had hesitated at the top of the descending escalator for just long enough to allow me to get on while she remained paralysed at the step-off point. I could now see a queue of people forming in the bottleneck behind her, but I was too far down to contemplate scrambling back to retrieve her. Grace had also noticed and was gesticulating wildly to me. 'Granny's stuck!'

'Mum!' I shouted as she receded out of view. 'Just step onto it!' But she was frozen in position, blocking the way for everyone else but unable to proceed herself. The queue behind her was starting to get restless; some were dissipating to the neighbouring escalator where a new lengthy queue was forming (partly due to people gawping at Mum and forgetting to actually move themselves) and one man in our queue appeared to be gently persuading or possibly wrestling my mother onto the moving floor in front of her. I then watched in horror as a well-meaning fellow shopper hollered from the foyer below, 'Wait there! Help is coming!'

The shouter, a stout and capable woman in her sixties, had noticed Mum's plight and proceeded to push past me in order to climb the descending escalator (no mean feat) but stumbled and fell *up* the stairs in her rescue attempt. I had reached the bottom by this point and just gazed on as the catastrophe unfolded.

Thankfully nobody was hurt. Mum (completely unperturbed and oblivious to the chaos) remained on the first floor until Grace (who had shown surprising initiative) reached her via the correct ascending escalator and accompanied her to the lift. We made a mental note to stick to traditional stairwells in future and it was only when we were back in the car that I realised we'd left the bloody leggings behind.

Grace sat in the back with Mum and chatted away to her, showing what she'd bought as we drove home. We collected Maisie from Darcy's party, where I was assured by Zahara that she had been a very good girl, and by the time we got home Sam and Tom were back from football. I followed the trail of mud into the sitting room to find them both on the Xbox playing *Fortnite*.

'D'you enjoy your shopping trip then, girls?' Sam's eyes were fixed to the screen as he leapt over tall buildings and took sniper shots at a pink rabbit that I assumed was Tom. 'Buy yourself anything nice?'

'I got some all right stuff, I s'pose.' Grace had appeared beside me and Sam dragged his eyes away, unused to engaging in actual conversation with his eldest daughter.

'Great! Stuff for the party was it? Nothing too "extra" or too "basic".' He did quote marks in the air, which isn't easy when holding onto a games-controller but he loves taking the piss out of her derisive assessment of other people's outfits.

She smiled. 'No. Just right, thanks.' She turned to leave the room and shouted over her shoulder, 'I don't think Mum had the easiest time though. She might need a cup of tea.'

Sam returned my stunned expression. OK, Grace hadn't actually offered to make me a cuppa herself but...

Had that been...

Actual empathy?

Chapter Thirteen

Another week, another dementia-related treat. Mum seems to be developing a problem with stairs, specifically coming down them. Once or twice I have found her motionless, poised, halfway down and unable to proceed – completely baffled as to where to go next. And in this scenario, extending a helping hand does not do the trick. She wants something substantial to hold onto; a wall, a railing, a post. Sadly, the lower part of our crooked stairwell is missing the banister – or as the estate agent described it, 'quirkily open-plan'. Nice in terms of flow and Feng Shui, but not so practical if you're a woman of a certain age and declining cognitive ability who has come over all wobbly and afraid.

I phoned the doctors' surgery. I explained that I did not need a medical appointment but that I needed some help with getting Mum up and down the stairs. I was put through to the secretary's office. I explained that I did not need a medical appointment. I was put back through to switchboard. I waited. I fed the dog. I waited. I noticed a message on my mobile: Grace had forgotten that Food Science was today – if she texted me the ingredients could I please bring them in? I replied in the affirmative and wished there was an emoji for a deep and exasperated sigh. I waited. I let the dog out. I spoke to a different receptionist who advised me to contact social services.

I let the dog in, put a wash on and emptied the dishwasher. I searched the county council website. I learnt a lot about the wheelie-bin collection dates and found the pothole emergency reporting number and noted it down – you never know when that might come in handy. The phone rang. It was school.

Tom had a temperature.

Did I want to collect him now or head over to school and administer some Calpol?

Could they not administer Calpol?

No. It was not in accordance with their medicines policy.

Really? I thought I'd signed that form…?

No. The form I was referring to had been pertaining to a particular school trip to Drayton Manor Park and Zoo and the instructions to administer Calpol, sunscreen or antihistamine cream were only relevant for that specific occasion. What was I thinking? Did I not realise that all hell would break loose if the school assumed my instruction from two months ago was still valid and applicable now?

I apologised to Mrs North for my error.

–

Two hours later, having purchased the alfalfa bean sprouts and cold pressed flaxseed oil that Grace needed immediately for Food Science, dropped them off at the school office in town, driven back to the village primary school and called in at that office clutching my bottle of Calpol to be told that Tom was feeling much better and was actually playing British Bulldog (did I want Mrs North to leave her post to retrieve him? Lord no. Heaven forbid), I found myself sitting once more in front of the clunky council website looking at their 'Care of the vulnerable and elderly' page. I completed their online form, all fifteen pages of it. I stalled at the question of whether an urgent assessment was required. Did I think the person was in immediate danger? Ummm. No? The egg-timer flashed up on screen. I waited. I made Mum some soup. I returned to the computer to be told that my session had expired and the form was now blank. Did I want to complete their short customer satisfaction survey?

I went back to the saucepan of boiling soup and contemplated sticking my head in it.

Chapter Fourteen

Wednesday, 26 February

Dad was having physio when we visited today. The 'rehabilitation suite' was actually a draughty terrapin hut, but it was surprisingly well equipped with rails, crash mats, treadmills and exercise balls; the accoutrements of rehabilitation. There was even a Mini Metro parked in the far corner of the room, presumably to allow patients to practise their manual dexterity and pedal skills as opposed to evidence of a recent ram-raid.

Dad was suspended between Ben and another physio, Neve, who were supporting his weight as he lowered himself gingerly back into the wheelchair. He looked absolutely shattered but managed a wobbly smile.

'Hellshp, Penshp.' The concentration on his face as he forced his mouth around the greeting was painful to see, but at least there was now something approaching vocalisation.

'Hi, Dad. Looks like you've been put through your paces?' I said, and he attempted a wonky smile.

'I'll just write up your notes and we'll get you back to the ward, Gordon.' Ben said. 'You've worked really hard today, mate. We'll have you up and walking in no time I reckon.' He gestured for me to follow him to the desk in the corner. I left Mum with Neve, who was wheeling

Dad over to the window, where he had a lovely view of the car park and distant incinerator.

'So,' I said, lowering my voice. Dad might have lost some of his motor function but his hearing was fine. 'How's he doing? Really, I mean. Don't put a gloss on it for me.'

Ben also lowered his voice. 'OK. Well. He *is* working really hard, that wasn't just motivational physio chat earlier. A lot of my patients aren't nearly as...'

'Bloody-minded?' I offered.

'Er, yeah. As bloody-minded as him. And that helps.'

'But?'

He smiled. 'You knew there was one coming. Yeah, he's really motivated, *but* the hip surgery on top of the stroke is a tough combination in terms of recovery. His speech and his manual dexterity are really improving, you'll have noticed that I expect?' I nodded. 'But getting him mobile is a challenge. The muscle wasting that's already occurred... the quads, the hip flexors. It's hard to build the strength up in those circumstances.'

I must have looked a bit alarmed because he hurriedly corrected himself, 'I don't mean it won't happen. It will happen, really. It's just...'

'It's going to take some time.' I finished for him.

He nodded. 'Yeah. Sorry. I know that's not what you wanted to hear.' He tilted his head over in Mum's direction. She was holding Dad's hand and staring out of the window as a parking ticket whirled past, caught in the breezy squall of winter's end. 'How are things going, with your mum? Looking after her on top of everything else?'

I suddenly found myself unable to speak. There was a lump in my throat that wouldn't budge. Ben just nodded.

'Yep. Thought so. My ex's dad had young onset dementia. It's a real bitch, isn't it?'

I snorted agreement through my nose, aware that a tear had escaped from my feeble eyes. 'Yes. It's pretty challenging,' I conceded. 'Not always. But most of the time it feels like a slow bereavement – and it's depressing as hell.' I told him about the difficulties we were having with stairs.

'OK,' he nodded, thoughtful for a moment, 'what you need is an OT, an occupational therapy assessment, which you'd arrange through—'

'Social services?' I interrupted him. 'Been there, tried that.' I told him about my wasted Monday and the frustration was clear in my voice. 'I just seem to be going round and round in circles all the sodding time. Everyone is trying to be helpful but nobody can actually *do* anything. Trying to access care is like a full-time job and I just can't do it while I'm actually being her carer and looking after three kids who are barely capable of wiping their own arses. Which is also my fault apparently, because I've indulged them. My brother, who's a doctor and therefore knows everything, reckons they're feral because I let them get away with murder, and my husband's never bloody home, and when he does get home I'm too knackered to even say hello...' I paused to take a breath and realised that Neve and my parents were staring at me from the other side of the room along with the bilateral amputee on the parallel bars.

'Oh, God.' I balled up a tissue into my eyes. 'Sorry.' I looked at Ben. 'You seem to be the one constantly on the receiving end of this. I'm normally a very together person. Well, maybe that's not true, but I'm usually a bit better than this bloody shambles anyway.' I stood up from my chair, noting his look of concern.

'I'm OK, really,' I said. 'I appreciate you being honest. I know it's going to take a while for Dad to get better. I know I can hang on in there until then, so don't worry. I'm not going to, like, throw myself under a bus or anything.'

'Jesus, Penny. Don't say things like that round here.' He looked over his shoulder towards the woman missing both her lower legs. 'We do see people who are suicidal from time to time.'

'Yes, of course, sorry. I wasn't meaning to be flippant.'

'No, I know. But seriously, depression is a really common part of being a carer. I saw it happen to my ex. You've got to get some support.' He rifled around in a desk drawer. 'You go and have a chat with your dad and I'll sort out some referrals for you, get some leaflets and things. There are people who can help. Not just social services; people who understand, who'll know what you're going through. And there are things you can do with your mum; art therapy, music therapy… Things that might help both of you.'

I raised my eyebrows a fraction but didn't contradict him. 'OK, thanks. That would be great.'

To be honest though, I failed to see how a bunch of leaflets were going to help me.

Spring

Chapter Fifteen

As per Ben's instructions, I dutifully phoned Alzheimer's UK and spoke to someone called Anita, who suggested we meet tomorrow in Hobbs garden-centre cafe. I toyed with the idea of going alone; trying to discuss my mother while the woman in question was sitting beside me was going to be a challenge. However, by virtue of her role, Anita was presumably well-versed in navigating this type of scenario and hopefully I wouldn't be required to explain Mum's diagnosis or behaviour. That in itself was a giant leap forward from most social interactions because to be honest, I was fed up of people throwing me questioning glances and judging my mother based on her erratic actions or loudly expressed and often offensive opinions. I can't blame them for staring; I certainly would. Mum telling a woman in the queue at the butcher's that her child is 'very ugly' does attract unnecessary attention, as does her laughing uproariously at the 'fat man' in the shoe shop. I always want to explain to these people that my mother is normally scrupulously polite, that these hurtful comments are a result of her illness and not her true character. But most of the time I simply don't have the energy. As a result, I often feel like I'm trapped at home – not because of Mum, but because of my own social anxiety and embarrassment.

Even worse than having to deflect insults aimed at total strangers is encountering casual acquaintances; people who know you well enough that they feel entitled to stop you in the frozen-food aisle, peruse the contents of your shopping trolley and enquire about your children, entirely unaware of the fact that the woman hovering nearby, tucking a packet of scampi and two tins of custard into her handbag, is your mother who has dementia. So it was that I stumbled across Lindi and Tiggy, two of the uber-mummies from school, whose presence did little to improve my supermarket shopping experience this afternoon.

Lindi and Tiggy are, shall we say, 'of a type'. They are ostentatious in their involvement with the school parents' association, always 'supervising a stall' or attending a committee meeting but never actually doing the boring stuff like getting the float from the bank or clearing up after the fete. These are women with a clear idea of hierarchy and a belief that one can never begin the process of scaling the class ladder too early – and by that I don't mean the class ladder that reception kids stick gold stars on when they do well at mark-making. In the world of social climbing, Lindi and Tiggy's children were kitted out with hard hats, crampons and belay ropes before their second birthdays. These mums make it their business to know everything about the relevant peer group and spend hours ranking each child in the school according to an ancient system, as follows:

- **Parental occupation:** Points for fathers who work in the City or have a recognisably 'good' job (doctor, lawyer, architect). Negative marks for tradesmen, farmers (unless very well-heeled 'gentleman farmers'), those who undertake shifts or travel extensively and are therefore not able to attend Father's Day breakfast or run the barbeque after Sport's Day. Mums who work tend to have marks deducted unless it's in interior design, floristry or upholstering niche items to display on Pinterest.

- **Appearance:** School uniform shop of origin – top marks for John Lewis and Clarks, low marks for Asda, Aldi or Primark (unless done ironically – not sure *how* you do this ironically but some of Tiggy's chums seem to pull it off). Tolerance for quality hand-me-downs as long as there is no evidence of white-board pen. Negative marking for earrings, other jewellery, garish book-bag decorations or attention-seeking accessories unless sported by their own offspring when seemingly normal rules do not apply.

  - *Subcategory:* State of school uniform during use – clean (by which I mean spotless bleached whites that smell delicious) and ironed to within an inch of their lives. Once a child has reached those heady pre-pubertal days of whiffy armpits, God help them, frankly.
  - *Additional subcategory for girls:* Hair – degree of maternal manual dexterity and ability to assemble hairstyle while not straying into attention-seeking hair accessories (see above). Top marks for immaculate French plaits, braids or complex fish-tails. No marks for lopsided and bedraggled ponytails or knobbly 'buns' held in place with rubber bands or an old pair of pants (believe me, I've tried).

- **Behaviour:** Boys – high marks for 'sporty' but low marks for pushing and shoving. For maximum points a boy must have exceptional ball-skills, speed and coordination and strike the perfect balance between competitive and aggressive – not easy when you are six years old. Girls need to be pretty (but not too pretty) and kind (but not too popular). Good to know that the gender imbalance remains deeply ingrained. As a side note, while Tiggy and Lindi would both consider themselves terribly woke and down with the transgender community, they will not tolerate boys with long hair or girls wearing trousers.
- **Academic attainment:** Moderation is key. Nobody likes a show-off, particularly if there is a suggestion that they might be further ahead in mastering phonics than Tiggy or Lindi's offspring, but then nobody really wants to be associated with the child who has had so little contact with actual books that they try to swipe their fingertip across the front page in order to move the screen along.
- **Family holiday destination:** Higher marks for long-haul and tropical luxury resorts (obviously) but also note that one can use the environmental card and garner decent marks by opting for an up-market vacay in the British Isles, particularly if one is staying in the Scottish castle home of a family friend or has access to a private beach, on-site nanny and organic catering facilities.

I could go on and I expect there are several criteria that I am completely unaware of – and therefore scoring poorly in.

Tiggy was the first one to spot me, although technically I'd seen her first. In an attempt to stave off the Spanish Inquisition that acknowledging her presence would involve, I paid a considerable amount of attention to the tinned clementine segments and sponge pudding bases that are always placed inexplicably on the shelf above the frozen vegetables. But needless to say, this was not sufficient defence against the eagle-eyed duo.

'Penneeee!' They greeted me with big expansive kisses to both cheeks.

'I was just saying to Tigs, that looks like Penny over there by the oven chips, wasn't I, Tigs?' Lindi was almost breathless in her excitement at actually identifying another school mum in the act of buying food.

'Yes,' I said. 'Chips and waffles. Although, I *was* looking for the quinoa, obviously.' I gave a nervous laugh, unsure where this was leading. Tiggy was peering into my trolley, her eyes wide as she took in the high proportion of value items and ready meals.

'Oh, but the quinoa's in the wholefoods aisle, just next to the nutritional yeast, Penny.' Tiggy's voice was momentarily reproving. 'Not that I ever have time to be messing around with nutritional yeast! God knows who buys it – vegans probably.'

'Not just vegans, Tigs.' Lindi was quick to correct her alpha, which may have been unwise. 'It's terribly good for people with allergies too, I use it all the time as a supplement in Chloe's meals. She's doing so much better since the naturopath diagnosed her combined gluten, lactose and sulphite intolerance, and school have said that she's performing at a level far more consistent with her ability.

It's *so* hard to see your child not fulfilling their potential because of allergies…' Lindi's sigh was loaded with the evident unfulfilled potential of her seven-year-old.

'Yes.' Tiggy screwed up her nose in sympathy, 'She has had some behavioural issues, hasn't she? Speaking of which…' She turned to me, 'How *is* Tom doing?'

She's a master of the Bridget Jones's conversational jellyfish, Tiggy. One minute you're swimming in the warm and shallow waters of small talk and the next, you've been stung into submission by an almighty Portuguese man-of-war. Either that or it's death by a thousand tiny cuts and you only realise on your way home that this is the reason you feel shit about your life. I was determined not to rise to it.

'Oh, he's fine, thanks. Doing well!'

'That's great.' (I could tell she wasn't going to leave it there because the contoured cheeks were pushing into a little moue of mock-sympathy.) 'It's so hard sometimes to keep these boys under control, isn't it? I lose track of the number of times I have to remind Reuben to *always tell a teacher* if somebody's being too rough in the playground, but I guess some of them just get a little carried away, don't they? I mean, there's often not much that the school can do about it of course, it's entirely dependent on what's going on at home, positive role models and so forth.' She puffed out a little sigh of self-importance. 'And I feel *so blessed* on that score, obviously.'

'Of course. Because…?' I was trying to think of the positive role models she was referring to. Surely not her blancmange of a husband?

'Because of John. I mean, he does leave me in charge of most of the discipline in the house.' (I bet he does.) 'But he has exemplary self-control and I think it's crucial that children learn the importance of that as soon as possible, don't you?'

'Oh yes. Although, Tiggy, I don't like to stifle their self-expression...' I left that one hanging there, knowing she'd be unable to refuse the bait. But Lindi interjected first.

'Oh *absolutely*, Penny!' she gushed. 'You must allow them to be themselves. I'm always encouraging Chloe to embrace her creativity and really release her inner child...' She trailed off before I had a chance to investigate exactly how an actual child was supposed to release their inner child. She had lost her main audience – Tiggy was no longer paying attention. Instead, that particular eye had been caught by the sight of my mother reaching up to a high shelf of meringue nests, revealing a large expanse of midriff and what appeared to be a pair of flesh-coloured tights trailing out of her waistband like an extra appendage.

My heart broke a tiny bit as I remembered how much care and attention Mum always took with her appearance before the dementia. She wouldn't have left the house without a full face of make-up, let alone allowed herself to be seen out and about in a mismatched cardigan and elast-icated trousers accessorised with superfluous hosiery. We all watched as the pack of meringues teetered on the edge for a moment before toppling to the floor. Mum regarded the broken nests with concern, nudged them with her foot and then picked them up, scrunching them into her handbag. She then shuffled across the aisle towards me and my lovely friends and I tried to discreetly remove the tights from her mid-region.

'Stop it, Penelope,' she said, batting my hand away. 'I need these for later.'

I left the tights dangling down between us like an embarrassed visitor as Mum turned her attention to Tiggy and Lindi, both of whom, to be fair, were smiling politely. Lindi, however, couldn't quite drag her attention away from Mum's handbag where the meringues were jostling for space with the scampi, tins of custard and what looked like a parsnip.

'Tiggy, Lindi, this is my mum, Mary. We were just about to head to the check-out, so...'

'Pleased to meet you, Mary.' Tiggy gave a gracious smile.

Mum narrowed her eyes and peered at her closely. 'Your dress is very strange,' she said.

A cloud settled over Tiggy's face, coming to rest in the only Botox-free space above her nose. 'It's Beulah, actually,' she said tightly and peered at the groceries in Mum's handbag. 'I assume you're going to pay for those?'

'Yes, of course we are. No need to call security! Ha ha!' I must have looked a bit manic as I grabbed Mum's elbow and manoeuvred her past the two women. 'Bye ladies. *Lovely* to see you. Sorry we couldn't stay and chat for longer but you know...'

'Snooty cow,' said Mum cheerfully as we moved in the direction of the check-out. It was a brief glimpse of the person she had once been, a woman who would not have tolerated Tiggy and Lindi's nonsense for a moment (although she'd have put them in their place a little more discreetly in the past) and I couldn't resist a tiny smile. Tiggy's smile, on the other hand, had become so thin that it looked as though she might have swallowed it entirely. But then the poor love probably needed all the calories she could get.

Chapter Sixteen

Tuesday, 4 March

I fully intended to shrug Tiggy's comments off with the casual disregard they deserved. However, yesterday evening I found myself grilling my son about acceptable playground behaviour, paying specific attention to the possible involvement of Tiggy's son, Reuben, in any scuffles, the reporting of such incidents to higher authorities and exactly what constituted a 'legal tackle' while playing football at breaktime. He assured me repeatedly that he had not been in any trouble and was in no imminent danger of disciplinary action, but the niggle of doubt remained. I emailed his teacher requesting a meeting to discuss my son's conduct. An email that was unfortunately seen by Tom prior to sending and which induced a barrage of hurt accusations: 'Why don't you believe me?!' 'I'm not in any trouble!' and, 'It's going to look like I am in trouble now when I'm not and that is SO UNFAIR!' All of which was true.

I felt terrible. After all, I had vowed long ago to ensure that my children always knew I was in their corner. I wanted them to feel that their opinion was valid, that they'd always be listened to and believed. But here I was doing the exact opposite. Bloody Tiggy and her stupid outfit and stupid words and stupid face. Of course, she'd really have the guns out for me now that my mother had given her sartorial verdict on the 'strange' dress, not to mention calling her a snooty cow, which was almost as great a declaration of war as the time that Annabelle Green had disagreed with Lindi about baby-led weaning.

On a more positive note, and despite my anxieties, today's meeting with Anita was, in fact, an enormous success. We left the garden centre with a date for a future meeting and a list of activities and classes so varied and numerous that I could potentially have made a full-time job out of simply driving to them. For example, on a Tuesday, Reminiscence Therapy at the library could be followed by a Dementia Coffee Morning in the church hall, with Macramé Pot Hangers before lunch at the soup kitchen and Line Dancing in the community centre afterwards. We could then have rounded off the day with a trip to a dementia-friendly viewing of *Dunkirk* at the local cinema.

In the car on the way home, Mum and I discussed the kind of things she might be interested in doing. I avoided talk of day centres and respite care – despite Anita having given me plenty of detail about those options – because I didn't want Mum to take umbrage at the whole process, but I kept the information to hand. Anita had made it clear that over time things were likely to get worse and I might find it harder to cope as a sole carer. Strangely, I didn't mind the implication that I might struggle hard to accept from her; she was so matter-of-fact about it that I realised feeling inadequate was an inevitable part of the process and not a judgement on my capabilities. I might need to share this insight with Sam, given the fact that I ripped his head off last time he suggested the same.

'She was nice, wasn't she?' I said to Mum as we pulled away from the roundabout. 'Had some good ideas. We'll have a look at all the things we could try, maybe give Grace a run for her money with the dance classes.'

Mum appeared to be contemplating this option quite seriously.

'I wonder what Anita's background is?' I mused. 'She's not that much older than me. Do you think she's got kids?'

Mum shook her head. 'I don't think she's married. She's one of those lesbeans,' she said with certainty. Mum has always pronounced lesbian *lesbean*, even before the dementia. Not that it was a word often bandied around the house. I've always found it quite endearing.

'Erm, I'm not sure you can assume that Anita's a lesbian, Mum, just because she's not married. And even if she was, she could still have children.'

'No, she talked about her girlfriend, Caroline. And she does have that kind of haircut.' She leant forward in her seat and rubbed at the raindrops on the windscreen. 'Of course, I thought about it once.'

'Thought about what?'

'Becoming a lesbean. "Going out" I believe it's called.' (Christ, WTAF?)

'D'you mean *coming out*?' I kept my voice light as I indicated and turned onto our road.

'Yes. Me and Bernadette Norris...' She sighed and looked out of the window. 'But, your father. You know.'

I most certainly did not know – and neither did I wish to.

119

Chapter Seventeen

In an attempt to stave off the creeping cabin fever of being trapped at home with only pre-schoolers, pets and pensioners for company, I've been trawling through the flyers and websites that Anita had suggested, looking for dementia-friendly activities that Mum and I can do together. And while I've reached the point where I'd probably do anything just to get us out of the bloody house, I am pretty pleased to have discovered Singing for the Brain – a local dementia choir and our destination of choice today.

I've never really thought of Mum as being a big fan of singing, but looking back, I guess there were times when I'd catch her bopping around the kitchen or warbling away to Diana Ross when she thought nobody was listening and I must have got my love of music from somewhere because it wasn't from Dad. Mum was the one who encouraged me to sing and took me to choir practice and music lessons. She was the one who stood over me as I attempted to master the flute, the violin and the bassoon before she and Dad capitulated and bought me the instrument I would go on to fall in love with, my very own piano.

I think music was originally my parents' way of giving me an identity other than just the sister of the academic and sporting legend that was my brother, and it meant that when their friends asked about me in a disinterested-but-obliged-to-comment way, there was at least something to discuss.

'*Oh, yes. Penelope is singing at the village hall in a couple of weeks. The choir are doing a Songs from the Musicals fundraiser for the church roof.*' Or, '*Oh, yes, Penelope is really enjoying the piano. She's just about mastered "Axel F" from* Beverly Hills Cop.' (I jest – I don't think they ever said that).

I could hold a tune, it's true. And I wrote my own songs; melodies that I hammered out on the piano once I'd finished practicing the scales and arpeggios that formed the basis of my tuition with Mrs Wiggins down the road. I loved Mrs Wiggins. She was mad as a box of frogs but she delighted in my music making. And I adored that piano – I really did. It's so much more of an intuitive instrument than woodwind or brass: a higher note is higher up the keyboard and a lower note is lower down. Easy. None of this, 'place your index finger lightly over the fourth key with your left thumb in the B-flat position while blowing into the embouchure hole with a consistent and steady exhalation in order to achieve anything other than a high-pitched screech' business. You just press the keys and a lovely rich melodic sound comes out. Pound harder for drama and press lightly for tinkling jollity. I could lose myself in music for hours at a time. If I was sad I'd play melancholy pieces while I contemplated the human condition, and if I was more chipper I'd play honky-tonk and pop on the electric keyboard. I'd reinvent theme tunes from television programmes, copy the melodies from my dad's old Beach Boys LPs and record the charts from Radio 1 on a Sunday night, playing the tape back over the following week in order to painstakingly recreate the most recent Top Ten. It was my party piece, my chosen method of communicating emotion and the perfect way to soothe my teenage soul.

In addition to playing the piano, I joined the school choir, I played recorder in the orchestra and I was even a backing singer in a sixth-form band (Ash-tray Mannequins) for a short while. Although this was mainly motivated by a desire to be in the company of the lead guitarist, Kev, an eighteen-year-old rock god with dark curtained hair and a ready supply of weed. Indeed, it was Kev who insisted that the Ash-tray Mannequins' playlist be composed almost entirely of Guns N' Roses covers in order to indulge his need for extended solos (that's not a euphemism – although it should be). And it was also Kev who broke up the band, pleading artistic differences with the lead singer, Jon, although we all knew deep down that 'artistic differences' in this instance meant, 'accidentally shagging Jon's girlfriend, Veena'. And thus it was that in the space of one day I lost my (already negligible) interest in eighties guitar music, my role as a backing singer in Ash-tray Mannequins and my virginity, as a grumpy Kev sought solace in the next best thing to Veena; that thing being a very available and completely smitten me.

Anyway, I digress. Suffice to say that I was talked out of pursuing a musical career by my parents and disillusioned about band politics thanks to a guitarist with a bad haircut and a casual disregard for monogamy. And, as is the way of most hobbies when you realise you can't make a career out of them, they fall by the wayside. The path of life is littered with abandoned childhood dreams and preoccupations; potential Picassos snuffed out by parental reaction to the suggestion of an art foundation course versus a career in dentistry, or those whose secret desires of becoming Kylie have withered and died when the realities of a degree in business studies come home to roost. I can't completely blame my parents; it was a reasonable and rational (if not magical and life-affirming) choice.

When I moved out of the family home I left the piano behind me, both physically and metaphorically. You simply can't have one in student halls of residence, I didn't even have room for my keyboard. I played when I went home for the holidays but without regular practice, the nightly scales and weekly lessons, my skills became rusty. When Sam and I moved into our first flat together there was no space for a piano and no time to play. I still sang on my own as I danced around our tiny kitchen and in later years I dragged the children to Musical Minis, harmonising 'Wind the Bobbin Up' with more gusto than is customary. I wouldn't want it to seem that I have been bereft of musical stimulation for the past fifteen years, but it has been an absence in my life. Occasionally I've seen adverts on local Facebook groups for community orchestras or singing lessons and my finger has hovered over the 'make enquiries' button. But deep down, I know I just don't have the time to indulge in something as frivolous as a hobby, so I usually shut the page down and walk away. Until today. Dah da Dahhhh! (Jazz hands.)

-

We arrived late, having spent half an hour with me coaxing Mum into the car and reminding her that she had to get her bottom onto the seat before both feet could move into the footwell. It is difficult to explain the level of mind-numbing, hand-chewing frustration involved in navigating transfers from one form of locomotion to another. Hence the delay and imminent migraine as we arrived at the centre of musical excellence known as Greatborough Community Hall to be met by a wall of sound. Not necessarily a wall of tuneful sound, it is true. Mum actually winced as I opened the double doors and gently nudged her through, promising it would be 'Fun!!!' with a lot of exclamation marks.

The woman running the show paused in her tambourine banging as the doors thudded behind us, and gesticulated wildly for us to join the motley crew assembled before her. Some were seated, some standing. One man was facing the wall in the far corner of the room but this appeared to be out of choice rather than some arcane punishment. 'Fizz', as she loudly proclaimed herself with an accompanying rattle of her tambourine and a jaunty wave of her many scarves, was 'delighted to have us here'. She was the self-styled choir mistress 'for my sins!' (raised eyebrows, comedy grimace) in charge of 'looking after this rabble!!!'. I tried not to hold the expansive hand gestures and over-effusive personality against her. She was doing a good thing; she must be a good person.

The other singers introduced themselves with names I promptly forgot, but luckily, this being a dementia choir, everyone routinely forgot each other's names and therefore had badges on. We nodded and smiled and stood around awkwardly. This is England, after all, and no amount of disinhibiting cognitive disorder can alter the basic psyche of a nation used to the crippling embarrassment of socialising with strangers. But Fizz was as good as her wafting scarves and colourful braids suggested and launched straight into an enthusiastic rendition of 'Roll out the Barrel' before you could say 'toe-curling exhibitionism'.

Much to my astonishment I noticed Mum tapping her feet beside me. I turned to look at her, knowing her distaste for those kinds of Mockney tunes, and found her belting out the melody with the best of them (in fact, she *was* the best of them). She didn't know many of the words, it's true, but neither did anyone – even Fizz got stuck after the second verse. But it didn't seem to matter a jot. Mum segued beautifully into 'My Old Man's a Dustman' following the lead of Fizz and her tambourine and then there was a brief pause where Fizz indicated that we would be moving from 'warm-up' into the 'vocal harmony' section.

By the end of the session we were both singing along to Adele's 'Rolling in the Deep' – everyone in the room was giving it the full power-ballad gusto – and I was happier than I'd been in months. The song choices had taken us through a vast and eclectic back catalogue ranging from 'Scarborough Fair' to S Club 7's 'Reach for the Stars'. You had to hand it to Fizz, there's not many women who could do that sort of mash-up justice on the Bontempi organ. It was an absolute riot.

I felt moved in an American-gospel-choir-type way to go and hug people afterwards. I didn't. Obviously (see previous 'This is England' statement). But the thought was there. Mum was beaming and both our faces were flushed from a combination of exertion and the lovely sense of communal sound that I remembered from my youth. We bade goodbye to a bunch of people (thank the Lord for the name badges otherwise I would have had to call them things like 'the wearer of snazzy jumpers' and 'the one with the Sellotaped glasses') and were invited to the extra weekly sessions held in nearby Chaldon. The Thursday class was for the 'advanced group' Fizz told us

Chapter Eighteen

The last day of term brings the joy of the PTA Easter-bonnet parade and cake sale. I have tried. Year after year after year I bring my paltry offering to the cake sale having slaved for at least two days making the godforsaken thing, plus at least two weeks worrying about it and planning it beforehand. But despite my best intentions something always goes wrong. Witness the chocolate Hansel and Gretel House which looked beautiful until you came to pick it off the table and realised it was as heavy as a lead-weight and needed an industrial saw to hack through the outer icing. Or take the Victoria sponge which, due to a topping of congealed cream and jam, ended up looking like I was serving up a placenta. The children don't ask me to make them birthday cakes anymore and who can blame them. But there is no getting out of the PTA cake sale. No way. Even when Caz had the temerity to be on holiday or when Julie was incapacitated by a broken leg, they were still expected to provide baked goods either in advance or from their sick bed.

'Just a batch of flapjacks or something really simple would be fine, Penny, seeing as you're eight months pregnant and have had a migraine for the past four days and Tom's been off school with flu,' Tiggy has kindly informed me in the past. 'It's just really important for us to raise as much money as we can so the kids can have their own individual iPads at school rather than having to share. And I'm sure I don't need to tell you how much better it is for the children to have locally sourced, home-baked products. That way they understand where their food comes from and we can make sure there aren't any allergy issues. Speaking of which, here is the double-sided A4 list of ingredients and possible allergens you'll need to label your cakes with.'

Well, this year I didn't have time. There. I've said it. In fact, it almost slipped my mind altogether as I have been avoiding Tiggy and Lindi at the school gate since the supermarket debacle and nobody else is bossy enough to prompt other mums in the same way. So last night when Caz dropped off a fruit loaf for me to take in on her behalf and Maisie asked whether I'd finished construction of her Easter bonnet yet, I muttered a few expletives and took myself off to the late-night Londis in search of ingredients for both hats and cakes. This morning, Maisie was the proud owner of a cardboard headband made out of a cereal box with two yellow nylon chicks splayed and stapled to the front in a manner suggestive of crucifixion, therefore appealing to both the secular and religious themes of the season. She had initially been sceptical, but sellotaping Mini Eggs to the brim, on the understanding that she could eat them all later, seemed to improve its artistic merits no end and she skipped into school having already scoffed at least four, leaving the bonnet a little lopsided but still a thing of immense beauty.

The cake situation was less easy to sort out. There was no time to rustle up a little something à la Mary Berry, so instead I bought some Mr Kipling French Fancies. I did toy with the idea of passing them off as my own but clearly that would be impossible. There is nothing that screams factory-processed carbohydrate more than a neon Mr Kipling cake, so I decided to brazen it out.

The sun was out and the last of the daffodils were nodding in the breeze as I walked Colin and Mum up to school late morning. I tied Colin's lead to the school fence so that he could see us and be reassured without actually entering the grounds, doing something unmentionable in the sand pit or eating the four-tier *Great British Bake Off*-inspired humble-brag cake offerings of Tiggy or Lindi. He was happy with a pile of kibble and the occasional self-important woof at passers-by, and we made our way into the school hall where there was a flurry of Cath Kidston print and Boden catalogue activity. It would have been hard to find more bunting at a wedding fair and the decorating team had truly surpassed themselves, although I suspected that the woman lording it over them had had little direct involvement with the drawing and painting of a family of life-sized chickens, the creation of enormous papier mâché Easter eggs or the construction of a three-foot MDF Easter bunny complete with piped musical accompaniment of 'Hop little bunnies, hop, hop, hop!' recorded at last year's Key Stage 1 Spring Concert.

Mum immediately crossed the hall to stare in wonder at the musical rabbit and I experienced a pang of anxiety as I carried my bag to the table in the far corner of the room. It wasn't far enough. Tiggy spotted my Londis carrier (itself an affront to all that was good and holy in the world) and shot over before you could say 'tasteful hessian tote bag'.

'Penny!' She looked discreetly at her watch. 'We thought you'd never get here!'

'Oh sorry, am I late?' I looked around me. To be fair, the level of decoration implied that a hive of workers had been busy since dawn – from that point of view I could probably be considered so late as to be entirely redundant. I went on the offensive to deflect from my shortcomings, using praise as my weapon of choice.

'The hall looks amazing, Tiggy. You've done a fantastic job.' I tried to sidle the Mr Kipling packs out onto the table. 'Was the bunny your work?'

She looked over to where Mum was now wiggling her hips along to the piped music. 'Oh! Your mother's dancing, how lovely!' (Delivered in a way that suggested it was very unlovely and not at all in keeping with the theme of the day to have an elderly woman jigging about near the decorations. If Mum had been sporting a quaint gingham apron and rosy apple cheeks she might have got away with it.)

Tiggy continued. 'No, the rabbit – not my project I'm afraid. I'd love to have the time to really indulge my creative side in that way and to be honest, I think if I'd been involved in the finishing touches I would have made him look a little less sinister.' She gave a tinkling laugh. 'But I shouldn't be ungrateful. Gina's done wonderfully considering the lack of space in that tiny house and I know that since Ian lost his job they've been struggling to make ends meet, so we can't complain if it's a bit rough around the edges!'

'But it looks amazing,' I said. 'We must make sure we reimburse Gina for the cost of materials if, you know, they're having issues with cashflow.'

'Hmm, yes. Although every penny counts for the school.' Tiggy shook her head. 'They've had individual iPads at St Bartholomew's for years. It's simply astonishing that we are so poorly resourced in comparison.'

'Well, yes, but St Bart's is a private school, isn't it? I don't know that we should be aiming to compete with their facilities...' I faltered slightly, seeing the look of horror on Tiggy's face.

'It is imperative that all children have the same opportunities, Penny, regardless of privilege or background. If they're to progress up the ladder and fulfil their potential, they need access to technology. You know me, I'm a great believer in social equality.'

'Hmmm, yes.' What I knew was that Tiggy would have chewed off her right arm if it meant she could get her children into St Bart's and mingling with the right sort. I've seen her glancing wistfully at their straw boaters and blazers when the schools all come together for the 'Arts 4 All Celebration of Young Creativity' (something of a misnomer, as you'd imagine).

'Oh!' Tiggy suddenly spotted the pack of French Fancies I'd managed to discreetly slide onto the table. She pointed one immaculate pale pink Shellac nail in their direction, 'Shop-bought cake. Who on earth brought those?'

I was sorely tempted to deny all responsibility for the purchase and almost caved before I realised that if I disowned them I would be left empty-handed or trying to claim someone else's offerings as my own. 'Um. Me,' I said in an undertone. 'I just didn't have time to make anything this year, Tiggy. It completely slipped my mind, what with Dad having his stroke, and looking after Mum and, you know...'

She didn't know. Her eyebrows would have shot clean off her forehead if there hadn't been a metric tonne of

Botox keeping them in check, certainly her mouth was open in astonishment at such an admission. 'Oh right, I see.' She nudged the box in my direction with a sympathetic smile. 'Thanks awfully, Penny, but I suspect we won't be needing them. You know we have very strict rules about ingredients; these look chock-full of additives and artificial flavourings.'

'True. But they are all handily listed on the box so no need for the completion of the allergen checklist,' I said brightly. 'In fact, it might make life easier for the parents, having it all detailed in such an accessible format?'

'Hmmm.' She turned her attention to a harassed-looking mum, currently balancing twenty-seven scones on a small paper plate. 'Melanie! Could you do something with these?' She gestured vaguely in the general region of the Mr Kipling box. 'Penny brought them,' she said for clarity, just in case there was any possible confusion as to their provenance. Then she turned back to me. 'I'd keep your plastic bag,' she said. 'Then you'll have something to carry them back home in after we've all cleared up. You are staying to help?'

'I… erm… I was thinking I might…'

'It's just that Reuben has to be at the orthodontist by midday so I've got to head off and I think Gina might need some help loading the rabbit and the papier mâché eggs back onto the van because we've got to have the hall cleared in time for Celebration Assembly.'

I nodded. Resistance was futile. 'Of course.'

–

A few moments later the children were released into the hall to parade their Easter hats and jumpers and spend their money on as much cake as humanly possible. Parents scattered in an attempt to encourage 'good choices' regarding food purchases. Not that it was particularly easy to see what would have been a 'good choice' in this instance but probably anything other than Penny Baker's shop-bought abominations. Of course, it was these that were selling the fastest – and for a significant mark-up on the purchase price, which I imagine will go some way to providing the little darlings with the individual iPad technology they so desperately need.

At midday I went to collect Maisie from the adjacent preschool building and managed to smuggle Colin one of Lindi's particularly inedible gluten-free buns, which he wolfed down in a single gulp. He seemed to have dug up a small shrub in my absence so I moved his lead a few panels down the fence in order to physically distance him from the crime. Maisie had eaten every Mini Egg that had been sellotaped to her bonnet and was looking a little green around the gills. It seemed that she had also consumed at least one of the yellow nylon chicks in her quest for food and thus her cardboard headband was now entirely bereft of Easter decoration, the other chick having been eaten by The Terrible Evangeline.

High-powered Joy had obviously chosen the 'throw money at it' option for the homemade bonnet and Evangeline was sporting a garish crown of plastic daffodils with diamante stems and a faux pearl swan with boss-eyes. By some miracle of modern transportation and business scheduling, Joy had actually arrived at preschool to collect her own child and caught my eye as I clocked Evangeline's headgear.

'Fucking hideous, isn't it?' she whispered cheerfully into my ear as the children were handed over by a sticky-looking Miss Janice.

A laugh burst from my mouth. I was surprised and, bizarrely, a little flattered to be drawn into Joy's confidence in this way. She probably had an ulterior motive, some kind of executive management strategy to make the underlings work harder, but I thought I'd play along and respond in kind with a little self-deprecation of my own – not that this was especially hard, given the circumstances.

'Yeah, I'm not sure I've got the moral high ground here,' I said, gesturing to Maisie's cardboard headband. Bolstered by Joy's snigger of appreciation, I then went on to share the horror of Tiggy's reaction to my shop-bought cakes back in the school hall, having some inkling that she would be very much in my camp in terms of home baking. I was right. Joy was suitably dismissive of such snobbery, describing it as 'pathetic mummy-shaming', which is a phrase I found particularly pleasing. She also admitted that she had once been on the receiving end of a lengthy email from Tiggy instructing parents of all age groups to contribute to various school activities. She had initially deleted the email but Tiggy, determined as ever, had followed up with another equally long missive complete with attached spreadsheet of duties.

'So I just told her I was far too busy to take on anything outside of work,' Joy said, while I marvelled at her extreme bravery. 'And I never heard from her again. It'd be interesting to actually see the woman in action.'

'She is *quite* something,' I said, suddenly unsure whether I was entirely comfortable bitching about another mum with High-powered Joy. Although I had to admit, it felt surprisingly liberating.

We marshalled our daughters in their assorted hats back to the school hall where all hell was breaking loose. It appeared that Mum, in an attempt to provide food for the starving urchins of Badger class, had commandeered an enormous tray of cakes and biscuits and was offering them free of charge to the swarm of children now gathered around her. Among the confectionary items were the last remaining Mr Kipling cakes brought in by notoriously bad mother Penny Baker, and the child who was reaching most eagerly for said cakes was none other than Lindi's daughter, Chloe – she of the multiple presumed, but as yet medically unproven, food intolerances. Chloe had clearly eschewed the gluten-free buns and vegan chocolate brownies that had been lovingly prepared by her mother and instead was intent on the toxin-laden processed cakery that had been smuggled in by my own fair hand. As I rounded the fire-doors it was as if I were witnessing an action movie in slow-motion; the hand of Chloe poised above a French Fancy, the cheerful smile of my mother as she shared her wares, and the protracted howl of 'Noooooooooo!' as Lindi charged across the width of the hall and knocked the cake out of Chloe's grasp.

The French Fancy wheeled up into the air, descending in a graceful arc to splat onto the rigid hairstyle of Mrs North as she crouched consoling a small boy who was crying about a missing flapjack. Like a ninja, and without breaking eye contact from the boy, Mrs North calmly removed the cake from her head, where it was impaled on a particularly lacquered spike of hair, and offered it to him with a magician's flourish. The boy laughed and promptly devoured the French Fancy in one gulp. Mrs North smiled. Lindi, having over-estimated her volleyball skills, fell over in a big heap. And Chloe's face crumpled as she began to wail.

Sensing that I was almost entirely responsible (what with the offending cake being mine, the cheery pusher of cake being my mother, and the fact that I'd just fed my dog one of the last remaining Chloe-suitable buns), I crossed the hall to embroil myself further in the drama, despite every fibre of my being shrieking at me to get the fuck out of there. Lindi was rubbing her knee and trying to explain to Chloe that the only remaining option was the vegan brownies, which were dairy-free, gluten-free and sulphite-free. One wondered what ingredients were actually in these cakes, there being so many absences.

'You know what the naturopath said darling,' Lindi winced as she extended her leg and tested her weight on it. 'Processed sugar is like crack-cocaine' (Chloe was looking like she might quite enjoy crack-cocaine as her mother continued). 'It's virtually a poison – plus the colourings and E numbers in those awful cakes could have long-lasting detrimental effects on your gut lining, your powers of concentration and even your future fertility'.

Chloe, unsurprisingly devastated by this news – or more likely the lack of pretty-coloured cake – continued to sob ostentatiously while I perused the remaining offerings on Mum's now depleted tray. Alighting on what I assumed was one of the brownies that Lindi was referring to (mainly because it was the only thing that hadn't been chosen by the other children). I picked it up with the reverence it deserved and crouched down next to Chloe.

'Wow,' I said. 'You're pretty lucky getting to eat these special brownies, Chloe. We usually save them for the grown-ups and the teenagers. Tom's big sister Grace, who's fourteen, always says they're her favourite.'

She eyed me suspiciously, as well she might, but eventually she wiped her eyes and took the brownie from my hand.

'I think Tom's granny was keeping this one aside, especially for you, but then everyone got a bit confused. Lucky we managed to save it, hey?'

'Thanks, Mrs Baker,' said Chloe seriously, as she took a large bite of her brownie. 'Cake can sometimes be extremely confusing.'

Beside me Lindi gave a shuddering exhalation as if the last few moments had been some of the most trying in her entire life. I knew it was time to man-up and admitted that the Mr Kipling cakes were mine. She gave me a brave smile.

'Thank you for your honesty, Penny,' she said earnestly. 'I didn't want to make a fuss – it's just so hard to ensure Chloe gets the appropriate nutrition.' (Her daughter was shovelling the remaining brownie into her mouth without pausing to draw breath.) 'Oh dear.' She dropped her hands down by her sides with the air of a broken woman. 'I think I have one of my tension headaches coming on. I suffer terribly – hopeless for days if I allow the pain to break through. Could you possibly get me a glass of water?'

'Of course. Would you like a paracetamol?' I said, rummaging in my handbag for the blister pack.

She winced. 'Oh no. Thank you. Astral, my naturopath, says I should avoid chemicals if at all possible. Conventional Western medicine does so much harm. I'll just need a Belladonna and one of my Kali Phos 6 Tissue Salts – they're in my emergency homeopathy bag.' She pointed to an Orla Kiely shopper by the canteen door, evidently too incapacitated to make the two-metre distance herself.

I went to retrieve her high-grade narcotics. 'Hopefully that's another potential crisis narrowly averted,' I said, handing over the stash. 'Now all we need is a nice tranquil Easter break!'

'Thankfully I have a ten-day healing-stone spa retreat booked,' she said, delicately massaging her temples. 'I'm not sure how on earth I'd cope otherwise. My chronic health conditions are particularly hard to manage during the school holidays.'

'Funny that,' I said, and I gave her a reassuring pat before going to find Tiggy and offering her twenty pounds in recompense for the tray of cakes my mother had given away for free. We always end up paying for our own cakes at PTA events anyway, just like the bric-a-brac stall where you buy back all the tat that your children suddenly decide they need again, having not played with it for four years. And anyway, I reasoned, at least nobody would need lunch. And I hadn't had to bake anything. Small wins.

Chapter Nineteen

Tuesday, 1 April

To celebrate the start of the Easter holidays, I brought Maisie, Tom and Grace along to Singing for the Brain this week. As you can imagine, this was not a voluntary outing – Tom and Maisie were forced to attend by virtue of being too young to be left home alone and Grace wanted to be dropped off at her friend Clark's house. The trade-off for transportation was enduring an hour of musical pensioners, which seemed pretty reasonable to me.

I was fully expecting all three kids to sit in the cafe staring gormlessly at screens, but Maisie was keen to parti-cipate in the singing. She has accompanied Mum and me to one of the art sessions from Anita's extensive list of activities and has clearly developed a taste for being treated like a princess (as if she wasn't indulged in this way at home). It was true what Anita had said – bringing a pre-schooler along to these sessions was like presenting the group with a precious gift or rare treasure and we were immediately bathed in radiant smiles and warm words. The only time I have seen it surpassed was when one of the key workers at the macramé craft session brought her six-month-old baby in and the group participants became apoplectic with joy; the older ladies in particular were entranced and every gurgle was rewarded with enchanted astonishment as if the very Lord himself had bestowed his individual benevolence upon these, the most devout of parishioners.

Maisie left her siblings plugged into their devices and strolled confidently into the middle of the group, already prepared for the reaction she knew was coming. She had barely made it as far as Fizz before she was drowning in a sea of outstretched hands offering Werther's Originals and Glacier Fruits. It was almost as if everyone over the age of seventy armed themselves with confectionery items before venturing outside on the off chance that they might encounter a small person in need of sugar. Or maybe they were all fearful of hypoglycaemic comas – not sure. There was likely some overlap to their thinking.

Mum picked up her favourite of the tambourines (the red one) and waved it in the direction of Ernest, a wheelchair-bound nonagenarian and man of few words – most of them extremely rude. His son Clive (late sixties), a quiet, unassuming man who can nonetheless unleash a formidable tenor-bass during the power ballads, waved a maraca back at Mum while Ernest nodded and mumbled a couple of choice expletives, which appear to comprise his own unique method of percussion.

Fizz suggested that Maisie accompany Mum around the circle with the box of instruments to ensure that every member of the company had ample opportunity to rifle through the bells, triangles and miniature cymbals and make their selection. Had I been the one to make this request of my daughter I would have been met with a resentful silence or a tantrum, but Fizz's larger than life personality has a habit of bulldozing young and old into participation.

I stood next to Tina, a smartly dressed woman in her early sixties who I'd talked to before. She was busy trying to persuade her husband, Bob, to choose an instrument instead of gazing vacantly out of the window, but was not having much luck. Prior to his diagnosis, Bob had been the chief executive of a large telecommunications company and was already married when Tina had started working as a junior in his office. She spoke in awed terms of how charming and erudite he had been when they first met. How he had entertained and surprised her with tickets to the opera and ballet, dinners at expensive restaurants and weekends spent in boutique hotels or travelling around European capitals. The divorce from his first wife, Helena, had been ugly and the children rarely spoke to their new stepmother, disgusted by the fact that she was only seven years their senior. But this second marriage had lasted beyond all expectations and now Tina's role had transitioned once more – from secretary to glamorous younger wife to that of full-time-carer.

'His kids love it, of course,' she'd confided last week. 'They think I've got my just desserts; that I was only ever after his money and now I'm saddled with, well, this.' She'd taken a tissue out of her pocket and dabbed at the corner of his mouth. 'But he's still my charming Bobby. I'd have married him if he was a pauper.' She gave his cheek a little squeeze and he beamed at her, eyes full of love as she continued to talk. 'And, even if I'd known he was going to succumb to this horrible disease; even with the angry outbursts and the times he gets terribly confused and thinks I'm Helena, or that I'm some awful ex-teacher of his who was a bit liberal with the corporal punishment, and he shouts or is cruel to me… I'd still have married him. I wouldn't change a thing.'

I asked her if Bob's kids had any contact with him and she told me that they visited rarely – 'usually if they need cash' – and that they would insist on her vacating the house prior to their arrival. 'It's important for him to still see them, I know that. They need to maintain a relationship with their father even if it's a fairly toxic one. And we have carers who can sit with him when I'm out – while he's waiting for the kids to arrive.' She smoothed a strand of hair over his forehead. 'But he gets really distressed when I leave, don't you Bobby?' She smiled at him sadly. 'I did wonder if I might suggest that I stay somewhere in the house when they come, just so he doesn't get so upset. It would be easier for everyone, but I guess it depends on how much they hate me; whether they are prepared to make that small concession to keep their father calm.' She had smiled grimly at that, as if the chances of having a reasonable discussion were very slim indeed.

–

Today, Tina was trying to encourage Bob to choose between a tambourine and a bongo drum without much success.

'Did you get a chance to speak to Bob's kids last week, about staying in the house when they visit?' I asked, after we'd exchanged the usual pleasantries. She shook her head and I realised from the set of her mouth that she didn't want to have the conversation in front of her husband, so I asked if she fancied a coffee afterwards. I knew that Fizz was very relaxed about us staying in the hall once the session had finished as long as we vacated before Jazzercise at midday.

'I could ask the kids to keep Mum and Bob entertained while we have a chat?' As I said this, I wondered exactly

143

how that particular deal would go down with Grace. But Tom and Maisie would, I was sure, be happy to prat about with the instruments for a while, particularly if there was an offer of screen time back at home.

'Yes, that would be nice, Penny. Thank you.' Tina looked pleased, but it was clear that Bob was not yet ready to engage in today's session and eventually she ended up asking Maisie to choose an instrument for him instead, a task Maisie took very seriously, presenting him with a small xylophone before returning to my side with Mum as we all burst into the opening verse of 'Life on Mars'.

After this it was the percussion special (Rolling Stones – 'Gimme Shelter') and with the sound of elderly voices singing about rape and murder, accompanied by an incongruous orchestra of maracas and bike horns, Fizz began to waft her scarves around in the way that indicated the song was reaching its denouement. We never manage to cease noise-making in a uniform fashion but once the majority of the racket had died down, Fizz clapped her hands. 'Right, choir. I was hoping to do "Bridge Over Troubled Water" next but unfortunately, I forgot to bring the sheet music with me and I haven't downloaded the backing track, so I think we'll have to pass and instead move onto a reprisal of Rihanna's "Umbrella", which I know some of you struggled with last week, so, sorry about—'

'Ooh, wait!' The words burst out of me before I could stop myself. I felt twenty pairs of cataracts focussing in varying degrees on my face, waiting for my next comment. 'Erm. I can play it.'

'The Rihanna song?' Fizz had her kindly voice on, the one she saves for the really cognitively impaired. 'Don't worry, Penny, I've got the music for that right here.'

'No. The Simon and Garfunkel. I learnt the whole album off by heart. Years ago.' It really *was* years ago; before my secondary school transition from 'easy-listening keyboard tunes' played in solitude to 'rock-band backing vocals' shouted to an audience of drunken sixteen-year-olds. Fizz moved away from the fold-out stool behind the keyboard and gestured me towards it as if it were the Iron Throne.

'Be my guest, Penny, dear,' she said graciously and I sat cautiously down in a plume of departing patchouli. Fizz always smelled like joss sticks. It was sort of wrong and so right at the same time.

I placed my fingers gingerly over the keys, noticing out of the corner of my eye that most of the singers were losing concentration and needed reining back into the musical fold. I played a few chords to warm up and focus their minds, humming the intro to myself. I was right, the tune was still there in my fingertips and by the time we reached the opening lines Fizz was beaming. It was immediately clear that this song had been an excellent choice, one that would really unite the group. Those who weren't singing were swaying gently, eyes closed. Ernest was humming along with the tune and Bob was playing the xylophone like a professional while watching Tina belting out the lyrics with gusto. It was loud, it was joyful and I like to think that it was profoundly moving, although I might be getting a little carried away. We concluded in a riot of sound and I even managed a flourish or two on the keyboard, which brought a cheer from the girls pouring tea behind the serving hatch.

'Excellent work, Penny. Thank you so very much for stepping in there. Looks like we won't need to revisit Rihanna this morning after all.' Fizz had already moved proprietorially back to the region of the keyboard and I vacated the stool with a modest 'it was nothing' flap of my hand. I resumed my place in the circle between Maisie and Mum. Tina whispered, 'That was fab-u-lous, darling!' under her breath, like Craig Revel Horwood. But before I had time to congratulate myself too thoroughly, Fizz had burst into a rousing chorus of 'I Want to Break Free' by Queen, prompting an air-guitar solo from Marie, a tiny bird of a woman dressed in soft pastels. By the time we finished the session our cheeks were flushed and everyone looked an inch taller.

Fizz was evangelical about the benefits of communal singing and had spent much of the previous week eulogising about the effects on posture, lung function and cardiac output, but I wasn't certain that I had previously taken much notice of the obvious physical changes until that moment. The sense of wellbeing was difficult to quantify but Mum summed it up as she patted Maisie on the head and said, simply, 'Good. Yes. We feel good.'

As people started to gather their belongings and Fizz alerted us to the fact that there would be no session next Tuesday due to the Easter break, I made my way over to the kids and Grace removed an ear bud. 'Saw you on the old *pianna*,' she said with a jaunty air.

I gave a modest smile, 'Yes, 'tis true.'

'Sounded good.' She went to replace the ear bud but I stopped her. 'Actually, Grace, Tom.' I pulled one of my son's headphones out to get his attention as well. 'I was wondering if you might do me a favour?'

I hadn't been optimistic but when I promised Grace that I'd take her to Clark's house as soon as Tina and I had finished our coffee, she rewarded me with a shrug and said, 'S'OK. Whenever,' as casual as a sandal. She and Tom

146

then went to see Maisie, who was chatting away to Mum, and I saw Tom asking Bob about his xylophone with an expression of such deep interest that it would have melted the hardest of hearts.

'What lovely children you have, Penny.' Tina followed my gaze. 'Just look at that. Bob loves being with kids that age. He never sees his grandchildren. Even before the dementia really kicked in.' She opened her purse and fished out two pound coins. 'Although some of that was our fault – we were so busy, always travelling… Anyway!' She looked up at me brightly, 'Coffee is it? How do you have it?'

We sat and chatted, clutching our Styrofoam cups while the children danced, mimed lyrics and cavorted around with the instruments under the watchful eye of Fizz and the adoring gaze of assorted older people. Without the attention of immediate peers and the need to seem cool, Grace morphed back into the relaxed easy-going girl I remembered from a couple of years ago. I could see her sitting on the floor of the hall, her long legs tucked underneath her as she pulled silly faces and mucked about, making Tom laugh until he was clutching his sides. Maisie was sat on Mum's lap playing some sort of clapping game with Bob.

Tina filled me in about Bob's children and we shared stories about the current challenges we were facing. It was an enormous relief just to be able to talk to someone who understood. At one point, Clive joined us, pulling up a chair and balancing his cup of tea on his knee.

'D'you think you can bring your kids along to every session?' he said, looking over to where Ernest was sat in his wheelchair, eyes closed, nodding along to Tom's tuneless rendition of the *Star Wars* theme on the recorder.

'Hmmm,' I said, taking a sip of my coffee. 'I *could* consider removing them from the education system and signing them up as a travelling entertainment company but it would very much be on their terms. Tom and Maisie would probably settle for payment in cake but Grace – she'd drive a harder bargain.'

'I bet she would.' Clive was laughing as Grace clowned around with Maisie, pretending they were both badly behaved horses in a pony show. 'God, they are a breath of fresh air though, aren't they?' He looked at Tina, who was nodding in agreement, and I watched them for a moment, my kids, being kind and helpful and funny.

'Yeah. I suppose they are,' I said, feeling proud. 'It's strange. I don't see them that way most of the time.'

'Well, you're lucky, Penny,' said Clive. 'I wish I'd had kids. I bet your life's a lot fuller because of them. Whereas with me, once Dad's gone,' he nodded over towards Ernest, who appeared to now be teaching Tom a new swear word, 'That's it. End of the family line.'

'Same with me,' said Tina. 'Once Bob goes, it's just me, rattling around that great big house.' She sniffed suddenly and Clive took her cup gently from her hand and replaced it with a tissue from his pocket. She looked up at him with gratitude. 'Thanks,' she said. 'It's an odd thought, isn't it? Sometimes just catches me unawares. I mean, I'm lonely most of the time even when I'm with him. It's not like we can have a conversation anymore. But the thought of him not being there at all… It's so strange, when someone has been a part of your life for so long.' She dabbed at her eyes and Clive offered to get her another coffee.

'I'm terribly sorry, guys, but I'm going to have to remove the impromptu respite entertainers,' I said, feeling really bad for introducing a practical aspect to proceedings given the fact that Tina was clearly having a moment. 'I've got to get Grace to her friend Clark's house. She's spending the afternoon there.'

'Oh, is that her boyfriend?' Tina's eyes were brighter now.

'No.' I picked up my bag. 'At least, I don't think so. Clark's a girl but she identifies as a boy, I think. Or maybe she's non-binary. She… I mean *he*…' I corrected myself quickly, 'I mean *they* don't define themselves as a boy or a girl. It's like a gender-neutral thing.' I laughed at the look of utter bemusement on Clive and Tina's faces. 'This is clearly a conversation for another day,' I said. 'I'll fill you in next week.'

Tina's face fell. 'Singing for the Brain's not on next week,' she said. 'Easter.'

'Oh, yes. I'd forgotten. But you could come to my house,' I said. 'My brother's over from Australia with his girlfriend for Easter weekend but he'll probably be gone by then and we could have an impromptu singing session maybe…' My face screwed up a bit as I tried to work out whether we could fit the whole group into my sitting room, including wheelchairs.

'Oh, no, come to mine.' Tina's face had regained its colour. 'We've got masses of room, we could get everybody in. I'll ask Fizz to make an announcement! It'll be perfect. I'll get some Easter eggs for the kids and, well actually, I'll get Easter eggs for all of us, and hot cross buns and… We've got a grand piano, Penny! You could play for us and, oh!' She clapped her hands together, her cheeks flushed. 'I'm really looking forward to it.'

'You had me at Easter eggs,' I said. 'I'd love to. Get Fizz to send out an email and I'll see you both next week.' I made my way over to the centre of the hall and put my arm around Grace, planting a sneaky kiss on the crown of her head, which was inclined towards Mum as they both sung along to a tune on her phone. 'Thank you,' I said, my voice muffled in her hair, which smelled of coconut. 'And you, Tom, and you, Maisie. And you, Mum.' I planted a little kiss on each of their heads, burying my nose in Tom's spiky fringe, Maisie's soft curls and Mum's greying, wiry waves. 'You're all lovely. OK. I know, I know. That's quite enough affection for one day. Bleurgh. Let's go.'

Chapter Twenty

Thursday, 3 April

The arrival of Captain Rory. And this time he's bringing Candice with him, the hot Australian doctor he's currently 'hooking up with' – i.e. shagging with no intention of settling down. I've never met the woman; the last time Rory returned to Blighty eighteen months ago he was single. But he never stays single for long, my brother, and from what I've seen on Facebook, Candice is a pretty spectacular catch. Ten years his junior, she appears to be that most intimidating combination of both clever and gorgeous. She works the surf vibe, lounging around in grungy hoodies and board shorts but then can miraculously transform into smart professional paediatrician or glamorous supermodel on Rory's arm at a military ball. I am obviously looking forward to meeting her but I suspect that, as with most of Rory's visits, tensions will be running high. Still, he must be marginally more serious about her than the other girlfriends if he's prepared to drag her across the globe to meet his increasingly shambolic family.

Rory's flight was due to arrive at Heathrow mid-morning and Sam had offered to collect them, given that he'd been attending some corporate event in London last night and could stay with a colleague who lived fairly near the airport. I'm hoping that this sets a husbandly precedent for 'general helping out with the guests'. Anyway, I texted him to let him know that the Qantas flight was on time and he replied that he was already at the arrivals gate with a large coffee – I expect last night's do was big one. I knew they'd been hoping to scoop a major new client and that usually warrants a hefty bar bill.

Just before lunch there was the familiar sound of Sam's car tyres on the drive and Maisie started squealing 'They're here! They're here!' at the top of her voice. She had made a banner to welcome her uncle and his new glamorous girlfriend, whose photos she'd already studied at length before declaring her 'a princess'. The banner had a collage theme and some of the pasta twirls had not been attached with sufficient care to the paper, which was now disintegrating under the weight of poster paint and the dried goods adorning it. Grace had reverted back to surly sloth mood and was still in bed despite it being midday, Tom was picking his nose while playing *Roblox* on the iPad and Mum was watching *Homes Under the Hammer* in the sitting room. I had told her repeatedly that Rory was coming to stay and she seemed excited each time I mentioned it but obviously forgot all about the impending visit after about five minutes, so this morning I had thought it best to just let her see for herself when he turned up.

I felt suddenly nervous as the car doors opened and Candice swung her long legs out of the front seat. Her face was turned back towards the car and she was laughing at something Sam was telling her. Rory emerged from the back seat looking grumpy as he brushed the dog hair off his trousers and stretched his arms up above his head. I noticed that he also had a crushed Wotsit stuck to the sleeve of his jumper, which had doubtless transferred itself from the car seat along with the dog-related debris.

Candice had sat in the front and therefore avoided the Velcro of inanimate, dog-hair-coated objects. Colin was not allowed to contaminate the front seat, except on very special occasions such as trips to the vet when he travelled in a state of splendour, resting his noble chin upon the dashboard, cocking an ear to his adoring public and manfully awaiting his fate.

I took in the length of Candice's skinny jeans (for a long-haul flight? I mean, what was she thinking? Did she not *do* bloating?), her cropped, pastel hoodie, her flower-patterned trainers. She looked comfortable, clean, stylish and athletic. Not like someone who'd spent the last twenty-four hours eating aeroplane food, battling jet lag and cooped up in a variety of vehicles. Whereas I looked exactly as one would expect a harassed, middle-aged mum of three, owner of an incontinent dog and daughter to a cognitively impaired seventy-year-old, to look. I ran a hand through my un-brushed hair and briefly contemplated the logistics of legging it upstairs, applying a full face of make-up, changing my outfit and undertaking a blow-dry in the time it took them to get their cases out of the car and decided that it was not possible. I'd brushed my teeth and I was out of my pyjamas – what more could they want?

I shut Colin out the back where he pined and scratched at the door, knowing that he was being excluded from something exciting. I then hollered upstairs to Grace to get a bloody move on, told Tom to get his finger out of his nose and wipe his hands before touching anything else, and positioned Maisie with her soggy banner directly in front of me as I opened the front door and cried out 'Hello!' in my most welcoming hostess voice.

Candice, to her credit, treated Maisie's welcome banner as if it was the newest exhibit at the Tate Modern; the full hands-to-mouth gasp of surprise at the level of creative genius that every four-year-old adores. Rory gave me a big muscular hug, patted Maisie fondly on the head and tried some sort of awkward wrestling manoeuvre on Tom that didn't look as though it turned out quite how he'd planned it (he also called him 'Tommo' for the rest of the day and while my son is not particularly precious about correct nomenclature, he did ask me whether Uncle Rory actually knew who he was). I went to hug Sam too, but he was struggling to get the bags in through the front door without coating them in poster paint as he brushed past Maisie's banner – a fate that had not escaped Rory's jumper, as it turns out. The crushed Wotsit now joined by a smear of purple lentils, glitter and glue all the way up his left arm.

I shepherded everyone into the kitchen and put the kettle on while clattering through the usual questions about their journey and enquiring about their itinerary for the next few days. I tried to mask my alarm at Rory's use of the phrases 'We'll just see how it goes' and 'No fixed plans', given that I had made extensive adaptations to the sleeping arrangements in the house in order to accommodate him for three nights and did not think that Grace would cope with being stuck in Maisie's room for any longer than that on a 'see how it goes' basis. Of course, I didn't say this. What I actually said was, 'Yep, sure – whatever works for you guys, stay as long as you like,' while I nearly sliced off my own thumb cutting into the hot cross buns.

In all the kerfuffle I'd forgotten about Mum until I heard a shuffling in the corridor outside. Her head poked round the door frame, a quizzical expression on her face. 'Breakfast?' she asked hopefully.

'No, Mum. You had breakfast, remember? Bacon, eggs, beans, mushrooms, cereal, toast, waffles, maple syrup, fruit juice?' She didn't look convinced. 'I'm doing hot cross buns now and then it'll be lunch soon,' I said. 'But look who's here!' I gestured to the table where Rory was pushing his chair out and standing up to greet her and I could see immediately that something was wrong. Mum's face was blank as Rory put his arms around her and she actually wriggled out of his grasp.

'Excuse me, young man,' she said. '*Who* are you?'

—

It didn't matter how many times we explained it to Mum, she just couldn't get her head around the fact that the beloved and adored son she spoke to occasionally on the phone was in fact the man now stood in front of her.

'It's Rory,' we said.

'It's me,' said Rory.

But she continued to regard him with suspicion.

'I have a son called Rory,' she said eventually. 'He's a doctor. In the army. Lovely boy. Do you know him?' Her face broke into a smile at the same time as Rory's face just sort of broke.

She pulled up a chair next to Candice, who was looking a little bemused by proceedings but, fair play, took the whole thing in her stride and introduced herself to Mum with a warm handshake. 'Hi there, Mrs Andrews. My name's Candice. I've heard so much about you. I've been really looking forward to meeting you and your lovely grandchildren.'

'Candice? Hmm.' Mum's eyes lifted at the corners and I could tell that she was quite taken with this young woman, despite not having a clue that she was dating her son. I've got so used to being with Mum now that I can quickly gauge her reaction and most of the time she's a good judge of character (instant dislike of Tiggy, for example) so this boded well. All we had to do now was convince her that the man seated beside her was her son and a glorious family Easter weekend would unfold. Simple.

–

After lunch, where a political discussion about our current prime minister had been rapidly brought to a close by Mum shouting 'He's a cock!', Rory stayed in the kitchen to help me clear up while Sam and the kids took Candice on a tour of the house (which lasted about forty-five seconds, given the size of it).

'Her dementia's really advanced now, isn't it?' he said, his voice casual as he gave the pan a cursory rinse under the tap. 'I mean, I had no idea how severe things had become.'

'Well.' I took a plate out of the dishwasher and reposi-tioned it. 'She has good days and bad days. Sometimes she doesn't recognise people, some days she does.' This was a partial lie – I'd never seen her completely mistake someone's identity before but I didn't want Rory to feel worse than he already did. 'She often thinks I'm called Sylvia, for example.'

'And is she still wandering? Stealing things?'

I was cautious. I didn't want to be disloyal to Mum and Rory was talking about her as if she was a stranger, which perhaps she was, at the moment. 'Like I say, she has good days and bad days. I don't make a habit of leaving her unattended but she's better now than she was; she's more used to being here with us. When Dad first had his accident, she was much more confused. Kept leaving the house and trying to walk back to find him.' I didn't say that she'd let herself out of the front door a few nights ago in an attempt to 'find that chap who stole all the spoons'.

'Hmmm.' Rory looked moodily into the sink. 'It's a ruddy shame, is all. Terribly tricky for the old man. We need to think it through; plan her care properly. Has she been assessed by a neurologist or is it psychiatry who run the memory clinic here?'

'Errr. Not entirely sure. She's on Memantine, um, and a calcium tablet I think.'

'But she's had a scan? A full cognitive assessment? She must have. I mean, I know it's the NHS but there's a basic level of diagnostics…' He sighed as he moved the bowls into the dishwasher. 'What's the name of her consultant? And when was her last review? Is there a letter from him?'

'I don't know, Rory. To be honest, I've been focussing more on the practical stuff. What she can do, what she needs help with, trying to keep her happy and calm, you know.'

'But she's… I mean, she's completely… Her brain's turned to mush, Penny. She's dementing at an astonishing rate… She's, I don't even know what to say. Surely you can see how serious this is?'

'I didn't know it was a verb,' I muttered, re-stacking the bowls so that they wouldn't weld together.

'What?' His voice was impatient.

'Dementing – I didn't know you could use it like that: I dement, we dement, she dements…'

'For Christ's sake, Penny. It doesn't matter how we describe it. She's completely loco, lost her marbles, got a few kangaroos loose in the paddock, whatever.'

'I didn't think doctors were supposed to talk about people with dementia in that way,' I said, more than a little annoyed on Mum's behalf. 'I think you should show a little respect. She's still our mother.'

'She doesn't know she's my bloody mother though, does she?!' He sighed. 'I take your point, Pen. But things are so much worse than I'd realised. And the real issue is, what are we going to do about it?'

I knew he was frustrated and I knew he was hurt by her reaction to him so I tried to cut him some slack, but honestly: what were *we* going to do about it? Who did he think had been doing everything up to now? Who did he think had been running themselves ragged *doing stuff*, left, right and bloody centre. Not him, that's for sure.

'Let's talk about it later,' I said. 'We'll see Dad tomorrow and—'

'And that's another thing.' He was back in practical attack mode. 'Why on earth is Dad still in hospital? It's been what, three months since his stroke?'

'Well. Not quite. Almost. But, you know, he had the fall, and then the stroke. And he's had a chest infection… They are looking at moving him to a rehab centre or a community hospital or something but there's no beds apparently…'

'But you need to get on at them, Penny. The longer he stays in an acute setting the more he's at risk of hospital-acquired infections, MRSA, Clostridium… It's like living in a petri-dish on those geriatric wards. You need to be—'

'Rory,' I cut across him. 'How about we discuss all the great many things I *need* to be doing a little later? Maybe after you and Candice have had a chance to unwind a bit? The kids have been really excited about seeing you. I thought maybe we could take the dog out for a walk later this afternoon, or you could just put your feet up in front of the telly, have a bath, have a lie down...'

He grunted in agreement. 'Yup, OK. Sorry. Bit upset, is all.'

'I know. Look, give me that jumper, I'll put it in the wash while you go and get yourself sorted out.' I gestured to the encrusted sleeve and he nodded absently as he pulled it over his head and handed me the scrunched-up bundle.

'Righto. I'll see where Candi's got to.'

'She seems nice,' I said as he left the kitchen and then lowered my voice to mutter into the recesses of the dishwasher. 'Although God knows what she's going to make of this omnishambles.'

Chapter Twenty-One

Easter Saturday, 5 April

As if life could get any more complicated, Rory has returned from his trip to see Dad in hospital with Mr Tibbs, my parents' cat. Sam drove Rory and Candice down yesterday morning while I stayed at home to coordinate the mountains of bedding and food necessary to accommodate our extended family. He dropped Grace off at her friend Rani's on the way and Caz came to collect Tom for some cricket practice with Alex. As a result, Mum, Maisie and I positively luxuriated in the vast quantities of vacated space, although my 'me time' was encroached on by requests to play 'Sleeping Princesses and Peas' in Maisie's room. The basic premise of the game involved lying on Grace's camp bed for a few moments and then leaping up for comedic effect when I found I had been resting on an item of plastic food from the play kitchen – it was a tempting offer, particularly the lying-down bit, even with the negligible discomfort of a plastic broccoli floret pressing against my buttocks.

Mum, I later discovered, had been unpacking items from Candice's suitcase and distributing them around the house in surprising and novel locations. Thus, Candice's toothbrush was finally uncovered beneath the laundry basket, her make-up was scattered across Tom's bed (this caused a few questions) and items of her underwear were to be found artfully draped across the hall lamp (the one Tom had broken in January that still hadn't been fixed).

Sam had popped into the hospital to visit Dad along with my brother and his girlfriend and they had then travelled the short journey to my parents' house where they had parted ways; the plan being for Rory to collect Dad's car, which had been idling in the garage for three months, and to drive it back to our place once he'd had a look through some of my parents' paperwork. I had suggested that, rather than hitting me with a barrage of administrative and legislative questions I was unable to answer, Rory might be better off searching through our parents' filing cabinet until he found what he was looking for. I'll admit there was also a part of me that wanted him to see the state of the house, although obviously this backfired because he held me entirely responsible for letting it go to rack and ruin since Dad had been in hospital. My attempts to point out to him that it had been in a far worse mess when I had originally popped in to collect Mum's things on that hideous day in January fell on deaf ears. However, the sight of the family homestead in such a state of dereliction did prompt a change of plan and it was decided that instead of taking Candice on a tour of the British Isles featuring luxury hotels and bijoux bed and breakfasts, my brother would proceed directly to Mum and Dad's after Easter lunch tomorrow to woo his girlfriend for the remainder of their stay in the far less glamorous surroundings of said dilapidated Edwardian terrace.

Rory and Candice puttered onto our drive in Dad's Corsa yesterday evening both looking flushed and happy in a way that suggested there'd been some hanky-panky going on. Given that they'd been at it like rabbits the night before (our house has extremely creaky floorboards that amplify most noises, particularly the repetitive nocturnal variety), it seemed implausible that they wouldn't have been unable to resist the urge to shag in a layby; they were grown-ups after all. Thankfully I didn't take them to task on their adolescent behaviour or make any lame innuendos because it quickly transpired that the reason for their rosy appearance was Mr Tibbs, who, angry at his enforced relocation, had shat in the pet carrier a few miles into the journey. My brother and his girlfriend had been forced to drive the remainder of the way with all the windows down and a howling Easter gale beating their reddening cheeks. Rory carried a furious and malodorous Mr Tibbs into the house, leaving the pet carrier out on the drive where it was later attacked by foxes. He then tried to explain his reasons for bringing said feline into our already tight domestic situation, a situation that was also ostensibly a 'dog-based' one and not an environment that necessarily leant itself to the addition of an elderly and already quite cantankerous cat. Did he feel there was currently an insufficiently carnival-like atmosphere? Were we not already teetering on the verge of Bedlam? Did we really need Mr Tibbs to push us over the edge completely? Yes, it appeared we did, or at least, Mr Tibbs needed us. Not that Mr Tibbs was aware of this.

I had told my brother that Agnes from next-door had seemed perfectly happy to continue to feed the cat every time I had seen her. I forgot to tell him that the last time I had seen Agnes was a month ago and it seems that as soon as she saw Rory arrive at the house she was round there like a shot, explaining that she was off to Lanzarote in a few weeks and would be unable to maintain her current duties.

To be fair, Rory recognised that she had been providing an invaluable service and turned on the famous 'Captain, Doctor and Bloody Nice Chap' charm. He had found an unopened bottle of Dubonnet in the drinks cabinet along with a dusty box of Ferrero Rocher, which may have been past its sell-by date, in the back of the kitchen cupboard and presented them to Agnes while assuring her that he, Captain Rory, would now be taking over proceedings, generally sorting everything out and being marvellous, and that she, Agnes-next-door, could rest assured that her kindness and faithful service to the family would not go unnoticed or unrewarded (although he failed to specify exactly what form that reward may take over and above the Dubonnet and dusty chocolates). He then located the ancient pet-carrier (which has since been savaged by our local vixen) and scooped a spitting Mr Tibbs into it, sustaining only minor injuries as a result. And now, here he was, larger than life and twice as pissed off (Mr Tibbs, not Rory, who was surprisingly cheerful despite the cat scratches and olfactory challenge of his journey. Maybe if you're an army doctor you've smelt a lot worse).

I was torn between amusement and incredulity, but could also begrudgingly see that we didn't really have any other option than to accommodate Mr Tibbs. He would have been even more furious to have gone to a pet-rescue centre, where he may have inadvertently been put down, and my parents would never have forgiven me if we'd had him rehomed. So, The Penny Baker Centre for Retired Pets, Feral Children and People with Alzheimer's was where he now found himself. Much to the delight of the resident canine. Colin has spent the past twenty-four hours in a state of near hysteria, so overjoyed is he to have received such a gift. The barking, chasing, careering into table legs, knocking things over and peeing on the floor in excitement has increased exponentially as Mr Tibbs' reaction becomes more disapproving. Colin seems to feel that it is his duty to alert us to the presence of the cat on a very regular basis, so last night we had continuous feverish barking from the kitchen to add to the bonking in the spare room.

The one silver lining is that Mum seems to be happier with Mr Tibbs restored to her. He sits imperiously on her lap, being petted and fussed over while Mum breaks my brother's heart by asking him if he's ever met her son, Dr Rory Andrews. I've suggested that he play along for now. Anita from Alzheimer's UK said it's far better to try and 'enter the world' of the person with dementia than to always insist on the accurate representation of a potentially distressing reality. And for Rory, trying to explain that *he* is this prodigal legend is exhausting and ultimately fruitless. It is much more fun to listen to her waxing lyrical about his virtues (so kind, so clever, *so* handsome) while Rory simply pretends that he is indeed an acquaintance of his actual self.

'Now you come to mention it, I think I *have* met your son,' he said this morning over breakfast. 'Tall chap? Quite good-looking?' Candice poked him in the ribs.

Mum was delighted. 'Yes! He's terribly handsome, my Rory. Always a one for the ladies.' She nudged him, winking, and I thought for one horrible moment that she was going to say something completely inappropriate in front of Candice so I clattered a large plate of bacon under her nose for distraction.

'Well, he told me a lot about you,' Rory continued, leaning over to get the marmalade. 'He said you were a fantastic cook.'

Her face scrunched up in delight. 'Oh, he would say that, my Rory. He always was a one for my baking.' She chuckled, pleased with herself and Rory smiled as he started spreading the marmalade onto his toast.

'He said his favourite was shepherd's pie, I think.'

Mum nodded with enthusiasm. 'Oh, yes! That and the puddings. He loved a pudding, that boy. Had such a sweet tooth.'

Rory paused in ladling yet more marmalade onto his toast. 'Ah. Yes,' he said.

Candice nudged him and whispered, 'A long-standing issue, I see.'

'Tell me more about him. Your son,' said Rory.

Mum's face lit up – this was her favourite topic, after all. She leant back in her chair, her attention diverted from her breakfast. 'He was a bit of a terror, really,' she said. 'Always getting into scrapes with that friend of his, the little lad with the red hair...'

'Joe Styles,' offered Rory.

'Yes! That's it, Joe Styles.' Mum patted Rory's hand, pleased. 'They used to climb the trees out behind the back garden, they were old trees those, planted long before the houses went up. Big spreading branches, perfect for climbing. Gordon built them a fort, it was just a few planks of wood really, balanced up in the boughs, a little rope ladder. Not that Rory needed it, such a nimble climber and so fearless. Of course, he fell out of there once or twice, broke his leg...'

'Arm,' said Rory. 'Right arm. I had to write with my left hand for weeks, d'you remember?'

'Yes! Of course. It was rugby, the leg. That was a nasty business. Still, I think that's maybe what made him want to be a doctor, all that time in the hospital. Happiest day of my life when Rory qualified.' She sighed. 'Of course, he's very busy now. We don't see him.'

There was a moment's silence. Rory kept his eyes focused down on his plate as he spoke quietly. 'I know, Mum. I'd like to have been around a bit more. I – I wish I'd made the most of…' He looked up and I realised there were tears in his eyes. Mum reached across and put her hand over his. 'Oh dear,' she said. 'Don't be sad.' And then her attention was caught by the sight of Tom tucking into the box of Quality Street that had appeared on the breakfast table like an Easter miracle. 'Ooh! Chocolate!' She stuck her hand out expectantly.

Maisie had also spotted the chocolates and, being a master tactician, knew exactly how to turn the situation to her advantage. 'Granny, can you talk more about Uncle Rory and Mummy when they were little?' she said, pulling the box out from under Tom's nose under the guise of 'offering them around' as she took one herself. She then went to go and sit on Rory's lap, sensing in the intuitive way of small children that here was a grown-up in need of a cuddle. She settled in against his chest and put her thumb in her mouth.

'How many times did Uncle Rory fall out of the tree?' She spoke around the thumb, which made enunciation tricky, but Mum got the gist and proceeded to regale her with stories; information recalled with such unerring accuracy that Rory and I found ourselves meeting each other's eye across the table and shaking our heads in disbe-lief. How could a woman who didn't recognise her own son when he was sat in front of her, still tell you what flavour lollipop he'd eaten on the beach at Clacton, thirty-five years ago.

wake up and want to chat with her big sister about Uncle Rory and Beautiful Candice and did Grace think they would get married, and did she think that she, Maisie, would be a bridesmaid and would she get a new dress and would it be prettier than the dress that Amy from preschool wore to her mum's wedding when she married Amy's dad who worked in the Plant Hire, and what was a Plant Hire anyway?

Grace might have indulged this in the past but there are limits to how many questions one can answer without losing the will to live and I know that Maisie can test those limits to their very extremes. In addition, Grace does not seem to be feeling particularly indulgent towards anyone at the moment – the only people she can tolerate being in the same room with are Mum and Colin. Thus, after a short while I would hear Grace hissing at Maisie to shut up, then there would be tears and, probably sometime around one o'clock, peace. This lasted until six in the morning when Maisie would wake up properly, try and get into bed with Grace, be pushed back out again with little ceremony and then make her way to clamber in with us. Add into this the overwhelming confusion of Mum being rehomed in Grace's bedroom, her complete inability to understand that she should sleep in this bed now and was not to enter the spare room under any circumstances (but particularly not in the middle of the night) and that if she did accidentally end up in the spare room she should certainly not attempt to get into bed with Candice and Rory or stand over them looking menacing.

By this, the third morning of their visit, there had been more overnight movement and bed-swapping than a college fraternity party. Grace was curled up on the sofa in the sitting room, Sam had moved into Grace's room and

Mum had got into bed with me, having been retrieved from the side of the spare bed before Candice's screams woke the remaining sleepers (the only person actually still asleep being Tom, who was quickly realising that one of the very few advantages of having a bedroom built for a hobbit was that he wasn't expected to share it).

After breakfast, I suggested that Sam, Rory and the kids took Colin out for a walk while I put the lamb in to roast, but in the time it took for them to get their wellies on and decide a route (my brother and husband poring over the Ordnance Survey map like they were about to scale the Eiger), Colin had helped himself to the majority of the Easter eggs and then thrown up in the sitting room. While the immediate evacuation of Colin's stomach at least meant that a trip to the emergency vets was unlikely to be required, Tom and Maisie were inconsolable at the loss of so many eggs. Sam jollied them out of the door with the promise that there would be loads for sale in the petrol station. He and Rory set off with the two younger kids in the back, an unrepentant dog perched between them thumping his tail against Maisie's arm and breathing chocolatey dog breath over Tom until they forgave him. Candice had seen my face fall when the information regarding the dog vomit filtered as far as the kitchen. 'I'll go get Grace,' she said. 'We'll give you a hand.'

I thought this was optimistic – Grace had relocated back to Maisie's room at first light and was likely cocooned on the camp bed in a comatose state. But a few moments later I heard laughter and to my absolute astonishment, Grace came into the kitchen with the bucket from the broom cupboard. 'I told Candice I'd bring her some warm soapy water,' she said, pulling on a pair of Marigolds and whirling the sponge cloth into the suds. 'We'll clean it all up for you.'

'Thank you.' I didn't know what else to say, this was most out of character. 'Um, did Colin scoff your chocolate too?'

Grace smiled. 'I'd put my eggs up on the bookshelf,' she said.

'Good thinking.' I poked the rosemary sprigs into the pink flesh of the lamb joint. 'So, you'll be happy to share yours with Tom and Maisie then?'

'Uh, absolutely *no chance.*' She carried the bowl out into the hall, laughing at such a ridiculous suggestion.

Once they had finished clearing up, Candice managed to persuade Grace to help set the table. She then poured me a glass of wine while she had a lengthy conversation with my daughter about K-pop and whether it was as big a deal here as it was in Australia. In a desperate attempt to appear cool and knowledgeable I tried to crowbar my way into the discussion, but Grace almost fell off her chair when she realised that I thought K-pop was a breakfast cereal.

'It's Korean pop music, Penny,' Candice said kindly. 'All the kids love it back home but you guys are often a bit ahead of us down under. I'd wondered if it'd had its day on the UK music scene.'

If I had even dreamed of uttering the words 'you guys' or 'music scene', Grace would have never spoken to me again, but seemingly Candice, being ten years younger and (more critically) not her hideously embarrassing mother, could get away with it. I nodded non-committally. 'We could see if Fizz would let us do some in the choir,' I said. 'What do you think?'

Grace snorted. 'Yeah, right.' But then her eyes lit up, 'D'you know, Mum, that's not such a stupid idea.'

'Wonders will never cease,' I muttered into the oven as I shoved the lamb in.

'There are some songs that we could do,' said Grace. 'I mean it's a bit old now but perhaps some of the BTS stuff. I'll just get it up on my... Oh, where's my phone? Must've left it upstairs.' She raced off to retrieve the device that was usually welded to her left hand and I raised my eyebrows.

'Well, you've got more conversation out of her in the last five minutes than I've managed in two years,' I said, trying to sound grateful rather than resentful, even though I was really a mixture of both.

'S'just teenagers, hey?' Her intonation went up at the end so it wasn't clear whether she was asking a question or stating a fact. (I nodded just in case.) 'We've got an adolescent unit at the children's hospital and I do a couple of clinics there? It pays to know your customer base, if you know what I mean?' (That was definitely a question so I nodded again, this time with more conviction.) 'Some of the kids we see, they're not mad keen to be there, they just don't want to talk to anyone? So, if you can get any kind of conversational opening you're onto a winner, right?'

'Sure, yeah. Well, cheers anyway,' I said, tilting my wine glass in Candice's direction. 'Much appreciated.' I noticed that her hands were empty. 'Have you got a glass?' I gestured to the wine bottle. 'It's the least you deserve after the past few days. Can't have been easy putting up with my brother and his crazy family – and you've managed to do it with a smile on your face the whole time. Even when Mum's gatecrashed your room.'

'Yeah, well. I think she got more of an eyeful than she'd bargained for.' Candice grimaced.

I didn't know what on earth to say to that so started stacking the dishwasher. 'Well, help yourself. To wine I mean. Or, you know, whatever, Tua casa, mia casa or whatever it is.'

'S'all right. I'm not a big drinker.' She crossed over to the dishwasher and started to help me put the breakfast plates in. 'I think you're doing an amazing job, by the way,' she said, holding up a bowl with Weetabix stuck to the side. 'Top shelf?'

'Erm. Yes. Thanks.' I smiled awkwardly. (Did she mean an amazing job loading the dishwasher? Not sure.) Grace returned, blaring out some tinny music from her iPhone. She linked it up to the speaker on the countertop. 'What d'you think, Mum?' She turned the volume up. 'Can you see Granny singing along to this?'

I listened. 'It's… got a good beat,' I said and my daughter corpsed with laughter. 'A good beat!' she wiped the tears from her eyes, 'Oh, Mum.' The look on her face was almost fond.

'I can imagine Ernest swearing along to it,' I said.

'Or Marie playing the air guitar here,' said Grace pointing to the speaker as the instrumental section kicked in.

We both laughed at that and it was Candice's turn to look confused, so Grace filled her in on the Singing for the Brain choir and suggested that they go and play the tune to Granny to see what she thought of it.

Two hours later and the dog-walkers returned, muddy and wet but triumphant. Maisie and Tom were both holding aloft two massive Easter eggs while Colin circled below them eager to pounce if one should drop. 'No way,

Colin my lad,' Tom gave the dog a wise smile. 'These eggs be miiiinnne…'

'Yeah, Colin,' Maisie chipped in. 'Feel the buuurrrn.'

'Half price,' Sam whispered excitedly as he dropped a carrier bag full of more eggs on the kitchen table. He was pretty pleased with himself and his bargain purchases.

'Nice work, Sam.' Candice high-fived my husband on her way out to the hall in one of the most awkward exchanges I have seen for many years, and I smiled into my second glass of wine.

'Yeah, *nice work, Sam,*' I said. I had been aiming for gentle mockery, an attempt to acknowledge that Candice was a bit Aussie and a bit cool and that we (the collective, us, a couple, united) were not really the type who said things like that or high-fived each other, but my voice came out as mean and whiney.

'That's a bit unnecessary, isn't it? She was only being kind.' A small frown line had appeared on Sam's forehead and I felt like one of the children being told off as he continued. 'Rory said that she'd really wanted to come for a walk with the kids but she stayed behind to help you.' He picked up the wine bottle and raised his eyebrows. 'Isn't this the one we opened last night? I thought it was almost full.'

'This is my first glass,' I said with dignity.

'Oh. OK.' He pulled off his wellies, releasing clumps of mud across the floor.

'Sam! For Christ's sake. Could you not…' I glared at him.

He picked his boots up and sighed as he left the kitchen in his wet socks. I heard snatches of 'Thanks for that, *Sam*, thanks for walking the dog and taking care of the kids and sorting out the Easter eggs…' as he muttered to himself.

I sighed. Things had been a bit tricky with Sam this weekend. Things had been a bit tricky with Sam full stop. We'd never really discussed the argument we'd had about Mum staying with us and I still felt, perhaps unfairly, that he was permanently looking out for evidence of my not coping well. This paranoia was reinforced by my brother's presence in the house. It was almost as if both the men in my life were colluding to squirrel my mother away in order to protect her from my ineptitude. I was determined to prove to them both that, while the current situation was not ideal, I was just as capable as either of them at managing it.

–

Easter lunch was a tense affair. Mum had returned to her initial mistrust of Rory and kept moving her chair away from him until she was virtually sitting on Maisie's lap. Rory was unusually subdued and didn't come up with a single anecdote relating to his own brilliance during the entire meal, which is unheard of. The lamb was not quite the perfectly seasoned, firm yet juicy texture I'd hoped for. The broccoli was soggy and the potatoes had burnt. The children were so full of chocolate that they refused to eat any of it and I was becoming increasingly annoyed with everyone. My period had arrived a week early and surprisingly the wine was not improving my mood.

Maisie was pushing a particularly gristly piece of meat across her plate with a lacklustre expression and Sam whispered to her. 'You don't have to eat it, love. Don't worry, the lamb is a bit tough.'

I jumped to my feet, fuelled by drunken hormonal outrage.

'It's nothing to do with the quality of the meat, *Sam*,' I snapped. 'And it's not about my skills as a chef, either. You guys were late back from the walk. As a result, the meal is over-cooked. If you'd be happier with restaurant-standard food then I suggest you book us into one for next year – or you could just try being on time, or cooking it yourself, or maybe not criticising every tiny thing I do...'

I tipped the last drops from my glass of Rioja into my mouth and began to clear the plates away despite the fact that Mum was still resolutely ploughing through her meal.

'Penelope, these potatoes are...' She was trawling through her unreliable vocabulary. 'They're... red, Penelope. Very red indeed.'

'The word you're looking for is burnt, Mum. And yes, I know they are. But luckily it doesn't seem to be impeding your enjoyment of them, does it.' I pulled Grace's plate away from under her disinterested nose. 'And Grace – what have I said about phones at the table?'

'Yeah, Grace!' Tom, who had been looking bewildered by my chippiness up until this point but was now on familiar territory. 'Mum says you can't have phones at the table. Not even grown-ups.'

I noticed my brother sheepishly sliding his own phone back off the table and into his pocket at this, but Grace did not respond to her brother's jibes. Her face had taken on an ashen hue as she stared at her screen.

'Grace, durr! Put it down! Oh my God, Mum, it is so unfair!' Tom turned to me, animated with the injustice. 'She gets away with things all the time. Just because she's a girl. You are all *so sexist*. I wouldn't be allowed to have my phone at the—'

'Shut up, Tom.' Grace's voice was quiet and empty. The words were merely an involuntary vocal response, slipping back into the reflex action of insult and counter-argument with her brother, but her attention was entirely focused on the screen.

'No! I will not shut up, you, you...' Overcome with impotent fury and unable to decide on the correct noun for his sister, Tom shoved her hard on her shoulder and grabbed the phone with his other hand, pulling it away from her and holding it aloft. 'Ha!'

Grace jumped up out of her chair in an attempt to reclaim the device but Tom was too quick for her and had already brought it back down to the table where he put on a mock grown-up voice and delivered the immortal lines that Sam and I have trotted out many times in the past. 'Let's have a look at what's so *important*, shall we? What was it that *couldn't wait* until after dinner?' He looked back at the screen and read exactly what was in front of him before his brain had time to engage.

'Hey buffet-slayer! Bet you be getting plenty lardy on all your chocolate but maybe leave my boyfriend's cock alone you blow-jobbing bitch.'

There was, as you'd imagine, a tumbleweed silence that seemed to stretch on for hours, possibly days. Tom, processing exactly how many banned words he'd uttered, pointed mutely at the screen as if to indicate that he was in no way to blame for what had come out of his mouth. Grace, trying to compose her face, wrestled the phone back off him and ran out of the door, slamming it behind her and yelling, 'Thanks for that piece of trademark fuck-wittery, Thomas, you massive tit,' as she disappeared up the stairs.

Sam and I exchanged paralysed glances, Rory and Candice looked down at their limp broccoli and Maisie piped up with, 'What's trademark fuck-wittery?' which, out of all the options she could have chosen from the preceding tirade, was actually less taxing on the ears than it might have been.

'It's, um, a quality put-down, to be fair,' said Candice. 'But maybe not to be repeated?'

'Blow-jobbing bitch,' Mum mumbled contentedly through her mouthful of lamb. I noticed a droplet of gravy poised on her chin and watched with fascination as it plopped onto her plate.

'What's…'

'Same.' Candice intercepted Maisie's next question. 'Not to be repeated either.'

Tom was on the verge of tears. 'But, but, but, it was what it said. I was just reading the message… I… Who would— *why* would someone send that to Grace?' he asked, also appealing to Candice as the adult most capable of speech at the present moment.

She shrugged. 'I dunno, mate. But it's a pretty lousy thing to do.' She stood up and started collecting the plates from their side of the table, gesturing for me to go upstairs, 'Penny, d'you wanna, you know, go after her?'

I was frozen in a combination of shock and embarrassment.

'Yes, God, Penny, maybe you'd better go and see if she's all right.' Sam's wide-eyed astonishment seemed to have defaulted back to the implication that I was terrible mother / cook / human being, which was nice.

'Yeah, thanks Sam, I think I know how to look after my daughter.' I put the plates back on the table with a crash. 'You're happy to sort out the rest of lunch then, yes? While I go and deal with this?' I couldn't quite override the keeping-up-appearances genes so left the room with a reassuring, yet apologetic smile to our guests, 'Sorry about that. It's not usually quite this tabloid in our house at Easter-time.' I gave a shrill laugh from the doorway. 'It's probably nothing, the way these teenagers speak to each other, you know, texting, Snapchat, Instagram sort of stuff...'

My random listing of social media platforms was not really convincing anyone that what they'd just witnessed had been in any way benign or innocent. Candice's sceptical face belied her, 'Yeah, I'm sure you're right – probably just banter.' As did Rory's raised eyebrows. It was safe to say that he had never witnessed an Easter quite like this while we were growing up. The thought of someone saying the words 'blow-jobbing bitch' over Sunday lunch with Mary and Gordon was laughable, but the idea that his mother would then repeat those words as if she were simply commenting on the vegetables was ludicrous. Anyway, I didn't really feel like laughing at the moment. I felt like taking myself off somewhere for a good cry. Instead, I raced upstairs calling for Grace and eventually discovered that she had locked herself in the bathroom again.

'Leave. Me. Alone.' The words were hissed under the door.

'Grace. Please. Let's talk about this...'

Silence. I tried again but no matter how much I pleaded and cajoled, Grace refused to comment further, or to unlock the door. I returned to the dining room feeling completely useless. My daughter was clearly in pain and yet could not bear to share it with me, her mother. I wasn't sure how much practical help I'd be able to offer – Tom might have been a better prospect if her plan was to compose an equally horrific reply to the text – but I needed to be at least given the opportunity to try.

Later that afternoon – once Rory and Candice had left for my parents' house and I had tried to pretend that '*everything was fine!*' – I headed to Grace's room, thinking she'd likely have relocated there. Sam, Tom and Maisie were settled in front of the telly watching *Mrs Doubtfire*. I'd forgotten how much swearing there is in some of those family films from my youth, but in view of the foul-mouthery that Maisie had already been exposed to today, I think we could safely say that this particular horse had bolted some hours ago and was now galloping away across open plains of profanity. Sam and I had been neither able nor willing to discuss the Grace situation or indeed any other situation, given the lack of privacy and general enthusiasm for such a debate. So I left him with the kids and a giant box of chocolates, made myself a coffee and knocked quietly on Grace's door.

'Grace,' I said. 'I won't come in unless you want me to but I do need to talk to you. We have to discuss this, because even if you don't feel it's a big deal, it really is. People shouldn't be sending you messages like that.'

There was silence. I tried again.

'Grace. I'm going to open the door and I'm taking your silence to mean that this is OK with you...' I turned the handle, confident that if I could at least get to her physically, I might be able to offer some support. But somebody had beaten me to it. Sitting on the edge of the bed, quietly stroking the hair of her eldest granddaughter, was Mum. Grace was curled up on her bed dabbing forlornly at her mascara-streaked cheeks with the sleeve of her jumper and cuddling Raggy Annie, the ragdoll she'd had since she was a baby and still used as a comfort blanket when she thought nobody was looking. She pushed the doll away and reached out for her phone as Mum stood up and crossed to leave the room.

'Penelope, you have been keeping us waiting for quite some time. I do need to get to the butchers for tonight's steak and kidney pudding.' She tutted as she closed the door behind her, but I didn't hear any footsteps heading back downstairs so assumed that the urgent trip to buy offal had been postponed. I raised my eyebrows at Grace and mouthed 'steak and kidney pudding?'

She gave me a watery smile. 'Granny came upstairs looking for some, like, onions or something.'

'Ah, yes. That's exactly what we need today. Onions.' I sat on the very edge of the bed in the spot that Mum had vacated.

'And then she got distracted and came and gave me a cuddle instead.' Grace shifted her position. 'D'you know the nice thing about Granny? She doesn't ask questions. She's just, like, there. D'you know what I mean?'

I nodded. 'Yes. I do. And sometimes it's quite soothing to just not have to think about stuff for a while isn't it? To just have a hug and a bit of a chat…'

Grace was pulling a horrified face. 'Erm, I don't need a *hug*, actually, Mum. But we can talk if you like.'

'Do I get to hold your hand or pat you on the shoulder? Any physical contact whatsoever? No. Righto. Why don't you start at the beginning. Spill the tea.'

She rolled her eyes at my comedy attempt at youth-speak, but I could see the corner of her mouth twitch in a begrudging smile so I pressed on. 'Who's the nasty little cow who sent you that horror-show of a message?'

The cow in question, it turned out, was one Jade Anderson, a fifteen-year-old potty-mouth who thought that her boyfriend, Dillon, wanted to hook up with my daughter.

'And does he? Fancy you?' I was intrigued. This was the closest we had ever come to any conversation about boys. We'd done the mortifying sex-education talk a few years ago and had since made veiled references to staying safe on the internet or discussing contraception in the context of the pill stopping period pain, but an actual mention of somebody fancying someone else? This was new.

'Nobody says they *fancy* people any more, Mum.' Grace's cheeks had gone pink. 'And, I dunno really. He's, like, in year eleven and, like, I chatted with him at, like, Millie's party.' The number of 'likes' in Grace's sentences was often directly proportional to the care she was taking not to reveal too much. For example, if she wanted to insult her brother or ask what was for breakfast there were no 'likes' involved, but if she was trying to cover up some minor misdemeanour the quantity of 'likes' could increase to the point where they accounted for every other word.

'And did you *just* chat with him?' I left the question hanging in the air as she mumbled something into her pillow. 'What?'

She sat back up. 'I kissed him.' She put her face in her hands. 'I didn't know he was seeing Jade. I wouldn't have… Millie had got these strawberry cider things and…'

I had a sudden vision of the words 'blow-job' and 'boyfriend's cock' and couldn't stop myself from blurting out, 'Did you only kiss him though? You didn't somehow accidentally…?'

What was I asking her? Whether she'd 'accidentally' performed fellatio? Whether a fifteen-year-old's penis had 'acci-dentally' fallen into her mouth? The whole concept made me want to barf and it looked as though Grace was having the same thought. 'Errrgh! God, Mum, no! I just kissed him, OK? There was, like, nothing illegal or anything.' She flumped back down onto her duvet. 'God, it was a lot easier when Granny was here instead.'

'Don't you believe it,' I said. 'The kind of stuff that she's been coming out with lately, you'd have been having a conversation on a whole different level.'

Grace smiled at that and I relaxed. Of course, my little girl wasn't doing anything sordid with random priapic teenage boys. She'd just had her first kiss, that was all.

Admittedly, in less than ideal circumstances.

And while she had been drunk on Koppaberg.

And with someone else's boyfriend.

But these were all issues we could deal with.

Chapter Twenty-Three

Tuesday, 8 April

Choir practice at Bob and Tina's house today. The kids all came along, although Grace's attendance was under duress. She barely spoke all morning, although she did rally slightly at the sight of the baked goods and confectionery items that Tina had clearly been slaving over a hot stove to produce.

'I've always loved cooking,' Tina said, watching appreciatively as Tom demolished another fondant truffle. 'We used to entertain a lot and I'd spend days planning menus and choosing ingredients, I really enjoyed it.'

'Mmmmf, these really are delicious, Tina.' Clive's compliment was muffled by the mouthful of warm, buttered hot cross bun. 'I don't think I've ever had a proper homemade one of these – usually just pick up a pack for me and Dad from the supermarket. It's like... another world.'

Tina laughed. 'I'm not sure about that,' she said, but her face glowed with pride. 'I'll put a few aside for you.'

'Really?' Clive was thrilled. 'That would be, well, marvellous. Are you sure?'

'Oh, absolutely. We won't get through these on our own, me and Bob, even with Penny and the kids' best efforts.' She smiled at Tom as his hand hovered over a cookie. 'Bob used to love my cooking but he's rarely hungry nowadays and I have to be really careful with what he has; he coughs and splutters so much with most things. The speech therapist says we're going to need to move onto a pureed diet soon.' Her mouth turned down a little at the corners.

'They said the same to us about Dad,' said Clive. 'But he told the girl to piss off and that he would eat whatever the fuck he wanted. Oops, sorry Penny,' he looked at Tom and Maisie. 'Little ears and all that. I'm so used to the language now, I forget it's not correct parlance.'

'I wouldn't worry,' I said. 'I don't think they can hear anything at the moment over their own internal monologue of *Cake! More Cake!*' I smiled as I watched Maisie examining her hands for traces of chocolate and licking them off. 'I can't pretend it's exactly a convent at our house anyway, they've heard considerably worse in just the past few days.' We moved away from the table and I filled them in on the story of our Easter weekend. I left out the specific wording of Grace's text message but I think they got the idea.

Once we'd eaten our fill, we went through to the drawing room. Grace was sitting in the far corner on a window seat that looked out through a large sash frame onto borders speckled with spring flowers. Her eyes were blank, looking but not seeing, and even the sparrows and blue-tits barging each other out of the way on the stone bird table didn't raise a smile. A polished grand piano occupied the opposite corner and it was around here that we congregated, although Tom and Maisie by now had taken to exploring the rest of the house, occasionally sliding past the drawing-room doors on the polished parquet floor and giggling as they fell over.

I've never seen such an amazing piano before, let alone played it. Every note seemed to reverberate through the body of the instrument before emerging, clear and rounded as it ascended to the high ceiling and filled the spaces between us. Even the disparate voices – the waverers, the warblers, the swearers and the dubious soprano from Marie – couldn't detract from the clarity and depth of the melody. It was as if the sound was pulsing through the floor to each singer, entering at their feet and coursing through their bodies until it burst from their throats in a rich and joyful expression of what it meant to be alive. Admittedly, without Fizz's extensive range of percussion instruments it was harder to keep some of the participants engaged beyond two or three songs, but those songs that we did complete were a prayer of thanksgiving, a celebration, a hymn to banish the demons of dementia. In all honesty, I don't think 'Wonderwall' has ever been performed with such anthemic vigour. And I've seen Oasis in concert twice.

–

I left Tina's feeling better than I had in days. Between songs, I'd had a good chat with Clive and the other carers about the awkwardness of Mum not recognising Rory and they listened sympathetically, offering similar stories of their own. It was so nice to be able to offload some of the stress and anxiety that built up over days of being a full-time carer, and to share it with people who really understood what I was going through. And if you combined this with the cathartic experience of singing and releasing all that stress out through your lungs, blasting all the negativity out to the ceiling, this was fast becoming my favourite part of the week. Mum was happy and relaxed, waving to everyone as we left with our goodie bag of leftover treats. The younger two children had also had a lovely day. Grace, however, remained unmoved. Tina and Clive both asked if she was OK and she was polite but reserved in her response. Gone was the sunny, carefree girl they'd seen at the last choir session and back was the sullen, overcast creature I was becoming more used to. I tried to reassure Tina that the mood swings were normal and that it was no reflection on her home or food offerings but I was embarrassed, for my daughter and myself, and this perhaps caused me to be a bit brisk with her as the session closed and I ordered her back to the car. Once we'd pulled off the gravel drive I thanked Tom and Maisie warmly for their good behaviour and left a long pause imbued with silent criticism of Grace's poor showing.

'I don't know what you're getting at me for,' she said eventually. 'I said thank you to Tina, I didn't get in anyone's way...'

'Grace,' I said. 'Thank you doesn't really count if it's delivered with a grunt and a face like a bulldog chewing a wasp. Tina had made an enormous effort today. I just wish you'd think about other people for a change. I know what happened at the weekend has upset you. But it's not *all* about you *all* the time.'

'God. Gimme a break.' She sighed loudly and looked back at her phone. 'Can I, like, sleep over at Clark's tonight? Seeing as you obviously, like, *can't bear* my company anyway.'

'Yes. That would be fine,' I said as I drew up to the roundabout. But then a thought occurred to me. 'What would the sleeping arrangements be? At Clark's.'

'What?'

'Well, I mean, would you sleep in the same room? In the same bed?'

'I dunno.' She snorted as if I was the most ridiculous woman on the planet. 'Why?'

Somebody beeped for me to move and I made a face at them before pulling out onto the roundabout. 'It's just that Clark sometimes identifies as a boy, yes?'

'Yeah, although mainly they're non-binary.'

'And you are a girl.'

Another colossal sigh. 'Yeeeeessss.'

I moved Mum's hand away from the air-conditioning controls as she had a habit of setting it to arctic blast when everyone least expected or needed it. 'So,' I continued. 'We're talking about a fourteen-year-old girl and a fifteen-year-old, who sometimes identifies as a boy, sharing a room and possibly a bed.'

I let that statement hang there for a moment.

'Oh my God, Mum. What. Is. Your. Problem?'

'I'm not sure, Grace. Genuinely, I'm not sure whether this is a problem or not. It's just that if Tom at fifteen wanted to have his girlfriend round for a sleepover I'd be saying no, wouldn't I?'

'Well—'

'I am *never* having a girl round for a sleepover, no way!' Tom interjected.

'I'm not saying no, I'll need to just talk it through with your father, that's all. Or maybe I could speak to Clark's parents?'

Grace sat heavily back into her seat between her brother and sister who were looking on with interest as she muttered into her hoodie, 'Man. I totally can't believe this middle-class, Cis-gender, heteronormative prejudice. It is, like, totally outrageous.'

I'm not sure that I've ever been accused of anything so wordy but evidently Clark's parents are less fazed by my heteronormative prejudice and I received a text from their mum an hour later confirming that the question has come up before and they have decided on a policy of separate beds in the same room if that was OK with me? I replied that indeed it was OK with me and that I was very relaxed about this type of thing and that the last thing I wanted was to make Clark uncomfortable or undermine their life choices or question their right to identify as a boy or a girl or indeed as non-binary... Until Grace pointed out that my reply was now so long that it was filling two screens and could I, like, just perhaps be a little less utterly mortifying about everything?

I did want to talk to Sam about it, but in the end he didn't get back from work until really late and I'd already gone to bed so didn't get the chance. It's these little snippets of life that I could really do with sharing; the kind of detail that composes the majority of my day looking after the kids and Mum, but often a decision needs to be made there and then, and when I come to recount the story it seems trivial and not worth the effort. So it was that by the time I did tell Sam about the whole saga, Grace had already been for the sleepover and my laughing about the awkwardness of not appearing to be 'woke' enough while also not wanting to place my daughter in a vulnerable position felt a bit hollow. Such is life.

Chapter Twenty-Four

Wednesday, 9 April

Rory called this evening. He'd evidently spent the last two days trawling through paperwork at my parents' house (lucky Candice) and had visited Dad in hospital. The good news was that Dad's speech was continuing to improve to the point where he could hold a full conversation with his son, albeit a laboured one. Their most recent discussion had resulted in Rory uncovering the existence of two savings investment accounts that could pay for longer-term residential care for Mum. The bad news was that he had also discovered more evidence of how serious her dementia had become, Dad having admitted under duress that she'd lost them thousands of pounds through some telephone scam (although I did point out that this could happen to anyone) and a combination of bizarre credit card purchases for, among other things, thirty square-metres of vinyl underlay, a set of monogrammed Hermès scarves and a life-size model of Geoffrey Boycott for the garden (I conceded that this probably *couldn't* have happened to anyone else). A conversation with Agnes next door had revealed that Mum had also managed to upset quite a few of the neighbours by variously uprooting their hardy perennials (Mr Elias at number 43), stealing their newspapers (Ms Collins at number 47) and posting underwear through their letterboxes (Mr Jennings, formerly of number 45, who has since moved house).

'She's really very confused, Penny. I mean, some of this is proper antisocial behaviour. Dad seemed to think it was all quite amusing, said he'd never liked Jennings anyway, but clearly it's just not on. It can't continue. She'll get herself arrested or worse.'

'She's not done anything like that since she's been with—'

Rory cut me off, reminding me of the shoplifting incident in the hospital and the fact that he, only two days ago, had caught Mum pouring herself a large glass of dishwasher rinse-aid as an evening aperitif. 'I don't know why you're being so resistant to the idea of her being cared for in a more suitable place. The money's there to find her somewhere nice, take the pressure off you, get her properly looked after...'

I knew that some of what he was saying made sense. And I knew from discussions at choir that there really were some lovely care homes out there. Both Herbert and Marie often attended with staff from their respective nursing homes and the affection on both sides was clear to see. But Rory was so bloody condescending. And such a know-it-all. Except he didn't know it all. *I* was the one who'd been living up close and personal with our mother for three months. Not Dad, not Rory, me. And *I* was the one who currently knew her best. It was me who understood her little foibles, me who knew what she would eat and what temperature she liked the bath, and finally, after forty-two years of living in my brother's shadow, it was *my* company she sought above that of anyone else.

'No. I'm sorry, Rory, but Mum is happy here. We had a lovely time with the choir at Tina's yesterday She might not get a chance to do that in a nursing home. She wouldn't be able to sit and stroke Gracie's hair when she's sad or put make-up on with Maisie or listen to grime artists with Tom. She'd just wander up and down the corridor feeling worried and nobody would know which days she likes to read *Hello!* magazine and which days it's *Woman's Weekly* or understand why she only wants to wear the cardigan with the daffodils on or why she wants to get all the bathroom towels out of the airing cupboard and pile them up in the hallway. They'd tell her off for breaking the rules and she wouldn't understand and, and, they wouldn't like her anyway because she'd tell them they were fat or that they had terrible teeth and…' I broke off, unable to continue because, against all better judgement, I was starting to cry. The first rule of combat with Rory is never to show any emotion and I already knew my line of defence was weak. By shedding a couple of tears, I would have let my entire regiment down and was probably due a Court Marshall. As expected, it came in the form of a clipped and efficient list, brutal as a bullet to the back of the head.

'Penny,' he barked. 'Mum doesn't know who anybody is any more. She won't miss stroking Grace's hair, she won't miss putting on make-up. She doesn't know *who she is or what she is doing*. She is effectively *in danger* while she is staying with you. She's a vulnerable adult and you cannot provide her with the level of care she needs. She's at risk of choking, falls and serious injury if she wanders outside. She could set fire to the house. She could accidentally take an overdose. Do you see? It is not safe for her to be with you when you can't restrain her or manage her problematic behaviour.'

'Rory, I don't think—'

'No. Listen to me. She's not there to entertain and soothe your children. She needs rest; peace and quiet. Your house is not a stable enough environment – and don't pretend that her being there is having a positive effect on your home life either. It's clear that she's causing plenty of tension between you and Sam, and you and the kids. You need to think about the impact this whole thing is having on them as well.'

'I *am*! The kids love having her here.'

Rory wasn't listening, he was in full flow. 'Dad's worried. The old chap's beside himself fretting about what could happen to Mum, and to you. It's actively impeding his recovery, the stress of it all. Your decisions here are affecting everyone. You're letting emotions get the better of common sense and this obstinate attitude is clouding your judgement about what's best for our mother.'

'Clouding my judgement? Rory, can you hear yourself? You don't think *your* judgement's been clouded by Mum not recognising you? I know it's hurtful, but dementia is random like that – I'm not an expert, as you're at great pains to tell me, but I've seen what *Mum's* dementia is like and she *does* recognise other people – and enjoys being in their company. Just because she doesn't recognise *you* doesn't mean that she can't appreciate being with other people that she knows.'

'Penny,' Rory tried to cut in, but I wasn't having any of it.

'No, Rory, shut up for once. Mum's not ready to go into a home yet and you've not been here for long enough to make *any* kind of decision about what's right for her. You're barely ever here. You swan over from Australia, having done bugger all to help look after either of them, having had hardly any involvement in their lives other than as a glory boy who turns up now and again for a pat on the back, and tell me what's best for "our mother" like it's some shared responsibility...' I snorted in disbelief at the arrogance of him and there was silence for a moment as he took a deep breath.

'OK, well you're clearly not in the right frame of mind to discuss this rationally, Penny.' He sighed. 'We'll just have to talk about it later. In the meantime, I've been looking through Mum's letters from the hospital and I can't find any evidence of her having seen a clinical neuro-psychologist or anything about her genetic assessment. Do you have a copy of either of those documents?'

'What? Neuro-what?' This was another classic Rory tactic; divert attention, destabilise and unsettle the opponent. I was not going to rise to it. 'No. I don't have any paperwork other than her medication list. As far as I'm aware, everything that's in the filing cabinet, that's it.'

'But...' He was now beyond incredulous at my incompetence. 'But she must have had genetic testing?'

'She must? Why?'

'Because she might have a hereditary form of Alzheimer's, Penny. For God's sake, this is serious. She's still young. It's not a classic age-related dementia and that makes it unusual enough to warrant testing. Her neurologist must have advised her to have a full genetic screen, mainly so you and I can work out our own risk – given that we are her offspring?'

I couldn't process what he was saying, although the words would come back to haunt me later. At that point in the conversation I just wanted to get him off the phone, pour myself a glass of wine and lie down in a darkened room. I tried to remain calm and not let my brother bamboozle me with science. 'It's the NHS, Rory. I don't think she has *her own personal neurologist* who advises on the minutiae of her condition. She was given the diagnosis and... I don't really know if she's seen anyone since.'

He sighed, managing to capture a world of frustration and anger in one simple exhalation. 'Well, that is just... ruddy typical. Yet another example of how this whole situation is not being managed properly.'

I managed to stifle a scream, but I'm sure it was fairly clear from my tone that I was now at the end of my tether. 'There isn't a way to *do things properly*, you idiot. I don't care how many sodding medical textbooks you've read or how many seminars you've been to. You don't know how to handle this any better than me and you're not the one here dealing with all the shit anyway, so why don't you stop making helpful suggestions, do us all a favour and run off back to Perth.'

'It's Brisbane.'

'Oh. Fuck. Right. Off. Rory!'

Chapter Twenty-Five

Thursday, 10 April

In an attempt to distract myself from yesterday's blazing row and the widening gulf between me and my brother (*and* my husband, *and* my daughter), I decided to go hunting around on Face-boast today. I'm a bit cross with myself because generally I try to avoid the platform as much as possible, mainly because both Tiggy and Lindi have managed to stray into my Facebook orbit and are officially (if somewhat erroneously) 'Friends' of mine. Accidentally catching sight of one of their #lifegoals posts is like opening up a portal into hell, and Tiggy in particular has been as busy this Easter as you'd imagine. She has posted fourteen times (basically every single bloody day of the holidays), with each post accompanied by approximately seventeen thousand photos and a list of hashtags as long as my arm. I don't know whether she's hoping to score some kind of social-media influencer role or if she is simply on crystal meth, but the outpouring of frankly delusional nonsense about her family is astonishing. It's almost preposterous enough to make you *not* feel worthless in comparison – almost, but not quite.

She starts with the school Easter bonnet competition and bake sale, photos of Zahara's glorious homemade berets strategically placed next to the faces of her own children to imply that she herself knitted them. (I'd tell Zahara but I know that she won't mind, she's far too nice.) Tiggy accompanies this with *#HomemadeIs-Best #HomemadeBonnets #LoveEasterCrafts #ABitOfLove-GoesALongWay #MakesMeWantToPuke* (spot the deliberate mistake) and throws in a couple of photos of the three-foot Easter bunny and school hall decorative extravaganza – again, none of her original handiwork but absolutely presented as such.

Below the post is the inevitable comment from Lindi regarding the cakes: *So glad I managed to find something suitable for Chloe – eventually! (eyeroll emoji) #MumsWhoBake #GlutenFreeMums #SulphiteIntoleranceMums #FoodAllergyMums* which has been loved/liked/hugged by everyone else in the Sulphite Intolerance Mum's Group – all seventy-nine of them.

It seems the first day of the holidays was spent at #HopscotchFarmPark mauling a variety of small mammals for selfies. There are photos of Tiggy rubbing noses with a fluffy rabbit that looks like it might take a chunk out of her given half a chance (good luck to it), and more commentary from Lindi about the availability of ingredient-free foods in the Hopscotch Farm Cafe *(#ConstantVigilance)*. Tiggy's husband John has been artfully airbrushed out of most of the shots, although I think I can make out his knee as their son Reuben catapults off it into the ball-pit and there is one shot of him holding all the bags in the background as Tiggy and her two children *skip* (yes) through a field of wildflowers (in reality this is more of a small yard area and half those flowers are plastic from what I remember).

Lindi obviously buggered off on her healing-stone spa retreat soon after Hopscotch Farm and her solitary post during this time is a YouTube clip of a waterfall with the word PEACE shimmering above (like the mirage that it is). Other highlights from Tiggy's feed include:

- The trip to the #StoryMuseum, where a photo of beautifully stacked bookshelves is accompanied by the hashtags #LoveReading #BooksAreBest #AboveAverageReadingAge #MustBeDoingSomethingRight (Reuben clearly visible in the background staring vacantly at an iPad screen)
- Friday Family Fun workshop in the village hall, where the children are pictured weaving paper baskets for the Saturday Egg Hunt #FamilyCrafts #VillageCommunity #BusyChildren #GoodFriday #Crucifixtion (sad face emoji)
- Easter Sunday churchyard, Tiggy and her daughter in matching lemon-yellow maxi-dresses, each holding a bunch of daffodils #MothersAndDaughters #FamilyTime #SundayBest #SoBlessed (Not entirely clear whether they set foot within the church or just used the backdrop)
- Trip to the #Waterpark complete with gratuitous shots of Tiggy in a bikini (so unnecessary), John's baggy swim-shorts just visible disappearing down a chute and Reuben clearly pushing another child into the Lazy River #Watersports #NoFilter (there is obviously a filter) #WhoCaresWhatWeLookLike (laughing emoji) #Waterfun #NotJustForTheKids #AdultWatersports (Careful with that particular hashtag, Tigs)
- Little Mix concert (at Wembley no less), Tiggy wearing a skin-tight tour T-shirt, both kids eating carrot sticks, drinking from Chilly's water

bottles and holding a banner that says 'We Love You Perrie' #HelloWembley #RockingOut #GirlPower #ShoutOutToMyEx (laughing emoji) #JustForLols #LoveMyHubbie (Reuben looking like he wants to kill himself)

I could go on, but you get the gist. Reading through the rest of Tiggy's filtered stream of consciousness, I did feel a tiny bit remiss that my children have not been taken to a wildlife park, music festival, laser-tag arena, dry ski slope, theatre or gallery this Easter holidays, but the Venn diagram of activities suitable or appropriate for a four-year-old girl, a ten-year-old boy, a teenager who hates everyone and a pensioner with mobility issues is essentially a picture of four completely separate circles – there is no overlap whatsoever. You'd think that might absolve me of some #ParentingGuilt, but sadly not. I did indulge in a brief fantasy where I posted a genuine #NoFilter item about my Easter holidays. Maybe a series of photos: Maisie having a tantrum on the floor while wearing her cardboard headband; Colin vomiting up the chocolate eggs; Tom losing one of his molars chewing through the tough lamb on Sunday; me looking haggard with red wine-stained teeth, perhaps with the following caption: *This was around the time that my teenage daughter received a text message about blow-jobs and called my son a fuck-wit #SoBlessed.*

One day I'll do it. I really will.

–

As if this wasn't enough #FacebookFun, I then made the mistake of glancing at Sam's page. Sam is much more relaxed about his social-media boundaries. He is neither susceptible to the timewasting effects of the medium, nor its underhand tactics of making you feel like your life is a pile of shite in comparison to everyone else's. As a result, his Facebook account is a link into a larger universe than mine. He doesn't post much and certainly avoids putting up photos of the family, but his page is a tempting portal into the lives of others and occasionally I get sucked in. Usually, I regret it. Today I certainly do.

A photo has been shared. Nothing unusual in that you might say, and you'd be right. But this is a work night out photo we're talking about. And yes, Sam does indeed go to work, he has colleagues, occasionally they go out for a drink and sometimes they take a photo. But it is extremely rare that anyone would go to the trouble of sharing it on social media.

The people in the photo are as follows (in order of appearance): Derek (sixty-two, the big boss and ageing lothario); Brian (fifty-nine, head of accounts); Veronica (mid-fifties – formidable, steely grey Lego-hair, tortoiseshell-rimmed specs); Sam (forty-three, handsome, slightly receding hair but he hasn't noticed yet, nice arse); Jenna (early twenties, supermodel); Steve (fifty-seven, marketing manager, twice divorced, crippled by maintenance payments)…

Wait a minute…

Rewind that a second…

The thing is, it's just a photo. It's just a photo of an immensely attractive younger woman with her arm around my husband. That's fine. I can handle it. But, I do need to have more information and my options here are limited. Do I ask Sam? I know immediately that I am incapable of dressing up any enquiry as to the history or provenance of 'Jenna' (honestly, what kind of *Love Island* name is Jenna anyway?) in a casual way. I don't have the dramatic aptitude to throw in an off-the-cuff, 'So… who's Jenna, then?' or 'I saw a photo of your new colleague today. She looks young/stunning/infinitely more desirable than your forty-two-year-old wife whose body has been ravaged by time, gravity and bearing your offspring.'

He'd see right through me and just think I was being paranoid or needy or a complete embarrassment. I may be all those things but I am also NOT STUPID and this girl has 'predatory threat' written all over her (not literally; that would be some tattoo). I needed to be a bit craftier and the obvious solution was to trawl through Jenna's Facebook posts. Luckily, she's friended my husband (how kind, what a good sport you are, Jenna, to open up your fabulous youthful life to your senior colleagues – I note that Derek, Brian and Veronica have not been 'friended' in the same way – can't think why).

And this is where the anxious paranoia kicked in. Because Jenna, it seems, 'really loves her new job' and thinks her boss is 'a great guy'. She describes 'Sam the Man' (I mean WTAF? Honestly?) as a 'right laugh' – says he's 'really laid back' and 'likes to party' and so on and so forth. And of course, he is all those things, my husband, he *is* a great guy *and* a right laugh. Most of the time. It's just we haven't seen that fun side of 'Sam the Man' at home very much recently. And his being 'really laid back' can often be confused with 'not taking things seriously enough' or perhaps, 'doing fuck all around the house'. So excuse me, Jenna, if I suggest that your puppy-dog adulation might be somewhat rose-tinted.

I'm not going to lie. It feels a bit shit. I checked the date and the photo was taken the night that Sam stayed over in London, just before he went to go and collect my brother and Candice from the airport. Just before the weekend of low-simmering resentment that resulted from a packed house, an angry teenage daughter and a schedule that allows no time for a long-married couple to spend more than a nanosecond together alone (not that we'd have known what to do with anything more than a nanosecond – probably discuss our council tax-bill, or whose turn it was to take the bins out).

It had been bad enough having a hot young Australian goddess in the house, but if I'd felt inadequate in the presence of Candice, I felt a hell of a lot worse looking at Jenna. I'd just have to hope that Sam viewed her as nothing more than a colleague; another one of the 'guys' in the office. Checking the photo again, this seemed unlikely.

Chapter Twenty-Six

The kids returned to school today in a flurry of mismatched uniforms, hurriedly packed and repacked bags, mislaid bus passes and shoes that have miraculously been outgrown in two weeks. I tried to have a chat with Grace last night to establish how she was feeling about the possibility of bumping into Jade, the jealous girlfriend of Easter Sunday text-gate fame, but she was non-committal and I didn't want to push it. Instead I focused on making the most of our trip to visit Dad, who was beaming – brimming with the news that he had been declared 'fit for transfer'. Not quite 'transfer back to an empty Edwardian semi-detached with no carer save for his cognitively impaired wife', but at least to a rehab centre, from where, according to him, it was a mere hop, skip and a jump back to his own house.

'Won't be long – backsh home together, Mary,' he said, the excitement causing some slurring of his recently improved enunciation.

Mum was caught up in his enthusiasm and clapped her hands with excitement. 'Ooh, back with the chickens. I *have* missed Agatha.'

Dad and I looked at each other, bemused, until Dad realised what she was going on about. 'No, Mmm, not house in Lydgate. That'sh where chickens – where you grew up.'

She looked worried. 'Is Agatha there? I hope the foxes haven't got in, that fence panel's completely rotted through. And the guttering's a state. Mother was expecting Old Varney to come and fix it. She's been fretting…'

Dad held her hand. 'That house alwaysh needed something sorting. D'you remember the front gate? Rusty hinges? N-nearly took my thumb off first time I came to pick you up…'

'For the dance?' Her face brightened. 'Yes, it's always been very temperamental, that gate. In the winter, when it's icy, sometimes I can barely slide the bolt across. We'll need to get some oil on it, come autumn.'

I know for a fact that Mum's childhood home was bulldozed in the eighties to make way for a block of bijou apartments, but as she was speaking to Dad it was as if she was right back there, sitting in the kitchen, dressed in her finery and waiting for my father to arrive and take her to the town hall.

'Your finger was bleeding,' she said, pulling him into her reminiscence. 'Wasn't it? You looked so embarrassed, wiping the blood off with your handkerchief so it didn't get on my dress. Mother laughed. Said it was the mark of a good man that you didn't give up, didn't let that gate beat you!'

I decided to make myself scarce, but – not wanting a rerun of the near-miss shoplifting incident – I chose to loiter around the nurses' station overlooking the only available exit from the ward. I'm a familiar face there now and Mandy, one of the staff nurses, suggested I make myself comfortable in a large vinyl upholstered chair in the neighbouring bay. 'Chap in Bed Four's just been taken down to the mortuary,' she said confidentially. 'So, his chair's free for a few minutes until the next patient arrives.'

I moved the hospital-issue carrier bag that was sitting forlornly on the seat and gestured to Mandy with a question mark on my face.

'Oh, yeah. That's his stuff. Give it here – I'll put it behind the counter.'

I dropped it onto the desk with a thud and a slipper fell out. 'Will his family be coming to collect his things?'

'Shouldn't have thought so.' Mandy's face was resigned. 'They never bothered to come while he was alive.' She picked the slipper up and tucked it back in the bag just as Ben came ambling up the corridor and thumped a large set of notes onto the desk. 'All right, Mand!' He smiled at her. 'I'm done with Mr Jenkins, he's put in some hard yards today. Might need a cuppa.'

He turned to me. 'Penny. Good to see you. Have you heard the news about your dad? The rehab unit?'

'Oh! Yes. It's great. He's so pleased,' I said. 'It's taken quite a while hasn't it, but he'll be so glad to get out of here – no offence, Mandy.'

'None taken, love. We'll miss him though, your dad. Proper gentleman. Always so polite.' She smiled. 'He'll be off in the next few days I'd expect, now physio's given him the green light.' She pointed at Ben, who nodded.

'Soon as a bed's available at Rookwood,' he said. 'Your dad's top of the list. Put him there myself and checked it again this morning.'

'I don't know what he'll do without you,' I said. 'I don't know what we'll all do without you to be honest. You've helped Dad so much. His mobility, his confidence...' I started to feel a tight, panicky sensation in my throat at the thought of not seeing these people again. They'd become like family, the nurses, the doctors, but especially Ben and Neve, who'd spent so much intensive time with Dad. It was a bit like that sinking homesick feeling when you're dropped off at Guide camp and you realise the only grown-ups left are the ones who don't care that you are scared of cows or that you don't know how to dig a latrine or put up a tent to their exacting standards (I left Girl Guides soon after this particular adventure). 'We'll miss you,' I said, a little sadly.

'I'll still see him once or twice a week,' he said. 'We run a community clinic there. No point in sending patients to a rehab unit to convalesce if there's no actual rehabilitation going on.'

'I suppose not,' I said, cheered by this news. 'Well, I'm glad he'll have some familiar faces around.'

'And logistically, visiting should be much easier. The parking's free, for a start.'

'Good grief,' I said. 'We'll be rich beyond our wildest dreams.'

He laughed. 'Well, make sure you pop in and say hello,' he said. 'Take care.' And he was off, heading back down the corridor.

–

I walked slowly back towards Dad's bay, not especially keen to occupy the chair of the recently deceased gentleman from Bed Four. As I approached the corner of the ward I paused, taking in the scene. Mum was chattering away to Dad, still holding his hand. She looked so animated and happy to be in his company. He was nodding and smiling at her, his eyes never leaving her face.

If you ignored the grey hair and wrinkled skin they looked like two young newly-weds, besotted with each other.

I know that in many ways I'm lucky to have had parents who've remained in love for these many years. But watching them together on the ward I couldn't help wonder how on earth this relationship works now? How can it function as an equal partnership when one half of the pair has undergone the irrevocable and fundamental change that dementia brings – when the person Dad fell in love with is no longer the same woman?

Way back in the mists of time, my mum and dad made an active decision, choosing to be together. They, like most of us, would have picked out traits in each other that complimented their own way of being, similarities in terms of preferences, beliefs and values that would suggest a compatible life partner. I'm not certain of which specific characteristics appealed to which parent, but when I first met Sam, for example, I was impressed by his sense of humour, his generous nature (he bought the first two rounds in the pub even though we were all skint students) and, let's be honest, his chiselled jaw and green eyes. And there were also more practical and tangible shared interests that allowed our relationship to blossom. We enjoyed rugby (him playing, me watching, but it worked), we liked dogs more than cats, we were the only people in our respective groups of friends who could see the merits of early eighties electropop and the only ones prepared to hunt high and low for a decent curry at one o'clock in the morning. If he had been a salsa-dancing fan of macro-biotic cuisine who listed to Country and Western music and played bingo, would I have found him so appealing? Maybe. Maybe I'd have adapted my interests to suit his if I fancied him enough, but I would have gone into that decision knowing who he was from the start. When someone changes their entire personality in the latter part of their life, as my mother has, what happens then? You can't very well ask for a refund or say that this isn't what you ordered when you said 'I do' forty years ago.

Until a few years ago, Mum was a quiet, unassuming person, happy to let her husband have more than his share of the limelight. She was contained, and dignified – bordering on prudish. She loved elegant restaurants and fine wine and she secretly judged people on the inferior cleanliness of their house. She liked to look good herself; enjoyed buying clothes, having her hair done, painting her nails and keeping trim. Now she is an overweight woman, bizarrely wedded to an egg-stained cardigan, who can't remember how to get into a pair of trousers. Her house is a mess, she shouts 'cock' in the middle of dinner and she's developed an uncanny flair for mimicry that often has me in stitches. It's fair to say that her behaviour has changed considerably.

And yet, looking at my dad's face today as he listened intently to her rambling stream of consciousness, seeing how he steered the conversation around to topics she enjoyed, how he showed his appreciation when she offered him a magazine or a spoonful of his own dinner, all I could see was love. He has reconciled himself to these differences; adapted in a way that I would never have thought him capable of. To be honest, he didn't have much of a choice, not being the kind of man who would ever turn his back on duty, but he seems to have found a new way to have a relationship with this woman who looks and sounds a bit like his wife used to, even if she no longer behaves like her. There remains an emotional connection that has endured, even as the equality of their

Chapter Twenty-Seven

Tuesday, 15 April

I spent a lot of last night thinking about that nurse's comment. Wondering what it is that forges such a strong bond between people, like I see with Mum and Dad. I don't know, and I guess I'm not alone. If someone had discovered the recipe for everlasting love they'd be a happily married billionaire by now. But I can't help but wonder whether my husband would care for me in the same way my father cares for Mum.

I think he would – and God knows I hope he never has to – but Rory's words about the inherited risk of Alzheimer's have been ringing in my ears ever since he threw them down the phone last week. The theoretical and provisional vows one takes during the marriage ceremony – 'to love, honour and comfort / cherish / protect / obey / whatever (can't really remember it), 'til death do us part' – are delivered solemnly enough, but it is very hard to imagine, when one is a sprightly twenty-six-year-old, how things will look in forty or fifty years' time. When you consider it, marriage is an astonishingly long contract, often entered into with the flimsiest of reasons: he looked good in his rugby kit / she laughed at my jokes / we both prefer a lamb bhuna to a jalfrezi. Is it any wonder that it so often it goes awry? When the rugby kit starts to look a little snug over the beer belly and she's realised that the jokes weren't that hilarious after all, in fact they're a bit annoying and couldn't he take things seriously once in a while? And he thinks she's no fun anymore and why does she always want to talk about things like home and contents insurance or social issues and feminist constructs, and when do they ever have time to go for a curry anyway? (Incidentally, Sam and I haven't managed to do so much as order a kebab in the past year.)

Does anyone, standing there in the glorious sunshine of an English spring morning with confetti stuck in their cleavage, really contemplate the prospect of becoming elderly and frail and needing to rely on the handsome chap beside you to take you to the toilet and feed you pureed food? I suspect not, because we are blessed with the arrogance of youth. We haven't witnessed our parents' slow decline and are as yet oblivious to the ravages of time and what they might do to our relationship. So, much as I want to believe that Sam would care for me if I became permanently incapacitated, I'm not sure how it makes me feel, the thought of that obligation and the resentment that would surely build up. I watch him with Mum, checking for little signs of disgust or irritation and wonder if he has the capacity to do this. I know he's kind; he's one of the kindest men I've ever met. And he can be thoughtful and considerate, generous, attentive... But is he reliable enough for this role he may be cast into? Is he strong enough? I examine the evidence:

- I've seen him care for the children. He can handle bodily fluids and functions. He understands what happens when little people fall ill or fall over. Good.
- He supported me when we were trying to conceive for the third time. And those years were tough,

as well as being more medically exposing than I'd anticipated. Revealing my nether regions to pretty much any gynaecologist who so much as blinked in my direction, discussing our sex life as if it were a British Rail timetable, putting up with the side effects of the hormone treatment only to be told that no, it hasn't worked this time, keep trying. All of that will put a strain on a marriage and we coped. He held me close when I cried, he put up with the snappy irritability of the cycle and he brought me tea, biscuits and heavy-duty pain relief when the failure and grief bled out of me. And he wept with relief when Maisie finally arrived. At least I think it was relief, but it may have been anticipatory horror. Still, good.

- He loves the dog. I know that if Colin was struck down with an incurable neurodegenerative condition, Sam would be the one refusing to take him to the vets to be put down. Instead we'd have ramps installed, we'd have Colin sleeping on our bed no matter what emissions he might make during the night, we'd have every medication and treatment that money could buy to keep our ailing canine alive. But then, I'm not sure whether this is good or bad. Maybe I'd prefer to be put down.

Of course, this is purely speculative. Children and pets are different – there is a duty of care and a shared responsibility (unless it comes to helping with maths homework). So, in order to further research my conundrum, I need to establish my own level of risk.

In the interests of pursuing this scientific endeavour I went to see the GP today. Not Dr Golding, but some other poor soul who was running forty minutes late and looked as though his eyes were melting into his face with fatigue. I brought Mum along, vaguely thinking perhaps I could leave her in the waiting room while I spoke to the doctor. But as soon as we arrived I realised this would be an error. The chances of her wandering off unnoticed were moderate to high, given the regular footfall and transient nature of the waiting room. The surgery doors opened out onto the High Street and although her usual rate of progress was painfully slow, she could put on a proper turn of pace if freedom beckoned. She'd have been in the butchers buying fifteen kilos of pig cheeks or stealing flip-flops from the Clarks display stand before I'd even made it past reception.

I knew that I would not be able to speak freely in front of her, so I wrote the doctor a short note, which he eyed warily until I explained what it was. He looked relieved as he took the paper from my hand.

'I thought it was a list,' he said. 'You know, like a fifteen-point, itemised catalogue of ailments. People seem to think it's reasonable to cover that number of things in a ten-minute consultation.' He raised his eyebrows and I chuckled sympathetically as I hastily scrunched up the additional sheet of paper with the myriad of questions relating to Mum's sore toe, occasional headaches, watery eye, halitosis and 'funny tasting tablets', back into my pocket.

The doctor leaned back in his chair and pursed his lips as he carefully read through my note. 'Yep,' he said eventually, folding the paper in half. 'I can refer you, no problem. The waiting time is around six weeks and the clinic likes you to fill in a questionnaire before they see you so they can assess your risk. In theory, you're supposed to be fully counselled prior to testing but in practice it can be a bit hit and miss so I'd suggest you have a look at these two websites for more information.' He scribbled the web addresses on a scrap of paper. 'And talk it through with your family, obviously.'

'Yes, of course,' I said, feeling slightly guilty as I hadn't mentioned any of this to Sam.

'Now, is there anything else I can help you with?' he said, turning back to his computer, 'because so far you've only taken six minutes. You've got a whole four left. Knock yourself out.'

I laughed. I liked him.

–

Later, with a paper bag brimming with alternative tablets, eye drops and mouthwash, along with a dental referral and an appointment with the podiatrist, we left the surgery and I took Mum to a dementia-friendly cafe that Anita had recommended for lunch. Mum pursed her lips as we sat down to order.

'Well,' she said huffily. 'I didn't think much of him! All he did was sit there reading his letters. We'd paid a great deal of money for the tickets to that dance performance and I'm sorry, I won't be thanking Andrea Dimmock for her recommendation.'

There was a beat as I picked up the baton, but by now I was pretty slick at stepping into Mum's world. 'No,' I said. 'I completely agree – a shocking lack of choreography and the stage-set was unconvincing. All very amateur really.' I handed her the menu. 'Egg mayonnaise or prawn cocktail, Mum? You choose and I'll go and get us a pot of tea.'

Chapter Twenty-Eight

Rory and I came to an uneasy truce today, before he returned to Australia. We had barely spoken since our row almost two weeks ago, limiting our exchanges to factual text messages. But, in a move that I suspect was generated by Candice, they invited us over for a hatchet-burying Sunday lunch cooked on our parents' ancient oven (which I notice has been cleaned very thoroughly) and everyone managed to get through the meal without insulting, harming or generally losing their shit with anyone else.

Mum coped surprisingly well with the confusing prospect of being in her old house, now almost unre-cognisable due to the restoration campaign undertaken by Rory and Candice. It was spotless. The broken cupboard doors had been fixed, new carpet had replaced the stained one in the sitting room, there were clean covers on the chairs and all the upstairs rooms had been given a lick of paint. The kitchen and bathroom looked as though they had been power-hosed and Candice described the fun afternoon that she and my brother had spent cleaning the oven, unblocking sinks and Dyno-Rodding the drains, up to their elbows in God knows what. They were both laughing as they recounted their renovation stories and I could see that such a project would be a satisfying one, but surely not how a young woman would choose to spend her vacation on the other side of the world. She must really care about him, I thought to myself as I watched them manoeuvring around each other in the kitchen; Rory assisting with the joint of beef, Candice handing him a glass of wine, both of them decorating the pudding with raspberries and occasionally popping one into the other's mouth. It was sweet and I felt a bit nostalgic for the times that Sam and I had been so wrapped up in each other that I'd have gladly sacrificed two weeks of my time to spend it unblocking drains with him. It also made me reminisce about the times that Rory had been in this same kitchen as a young man, me sitting at the table doing my home-work and him rifling through the fridge for something to eat, having come back from some rugby tournament or other. Mum's presence back in the old house only added to the sense of family reunion and I daydreamed of a parallel universe where my mother didn't have dementia and my father wasn't convalescing from a combined hip fracture and stroke. Instead they were both here, dishing up Sunday lunch for their kids and grandchildren, meeting their son's girlfriend for the first time, Mum's eye glinting with excitement as she contemplated the prospect of her Rory settling down with a nice girl and whether she'd be in need of a new hat any time soon.

Sam seemed to sense that I was feeling a bit conflicted and he gave my shoulder a quick squeeze. 'You all right, Pen?' he asked. 'Shall we go for a wander down the garden?' But then Maisie ran up and insisted that he take her to see the tree that Uncle Rory had fallen out of and Tom asked if it was OK to play football if he promised to stay away from the greenhouse and Grace asked if we knew what the WiFi code was. And the moment was lost.

I helped Candice set the table in the dining room, which had undergone a similar transformation to the rest the house while still retaining its inherent Andrews' family magic – i.e. masquerading as a shrine to Rory's academic and sporting achievements.

'How's Grace?' Candice asked with her usual lack of preamble as she pulled the knives from the 'best cutlery' drawer.

I was going to make my usual, breezy 'everything's fine' reply, but then I thought, sod it, I'll probably never see this woman again, Rory will have moved on to a different girlfriend by the next time he visits, likely in about four years or so. I might as well be completely frank.

'It's the mood swings,' I said as I took the glasses out of the cabinet and gave them a quick dusting with my sleeve. 'Sometimes she's my lovely little Grace and sometimes she's an absolute nightmare. It can change in the blink of an eye. I don't know what to do with her. But whatever I try, it seems to be the wrong thing.' I put the glass down on the table and stuck the heel of my hand into my eye socket to push away the teary sensation.

Candice put her arm around me. 'It's just because you're her mum,' she said. 'She knows she can be a bitch to you and you'll still love her. It's hard but her brain is just wired differently at the moment.'

She told me about the research that's been done into teenage neurodevelopment, how the adaptability of the brain is the same as that of a toddler and how it can change at the same rate. She lost me a little when she started talking about neuroplasticity and cortical pathways but I nodded knowingly.

'It's funny isn't it,' I said. 'I watch Maisie, and she's developing all these skills, reading, writing, speech…' I paused. 'And then I look at Mum, and she's losing all these skills, like her coordination and how to get dressed, and whatever you call that sort of social awareness that adults generally have…'

Candice nodded, 'Yeah, she's a bit disinhibited.'

'But I'd never really thought about Grace's brain undergoing a massive transformation as well,' I said. 'It's sort of interesting.'

'Your family's like a little case study all of its own?' Candice offered helpfully.

I laughed. 'I guess so. We've probably been called a lot worse.'

'Well, I think you're all great.' She beamed. 'Really, I do. And if you ever want to talk about Grace, or any of the kids, or your mum or whatever, we're only a phone call away.'

'Thank you, Candice. You've been a big help.' I smiled as we made our way back into the kitchen to bring the food through.

'I'm not sure about that,' she said, noticing Grace curled up in one of the kitchen chairs looking mutinously at her phone and muttering about *using up all of her roaming data*. 'It's pretty easy to dish out advice when you're not the one having to act on it.'

–

After lunch, it took us half an hour to release Mum from the downstairs loo, where she'd locked herself in using Rory's newly mended bolt (subsequently rebroken to facilitate escape). I managed to cheer her up by running through a few songs from choir on the now completely tuneless (but extremely well-loved) piano of my youth, and then we went to go and visit Dad in his new residence. I'd already taken Mum to see him the day after he moved to Rookwood and he seemed to be settling in well. Ben was right; the more relaxed atmosphere was immediately noticeable and the focus had shifted from recovery to rehabilitation. There were kitchen facilities where residents could make drinks for their guests and Dad was becoming quite adept in his wheelchair. There was a residual weakness in his arm that meant each cup of tea had to be individually and painstakingly filled to the halfway point with a specially adapted kettle on a lowered counter, but he was determined to provide hot beverages for all the adults and even managed to locate some squash for the kids, which Grace, to her credit, accepted with something approaching enthusiasm.

Given that it was such an unusual event, having all of us in the same building at the same time, we asked one of the staff to take a photo and although the nurse's thumb is obscuring the bottom corner, and despite Mum looking as if she is about to walk out of shot, Grace staring contemptuously at Maisie, who is grabbing my left breast, and Tom having his finger wedged in his ear, we look like a happy family. Dad is in the centre, sitting in his wheelchair with his good hand raised in a cheerful wave, Rory and Candice are smiling at each other in a nauseatingly soppy yet sexually charged way, Sam and I are separated by the bodies of our children (insert your own allegorical interpretation) and Mum has the majority of her clothes on the right way around and is showing no ill effects from being recently imprisoned in her own toilet.

It's a nice picture.

It was a good day.

Chapter Twenty-Nine

Thursday, 24 April

Fizz was full of excitement at today's Singing for the Brain session. She clapped her hands with even more flourish than usual and once she'd got our attention, she made her big announcement.

'We.' She indicated round the room with her scarves. 'All of us here.' She paused for dramatic effect. 'Are going to put on a concert. A musical extravaganza!' More wafting of scarves. 'It will be a summer event. July nineteenth, and we will be raising money for Dementia UK. What do you all think?'

She was breathless with anticipation but the reaction from the room was initially muted. Marie was squeaking with excitement but she tended to mimic the emotions of others and I suspect she was simply picking up on Fizz's enthusiasm; many of the other singers were either gazing out of the window, picking fluff off their clothes or looking worried. The carers were all busy trying to work out whether they would be expected to join in.

Fizz's response to this underwhelming reaction was predictable. 'IT. WILL. BE. MARVELLOUS,' she boomed. 'A tour de force. Don't be fearful, my talented friends. You will *shine* like the stars that you are. I have every faith in you.'

'Balls,' shouted Ernest from his chair and Marie started clapping in delight as Fizz handed out the new rehearsal schedule. 'With only three months to go,' she said, solemnly passing me my copy, 'we have to increase the work rate. Make sure we are absolutely pitch perfect. I have the set list here. You'll be pleased to know that there are many old favourites, but I have snuck in one or two little surprises to keep you on your toes.'

Great, I thought. Because that's exactly what we all need, to be kept on our toes. It's not as if most of the people here aren't troubled enough by simply getting food into their mouths or recognising their family. I snuck a look across at Tina to gauge her reaction but was surprised to see that she was gazing listlessly at the floor. Usually Tina could be relied upon to, if not match Fizz's ebullience, at least bolster it with an encouraging smile. Not today. I walked over to where she was stood next to Bob's chair and touched her lightly on the arm. 'Hey, Tina,' I said. 'What d'you think about this concert then? *Hello Wembley!* et cetera.'

She flinched as she moved away, smiling politely. 'Yes, sounds fun.'

'Are you OK?' She was holding her shoulder awkwardly. 'Have you hurt yourself?'

She nodded. 'Just some silly little thing,' she said rubbing her arm. I could see the edge of a dark purpling bruise where the short sleeve of her blouse was gaping. I gestured to it. 'God, Tina. That looks…' I lifted the fabric slightly to reveal three thick bands of bruising across her upper arm and now that I looked more closely, I could see that her cheek, underneath a layer of foundation and powder, was puffy and discoloured too. 'What happened?' I said. 'It looks like someone grabbed you?'

'Oh, I bruise really easily,' she said and tried a little laugh which came out hollow. 'It's nothing.'

'Tina…'

She sighed, realising I wasn't going to let it lie. 'It's just when Bobby gets a bit confused, you know, when he thinks I'm someone else, or he thinks *he's* someone else. You know.' She pulled her sleeve down below the bruise.

'Tell me,' I said. 'Just tell me everything.'

'Well,' she said. 'It's usually in the evening. He decides he wants to go home and he gets really upset when I tell him *we are home* or try and stop him leaving.'

I nodded. 'Yep, I've had similar conversations with Mum.'

'I've put deadbolts on the door,' she said. 'Because it was getting harder to stop him and I'd wake up some nights and find him halfway down the drive, but he'll hammer on that door for hours now; he cries like he's terrified. It's horrible. He thinks he's trapped, he shouts about getting home to his mother. I just got in the way this time, it was my fault.'

'Oh, my God, Tina. It's not your fault. How can this be your fault? Does anyone else know?'

'Now, now ladies,' Fizz called peremptorily from across the floor. 'Less chat and more singing. How about we move into the vocal warm-up?'

I turned back to the group and joined half-heartedly in the rendition of 'Son of a Preacher Man'. Between lyrics I whispered urgently to Tina. 'How often does he get like this? Is it maybe… his medication?'

'Not often,' she whispered back. 'Well, maybe a little more frequently now. It's definitely getting worse.' She reached over to help Bob with his maracas. He gazed back at her in adoration and she squeezed his hand. He smiled, looking every inch the harmless little old man. It was hard to imagine that he could inflict this sort of injury on his beloved wife.

'Speak to Anita,' I said when the song had finished and we were all selecting different instruments. 'She might have some ideas. Or your GP, or an Admiral Nurse? There's a helpline?'

She smiled. 'That's a good idea,' she said. 'Thanks, Penny. I'll do that. And please don't worry. It looks worse than it is. I'm not afraid of him or anything. He'd be devastated to think...' She looked across at Bob, whose attention was fixed on the motes of dust dancing in shaft of sunlight. 'I'm worried that if I tell someone,' she said quietly, 'they'll take him away from me.'

She looked so sad. I felt my eyes stinging but the last thing she needed was my tears. 'Just promise me you'll call someone?' I said. 'For advice. There might be a really simple solution and you can make him less distressed...' (And make you safer, I thought to myself.)

'I will. I promise.'

She closed the conversation down and we carried on, swept up in the music and the zealotry of our song-mistress for another really enjoyable session. Last week Clive had mentioned the success of our impromptu Easter singalong at Bob and Tina's house, and Fizz has since gallantly suggested that I take over the piano accompaniment on some of the songs (Clive was very diplomatic obviously, making sure Fizz knew she was still the main maestro). As a result, I've been brushing up on my skills and practising at home on the ancient keyboard that Sam pulled out of the attic. I had idly mentioned retrieving my old and un-tuned piano from Mum and Dad's, possibly squeezing it in next to our widescreen TV in our not-very-wide sitting room, but Sam's expression of panic was enough to halt me mid-sentence.

We left the session with our set lists tucked under our arms and I added them all to a Spotify playlist and ordered the sheet music as soon as I got home, so that Mum and I could practise both playing and singing. The date for the concert was circled on the calendar. It was, I noted with slight trepidation, scheduled for a week after Sam's summer work event, one that I had promised I would attend this year; the great and the good of actuarial insurance coming together to get razzed up on cocktails and talk shop. The two events were likely to be polar opposites of each other, but I already knew which one I was looking forward to the most.

Chapter Thirty

Tuesday, 29 April

It was that time of the month again. Not my period, just my designated slot on the rota to provide childcare to The Terrible Evangeline. I'd received my email instructions, made my traditional excuses, had my appeal for leniency overturned, and here we were. Unwanted playdate. But having thrown down the gauntlet over stolen-glitter-pen-gate last time, I was quietly confident that I could handle the monster-child today. Which, given the fact that she's only four years old, is probably not something to be enormously proud of.

Things started well. I'd ensured that there was an equal supply of glitter pens by buying an additional pack of exactly the same brand and then mixing the old pens with the new pens and dividing them for absolute fairness. Of course, neither child wanted to play with glitter pens today – of course not! What was I thinking? No, today the activity of choice (Evangeline's choice, natch) was 'Dolly Picnic'.

'We can use your big sister's dollies,' stated Evangeline with unwavering conviction. 'Your dollies is just for babies.'

Maisie wasn't entirely sure what to make of that, but her look of alarm indicated that she knew what would happen to her if she was caught rifling through Grace's bedroom for toys.

'Grace doesn't have any dollies,' I said gently. 'Sorry, Evangeline, you'll just have to play with Maisie's.'

'She does,' said Evangeline. 'I seen dem. On her bed.'

'You don't mean Raggy Annie?' I said, as Maisie gulped. Raggy Annie was Grace's ragdoll from early childhood – a never-mentioned but always-present comforter. She'd actually been made by Mum, rustled up on the ancient Singer sewing machine (in the way that mothers of yesteryear seemed to just *do*) and presented to a one-year-old Grace with a full wardrobe of hand-sewn outfits. She's a well-travelled and extremely well-loved doll, having accompanied us on every family camping holiday, every trip to the pantomime and every hospital appointment when Grace had grommets. She was also once savaged by a juvenile Colin and two of her limbs have never been the same since. Now a fragile, fraying, bilateral amputee, she was definitely not a robust enough guest for a pre-schoolers' picnic party.

'Raggy Annie lives on Grace's bed,' I said firmly. 'She's not even a real dolly. And she doesn't like parties. Or picnics. At all.'

Evangeline gave me a calculating look. 'But I wants her,' she said, challenge in her eyes.

'Well, you can't haves her,' I said. 'And that's that.'

-

A few hours passed and the girls were playing happily in the sitting room, arranging teddies around the motheaten tablecloth I had found in the cupboard, while I made picnic tea. Once all the tiny sandwiches were prepared, squash poured into beakers, Party Ring biscuits displayed on a plate and paper napkins tucked beneath, I carried the heavily laden tray into the picnic area to be met by two little girls, one defiant, one clearly terrified, and every stuffed creature that has ever set foot in our house (in the interests of accuracy, some of them don't actually have feet). In pride of place, propped up on a velvet cushion, head lolling alarmingly with a small amount of stuffing protruding from her almost-severed neck... was Raggy Annie.

I looked pointedly at the ragdoll on her cushioned throne.

'Did you go into Grace's room and take Raggy Annie?' I addressed both girls, but my body language was screaming, *Evangeline, I mean YOU!*

'No, Mrs Baker,' Evangeline lisped sweetly. 'I didn't.'

'I did,' said Maisie, breaking into a sob. 'Evangeline made me do it. Don't tell Gracie, Mummy. She might murdle me.' She hiccupped and a bubble of tearful snot popped on her upper lip.

'Grace won't murder you,' I said. 'But you have broken the rules. Both of you.' I glared at Evangeline, who was starting to suspect she might not get away with having distanced herself from the crime scene. 'And so,' I looked around for some leverage and my eyes alighted on the plate of Party Rings, 'no pudding.' I lifted the plate off the tray and carried it towards the door.

'No!' yelled Evangeline in outrage. 'We *need* dem Party Rings. It's a *party*.' (You can't argue with the girl's logic.)

'And it's your bad behaviour that has spoiled the party,' I said calmly. 'No Party Rings. That's the punishment for breaking and entering.'

Evangeline, eyes ablaze, picked up Raggy Annie and threw her in my general direction. 'She's a stupid dolly anyways,' she said. 'I hate her. Stupid, stupid ugly dolly. Stupid party.' She folded her arms across her chest and glared at me.

Raggy Annie is not terribly aerodynamic at the best of times and I retrieved her from where she had fallen in a saggy heap, scattering stuffing at my feet.

'She is *precious and special*,' I said to Evangeline, feeling like I was making a wider point. 'Even if she doesn't look very pretty. And besides, she doesn't belong to you. You shouldn't have taken her. *No Party Rings*.' And I left the room with the kind of gravitas that only a forty-two-year-old enforcer of iced-biscuit sanctions can pull off.

–

Evangeline appeared to come to terms with the biscuit deprivation fairly swiftly, managing to polish off three rounds of cheese sandwiches, half a punnet of strawberries, a packet of Quavers and a banana before the majority of dolls and teddy bears had even made it to story time. Both girls then went to put on onesies and by the time Joy arrived they were huddled up on the sofa beside Mum, partially submerged beneath their inanimate party guests and watching the television, tranquil as a pair of doves beside a summer pond.

Being a glutton for punishment, I again felt compelled to inform Joy that I had had stern words with her daughter, just in case Evangeline reported it back with embellishment (I had visions of her telling her mother that I had threatened to *murdle* her, as well as imposing starvation rations).

'So, I basically told them, no biscuits,' I said as I shut Colin in the kitchen (he *really* has a thing for Joy's shoes). 'And they've forgotten all about it now. Both sat watching telly.'

Joy's mouth tightened. 'Evangeline may appear to have forgotten all about it, Penny, but that's often just her outward display. She's a sensitive child, as I've said before. I'm always very careful with the language I choose when discussing behaviour. She's probably been affected quite deeply by your harsh words, even though she might have been too frightened to show it at the time.'

'There were no harsh words, Joy,' I said wearily. 'I simply told them that they'd broken the rules and therefore they didn't deserve a treat, which in this instance was biscuits. They've had a lovely time otherwise.'

'I'd really prefer it if you didn't use withdrawal of food as a punishment in future though,' Joy persisted. I could see where Evangeline got her dogged determination from. 'Evidence suggests that young girls who grow up seeing food as a means of control often go on to develop eating disorders.'

I picked up Evangeline's coat and handed it to her mother. 'I'm sorry, Joy,' I said. 'I didn't really have time to come up with an alternative. I didn't think the naughty step would be appropriate for someone else's child and to be honest the Party Rings were just the first thing I could think of.' I moved towards the sitting room intending to retrieve the delicate flower whose feelings had been so damaged by my intervention, but then I turned back, propelled by righteous indignation.

'Look,' I said. 'They were both in the wrong and there-fore I had to tell them off. Maisie's no angel but she didn't act in isolation and they both need to know that there are consequences for their actions. And today that meant no pudding. I understand what you're saying about using food as punishment and if that means you'd feel uncomfortable about me having Evangeline to play after preschool in the future, I entirely understand.'

My extreme bravery was glorious to behold, although it was somewhat belied by the hives that broke out across my neck.

Joy went very pale. 'Oh no, Penny... I, um, I didn't mean that.'

I bet you bloody didn't, I thought to myself.

'No, Joy,' I said cheerfully, 'I get it. Sometimes the rules in one house are different from the rules in another. It's nothing personal and I'm not remotely offended. It's probably better if she goes to play with friends whose parents discipline their children in a similar way to you. I'd hate for you to be worrying about my choice of sanctions and their impact on Evangeline's *sensitive nature* if she came here for a playdate again.' *Boom!* I thought. *Fuck you, High-powered Joy. You've just talked yourself out of the Baker child-minding service.*

I went to move but stopped when I felt a hand on my arm. Joy's eyes were looking distinctly puffy and red. She sniffed.

'I'm sorry, Penny,' she said. 'I'm a bit paranoid about eating disorders. For – uhm – for personal reasons. I – I didn't mean to imply – I'm, I'm really very grateful for everything you do.'

She spoke in a rush as if those types of apologetic words were not in her normal lexicon and she had to rid herself of them as quickly as possible. Her nose was going red too. Joy suddenly looked as though she was about to make the transition from High-powered to Ugly-crier.

'Joy?' I said. 'Are you OK?' She shook her head, lips pressed tightly together as a tear escaped down her cheek.

'Would you like a glass of wine?' The words were out of my mouth before I had time to think.

She gave me a watery smile. 'That would be... *really* nice actually. I've had an absolute bitch of a day. If you're sure? I realise that I've...' She trailed off.

I opened the sitting-room door to reveal two little pairs of human eyes glued to the television, along with seventeen pairs of plastic and fabric eyes. Mum's were closed and she was snoring quietly. The door shut behind me and I gave her my best reassuring smile. 'They'll be fine in there for a little longer,' I said confidently. 'Come and have a sit down.'

–

We'd got through a bottle of wine before Sam got back from work and the entire evening was something of a revelation. Joy, far from being the uber-confident power-house we had all assumed, was in fact a gibbering wreck of anxiety. She had suffered with significant postnatal depression when Evangeline was born and the guilt of not bonding with her child had never really left her.

'Going back to work was the only thing that made me feel human again,' she said. 'Isn't that awful? I mean, what kind of mother says that? We'd tried so hard to have kids and I'd got to the stage where I thought maybe it just wasn't going to happen.'

I nodded in sympathy, recalling the time it had taken Sam and me to fall pregnant with Maisie, most of which was spent squatting over ovulation testing kits, checking my mid-cycle temperature and scheduling emergency sex into an already hectic life.

'And then it did happen,' Joy continued. 'And we were thrilled. I carried on working through the pregnancy. I felt fine. And then, I was in a meeting one day and my waters broke, and I thought, *It's too soon, oh my God, I'm going to lose my baby*. That, and *I can't quite believe I've just dropped a load of amniotic fluid into this designer maternity suit.*' She took a big gulp of Pinot Grigio and winced. (I had already apologised for the quality of the wine, before reminding myself that I didn't need to apologise because I was in fact doing a really nice thing by merely listening to the woman, let alone providing beverages. However dubious the vintage.)

She forced the wine down by some miracle of necessity over good taste and continued. 'The labour was hideous, stop and start, stop and start, so stressful, not knowing what was going on and the pain, well, total fucking agony really. I mean why does nobody ever tell you?' She raised her eyes to me and I nodded sympathetically as she continued. 'And everyone prodding and poking the shit out of me. And something seemed to close off. It was like, I wasn't in control and I hated it so my body just went *Right, that's it, we've got no more emotional energy to give to another human being at the moment, that's your lot*. And by the time Evangeline was off the ventilator I felt as though I'd shut down.' She shook her head. It seemed that she had deliberately avoided revisiting these memories for some time, but now it was like someone had flicked a switch and out it all poured. Amazing, really, what people have bottled away inside. I tore the lid off a Pringles tube and wafted it in her general direction as a gesture of solidarity, but she was on a roll.

'I tried to feed her and I couldn't. Just sat there with my tits out, nipples bleeding, baby screaming, turning her head this way and that… I felt like even more of a failure. Bloody health visitor Nazis with their "best for mum, best for baby" shit. I was like, *I'm trying, I'm really trying!* And one of them said to me "It's always the career mums who struggle, dear. You treat having a baby like a work project and babies just don't behave like that." She said it just like that; that tone, everything. So I told her to fuck off… patronising bitch.'

I spat my wine out. 'Bet that went down well!'

Joy smiled, 'Yeah, brilliant. It now says in my medical notes "Mother not engaging with healthcare professionals – rude and abusive", which is nice.' She shovelled in a couple of Pringles. 'And it just feels like it's been downhill from there.'

'Oh, Joy, it sounds bloody awful.' I rested my chin into my hands. 'I had no idea you'd been through all that. You always seem so… I don't know. Efficient. Sorted.'

'Yes, I know.' She gave a long sigh, her elbows propped up on the table. 'That's how I've always been – "hard-nosed", "dynamic", "career-minded" – all those words people use to describe women who enjoy their job. Except the most important job – the whole "being a mum" routine that everyone else seems to manage so effortlessly – I'm shit at.'

'You're not!' I drained my glass and poured out another. 'Never say that. We *all* think that about ourselves and it's so unhealthy, this obsession with whether we're good enough, whether we're as perfect as the next person. Lots of women will be looking at you, measuring them-selves up against your successful career and feeling inferior as a result.' (I didn't add that I have been one of those women.) 'Just like you're looking at other mums and making comparisons. It doesn't do any of us any good.'

'I know.' There was a pause. 'I just wish I enjoyed spending time with my little girl.' She started to cry again, big Pinot Grigio-imbued sobs.

I reached across the table and held her hand. 'Joy, I've been there. I know about those times when you really don't like your kids very much. And you feel like a crappy person for it. But the reality is, you do still love them, even when they're not being especially loveable.'

Joy sniffed noisily and pulled her hand away from mine. 'She doesn't make friends easily though, does she? She's got that from me.'

'Look,' I sat back in my chair. 'I'm not an expert, by any means, but I've found that when they're this little you can encourage friendships just by inviting kids over to play. They soon find something they can do together and then they decide they're best mates, it's as simple as that.'

Hearing Sam's key in the door, I stood a little unsteadily. 'I'd make the most of it while you've got the chance,' I said, crossing to the oven to get his dinner out. 'You don't have a hope in hell of engineering anything social after a few years of school – that's when you'll start getting the awkward "only wanting to invite half the class to the party" scenario. It's hideous.'

Joy looked thoughtful. 'Yeah, that makes sense. You're right, she should have a friend over. Maybe Wednesdays after preschool, that's my half day.' She tapped her hands down onto the table in a decisive action, the merest hint of a plan flooding her face with new enthusiasm. High-powered Joy restored. 'How about next week? Would Maisie like to come over to our house?'

WTF? I nearly dropped dinner. This was a spectacular first – Joy offering childcare *to me*. I had inadvertently struck gold by suggesting playdates as the solution to

Evangeline's social woes. (Although also, WTAF? Joy has a half day off *every* week and not once has she offered to reciprocate the favour so many of us provide on a regular basis? Oh well, better late than never.)

Sam looked confused to find both of us in the kitchen with an empty bottle of wine and the girls asleep on the sofa with Mum, but he took it all in his stride and suggested that he drop Joy and Evangeline back home when they were ready.

I was pleasantly tipsy by the time he returned and we opened another bottle of wine while I regaled him with stories of my day on the domestic frontline. He listened appreciatively, having the good sense to laugh and commiserate in all the right places and didn't appear to mind that, yet again, dinner was dry and over-cooked, having spent far too long in the oven while I listened to Joy's sad tale. I realised with a pang that we hadn't sat down and had a relaxed chat like this for a while. Awful as it sounds, there is nothing like witnessing someone else's distress to make you a little more appreciative of what you have. The twinge of anxiety regarding Jenna the supermodel-work-colleague had faded slightly since I banned myself from Facebook, and I started thinking especially warm thoughts about Sam and his general relaxed, laid-back attitude, which normally winds me up immensely. He must have picked up on the fact that he was likely to get lucky because he started shovelling dinner in at quite a pace, particularly given that it was almost inedible due to extreme chargrilling. There may have been a white-wine tinted glow to some of my fondness, but once I'd got Mum settled upstairs and ensured that the older kids were safely ensconced in their rooms, Sam and I shut the sitting-room door and

Chapter Thirty-One

Monday, 5 May

Yesterday was Mum's birthday and while Sam was at football with Tom, I suggested that we treat Granny to a 'home spa experience'. I know how much Mum used to love going for beauty treatments and the girls were quite taken with the idea, setting up an area in the sitting room with a choice of nail varnishes and a selection of magazines while I ran the bath. Maisie's choice of bath bomb was one of the more vibrantly coloured options available and the room was quickly filled with the scent of blackcurrant as the water turned bright purple. Undeterred, I helped Mum get undressed and she stepped into the Technicolor froth with a smile. I washed her hair and all seemed to be going well until I suggested that it was time to make her way down to the 'nail bar' and it became suddenly obvious that Mum didn't have a clue how to physically get herself out of the bathtub.

I called Grace upstairs to give me a hand, but despite our best efforts we simply couldn't persuade Mum out. She smiled and nodded and seemed very willing to help but she simply did not know what to do. It was like the time she'd frozen at the top of the escalator. After a couple of attempts to physically pull her towards us I felt a twinge in my lower back. I looked at Grace, who was rubbing her elbow, and realised that we were going to need reinforcements (i.e. Sam), so we brought the manicure to Mum while we waited and made sure the hot water was topped up at intervals.

When Sam came home he paled slightly at the prospect of lifting his now aubergine-hued mother-in-law out of the bath, but he could see that Mum wasn't in the least perturbed. And in fact he seemed to relish the opportunity to take on such a challenge of engineering. After a few calculations around mass, velocity and leverage, the strategic placement of towels to cover modesty, and the assistance of every family member including Colin, who barked words of encouragement, we managed to release Mum from her spa-experience. She glided back down the landing trailing purple bubbles, as stately as a galleon.

However, despite the fact that the situation had been resolved with limited trauma, I was left concerned by what this most recent deterioration in mobility meant, and how it might be used by my brother as further evidence of Mum being unsuited to living with me. I also continued to feel the physical effects of the forced bath evacuation as the day wore on, the tightness in my lumbar region increasing by the hour. By early evening I was really struggling to walk and this morning it took me ten minutes to get out of bed. I found an old tube of Deep Heat in the medicine cabinet which I applied liberally, forgetting to wash my hands before rubbing my eye and nearly making myself go blind.

By the time I'd driven down to Rookwood, I was feeling a bit sorry for myself. Luckily Ben had finished his morning clinic and noticed my predicament as I made slow progress around the courtyard. My parents were enjoying the sunshine with a cup of tea, Mum proudly showing dad her nails at regular intervals.

'I may not have the most highly-tuned clinical skills but I think I'm right in saying you've hurt your back?' Ben said as I hunched over the garden bench like a crone.

'Indeed, I have.' I lowered myself gingerly onto the seat and told him about the process of extracting Mum from the bath.

'Have you… don't take this the wrong way,' he said quickly, 'but have you had any training or advice on how to lift people?'

'No, Ben. I haven't.'

'It's not a criticism.'

'I know, honestly. It's just yet one more item on the list of myriad things to do. When the OT came to help us with the handrail for the steps we didn't get around to discussing the forcible extraction of my mother from a bathtub. And I'm not trying to be facetious, it really was not on my mind that this would be an issue. So many aspects of home care don't occur to you until they've actually happened and you're just sat there thinking, *Bollocks, what do I do now?*'

He laughed. 'Fair enough – and to be honest, there is no "ideal" way to get someone out of an un-adapted bath. I guess, from what you've said, rails wouldn't have helped?'

'No.' I shrugged as much as my back and shoulders would allow. 'She simply wouldn't have been able to carry out the instructions to hold them and pull herself up.' I took a sip of my tea. 'The way her brain works, or doesn't, is both fascinating and upsetting.'

Ben gave a thoughtful sounding sigh. 'It's really difficult to know what to suggest. If her mobility is that unpredictable then the chances of you injuring yourself by helping her are pretty high. Have you thought about a more *residential* option? Even just for a brief period while you get a care package sorted?'

'Putting her in a home, you mean.' My heart sank. This is exactly what Rory would suggest.

'It's not necessarily *the wrong thing*, Penny. It's certainly worth looking at all the options and there are some great care homes out there...' He sighed again. 'Look, I can tell from your expression that you're not enjoying this conversation. I get it. You don't want a stranger telling you what's best for your parents.'

'No. It's not that, Ben. It's just there seem to be an awful lot of men in my life who feel that they know *exactly* what I should be doing and *exactly* where I'm going wrong. It gets a bit wearing. I know you mean well, but—'

'The thing is Penny, I'm not really directing this at you. I'm thinking more about your dad.'

'And I'm not?' I was a bit sharper than I'd intended.

'No. Of course you are.' His voice was conciliatory. 'You're having to consider everyone else. I know that. But I have the luxury of being able to focus on one person, and that's your dad. He's a strong man, well-motivated, and he's recovering well so far. But he's in his seventies, he's had a stroke and a replacement hip. He's not going to be able to continue being a full-time carer for your mum indefinitely.'

I knew he was right. I just didn't know what to do about it.

–

The cherry on the cake was that today's slow progress to and from Rookwood resulted in me missing Tom's parent-teacher consultation, which had been scheduled for straight after pick-up this afternoon. Having spent yet another day stuck in a hot car with broken air-conditioning, ferrying various family members to and from their destinations of choice, I have now managed to rile the formidable Mrs North and there is a message in my email inbox as follows:

Dear Mrs Baker,

Sorry not to have seen you at the scheduled time of 3.30 p.m. for our parent-teacher consultation today. I can only assume you were unavoidably detained by more pressing business. It is essential that we maintain good links and communication between the teaching body and those in parental custody or guardianship of our pupils. Therefore, if you would kindly get in touch with the office regarding arranging a mutually convenient time for a further appointment that would be most appreciated.

I also note that Thomas was the only child in the school not to have participated in the fundraising event last Friday, where the children were encouraged to attend school dressed in mufti and pay a nominal donation towards our charity, Waterfall, which, as I am sure you know, is raising money to build a well for a small community in Uganda. It may be that you take exception to our choice of charity this year and are not willing to assist in the fundraising process or that the event escaped your attention, although it was extensively publicised in the school newsletter. Perhaps we can discuss when we meet.

Chapter Thirty-Two

Wednesday, 7 May

Tom wasn't unduly distressed that I missed his parent-teacher consultation, but today I have managed to compound the problem by being unable to attend the presentation of the spring season sports trophies. Tom came second, missing out on the top spot to Alex, but I was one of the only parents who was not present at the awards ceremony to see my son collect his plastic replica cup, and the shame and humiliation is evidently not to be borne.

I have explained to Tom that the reason I missed the ceremony was because I had taken Granny out to Wilton Woods for a dog walk with Colin and managed to lose the dog, Maisie and my mother in a never-to-be-repeated game of hide and seek. By the time we arrived at school, muddied, scratched and bruised, the last few medals were being distributed to the children who had 'tried really hard all term'. I had hoped to be able to sidle into the back of the hall and pretend to Tom that we'd been there for the whole presentation, but alas Mrs North noticed our motley crew and loudly proclaimed our arrival.

'Mrs Baker! Good of you to make it. Sadly, you've missed Thomas's award. Hmm, your arm and face appear to be bleeding. Do you need a sterile-dressing?'

A few moments later she added, 'Mrs Baker, while we love to have younger siblings attending school events, I would ask that if your daughter keeps running around in circles pretending to be a helicopter, you may wish to take her back outside. And,' she smiled delicately as she turned to Mum. 'Mrs, um…'

'Andrews,' I prompted.

'Mrs Andrews,' she continued. 'If I could just ask you to leave the spring display area alone for now? Those paper daffodils took the year twos quite a few weeks to construct and they're actually quite fragile. Could you perhaps… put them back?'

—

Tom didn't say anything in the car on the way home. I tried to make a big fuss of the trophy and phoned Sam when we got back so that Tom could tell him about it, but a female voice answered the mobile. *Interesting.*

'Hello?'

I looked at the phone in confusion. 'Oh, hello. Sorry. I think I must have called the wrong number. I wanted to speak to Sam Baker.'

'Oh, no problem. Sa-am!'

I heard a rustle of static as the phone was passed over and Sam's voice said 'Thanks Jen' away from the receiver. 'Penny,' he said. 'Everything OK?'

'Yes. Who was that?' I tried not to sound neurotic.

'Oh, nothing, don't worry. What is it?'

I frowned at the phone but didn't really have any reason to push for more information. Besides, the reason for the call was currently sulking in front of the Xbox console and I desperately wanted to cheer him up.

'It's Tom,' I said in an undertone. 'He won a trophy today and I didn't get to see it. I was—'

'Oh, love. I bet he's gutted,' Sam said. 'Sorry, I'm not trying to make you feel bad but he's been talking about the presentation ceremony all week. What did he get? Did he win? Oh, I'd have really liked to have been there. Can I talk to him?'

'Well, yes, that's what I was hoping,' I said, a little stung by his implied criticism. 'It was just that I was out walking with Mum and the dog and—'

'I know, love, don't worry, I know what it's like. And you've got so much on your plate at the moment.'

'It is a bit hard to keep all the balls up in the air,' I admitted. It seemed easier to do this with Sam on the end of the phone than face to face. 'Maybe Tom's the ball that just got dropped.' My voice had gone a bit wobbly and I heard Sam shuffling about, presumably moving somewhere quieter.

'Penny, sweetheart,' he said. 'Don't beat yourself up about it. You're doing a great job and the kids all know that you love them and that you're doing your best. How about I have a chat with him now? I can make a big fuss about the trophy and you know what he's like, he'll have forgotten all about it in a few days.'

I nodded a little sadly. Sam was probably right but I couldn't shake the image of Tom as a forlorn juggling ball, languishing on the ground while his mother continued her circus tricks, utterly oblivious.

Chapter Thirty-Three

Thursday, 8 May

Choir rehearsal. Thank God. Any time I feel as though my life is particularly rubbish, I can come along to one of these sessions and let it all wash away. We've stepped up to practising three or four times a week now and each time I walk into that village hall, I feel the tension slip from my shoulders just a little. I love reconnecting with the musical side of things, obviously. Playing the piano in front of a small group of enthusiastic pensioners makes me feel like Elton John and singing really does release the stress. I also enjoy seeing the other carers like Tina and Clive and feeling a sense of unspoken understanding that comes from being in their company. And I like getting to know the paid carers and the volunteers; they're an incredibly useful resource when you've got a specific question about cutlery or mobility scooters or whatever.

But the thing that surprises me most is how fond I have become of the people these carers bring with them. Which is odd, because I wouldn't have said that I needed more people with dementia in my life; one feels like it should be enough. But I love seeing Marie dancing away in her own little world and I thoroughly enjoy hearing Ernest swearing his head off. Even Bob, who I have been keeping a closer eye on since Tina's revelations, has become a reassuringly familiar presence. He doesn't do much or say much but Mum talks to him like a long-lost brother, laughing and joking about all sorts of nonsense while he holds Tina's hand and smiles.

And Fizz is, of course, always a treat. Her love of life is infectious, her ebullience lifts everyone's spirits, and despite not currently being an active carer for someone with dementia herself, her knowledge and ability to rally people along makes me think she must have some experience of dealing with Alzheimer's over and above her weekly singing sessions. Maybe a relative or friend who lives elsewhere, or perhaps a loved one who has since died. Of course, it may be that she has no direct link, just bags of empathy instead – but she really seems to get inside the damaged minds of those attending her classes, and deals with each unique set of requirements appropriately, knowing when to take someone seriously and when to turn a blind eye. She understands that it is often better to go along with someone else's reality than to insist on reminding people of the brutal truth, and so when Edith talks about her father as if he's still alive, Fizz, instead of saying 'He's dead, Edith', simply nods along and asks whether he's still enjoying the gardening.

Like Fizz, I am now more *in tune* (see what I did there) with the likes and dislikes of other choir members. I've found that the regularity of these sessions means that I can tell when someone is having an off day, be they the person with dementia or their carer. Equally they can tell if Mum or I are out of sorts, and even when the problem is outside of their area of expertise there will be somebody ready to listen and offer a shoulder to cry on if needed. And sometimes I have needed. Believe me.

I've told people at choir a lot about my life. I've shared stories about the children, when they've brought me joy and when they've made me so furious that I could slap them, and how bad that makes me feel. I've told them about Rory and what an arse he can be, about Candice and how she seems to be rubbing some of the arsiness off him (which sounds like something they might do in the privacy of their own home). And I've talked about Dad and his slow recovery, how brilliant the rehab hospital is, how much I miss seeing him and wish he was nearer.

In return, I have heard stories of unrequited love, exotic travels, illicit affairs, lost children and reunited families. I've learnt about acts of heroism, sacrifice and the ravages of war. It turns out that as a young teenager Ernest rescued three generations from a burning building during the Blitz, and that Marie at twelve was left in charge of her four younger siblings while her mother worked in a munitions factory. Herbert was evacuated to a farm in Kent where he went on to develop a love of horticulture, and has since had multiple exhibits at Kew Gardens and Chelsea flower show. Gertie once met Elvis Presley and Edith was a Tiller Girl, performing at the London Coliseum during the fifties – which might explain some of the attempted high kicks.

All these lives lived, all these fabulous stories and memories are here, buried deep perhaps, but here nonetheless. And for every person dancing in their wheelchair, for every frail old man shaking his tambourine, for every elderly lady humming along to the tune, those memories seem closer to the surface when they are here, together, making music. The carers all say the same thing; that the person they care for comes alive when they sing, the person they once knew is almost within touching distance. It doesn't need to be an old war song to trigger this sense of wellbeing. It's not as simple as tapping into auditory memory and familiar tunes; melody and harmony and rhythm have their own unique way of getting through these tired neural pathways, whatever arrangement they're in. Even if it's Bon Jovi.

Chapter Thirty-Four

Saturday, 10 May

Sam suggested that I take Tom to football this morning, although I'm not sure whether his intention was to give me some quality time with my son or just because he fancied a lie-in (I'm being harsh — I think it almost certainly was the former). I wanted to be involved in this important part of my Tom's life but, right from the off, I was out of my depth. The windscreen wipers were bobbing furiously as I peered through the murk trying to locate a sign for Hendon community pitches, while Tom and Alex were busy debating the potential challenges ahead.

'One of their midfielders, he's a massive unit. And dirty,' said Alex with some urgency. 'D'you remember when we played them last month? And he panned Archie? Ref didn't see it.'

Tom murmured in agreement.

'Is there often a bit of foul play?' I asked knowledgably from the front.

There was silence until Alex chipped in. 'Uh, yeah, Mrs Baker. Sometimes. Depends who's playing.'

I nodded and tried again. 'And did you beat them last time? Hendon?'

'No,' said Tom. 'Their goalie, he's good. They're top of the table.'

'Ooh. So, it's an important match then?'

'Uh, yeah?'

'That's exciting. Well,' I turned into the waterlogged carpark, which was essentially just a muddy field itself. 'I'm really looking forward to watching this.' I tried to force some enthusiasm into my voice, but I hadn't really banked on the weather being this catastrophic in May and had only brought a light summer cardigan and flip-flops. However, I was here to support my son and support him I would.

The boys scrambled out of the car in a jumble of shin-pads and polyester and ran straight for the pitches, where the rest of the team was warming up. My back was still feeling a little bit delicate so I eased myself slowly out of the front seat. Unfortunately, I'd parked next to an enormous puddle and didn't feel nimble or sprightly enough to jump over it. Instead, I had to plough my flip-flops straight through the icy water and slipped my way through the mud to join the other parents on the side-line. I noticed that several mums and dads were wearing full-body waterproofs and clutching Thermos flasks. They all seemed to know each other and were chatting happily together. Feeling that familiar awkwardness of not knowing the ropes, I did what most adults in the same scenario would do; I stood a little way apart from everyone else, pulled out my phone and looked at it intently. While I was doing this, a misdirected football went sailing a centimetre past my ear and I shrieked, crouching down with my hands over my head like a Dickensian urchin fearing a beating.

'Sorry, Mrs Baker!' Alex ran over to retrieve the ball.

'No problem, Alex.' I called back gaily as the whistle blew for kick-off.

I did my best to follow the game while listening carefully to the comments being shouted by the other parents. Occasionally I tried to throw in one of my own, although I can't pretend that I wasn't basically copying whatever I heard.

'Beautiful pass, Ronnie,' shouted one of the dads.

'Beautiful.' I nodded my agreement.

'Man on! Man on!' screeched one of the mums.

I shook my head and tutted. 'Man on,' I said quietly, not being entirely clear as to what this meant.

I did at least know to clap and cheer when a goal went in. Although unfortunately it was the other team that had scored so my whooping drew the wrong kind of attention. It had also started to rain very heavily and my cardigan was stuck to my skin. One of the mums from the knowledgeable cagoule-wearing crowd gave me a wave and pointed to her umbrella with a querying look. I closed the four-metre gap between us, feeling very brave, and stepped under the shelter she was providing.

'Clearly hadn't thought this through,' I said gesturing to my blueing toes sloshing around in my muddy flip-flops and chattering my teeth together.

'I've got a spare coat in the car,' she said. 'One of the boys always forgets their shin pads or destroys a pair of tracky bottoms or snaps their bootlaces so I basically travel around with a spare set of everything. I'll go and get it at half time, you can borrow it.'

'Oh, thank you,' I said. 'Are you sure?'

Her attention had returned to the pitch where she was focusing intently on a rangy lad flailing his limbs about as he tried to make contact with the ball. 'COME

ON, DEESH!' she yelled like a woman possessed. 'PACE! PACE!'

Deesh appeared to be doing his best to heed his mother's advice but a defender from the other side beat him to the ball (at least I think that's what happened) and scampered up the other side of the pitch with it. The woman groaned loudly and put her head in her hands. 'Jesus wept,' she muttered.

A tall man wearing an enormous overcoat was standing beside her. 'They've got no depth in the squad,' he said, shaking his head sadly. 'Even if Deesh had got a touch, there was nobody up there with him.' He sighed, puffing out a little cloud of coffee-scented frustration.

Another woman chipped in. 'If they don't sort out the formation we're never going to progress through the league,' she said. 'How many matches have we got left before the end of the season? Three? There just isn't the time now to work on the squad fitness – they're all out of condition.'

'They look like they're all enjoying themselves anyway,' I said brightly, and was rewarded with what can only be described as incredulous silence.

The whistle blew for half-time and the team gathered in a disconsolate huddle, squirting water from their muddy bottles directly into their mouths and rubbing at sore patches on their knees and elbows.

'Well done, darling.' I waved enthusiastically at Tom and gave him a thumbs up.

'Oh, *you're* Tom's mum,' the lady holding the umbrella said as we walked to her car. 'We usually see Sam.'

'Yes. I know,' I said. 'I rarely get a chance to see Tom play. I'm often busy doing stuff with my girls or...'

'And Sam likes to be involved anyway, doesn't he?' she said. 'He certainly seems very hands-on – he and Tom are very close, always chatting about the game and tactics and skills-training. It's nice.'

'Yes,' I said, feeling a little sting of irrational jealousy towards my husband. 'It really is.'

'Not like my ex. He can't be arsed to come along and stand in the rain watching his son run about in a second division under-elevens side. He'd rather be in the pub.'

We'd reached her Volvo estate and she pulled a mud-spattered mac out of the boot, brushing off the dog hairs. 'This do you?' She held it up.

'Perfect,' I said. 'Thanks.' I pulled it on over my sodden cardie.

'It's my older boy, Arjun's. He's playing away at Kenton, kick-off in half an hour so I'll be heading over there next. And then we'll be off to the club after to watch the first team play-offs.' She clocked my expression. 'Yeah, s'just how I spend my weekends now. My boys, they love their footie, so if I want to see them, I've got to love it too. Can't spend the whole day discussing bleedin' *Fortnite* can you!' She looked down at my flip-flops. 'Not much I can do about those though, love. There's a pair of wellies in here but they're a size nine. You'd look a right state.'

I squelched my way back to the touchline where the second half had begun and spent the rest of the match being instructed in the basic components of the game by Neelima, Deesh's mum. It paid off. In the car on the way home, Tom and Alex were arguing about territory and how many points they'd conceded.

'You probably just need to have more of your defenders goal-side,' I said over my shoulder. 'And your midfielders need to pass. They're hogging the ball.'

There was a stunned silence before Alex said, 'Ye-es, actually, you're right Mrs Baker. They do.'

'Lovely outside curve on that shot from Jason though,' I said. 'And I thought you both put in some excellent tackles. Alex, getting possession off their number seven wasn't easy and Tom, when you nutmegged their number ten? Beautiful.' I registered my son's open-mouth astonishment with a smile.

Mission accomplished.

Chapter Thirty-Five

Urrrgh! Woken up with a *tiny* hangover due to over-consumption of booze with Zahara, Caz and Joy last night. What larks! What lolz! WTAF was I drinking?

Zahara had suggested that we 'deserved' a night out as a basic human right (as per Geneva Convention and Amnesty International guidance) and I have sorely missed the company of women my own age over the past few months, so was eager to agree. The plan had been to meet at the village pub, The Cock – source of endless puns that my husband and older children continued to find hilarious, in contrast to most of the village who are a bit more, *Yeah, yeah, it's called The Cock, whatevs* – but we decided to head for the bright lights of TOWN and WINE BARS when Joy invited herself into the mix. Zahara did her best to be accommodating but I did register a flicker of mild annoyance on her face when, at preschool pick-up, Joy leapt on my lukewarm suggestion that she join us for the evening. Caz was so excited to escape from the house that she would have happily shared a pint with Attila the Hun and so it was that this unlikely foursome hit the big city, otherwise known as the high street of a small market town.

It may have been the slight tension in the air that caused us all to neck our gin and tonics a little more rapidly than usual. While Zahara is one of the kindest people I know, I forgot that she hasn't shared the moment of affinity with Joy that I have and I suspect she harbours residual ill-will about Joy's lack of regard for fellow preschool mums when it comes to childcare and other forms of support. I have mentioned to her that some of Joy's apparent indifference is actually borne out of low confidence in her own parenting skills, but Zahara's reply – that this was 'a poor excuse for treating people like shit all the time' – leads me to believe that there may be a smidgen of persistent resentment, which is fair enough. Joy, on the other hand, finds Zahara a bit 'too perfect' and this doesn't exactly bolster a burgeoning friendship. So it was left to me and Caz to mediate – basically pour gin down their throats until everyone got along.

I can fully understand Zahara's ambivalence towards our newest addition, but there is a part of me that sees Joy's point as well. Zahara's life *is* perfect. Her family are like something out of a Boden catalogue. She scores highly in all of Tiggy and Lindi's ranking categories while also not falling into the trap of being a smug cow. Her children are kind and polite without being insipid or weird (not easy) and are always immaculately dressed but still happy to muck about in the garden playing wholesome games of tag and hide-and-seek instead of *Grand Theft Auto* or *Smack Your Bitch Up* (I've made that up – it's not actually a computer game as far as I'm aware). Her house is, as I've mentioned, glorious: clean, tastefully decorated in pale neutrals and tactile natural fabrics and always smells like an exclusive department store. Her job is rewarding, fun, surprisingly well-remunerated and fits beautifully with childcare and school hours. Her husband is attentive, witty, intelligent and devastatingly handsome. He adores her. I mean, really adores her. He showers her with gifts; whenever he's been on one of his business trips we know Zahara will be getting some expensive bit of jewellery or a spa day to compensate. In fact once, when he was over in America for two weeks, he sent her a dozen red roses every day until he returned. He compliments her appearance, helps around the house, takes the children out for the day so that she can have some 'me time' and respects her opinions on everything from politics to hairstyles to what's good on Netflix.

Hugh is also charming and considerate with her friends and all the school mums adore him to the point where some of their own husbands probably feel a little less than enamoured with him. It doesn't hurt that he's very easy on the eye, and if I had one teensy criticism it would be that he is a bit vain, a bit too concerned with appearance. Zahara has admitted that one of the gifts he offered her last year was a voucher for cosmetic surgery, just in case, you know, she felt like getting a boob job or whatever, since having the kids, perhaps she might want to…

Maybe he thought he was being kind. He did say that many of his colleagues' wives were constantly on at them to fund various nips and tucks. And this was his only misstep in ten years as an otherwise exemplary husband. But it was, most definitely, an error of judgement, because Zahara isn't *one of those wives*. She is, as only the truly beautiful can be, completely oblivious to, and unconcerned by, her appearance. As I said to her, on learning of this outrageously misjudged 'gift', you can't enhance perfection.

And she is perfect. She is tall and slender and has the smooth, pore-less complexion of a teenager – a beautiful, as opposed to acne-riddled, one. In fact, I was once with her in the supermarket when she was asked for age iden-tification when buying a bottle of Chablis. A request that she was later embarrassed to admit to, as opposed to me or any other woman in their forties who would have been shouting from the rooftops that the lad at the checkout thought they might not have turned eighteen yet.

The thing with Zahara is that she knows she's lucky and she wears her privilege lightly; she doesn't indulge those who only want to be friends with her because of her lovely life, but neither is she ever rude to them. Everyone likes her. Everyone, that is, apart from maybe Joy.

'I just think sheesh holding something back,' Joy slurred to me as she tried to touch up her lipstick in the gin bar toilets, squinting into the mirror and then scrunching up her nose, 'Ugh, I look vile. My mouth's like a cat's bum. Gonna get something done.'

'You'll end up like Tiggy,' I said. 'Don't do it. You don't need Botox anyway. You look fine.'

Joy pushed her face closer to the mirror in drunken contemplation. 'Wasn't thinking Botox, it's *so* noughties. Thought maybe fillers?' She squished her lips with her fingers, 'Plump them up a bit?'

'Yeah, but that can go wrong too. You really don't need—'

'Yourright.' Joy rested her forehead against the cool of the mirror. 'I'd end up with trout-pout instead of cat-bum knowing my luck. Bet Zahara doesn't have to worry about this crap.' (I immediately thought of Hugh's gift voucher, but Joy was on a roll). 'Did you see the lads at the bar giving her the eye? They're half her age!'

'I know,' I said. 'One of them came up and asked me for her number when she was on the dance floor. I told him she was happily married and the mother of two children. Didn't seem to put him off though.'

'Men.' Joy had a derisory tone but seemed incapable of expanding further. She grabbed my arm as we made our way out of the loos. 'Another thing,' she said. 'Those kids of hers. How'd they get to be so bloody perfect?'

'They're just lovely kids, Joy,' I said, my voice firm. I wasn't going to have her jealousy spill into a character assassination of my best mate. It's far too easy to get caught up in a bit of bitchiness, colluding in the slagging off without meaning to and then you hate yourself the next day. 'She's a great mum and she has lovely kids. End of.'

'They don't have *character* like my Evangeline though.'

'You could put it like that.'

She laughed. 'Yeah. Ignore me,' she said. 'I'm just a jealous cow. Those kids are sweet. They'll do well at St Barts.'

I pulled to a stop in the corridor. 'They're not going to St Barts,' I said.

Joy leant heavily against the wall and nodded with drunken fervour, 'Yeah, yesh. They are.' She saw the look of scepticism on my face and began to nod even more violently, 'Oop, feel bit sick. But they are. She definitely said. Hugh, Hugh? Hugh thinks it'll be better for them apparently.'

My eyebrows lifted. This seemed very unlikely. 'But I thought she was happy with the school,' I said, my voice small with doubt.

Joy shrugged, 'Clee-early not.' She prised herself off the wall. 'Let's get another drink. S'my round – I'll get Lovely Zahara something special for being such a gorgeous bleedin' superstar anyways.'

'Can I have something special too?' I put on a whiney voice.

'Course you can, missus. You're a bleedin' superstar too, inviting me out on the razzle. What'll it be? Cosmopolitan? Manhattan?'

'I'll go for a Gimlet,' I said.

''Course you will. Gin, gin, gin. A Gimlet it is.' We took a few more steps. 'There is *something* though,' she said, wobbling slightly against me as she returned to her obsession. 'With Zahara? It's not all roses I reckon. Take it from me.' She tapped the side of her nose conspiratorially. 'I know how to hide crap from people and I can sniff it out when someone's doing the same.'

'I think that's just the Gents,' I said, steering her down the corridor.

–

Later, we dropped Caz and Joy back at their respective houses: seventies mid-terrace and Georgian rectory – Zahara's eyes had lit up at the sash-windows and pillared portico as Joy threw a twenty-pound note at us and fell out of the taxi onto the pea-shingle.

'Byeee ladeez!' she hollered as she made her way unsteadily across the drive.

'D'you need a hand?' I wound the window down after watching her unsuccessfully tackle her own front door for the third time.

'Nope! Shimple matter of… Just. Getting. In. To. My. Own. House.' She punctuated each word with a stab of her key in the general direction of the lock until she hit the target. 'Aha! Easy-peasy! Quiet now.' Her voice had reduced to a very noisy whisper and she brought her finger to her lips in an exaggerated gesture as the door creaked open and the warm lamplight spilled into the porch. 'Smashing night, ladies. Thank you. Inviting me, you know. Nishe friends. Really, really, *really* nishe friends...' She was still muttering to herself as the door shut behind her and the taxi reversed past the box hedging back down the drive.

'She's a real laugh, isn't she?' Zahara's voice was warm but I knew it had been quite an effort to ignore some of the thinly veiled barbs of jealousy thrown her way during the course of the evening. Joy had gone on and on about the guy who'd asked for Zahara's number – I really regretted having told her. And Zahara had clearly felt awkward when Joy had asked the barman to try and guess their respective ages and then been incensed by the result. Although suggesting that Joy was old enough to be Zahara's mother was a schoolboy error on his part – I don't think he'll be making that sort of mistake again in a hurry. Thankfully we were saved by Caz's suggestion of tequila slammers before it turned ugly, but I felt some degree of responsibility for having invited Joy along.

'She is,' I agreed. 'But she's also a bit abrasive.'

Zahara breathed out with relief. 'Yeah. And – sort of exhausting. Not in a bad way,' she hurried on. 'Just, you know.'

'Yeah. I know. And it does alter the evening a bit, doesn't it? She didn't half bang on about that *youth* chatting you up, although, to be fair, he was *pret-ty* hot. I'm not surprised she's a bit jealous. Have you seen her husband, Simon? He's got to be mid-fifties. I expect she just fancies a bit of toy-boy action now and then. And there's you, being offered it on a plate everywhere we go!'

Zahara looked uncomfortable. 'That's not true. It was just that one guy. And it was *really* dark in that bar.'

I put my arm round her. 'Oh, my modest, lovely chum!' I said. 'You really are too sweet. And I'm sorry we didn't get much of a chance to chat tonight.'

'So am I. I was really wanting to find out how everything's going with your mum. I barely see you now, and I just wanted you to know if you need any help, someone to have Maisie for a few hours or walk the dog or, even to keep your mum company if you want to pop out...'

I found myself welling up a bit at that, although I blamed the tequila. Anyway, we agreed to go out again, just the two of us to catch up, and I skulked into the house feeling drunk and giggly. That was until I read Sam's note, which he'd left propped up against the lamp on the hall table.

> *P – Sorry. Couldn't persuade your mum upstairs. Waited up as long as I could but knackered and T has match 8am start so have headed off to bed. She seems fine, left her with a glass of Baileys watching TV. Hope you had good night with the girls XX*
> *S*

I looked at my watch – it was only half-eleven. Could he really not have managed to sit up with her until now? That was just Sam all over. I remembered the nights of being awoken by babies crying and lying there silently praying for Sam to be the one to haul his arse out of bed, all the time knowing it would be me. It was always me. That was the unwritten rule. He always had work the next morning, or if it was the weekend then he would obviously be in greater need of rest, having slogged through another long week of commuting. His sleep was inevitably prioritised over mine. By the time we got to holidays, where I could have legitimately claimed a more equal share of rest and relaxation, the children would only settle if it was me getting up to attend to their various night-time needs (too hot, frightened of the noise in the cupboard, felt sick, wanted a cuddle...) and thus our summer vacations were often spent with me collapsed in a greying heap of knackered mum-ness while Sam, reinvigorated and refreshed, leapt about in the waves, built epic sandcastles and ordered extravagant ice-creams, perfectly assuming the role of 'Fun Dad'. Yay!

I knew that this situation was different, of course. This was *my* mother, not a shared childcare responsibility. But this was my first night out in months — certainly the first time I'd had away from Mum since the awful night of Dad's stroke — and I wondered if the roles had been reversed and we'd been looking after one of Sam's parents, whether there would be some automatic expectation that I would pull my weight on the caring front. I doubted that it would be considered OK for me to just pop off to bed leaving *his* mother unattended (she'd be appalled by my rudeness for a start) and that was despite the fact that neither of his parents were remotely incapacitated. It was just an assumption, based on societal norms, that I, as the woman of the house, would undertake the lion's share of caring duties for young and old, blood relative or casual acquaintance.

I sighed wearily and levered my shoes off with my toes, kicking them into a corner where they would be doubtless tripped over by Tom in his rush to get ready for football tomorrow morning. I tiptoed into the sitting room where Mum was now sleeping; the glass of Baileys had tipped in her lap and was trickling drops into a pale sticky puddle on the carpet, so I went into the kitchen to get a cloth and let Colin out. The place looked like it had been evacuated in a nuclear emergency, but it was simply that nobody had thought to clear up after supper. Pots and pans were lined up on the hob, their contents crusting nicely around the edges, dirty plates were on the table, ketchup congealing in red blobs and streaks like something in an abandoned art lesson. A bottle of wine was open on the side so I poured myself a cupful, not being able to locate a clean glass and proceeded to stack the dishwasher and wipe down the surfaces. The cereal cupboard was open and Colin had evidently helped himself to a breakfast selection, scattering Alpen across the floor so I cleared that up, closing cupboard doors and moving stray shoes as I worked my way around the room. By the time I finally got to bed I was feeling pretty sorry for myself and I'd also consumed two further mugs of wine and the rest of Mum's Baileys. Which might explain the epic awfulness of my hangover.

Summer

Chapter Thirty-Six

Summer half-term begins and obviously it's pissing it down with rain. But astonishingly, the kids have all agreed to come to the cinema to watch the new *Star Wars* film with me. Ostensibly this is meant to be a treat for Tom as he is the most enamoured with the franchise, but Maisie is enormously excited to be going to a 'big person's film' and Grace will never knowingly turn down the offer of pick 'n' mix, so everyone's happy. Remarkably.

Despite a two-hour lead time, we were already cutting it fine as we arrived in the cinema foyer. Mum was confused by some of the promotional material on display and insisted on looking intently at an advert for the next *Minions* film while Maisie shouted 'Banana!' at the top of her voice. No matter how many times I suggested we move through to the actual film we were there to see, she remained fixed to her spot, resolutely peering at the cartoon. 'They're yellow,' she said very seriously to me when I went to steer her away.

'Yes, Mum. I know.'

'But, Penelope. They're yellow.'

'Yes, they're not real, Mum.' Jesus, how was she going to cope with a CGI stormtrooper?

By the time we arrived at screen four the lights had gone down and the trailers had almost finished. The cinema was packed, which didn't help as we made painfully slow progress to our seats (at the back and accessible only via trampling over the feet, or falling into the laps, of twelve other people) but eventually we were seated just in time for Maisie to spill her popcorn and announce that she needed the loo.

'Grace, can you take her?' I asked my eldest daughter, who was staring firmly ahead at the screen and trying desperately to disown us all.

'No,' she hissed under her breath. 'God, this is so embarrassing.'

'Ssshhhh!' a large man from the row behind leant forward and pointed to the screen, just in case we weren't aware the film was about to start.

'Yes, thank you,' I said. 'Sorry for the disturbance.'

'Mummeee...' Maisie wriggled in her seat 'I really need a wee. It's *urgent*.'

'Right.' I took Maisie's hand and began my apologetic return journey past the same twelve obliging people whose toes had been crushed by my family on our way in. I was a little nervous about leaving Mum behind, but she was with Grace and Tom. What could possibly go wrong? Still, I legged it out into the main concourse and into a toilet cubicle, dragging my youngest daughter with me, digging my nails into my palms as I waited for her to finish.

She pulled a face halfway through. 'Mummy, I think I need a poo...'

'Jeez, Maisie. Really?'

She nodded and squeezed her eyes shut as she pushed. 'Sorry,' she said through gritted teeth. 'I'll be quick.'

Ten minutes of extended wiping, thorough hand-washing, protracted use of the Dyson hand dryer and endless conversation about each activity later, we raced back into the screen where I noticed that a group of teenagers had occupied the seats beyond ours. I leant over to Grace and whispered in her ear, 'Did Granny move to let those people through?'

She shook her head and looked mortified. 'No,' she whispered back. 'She just didn't know what to do. Tom and I kept trying to move her or get her to stand up or anything. Eventually they just had to clamber over her. It was awful. She told them off and they were, like, *Why don't you just move, you stupid woman?* and she was like, *That's quite enough out of you, Norman*, and I was like, *Granny, I don't think he's called Norman*, and she was like, *That's no excuse*.

She put her head in her hands and I grimaced.

'Sssshhhhh!' said the man behind us, leaning forward with his nachos and spraying saliva and salsa into my face. 'This. Is. A. Cinema!'

I wiped my cheek. 'Yes,' I said. 'Thanks for pointing that out.'

Mum appeared to enjoy the film although we had to swap seats when she started nicking her neighbour's Jelly Babies. I gave her the rest of Maisie's popcorn which she chomped on for a while, but halfway through yet another climactic battle scene she started coughing and spluttering. The people sitting around us had obviously been under the misapprehension that there was to be no further disruption to their viewing pleasure. They were wrong. Mum wasn't delicately clearing her throat. Her nose and eyes were streaming and she sounded more like she was coughing up an entire lung.

'Mum,' I said, thumping her hard on her back. 'Are you OK?'

'Granny?' Maisie's voice quavered. 'Is she dying, Mummy?'

'I don't think so, darling,' I replied as cheerfully as I could while whacking Mum between the shoulder blades for the second time. 'You enjoy the, um, space battle.'

Thankfully the piece of popcorn dislodged itself and sailed through the air to land on the scarf of the lady in front before I needed to implement the full Heimlich manoeuvre. Mum sniffed and settled back into her seat, going from imminent respiratory failure to happy cinema-goer in a matter of moments, staring at the screen as if nothing had happened. The rest of the viewing public threw us a mixture of concerned and annoyed glances before returning their attention to the screen and I closed my eyes and breathed deeply. We were reaching the denouement of the film now, I felt certain. We'd been in there for at least two hours, although it felt like forty, and all I wanted to do was get home. Sadly the off-screen drama was not completely finished because once the credits had rolled and we had made our way blinking into the bright lights of the main concourse, Grace began patting her pockets with the fervour of a drugs-squad search team.

'Shit,' she said under her breath.

'What is it?' I put a restraining hand on Maisie, who was about to dart off to the pick 'n' mix for a second helping, and another on Tom who was doing keepy-uppy with his scrunched-up popcorn bag.

'My phone,' she said, her voice panic-stricken in the way only a teenager missing their life-source and sole means of communication can be. 'I've lost it.'

So began a wearisome traipse back to the seating area of screen four, where the cinema attendant had to cease his hoovering while I called Grace's phone from mine, hoping the tinkling ringtone would give away its location, from there back to the ladies' toilets where we repeated the exercise, and then on to the main reception where we handed over details of Grace's phone make, model and cover, along with my contact details, before racing back to the car to find the bloody phone in the footwell of the rear seats and a parking ticket on the windscreen because we'd overrun our four-hour maximum stay.

Ruddy marvellous. I don't think I've ever enjoyed a cinema trip less – and I've made the mistake of paying for premium seats to see the film version of *Cats*, so the bar is pretty low. As soon as we got home I updated our Netflix subscription and told a sheepish Grace that if I ever suggested another multi-generational trip to the cinema she was to restrain me until the urge had passed.

Chapter Thirty-Seven

I'd like to say that the cinema trip was the pinnacle of my half-term holiday stress, but to be honest it was pretty much downhill from there. Mum went on to develop a urine infection, Grace was still anxious about school and refused to talk about it, while also being crippled with period pain, and Tom, not to be outdone, twisted his ankle at the trampoline park. So the majority of my week was spent tending to the sick and needy – and believe me, they were all *very* needy. Maisie wasn't ill but she was appalled that her share of attention had been so dramatically reduced and set out to find ingenious and highly irritating ways to alert me to her presence, including spilling a bottle of nail varnish over her chest of drawers, making up complicated dance routines that had to be watched and appraised immediately and 'doing fashion', which basically involved cutting great chunks out of her clothing with a pair of kitchen scissors, turning a perfectly respectable T-shirt into a bra-top that barely covered her nipples and shredding her shorts into a ragged thong. She spent most of the week looking like a cross between a Flintstone and a low-budget porn star.

But we made it through and I packed them back off to their educational establishments rested and restored (them, not me, obviously). And so, as it is with the yin and the yang of life, this plague of illness and injury has ended and a new calamity has befallen us. Well, not us for a change, but Fizz. It seems that during one of her recent motocross competitions (she fits this in between singing classes and her cabaret show – I'm not sure if they ever combine), her Kawasaki Ninja 125 slid out from beneath her on a patch of loose chippings and dragged her into what she described as 'a fairly small' ravine. She sustained a fractured collar bone, a dislocated shoulder and a broken jaw so her ability to sing and waft her scarves about is now much more limited. Miraculously her legs, pelvis and abdomen appear to be entirely preserved and despite blacking out for a few moments, there has been no obvious brain damage. All things considered, she's pretty lucky and she knows it.

Fizz's jaw is slowly repairing, so most of our communication has been via email, where she remains as ebullient as ever, even via the medium of the typed word. There are more exclamation marks in a single WhatsApp message than one would expect to see in the entire script for a stage production of *Whoops! Vicar! Where's my knickers?!!!*. But she saved her most interesting communique for our face to face, when I took Mum, Tina and Bob around to her house to drop off some flowers and cards from the group.

'Penny!' Her left arm was fully functioning as she answered the door, welcoming us in with a lopsided hug. 'And Mary! Tina! Bob!' Our names were announced through the wiring of gritted teeth; it was a little like being introduced by Hannibal Lecter. However, I am now quite adept at understanding those whose conversational skills are impaired, whether it be through cognitive or mechanical means. Dad with his stroke, Mum with her muddled vocabulary; I'm a veritable multi-linguist.

Fizz's partner, Doreen, was also home and fussed around with a fruit cake she'd made. 'None for you, Fizzy,' she said. 'The almonds won't get through the grille. But for the rest of you, a large slice each?' She didn't wait for an answer and we were all served a slab of cake with our tea. It was delicious, although I did feel the waistband of my trousers cutting into my stomach as I sat in one of their flamboyantly decorated armchairs (orange embossed flamingos on a velvet backdrop of verdant palm trees – pretty cool, actually, but wouldn't survive a day in our house).

We discussed the obligatory details of the accident and the recovery. Doreen filled us in on the more macabre aspects – 'Her face was completely mashed in, the surgeon only just managed to save her eye...' et cetera. Then Fizz turned to me with an urgent look. 'Penny,' she said through the wiring. 'The concert.'

I was surprised that she had even given the singing group a second thought, but this was Fizz and she was nothing if not committed (*should* be committed, perhaps, in an institutional sense). 'Fizz, don't worry about it. We'll just cancel. People will understand. I mean, look at you.' I gestured towards her arm in its sling. 'It would be impossible.'

Her face fell despite its external scaffolding and Doreen sat forward in her chair (upholstered in a damask velour decorated with large pomegranates). 'I think she was hoping you'd take over, Penny.'

I stared at them both blankly. 'Me? Take over? How?'

'Well,' said Doreen. 'You know all the songs, you know the musical accompaniments, you have the set list pretty much off by heart.' She looked over at Fizz, who was nodding fervently. 'And Fizz says you're very talented and also very organised.'

'Organised? Me?'

'Kids,' Fizz said through gritted teeth.

Doreen nodded. 'Yes. Those kids of yours, I heard they made a big difference to the singing group when they came along for the Easter session, really raised everyone's spirits and it's so lovely to have the younger generation involved.'

'Keep the momentum,' Fizz said.

'Yes.' Doreen paused and turned to her, 'What?'

'Momentum!' Fizz hollered despite the clenched jaw.

'Oh yes, and we thought, well, Fizz hoped, that you would feel the same desire to see this through, to carry on the good work. It would mean the world to her. And to me. And most importantly, to all of those for whom the choir is their only means of communication.' Doreen stopped, pleased with the way she had managed to both flatter me and make it sound as though Fizz was Mother Teresa, crusading against choral injustice.

I looked down at the crumbs of my fruit cake and Tina, who'd been silent up until now, cleared her throat. 'Penny, it would be lovely if we could keep it going. We could have extra practices at our house. I had the piano tuned again recently. I hadn't bothered for years but after Easter, well, Bob loved hearing you play it and you've definitely got the talent to get us all through the performance. Just like Fizz,' she said quickly. Fizz and Doreen nodded graciously. 'You can encourage us all, help us out with the harmonies, chivvy us along, keep us motivated…?'

'Uhhh. The thing is…' I dabbed at half a glacé cherry stuck to the corner of my plate.

'We'll understand if you say no,' said Doreen, with very little understanding in her voice. 'But you can see just how much it means to everyone. They need a focus; the performance is giving them hope…'

This was pushing it a little, but Tina was certainly looking a bit dejected as she considered the possibility that the show might be cancelled. 'It's the one thing that Bob talks about with anything approaching excitement now,' she said, rubbing a yellowing bruise on her wrist. 'Everyone's practised so hard already…'

What was I going to say?

'I'm already incredibly busy / I'm barely keeping body and soul together as it is / My son thinks I don't care about him / My eldest daughter's moods are like a meteorological force / My youngest daughter is a tyrant with no boundaries / My husband is barely home and appears incapable of helping out in any practical or tangible fashion / I'm already so worried about my own risk of degenerative neurological disease that I think I might be giving myself an ulcer / I drink too much and am generally spending half my day as a borderline alcoholic / I eat too much and look like a massive blimp although that's not especially relevant to this discussion / My mother doesn't recognise half the members of her own family and struggles with basic mobility / I barely have a moment's peace in the day and often find myself losing the will to live.'

Or I could just say, 'OK. I'll see what I can do.'

Which is what I did.

God help us all.

Chapter Thirty-Eight

Friday, 6 June

I went out for a drink with Zahara tonight. Just me and
her this time. I'd asked Sam to try and get home for a reasonable hour but, as eight thirty came and went, I pulled on
my boots and announced to Grace that she could babysit
instead. I was only going to the neighbouring village and
Maisie was already in bed, so all she needed to do was sit
with Granny and make sure Tom got to bed by nine. She
still insisted on being paid current market rates though,
telling me that it wasn't fair to limit her opportunities of
earning money babysitting elsewhere and not reimburse
her for the inconvenience. I wanted to point out that
she did not currently have any babysitting work outside
the house, paid or otherwise, and that looking after her
siblings and grandmother could be considered to be just
a part of family life, but she looked so mutinous that I
agreed to five pounds an hour and hurtled over to The
Red Lion in Amberley as fast as you could say 'massively
taken advantage of by a teenager'.

Zahara was already at the bar and had just bought a
bottle of red to share, so I decided to leave the car there
and collect it in the morning. It was a chilly evening for
June and the rain was starting to lash against the windows,
so we made our way over to a table by the fire. The pub

was relatively empty other than a few locals neither of us knew and I wondered why Zahara had chosen this as a venue.

'I wanted somewhere private,' she said ominously. 'I can't talk at home and if I opened my mouth in The Cock—'

'Or around it…'

'What?'

'Never mind,' I said. 'Too much time with my husband and his hilarious innuendos.'

'Well, that's the opposite of my problem.' She poured us both a large glass of Cabernet Sauvignon. 'I've evidently not been spending enough time with my husband.'

I must have looked a bit bemused.

'Not enough time to stop him having an affair, anyway.'

The bombshell had been dropped. I spluttered into my drink. 'What? Are you sure?'

She nodded in that horribly wise way of the cynical and betrayed. 'I am sure,' she said. 'He admitted it.'

'Fuck.'

'Quite.'

'Oh my God, Zahara! Are you OK?' I was trying to gather my thoughts. The lovely Hugh? The lovely, handsome, charismatic Hugh? The devoted husband, the attentive, flower-buying, spending-time-with-the-kids and charming-the-ladies-of-the-village Hugh? I couldn't believe it. Except, now I came to think of it, maybe I could. My thoughts returned to Joy's drunken comment before the half-term holidays; she knew something wasn't right. A virtual stranger had sussed it out before Zahara's supposed best friend had. How awful. I took a gulp of my wine and reached out and grabbed her hand across the table. 'When did you find out?'

'Couple of weeks ago.' She smiled sadly. 'I'd had my suspicions for a while, I think I just knew but I didn't want to confront it, to make it real. Because once it's real you've got to have all the shit conversations, the ones both of you would rather avoid. *Do we really love each other? Have we ever loved each other? Is it just about the sex? Is it that this 'Nadia' woman is fifteen years younger than me?* And of course, the biggest question of all: *What do we do now?* I mean, What. The. Fuck. Do. We. Do. Now?' She turned to me as if I had the answer. I took another gulp of wine.

'Shit. Zahara, I just, I don't know. What do you want to do? Can you forgive him? Can you move on from this in, like, a positive way?'

'What, like a Gwyneth Paltrow, Chris Martin "conscious uncoupling" way?' she asked with a wry smile.

'Not necessarily. I mean, not necessarily *uncoupling* – clearly it would be good if whatever you do is *conscious*. But – are you, are you going to leave him?'

'No... Not at the moment.' She ran her fingertip around a circle of condensation on the table and looked thoughtful. 'We felt it would be best for the kids if we didn't do anything drastic. Well, Hugh thought it would be best anyway.'

'I bet he bloody did!' Suddenly I was furious, really punch-him-in-the-face furious. How dare he do this to my friend, the best of women? What an absolute shit. 'Shame he didn't think about how *drastic* shagging someone else might be and whether that perhaps might not be *best* for the kids.'

Zahara winced.

'Oh, mate. I'm sorry. I didn't mean it to come out like that, but honestly, what a complete tool.'

We talked for hours and made our way through two more bottles of wine. The alcohol seemed only to stoke my righteous indignation, but Zahara remained calm and reasonable, listing the instances of betrayal as if she were reading from a catalogue. I wasn't sure how she could be so sanguine about the whole scenario but I guess she had had a couple of weeks to at least become accustomed to the idea, if one ever gets used to the fact that their husband has cheated on them. At some point my phone buzzed in my pocket. It was a message from Sam saying he was really sorry he'd been so late home and to give him a call and he'd come and collect us whenever we were ready.

'I expect Hugh would happily charter a private jet to collect us if he thought it would go some way to making amends,' Zahara said. 'He's being really attentive at the moment, nothing's too much trouble. I'm tempted to see how far I can push it really. Holiday for one in the Maldives? New car? What d'you reckon?'

'I just... don't know how you can be so relaxed about it,' I said truthfully. 'If it was me, I'm not sure I could forgive him.' (God, I fucking hated Hugh – I didn't want her to forgive him, the absolute bastard.)

She looked thoughtful. 'I used to think that,' she said. 'I always thought that I was the sort of person who couldn't tolerate infidelity in my partner and that even him snogging someone else would be a red line for me. I thought that women who took their husbands back after an affair were somehow devaluing themselves and sending out this message like, *Yes it's OK to mess me about, I'll still be here like a faithful dog when you come home.*'

I nodded, because that's exactly how I felt.

'But it's funny how you react when it actually happens,' Zahara said. 'You look at what you've built together and it seems madness to throw it all away because of a mistake.' She took a sip of her wine. 'Not *my* mistake, admittedly, and of course I am furious about what he's done, but you start to question how much of your response is about punishing the other person. Is it worth uprooting the family just to make a point?'

'And it definitely was a mistake? He's finished with this 'Nadia'? You're sure?'

She nodded. 'I heard him on the phone to her.' Her voice was tight as she relived the evening when she'd discovered the affair. 'He told her that his family were more important to him than she was. Which shouldn't have needed to be explained, but there you go.'

'Can't have been an easy conversation to listen to?'

'It wasn't. I made him put her on speakerphone so I could be certain she'd understood. Hearing her voice… that was… hard. She was crying and… Hugh was pretty brutal.'

'Well, my brilliant friend,' I raised my glass in her direction. 'You are a better woman than me. As if that were ever in doubt. But honestly, good for you, looking at the bigger picture and everything. I hope he spends the rest of his days making it up to you.'

Later, when Sam came to pick us up, I clambered into the front seat and planted a big kiss on his cheek. 'You lovely, lovely man,' I whispered in his ear. 'Thank you so much for collecting us. I don't care if Mum's asleep in the sitting room and has spilt Baileys all over the floor again, I don't care if you've left the kitchen in a state or not managed to get the kids into bed. I do really, really love you.'

Zahara had sworn me to secrecy, saying that it wouldn't be fair on Hugh if the other blokes in the village knew

283

what had happened. The only way their marriage stood a chance of survival was if everyone treated them exactly as they always had done. She had a point – I was going to struggle to stop myself kneeing him in the bollocks next time I saw him. But as a result my husband had no real idea of where this little burst of affection came from and probably just assumed I was drunk. Which was a shame, because tonight's revelations had only added to my lurking unease about Sam's predatory work-colleague Jenna and the increasing emotional distance between us. I realised I probably needed to up my game. But how I was going to find the time and energy to lavish this much-needed attention on my marriage, I had absolutely no idea.

Chapter Thirty-Nine

I've been keeping pretty busy the past few days what with having to *run an entire bloody concert* in five weeks' time. I've had a look at the set list and made a few minor changes based on what I know of the choir and where our strengths lie, such as they are. I've slipped in a couple of extra Rolling Stones tracks because they have such great percussion, and The Beatles likewise. And I've taken out Rihanna, much to everyone's relief. Some of those sensual lyrics and Bajan rhythms just do not sound the same coming out of the mouths of doddery nonagen-arians. 'Umbrella' was fine, but Edith's rendition of 'S&M' was unsettling to say the least. Instead I've brought in 'Survivor' by Destiny's Child and Lynyrd Skynyrd's 'Sweet Home Alabama' (partly because it has a fantastic keyboard solo – I'm not going to lie), which is a big favourite as the chorus lyrics are simple, the melody joyful and if one gets lost in the song a few well-placed whoops and hell-yeahs fit the gaps quite nicely.

Grace has grudgingly agreed to help me with some of the evening rehearsals (to be honest, I just wanted to get her out of the house – she seems so flat at the moment) and Clive has asked the son of a colleague to assist with the lighting and sound on the night. Fizz, in a classic burst of optimistic enthusiasm, booked the town hall for the event months ago. It's a bit of a step up from the small community venue we've been using up until now, but at least they have a proper piano and a (gulp) stage.

Anyway, I have to admit that despite my anxiety around taking this on it's actually been lots of fun to have a project, particularly one that involves my family in a positive way. I've tried to include Grace in decisions about song-choice ever since she first showed signs of interest at Easter with the K-pop discussion. It seems a neutral way of engaging with her (in that it doesn't tend to lead to hideous rows) and we've spent much of the past few evenings sitting around the kitchen table – me, Mum and the older two kids searching up tunes and deliberating whether they should be included. Tom's request that there should be at least one featured rap artist was overruled when we established in no uncertain terms that there wasn't a single performer capable of, or willing to, undertake such a task. Tom offered to *over-dub some sick rhymes* if we threw a Childish Gambino track in, but I had literally no idea what he was talking about and Grace just rolled her eyes in my direction and whispered 'OK, Boomer', which caused Tom to almost piss himself laughing.

'I am not a Boomer,' I said, outraged. 'Baby boomers are Granny's generation.'

'Sorry, mate, it's anyone over forty,' Grace said with a *What can you do?* face. 'You're Boomers, we're Snowflakes. It's, like, the law.'

I ignored them and lined up John Denver as my next track. Ha, that'll show them.

–

We were all still laughing about each other's song choices when Sam got back from work at eight. He came and joined us and I shamelessly pounced on the opportunity for 'quality time', opening a bottle of wine and playing songs from our university days to properly educate the offspring. When we were certain that they had mastered the fundamental differences between The Stone Roses and The Charlatans, and that they realised how much artists like Jay-Z were indebted to Public Enemy and N.W.A, we let them go to bed.

I was hoping that this fond musical reminiscence session would act as a kind of couples therapy, reinforcing the marital bonds and perhaps leading to a bit of marital action, but unfortunately Sam had to take a call from work just after nine so I stayed in the kitchen scribbling ideas down for breaking the choir into harmony groups instead. This was an ambitious task, because any of our singers (with or without dementia) could decide on one day that they were an alto and the next a tenor-bass. It had even been known for both Margaret and Jan to drop two or three octaves within the same song before they 'found their voice', as Fizz called it. But there were some natural groupings and several of the carers were quite musically talented themselves. Tina, for example, was an obvious contralto but could manage a mezzo-soprano and would probably be able to rein in Marie, whose vocal range was somewhere in the zone only dogs could hear. Clive, on the other hand, had a lovely rich baritone and Ernest was marginally less likely to swear if his son was leading that section.

We had a practice session yesterday and I implemented some of my changes. The group are disappointed that Fizz is no longer leading us – I don't have quite her level of eponymous effervescence – but they all seem extremely happy with my keyboard accompaniment. This is gratifying, I won't lie. Having my musical skills appreciated by a group of pensioners takes me right back to playing the recorder at Wellhouse Nursing Home aged eight. There's also a great deal of enthusiasm about the fact that we are going ahead with the performance. Not least from me – I'm enjoying the preparatory work immensely; relishing the challenge. The show must go on, et cetera. Sam's very tentative suggestion that I might be taking on a bit too much was roundly rebuffed by me and the kids – and Mum, if you include being hit with a slipper as a rebuff, which I think you can. To be fair, he was only echoing my initial thoughts when Fizz had made her proposition, but doubts about my own capabilities are very much *my* domain, and for personal use only, thank you very much.

Chapter Forty

Mum and I had our appointment at the genetics clinic today, which was neither the challenge nor the moment of epiphany that I had anticipated. Over the past couple of weeks, I had been stewing over the probability of my own imminent cognitive decline and having a near heart attack every time I forgot the name of the person I was talking to, or walked into a room and couldn't remember why I'd gone in there. However, today I was rapidly disabused of the notion that there was a simple test to either confirm the worst or put my mind at rest. Dr Carlton, an elegant woman in linen, advised us that the genetic risks of dementia are difficult to predict in the majority of cases and blood tests can only check for a few specific markers thought to be linked to familial Alzheimer's and something called frontotemporal dementia.

'You're unlikely to have one of the directly inherited single-gene mutations,' she said, speaking to Mum as she flicked through the questionnaire we'd completed via the GP. 'Given that you're the only person in the family with the condition. But we'll test you for them just in case.'

'Hmmm?' Mum started to pluck at her trousers, an early warning that she was feeling unsettled. I rested my hand gently on hers to still them as Dr Carlton continued.

'As I understand it, Mrs Andrews, you were only sixty three when the dementia was diagnosed?'

The plucking of the trousers intensified, as did the pressure of my hand over hers.

'And at that time no genetic testing was requested?' Dr Carlton looked back towards me. 'I'm intrigued,' she said. 'What's brought you here now, seven years later?'

I stifled a sigh. 'My brother mainly,' I said. 'He's a doctor. He said we should get some baseline genetic information about Mum's condition and that it would be worth assessing my own level of risk.'

She nodded.

'It's not just that though,' I said. 'I suppose now that Mum's living with me I've seen what the condition entails.' I puffed out my cheeks. 'So I wanted to know whether I might end up with the same thing, whether the kids are at risk. I just need a bit of clarity.' As I voiced my concern about the children, I realised that I still haven't had a conversation with Sam about the fact that I was investigating my own risk of hereditary Alzheimer's. I guess I'm hoping the tests will be clear, thus avoiding the need for lengthy discussions about my husband's potential willingness to care for me long term as I develop an incurable, debilitating condition. Let's face it, that's not a conversation anyone wants to have over a rushed microwave dinner.

We talked about the practicalities of testing and decided that the best place to start was the index case – or Mum, as she is otherwise known. Dr Carlton advised again that the chances of her testing positive for a directly inherited trait were low. 'You may have heard of variant testing?' she said. 'The APOE gene?'

'Not really,' I said, not wanting to admit that I had been googling these things for the past four weeks and had already convinced myself that I had Parkinson's, Huntingdon's and a rare form of absence seizure syndrome.

'The APOE testing is not especially helpful at the moment,' she said as she labelled up a bottle for the sample. 'Lots of false positives, poor predictive value and it's not available on the NHS. You can buy self-testing kits commercially. I would advise against it, but if you do, make sure you go through an accredited organisation. There are some horribly unscrupulous individuals out there.'

I know, I thought to myself. *I've joined the mailing list for half of them.*

–

Before we left, Dr Carlton took me to one side and reiterated her concerns. 'We're only testing your mother,' she said. 'But if her sample does show one of the rare gene mutations it doesn't necessarily mean you need to get yourself tested, or your brother, or your children. Each person can make their own decision and there's no right or wrong answer.' She smiled. 'Knowledge isn't always power.'

Chapter Forty-One

Friday, 13 June

Tonight I went out with Zahara again. We managed one night out with Joy and Caz last week, but there wasn't really an opportunity to chat because the night in question was the living hell of a PTA fundraising trip to a local art installation, where Tiggy and Lindi asked parents to part with a princely sum in order to gaze in wonder at an unmade bed.

'Um, is this not a bit derivative?' I'd muttered to Caz in my best art-critic voice, which clearly carried further than I had intended because Tiggy piped up immediately.

'The more discerning among you will have certainly noticed that there are some similarities between Indi's work,' she put her arm around a startled-looking millennial, 'and that of Tracey Emin.' She looked over to me with a sickly smile. 'But if you look closely there are some *subtle* differences that some of you may not have picked up on.' She laughed. 'I'm lucky, people say I have a bit of a natural eye for these things, but I know that true art doesn't speak to everyone in the same way. As Indi said to me only this evening, "Not everyone can be as intuitive as you, Tiggy!" And she's right.' She gave a little toss of her hair and I watched Joy reach over for another glass of lukewarm prosecco and swallow half of it in one gulp. 'In fact, sometimes I wonder if it's perhaps more of a curse than a blessing, to have such a *communion* with one's inner artiste.' Tiggy gave a rueful smile.

'Is she on crack, d'you think?' Joy leant over and asked me. 'I mean, seriously? What the actual?'

'She wouldn't sully her body with crack cocaine, Joy,' I said. 'Now, her inner artiste, that's a different story. I bet her inner artiste is a massive caner.' Joy snorted her mouthful of prosecco up her nose and began coughing while I smiled back at Tiggy, nodding with interest as she warbled on about taking art in new directions and how fortunate we were to be raising such a talent in our midst.

'Indi has kindly agreed to run a session with the children in Badger class later in the term and I for one can't wait to see what my little Reuben will come up with.' Tiggy crinkled her nose up in delight at the prospect of her son's artistically unmade bed. I'll have to alert her to the fact that this is a regular feature in our house if she ever wants to come around and commune with her inner artiste in Tom's room.

We enjoyed ourselves in spite of, or perhaps because of, Tiggy's ridiculous affectations. I have found that since the encounters between my mother and the leader of the mummy-coven, I have felt a lot braver about confronting some of Tiggy's bullshit. OK, maybe not *confronting* it exactly, but not caring so much about what she, or anyone else, thinks. I've thrown down the gauntlet of bringing shop-bought cakes to the Easter bake sale. I said an outright 'No' to spending my Saturday cleaning out the village-hall toilets so that she could run a fashion show (which she was modelling in). I turned down her kind offer of maintaining the school allotment in my free time; walked away from the role of parent helper at the after-school embroidery club and did not reply to the email requesting volunteers to collect fees, order the bus and check the parachutes for the half-term trip to the hang-gliding centre.

Instead, Zahara, Caz, Joy and I make it our mission to support the school by attending PTA events wherever possible (no matter how bonkers they may be) and we spend a lot of money at the bar, which, as we all know, is the biggest source of revenue. The amount Joy alone has spent on warm sparkling wine would pay for a new wet-play area and Evangeline is yet to start school. By the time she leaves year six, Joy will probably have paid for an entirely new wing of the building (maybe it could be a school pub?). We embrace fundraising within the constraints of our own family lives. Perhaps because my home life is now more manic than I could ever have possibly imagined, the school run no longer fills me with dread. What does it matter if Maisie's entry to the best-dressed wheelbarrow competition is literally a wheel-barrow with a dress on? Why would I care if Tom's shirt looks as if it has been dragged through a hedge? It probably has. As long as my kids get to their lessons and come home again in one piece without having inflicted distress upon anyone else or caused significant disruption, I'm happy. It's not setting the bar very high, I know, but when life is full to bursting with genuine emergencies and crises, the little things pale into insignificance.

–

Zahara, it appears, is having a similar epiphany to me, but hers has been initiated by an errant husband rather than a mother with dementia. She too has eschewed some of the trappings of her perfect life, having now realised it was not quite as perfect as she had previously thought. The kids and the house still look immaculate but the insane level of wholesome craft activity has been replaced with a bit more time on the Xbox. And Maisie revealed the shocking news last week that Darcy had come to preschool with a Cadbury's Mini Roll in her packed lunch. I chose not to mention this significant lowering of standards when we met for a drink this evening – *let he who is without sin* and all that. We returned to our previous haunt of The Red Lion, except this time we were able to sit outside for a few minutes with the late evening sun warming our cheeks. We even ordered a bottle of rosé, so it must be summer.

Zahara looked gorgeous. Five feet and nine inches of tanned, toned loveliness that half the aged population at the bar could barely take their eyes off – women included. I felt pasty and dumpy in comparison – like a lump of old dough. But behind the Dolce & Gabbana sunglasses, Zahara's expression was one of a woman scorned. And indeed, Hell hath not seen fury like it.

'The fucking useless son of a bitch who can't keep his dick in his fucking trousers…' was how she began her description of Hugh. And it only got worse. He'd been at it again with Nadia-the-twenty-eight-year-old and evidently the 'my family comes first' line had been superseded by 'Hugh comes first – and usually inside Nadia'.

'He was back on the phone to her a week later and shagging her again the week after that,' said Zahara, clinking the ice cubes in her glass for me to top it up. 'So, a "conscious uncoupling" it is, to use your phrase. Hugh's moved in with Nadia, who still lives with her parents, so that should prove to be an interesting set-up. I've been to see a solicitor and the divorce papers are being prepared as we speak.'

'How are the kids?' I asked. 'How much do they know?'

'Well, if you're asking whether they realise their father is a cheating, lying scumbag then the answer is no. We've told them that Mummy and Daddy realised they didn't love each other anymore and that Daddy found someone else he thought he might love, or maybe not love, maybe just enjoys sticking his dick into – obviously didn't say that – and they seem OK about it. They've got enough friends whose parents live apart to understand and most of their concerns are practical, you know what kids are like, even sensitive little souls like mine. Rex wanted to know whether he would be able to take his games console to Daddy's new house and Darcy made him a collage to stick on his wall in case he missed us and then asked if we could get ice-cream the next time we went to the supermarket.'

'They're a great leveller,' I said. 'You can't get too immersed in your own sorrow when there are kids around.'

'Ain't that the truth.' She sighed and rested her head back against the red brick of the pub wall. 'And at least they don't have to move schools now. Hugh was all for them starting at St Bartholomew's, wanted to get them into the prep system ready for Common Entrance like he did. I mean Darcy's still at preschool, for God's sake. Anyway. I've put the brakes on that. Argued that they needed stability, although the truth is I simply can't face the thought of Rex wearing one of those ludicrous boaters.'

The selfish part of me was inwardly rejoicing that Zahara's kids would still be attending the same school as mine and that she wouldn't have to go and socialise with all the St Bart's mums (who I'm sure are very nice but they do like to set themselves apart). 'Yeah,' I said. 'But it might have been worth it just to see Tiggy's face. Can you imagine casually parading Rex through the village wearing the hat and blazer? Catch the woe, as Grace says.'

Zahara laughed. 'To be honest, the whole thing's a bit of a relief, not just the school issue.' She sat forward and swirled her glass. 'I wonder if we've been living a lie for a long time now. It's like I was sleepwalking, all those years, going through the motions, and now I'm awake.' She nodded. 'It's good. Or at least, if not good, it's OK.'

I had to concede, she did look as though a weight had been lifted from her shoulders. She was angry, of course, who wouldn't be? To be lied to and then lied to again, by the person who was supposed to be in your corner, that was tough. But her anger is a grown-up version; tempered and pragmatic. It's as if Hugh has only confirmed her suspicions that he was never good enough for her and now she's had verification, she can move on. There was something about her cool detachment that made me feel, not envious exactly, but a bit naive. As if the notion of a lasting relationship and a faithful husband was childish, a false aspiration foisted upon girls from an early age, and once you'd grown up a bit you realised that you didn't actually need a man at all and independent living was the ultimate goal. I felt as if suddenly she was further along life's journey than me and was therefore more knowing, more sophisticated and more mature. While still looking like a teenager.

When I got home later that evening, Sam was with Mum in the sitting room watching the television.

'Zahara and Hugh are splitting up,' I said, dropping my coat on the chair.

Sam raised his eyebrows. 'God, how sad,' he said. 'I thought, I just assumed they were...'

'Happy together? The perfect couple?' I finished for him. I was cross and I didn't know why. 'Evidently not. He's been having an affair with a much younger woman apparently.' I checked Sam's face carefully for tell-tale signs of a *Go on my son!* response, but there was none. 'You'd better never even *think* of doing that to me,' I said, still feeling unnecessarily belligerent.

'God, Penny. Don't be stupid. 'Course I wouldn't. Don't have the energy for one thing...'

I smiled and gave him a peck on the cheek. 'I know, old man. Just checking.'

He got up out of his chair. 'You have a sit down here with your mum. I'm just going to pop Colin out and then I'll head off to bed.' He kissed my forehead. 'I'm glad you saw Zahara tonight. Sounds like she needs a friend at the moment. Sorry to hear about her and Hugh.'

'Well, it's never the ones you expect, is it.' I said a little sadly. 'Night, love.'

'Night.' He raised his voice slightly and called over to Mum, 'Night, Mary.'

Mum didn't acknowledge him but this wasn't unusual; I wasn't entirely sure that she knew her own name anymore. I sat down next to her on the sofa and she reflexively put an arm around my shoulders, eyes still fixed on the screen. For some reason, tears had started to roll down my cheeks. The realisation that Hugh could be such a bastard, and a repeat offender at that. To my lovely friend, the best of women. And that I had fallen for the veneer of marital perfection when in reality their relationship was riddled with cracks and sink-holes like a mansion with subsidence. I lay my head against the reassuringly solid warmth of my mum and closed my eyes.

'Shush, shush, dear,' she said, her voice soothing, bringing back memories of grazed knees, failed exams and broken hearts. 'Everything'll be all right.'

Chapter Forty-Two

Saturday, 21 June

A beautiful sunny morning for choir practice at Bob and Tina's. I feel like we're really coming together as a cohesive group now. Our sound is more rounded and developed, and the enthusiasm and commitment of all the singers is self-evident. Edith breaking off into a provocative dance routine certainly lifted everyone's spirits and Clive had brought two packets of sherbet lemons, which he distributed eagerly once we'd finished rehearsing (it being extremely hard to enunciate with a sherbet lemon in your mouth, let alone sing). The weather was glorious and the sash windows in the drawing room were opened to their fullest extent so that half the town were treated to our rendition of 'Livin' on a Prayer'. It even prompted the gardener to stop his pruning for a moment and sashay among the roses when he thought nobody was looking (I was).

–

Zahara and I went shopping this afternoon and left Sam optimistically filling up the paddling pool. He had initially queried my request for a new outfit for his work summer party, suggesting that I had 'loads of clothes that would be suitable' but I countered this with the old *important that I look the part* routine – saying that I needed something a bit more up-to-date and appropriate in order to mingle with the other partners. The truth was that fitting in with Sam's colleagues' wives was the least of my worries compared to fitting into my old dresses. During the week I'd tried on a couple of stalwart favourites, dresses that could usually be relied upon to cinch in a waist or cover up a tummy. Clearly, however, I was confusing reliable with magical. After I'd split a hole in the seam of one garment and trapped my back fat in the zip of another, I burst into tears and collapsed in a big heap on the floor, vowing to purchase something glamorous to accommodate and disguise my lardiness, as it was now too late to diet. Honestly, it's so annoying. I thought that anxiety and stress was supposed to make you thin. Clearly that advice doesn't apply if you use cake and wine as a coping mechanism.

The trip was moderately successful. I've ended up with a dark green, ankle-length slip dress, which, when teamed with a new shrug to cover the bingo wings and a pair of sparkling red three-inch heels (I know!) for extra height, makes me look a little more elegant. The green and red do lend an unintentional Christmassy feel to the outfit, which is probably why both items were reduced and therefore affordable. Although the red heels may have been cheaper simply due to the fact that they are almost unwearable, as I have found since returning home and actually taking more than a few dainty steps around a cubicle. No matter. I shall be tall and therefore slim – who cares if I can walk?

The trip was also a success due to a conversation with Zahara over coffee when we were both exhausted by retail and I needed a break from staring at my wobbly body, split-ended greying hair and leathery face in three-way mirrors. It turns out that she is finding the weekends when Hugh has the kids less of a blast than she expected; perhaps originally anticipating some kind of high-octane social life emerging from the wreck of her domestic idyll. Instead of going out clubbing and partying until dawn, Zahara spent the first weekend *sans enfants* sitting in her tracksuit, eating an entire M&S choux-pastry platter and sobbing in front of the television. She related this tale with trademark sincerity and her frankness almost made me weep.

'It was astonishing,' she said, looking truly outraged at her own lack of resilience. 'When I think of all the design work I could have got on with; there are two chairs that need re-upholstering, a mood board to update, fabric swatches to source, colour schemes to create. Or I could have gone to the cinema, or a park, or the gym, or a spa... But I just couldn't get out of the house. I felt as though leaving the immediate vicinity of my children's bedrooms might somehow jeopardise their return; that they might need me to be available at any given moment, that Hugh might completely forget how to parent while he's with Nadia.' She toyed with a napkin. 'Or worse still, that they might like Nadia more than me and decide to move in with her permanently.'

'Well, that's understandable,' I said. 'Both the anxiety of separation and the concerns about Hugh, although I think we both know that Nadia is unlikely to provide much in the way of maternal challenge; not now, not ever.'

'Yes, but logic went completely out of the window. Which is why I need to make sure I have a cast-iron reason to be out of the house next time.' She gestured to the waiter for the bill as I finished off the rest of her Eccles cake.

'So, I was thinking,' she continued once the waiter had spotted her and signalled that yes, he would be with us imminently. (Zahara is always completely oblivious to the speed with which mere mortals of the male persuasion respond to her every whim. She doesn't have any concept of the eternity that it takes most of us to be served at the bar or attended to in a shop or restaurant scenario.) 'I was wondering, given your tricky situation as regards what to do with your Mum and the kids when you're at this work do, why don't I babysit? You'd be doing me a favour really.' She smiled up at the strapping gap-year student currently poised with the contactless payment machine and tapped her card gently along its side, unaware of the effect this simple action was having on him.

'You don't need to do that, Zahara,' I said (really thinking that this would be the most perfect solution to what was proving to be a complex conundrum: what to do when you need a babysitter and a respite carer on the same evening). 'It would be a massive undertaking, the kids are tricky enough, but Mum…'

'I know your mum,' she said, tucking her purse back in her bag. 'And she knows me. The kids know me. It's not like getting some teenager only a few years older than Grace to come along and eat all your snacks and do bugger all. In fact, the easiest thing would probably be for me to stay over. You said that Sam's company had a block booking on a hotel for the night? Well, how about, instead of you guys having to leave early and come home in the small hours, I stay over and you have some "quality time" together overnight.' She gave me a broad wink and a nudge.

'Quality time in A&E if those heels have anything to do with it,' I said, although I was starting to wonder if she might be on to something. When was the last time Sam and I had a night away together, anywhere, let alone a swanky London hotel? And we could go for breakfast in Soho the next morning like we used to before the kids came along and reduced our leisure time to endless trips back and forth from sports pitch to play park. Maybe this was the opportunity I'd been looking for – a chance to reconnect with my husband?

'You would be doing me a favour,' Zahara repeated. 'Honestly. I need something to keep me occupied.'

'Well, my family can certainly be relied upon to do that,' I said, little realising how ominous these words would prove to be.

–

When I got back home, Sam had taken Maisie, Tom and the dog to the park. The paddling pool was a soggy plastic puddle where Colin had punctured the inflatable part of the wall and the water had oozed slowly into the lawn. Grace was curled up on the sofa with Mum, who looked up in concern at my arrival. She pointed at Grace.

'She's feeling a bit,' she paused, 'grey?'

'Sad?' I said, sitting down next to them both. 'Are you feeling sad, Gracie?'

Grace nodded glumly. 'S'pose. A bit.'

'Do you want to talk about it?'

'No.'

'OK. I'll go and unpack my things and get the kettle on. There are some lollies in the freezer. Do you want one?'

She nodded and ambled off to the kitchen.

'Phone,' Mum said, her expression worried again.

I picked up the offending article. 'Hmm, the root of all our woes,' I said and took it through to Grace, thinking that it might act as a prompt. 'Looks like you've got a couple of new messages,' I said. She shrugged and made no move to take the phone or look at it.

'I'll just plug it in over here and let it charge,' I said. 'Could you get me a Twister please?'

She pulled two lollies out of the freezer. 'I'm not going to look at it for the rest of the weekend,' she said, gesturing towards her phone as she ripped the wrapper off her Fab. I nodded non-committally and left a long pause for her to fill.

'Looks like Dillon's got back together with Jade,' she said eventually. Her mumble was almost indecipherable.

'Dillon, was that the boy who…'

'Yeah.'

'And Jade was the one who… Easter Sunday…'

'Yeah, that's her.'

'They'd split up, had they?' I peeled the wrapper off my Twister.

'Well, that's what he told me. Dickhead.'

'Grace!'

'Well. He is.'

I went to go and put my arm around her, which she managed to just about tolerate. 'Sounds like they deserve each other then, hey?'

She nodded. 'S'pose.'

'Do you want to see if Clark or Rani want to come for a sleepover tonight? Maybe you could watch a film, I'll do some popcorn?'

She smiled and gave me the tiniest of squeezes before moving away. 'Yes, thanks Mum. That's a good idea.'

So, Clark came over to stay and Dillon was discussed *at length*. Mum managed to avoid causing the level of offense she did last time, when we had many loud conversations along the following lines: 'I know Clark looks like a girl, Mum, but she, *they*, don't identify as one. No, don't tell them it's a shame that young ladies don't wear pretty things anymore or ask Clark why they've had their hair cut like that.' This time Mum simply gave Clark an unprompted cuddle when they walked through the door and made no further reference to their life-choices or self-identification.

'I like your gran,' Clark was overheard saying to Grace as they sat in the kitchen trawling through their phones. 'She's a bit, like, bonkers. But she's all right.'

Yep, that just about covers it.

Chapter Forty-Three

Another rehearsal and this time on the Sabbath – how appropriate for our choir of angels. I persuaded all the children to come to over to Bob and Tina's again, but this time using the lure of the indoor swimming pool. Apparently, we're doing Tina a favour because since Bob stopped his twice-daily backstroke, the filter has been clogging up due to lack of use, So, similar to Easter when my children were invaluable in hoovering up the excess baked goods and confectionery items in Tina's kitchen, they are now equally instrumental in maintaining the pool to a high standard simply by splashing around in their armbands doing doggy paddle and bombing into it. It's a hard life.

Clive had brought George – his colleague's son – along today to discuss our lighting and sound-engineering requirements. He's at the local tech college in town doing a diploma in stage management and production so he knows his stuff, but he's painfully shy. I don't know who felt more awkward, him or Grace, when they bumped into each other in the hallway. She, clad in her bikini and shorts, ready to head for the pool, and him, shuffling awkwardly through the front door with his sound deck. It certainly made a difference to the vocal performance though and I think George came away with a better idea of the calibre of musicians he was dealing with. I heard him muttering about a special high-frequency microphone for Marie and perhaps a muffler for Ernest, so you've got to commend his grasp of a situation.

Once we'd had a chance to practice with some of the equipment, I talked George through the set-up at the town hall and he sketched out a plan for us. It was warm in Tina's drawing room. The sun was streaming through the windows throwing large squares of light onto the parquet flooring and George was looking a little flushed, so I suggested that he have a swim as well. He sheepishly withdrew a pair of trunks from his bag and said that Clive had mentioned the pool.

Tina watched him wander off to the bathroom to change, his shorts loose around his hips, his gait shambolic. 'He's just at that age, isn't he?' she said. 'Part awkward teenager and part young man. Still, I can't tell you how glad I am to have the pool being used. You tell those kids of yours to stay as long as they like and come back any evening or weekend they want.'

I smiled. 'They'll never want to leave. What with your baking and the pool, it's like the ultimate luxury retreat.' We were now in the vast kitchen and I sat back in one of the armchairs, closed my eyes and felt the warmth of the sun beating through the window onto my cheeks.

'That's a lovely thing to say,' said Tina. 'I've always wanted a home where people felt like that. Mind you, I'd better not leave Bobby for too long…' She stuck her head around the door where she had sight of the drawing room.

'They'll be fine,' I said. 'Clive's in there. And a few moments away from Bob won't hurt.'

Tina had put the kettle on and pulled up a chair alongside me. 'No, I know. It does help, having everyone here to keep him occupied. Allows me a moment to catch my breath.'

I looked at her closely. She was wearing a short-sleeved blouse and there were no signs of the ugly bruises from before. 'Have you been finding things difficult?' I said. 'Any more difficult than usual, I mean.'

She shook her head. 'No, we're OK. I promise. I spoke to Anita and we've got carers coming in during the evening now, which is when he used to be most agitated. They help me get him upstairs and ready for bed.'

'Result.'

'Yes.' She smiled. 'Although to be honest, it won't be long before he can't get upstairs. I'm thinking we'll either get a stair lift or maybe just relocate to one of the downstairs rooms in the east side of the building.'

'How many rooms have you got?' I asked. 'Sorry, I'm just being nosy.'

She laughed self-consciously. 'Fourteen bedrooms if you include the stable block and the gatehouse. I know, it's ridiculous isn't it?'

'Whoa! Fourteen bedrooms *and* the swimming pool.'

'And the tennis court and the acres of garden… I know. It was our pride and joy this house, still is, but no amount of money buys you a cure does it? I'd live in a cardboard box if it meant Bobby didn't have dementia.' She spoke without sentiment, simply stating facts. And I believed her. The luxury of their surroundings only served to throw their losses into stark relief. We sat in silence for a while before Tina shifted in her chair. 'Come on,' she said. 'Let's rescue Clive and then we can go and see how the kids are getting on in the pool.'

I groaned as I stood up out of my chair. 'Must we?' I said. 'Feels like you've just told me the holiday's over.'

Tina took my mug. 'I'm not sure my kitchen qualifies as a holiday destination,' she said, smiling.

'You'd be surprised.' I stretched my arms above my head. 'A trip to the dental hygienist feels like a vacation at the moment. Anyway, your house is one of the only places I'm confident leaving Mum and the kids on their own. It takes the worry out of everything.'

'I know what you mean,' she said. 'Having you all here makes it more relaxing for me too. It's nice having company for a start, but I don't feel like Bob or I have to put on a performance for anyone in the choir group.'

'Well, there is the small matter of an *actual performance* that we are putting on...' I said as we crossed the hallway, pausing by the window to the pool area where we could see the kids and George racing each other up and down the swimming lanes. 'But yes, it's easier here – being around other people who *get it*. Wouldn't it be great if it could always be like this? Just a whole heap of us together like a commune or a – I don't know...'

'A dementia spa hotel?'

'Exactly!'

She laughed. 'Come on, let's see what they're up to,' she said, crossing to the other side of the hall. 'Once more into the fray...'

We entered the drawing room and were greeted with a chorus of The White Stripes' 'Seven Nation Army', conducted by Clive who was chuckling away as he picked out the introductory notes on the piano. Tina and I looked at each other and smiled.

'Good to see that there's still joy to be had,' she said.

Chapter Forty-Four

The past few rehearsals have been going well and in addition to our twice-weekly sessions in the village hall we have at least two at Bob and Tina's, so most of our singers are now familiar with the songs and the lyrics, if not the correct order to put them in. I'm really enjoying the process of bringing the event together; it's a long time since I worked on a task that had a definitive completion date and a logical sequence of events leading to it. There are random elements, of course – any time I become too complacent one of our singers will wander off, insist on performing in the car park or simply refuse to participate. But generally, having a planned timetable and working towards a tangible goal is really satisfying. Perhaps more so than other aspects of my life, such as the unending chaos of running a household or the unpredictability of raising children.

I think maybe I've forgotten what it feels like to have an element of control over a project. While I've never exactly been a high-flyer, I have in the past enjoyed being part of a team and working on a shared venture. To me, the summer concert feels like I'm dipping a toe back into the turbid waters of industry. That probably sounds ludicrous and my brother would have a field day sneering at my self-aggrandisement. But despite it not being my first choice of undergraduate course, I did put my business studies degree to good use and in my twenties, when Sam and I were both living in London, I relished the hustle of working in a big office. I wasn't the one setting the targets or leading the projects, but I was involved, learning the ropes, climbing the ladder (and other PE-related metaphors). I also enjoyed having my own salary, although that diminished significantly when I went part-time after having Grace, and once I'd had Tom I gave up work entirely. There just seemed so little point in fitting the needs of two very tiny people around what by then was purely an administrative role. I was unfulfilled on two counts, as a mother and as a worker. Better to concentrate on one thing I could do well. At least, that's what I thought.

–

I was out with the girls tonight. We were round at Joy's for what was supposed to be 'a glass of Pimm's' but, given the fact that High-powered Joy herself was in charge of weights and measures, the glasses were actually *full of Pimm's* with only a splash of lemonade and a token cucumber slice to absorb the alcohol. Joy had over-imbibed while checking her dilutions, or lack thereof, and was wanging on about the stresses of her career. But even mid-description of a particularly demanding client, she did acknowledge that having a job gives her another string to her bow and that sometimes, when Evangeline is being a pain or she contemplates a time when her daughter flies the nest, she has the inner security of knowing there are other roles for her and alternative ways to occupy her time.

Zahara agreed. She has become more accepting of Joy's brusque attitude now and after a few stern words from our high-powered friend about standing up to Hugh, she has come to see the benefits of having a fierce ally in your corner (as well as a job to provide distraction from her car-crash of a marriage), although she admitted that she is not managing as well as she'd hoped. Hugh has told her that they need to sell the house so that he and Nadia can buy a flat together, and throwing estate agents into the mix along with divorce lawyers and precarious finances has resulted in a trip to the doctors and a prescription for antidepressants.

'We can't all be copers like you,' she said, plucking a soggy cucumber slice from her glass.

I tried to correct her. 'You mean Joy,' I said. 'We can't all be like Joy.'

'No!' Zahara lurched in her chair and her Pimm's sloshed ominously. 'No offense, Joy,' she said, tilting her head in Joy's direction. 'I mean you, Penny Baker. All the stuff that you've got going on with the kids and your mum's dementia and your dad in hospital and your crazy dog and running the choir... It'd make my head explode.'

'She's right,' said Joy. 'I see you sorting things out for your mum, chasing after social services and carers and therapists, how you're tenacious and determined and committed. *And* you still manage to keep a smile on your face. You,' she jabbed a finger in my direction, 'are a plucky little trouper – like one of those heroic cartoon dogs.'

Zahara laughed and this prompted a lengthy discussion of exactly which animal would best represent each of us in an animated film biography, but I really felt I had

313

to correct their misapprehension of me as someone in control of her life.

'I am not that person,' I said. 'No, I'm really not. What you maybe don't see is that most of the time I feel like I'm completely falling apart. I just seem to lurch from one disaster to another, making mistakes, dropping the bloody baton, over and over again. You ask my kids. And my husband. And my brother for that matter. I don't think they'd agree that I'm coping. They'd tell you I'm a shambles,' I laughed. 'And they'd be right.'

Joy was shaking her head. 'Mate,' she said. 'You are a coper. You are the definition of a multi-tasker and, make no mistake, you're more resilient than the rest of us put together.'

'Amen!' Zahara clinked her glass against mine. 'You, Penny, are the master of your own destiny, you are the author of your own story...'

I took her glass off her and put it down firmly on the table. 'And you, my friend, are very, very drunk.'

–

I got home to find that I'd missed a call from Rory. 'He's flying back over here again in a couple of weeks,' said Sam, writing it onto the calendar. He clocked my expression. 'I wouldn't read anything into it,' he said. 'Probably just wants to see your dad. He's not checking up on you.'

I smiled. 'You know me too well,' I said and gave him a squeeze. 'Is Candice coming too?'

'No. Couldn't get leave apparently.'

'Hmmm. Or the relationship's in trouble and he's fleeing the country for "a bit of space". You know what he's like.'

Sam shook his head. 'No, didn't sound like that. She probably just really can't take any more time off work. I'm surprised Rory can, to be honest. Anyway, Grace wanted to know if you were going to Tina's tomorrow? She mentioned something about swimming?'

'Oh, yes, we've got another choir practice booked and I'm sure Tina would be glad to have her there. We could all pop over as a family?' I said hopefully. 'It would be so nice for you to meet them all and you should see their place, it's just amazing; the pool, the grounds. It's great fun.'

His face fell. 'Oh, Pen, I'd have loved to.' He sounded as though he genuinely meant it. 'I've got to work. It's this project that Brian wants finished and I just...'

'On a Saturday?' I frowned as a thought occurred to me. 'Are you going into the office?'

'I might need to.'

'Just you, or other *colleagues*?' I almost stumbled over the word.

'Just me,' he said, looking confused. 'I *will* try, Pen. I know I'm working a lot at the moment but I'm doing it for us. For the family. With your mum here – well, money's a bit tight... I'll see if I can clear the decks by midday and maybe join you over there?'

'Yep.' I tried not to stomp as I went upstairs or mutter *what-ev-errr* too loudly, being aware that my daughter must get it from somewhere. But I was unconvinced about the likelihood of his making an appearance as well as being annoyed that he was trying to blame Mum for our precarious finances, and slightly anxious about who he would be spending the day with instead of his family.

Chapter Forty-Five

I was right. At least about Sam not making it to Bob and Tina's. The kids and I were there well into the afternoon. What with the weather being so glorious, Tina had opened up all the bifold doors and the roof-lights over the pool, and even I had brought my swimsuit. Once the singers had departed with their various carers and relatives, the kids and I (along with George, who had also made another appearance despite there being no obvious lighting or sound requirements to address) had an hour's swimming while Mum sat on one of the loungers next to Tina. Bob had only been able to make a limited contribution to one or two songs before he fell asleep in his chair, but Tina wheeled him out onto the patio near the open pool doors so that he could feel the sun on his face and hear the happy cries of the children as they splashed in and out of the water – and my less happy cries as I was catapulted out of my inflatable unicorn and into the deep end by my son.

When we got home, we discovered that in an attempt to redeem himself Sam had stopped off at the garden centre and bought a new paddling pool with sturdy, Colin-proof sides. I thought that the kids, fresh from their contact with a heated, chlorinated and properly filtered swimming pool, would turn up their noses at the ice bath now on offer (which already had half a ton of dry grass floating in it, how was that even possible?), but I was underestimating the power of The Paddling Pool In Your Own Actual Garden. Daddy had nailed it (not literally) and they all leapt straight in. Sam poured me a Pimm's (normal strength as opposed to Joy's oesophageal burners) and asked all about the choir session, how everyone was doing, whether Bob was still going downhill and whether Tina had baked anything special, until I forgave him.

–

The only thing that put my nose slightly out of joint was later this evening when I had a trawl through Facebook on the laptop again. There was nothing interesting on my home page, just the usual *Beautiful holiday for a beautiful family* comments under Tiggy's carefully-curated photos of half-term in the Maldives, so I sidled onto my husband's page, trying to be discreet. (Although Sam was glued to the television and wouldn't even have noticed if I'd been cruising Tinder, so there was no real need.) Lo and behold, there was supermodel Jenna, having this time messaged him about outfits for the summer party.

Hola! Sam the Man! began her fashion query.

> Haven't been to one of these big work events before, bit of a corporate-social virgin really!

(Really?)

> Was wondering what the score was in terms of dress code. Thought better ask you rather than Vron (!)

(Classy – taking the piss out of Veronica's fashion sense.)

And then helpfully, Jenna had posted a couple of photos of herself in different outfits, each captioned to assist my husband in his decision.

Too revealing? next to a picture of Jenna in a minuscule bandage dress, with just a glimpse of areola visible over the scrap of Lycra designated to keep her breasts modestly covered.

Too serious? next to a shot of her in a figure-hugging 'suit', peering over her glasses like a seventies Miss Moneypenny.

Too much? next to a frankly stunning ballgown that she clearly could have worn to the Met Gala in New York. Corporate-social virgin, my arse. If she's had the need for a dress like that she's more of a social-function expert than Paris Hilton.

She'd posted the photos on her own timeline, as well as thoughtfully sending them via direct message for Sam's personal perusal, and the public shots had attracted comments from far and wide, mostly from female friends who could barely contain their verbal diarrhoea: *Omigod-you-look-SO-amazing-all-of-those-dresses-look-stunning-the-bosses-won't-know-what-hit-them-are-you-after-a-promotion-?-wink-emoji-there's-only-one-kind-of-figure-they'll-all-be-looking-at-and-it's-not-on-a-spreadsheet-not-yet-anyway!-wink-emoji-hearts-for-eyes-emoji-heart-emoji-heart-emoji*, et cetera, et cetera. My husband had so far not replied to the direct message. It is possible that he might not have even seen this borderline porn on his timeline and there was a tiny part of me that toyed with the idea of replying on his behalf. *You look like a prostitute. You're fired – angry face emoji.* And then blocking her. But I knew that would catch up with me.

Instead I left the screen open on the Jenna-wank-page (as I shall now refer to it) and wondered if Sam would mention it. He hasn't so far.

Chapter Forty-Six

Thursday, 3 July

Letter from the GP surgery addressed to Mum. I took it to her and watched her open the envelope and look completely bemused at the contents before handing it back to me. 'Put it with the rest of the luggage please, Penelope. I'll deal with it after our tennis lesson.'

'Righto' I said. We obviously don't have a tennis lesson booked today or any other day. 'OK if I read it first?'

She shrugged. 'I think it's Barbara's tax return. I'm sure she won't mind.'

I nodded. 'Barbara?'

She puffed out in exasperation. 'Barbara. You know? Barbara. With the hanging baskets. And the thingy, with the moustache.'

The letter wasn't about Barbara, her tax, hanging baskets or moustache. It was a brief two lines asking Mrs Mary Andrews to attend the surgery to discuss her results from the genetics clinic. I read it out to Mum and she nodded. 'Yes. Exactly as I'd said, Penelope,' she said crossly. 'The doctors. And the... yes. Hmm.' She wandered into the hall and stood looking blankly at her own reflection in the mirror.

I'm not sure whether her difficulties are limited to correctly articulating the information she's gleaned or if she is now struggling to actually read. She won't admit to either of course, but I have noticed that when Maisie asks her to read a bedtime story she spends most of the time pointing to the pictures while Maisie trots out the lines she knows off by heart. They both enjoy the experience, but it seems that as quickly as my daughter gains vocabulary, my mother is losing it. Basic nouns and adjectives are often replaced with increasingly outlandish words and the result is sometimes total nonsense delivered in an utterly serious tone. I worry that one day she might not be able to communicate with us at all and keep thinking maybe I should ask her about all the important stuff now so that her useful knowledge, her memories and life experience are not lost forever. I read on an Alzheimer's website that one man had recorded interviews with his father over a period of years, detailing his thoughts and feelings about topics as diverse as the Suez crisis to what was his favourite cheese and why. Maybe that needs to go on the to-do list as well. Maybe I'm already too late.

Chapter Forty-Seven

The morning of the big work summer event dawned bright and sunny and all appeared to be right with the world. The children were on good form. Grace has perked up a bit in recent weeks with a combination of the choir sessions, swimming and possibly the attention from a certain sound and lighting expert – I saw George give her his number last week, *just in case she had any technical queries regarding the concert* (obviously). Mum stayed in bed until ten but with my help navigated her way in and out of the shower in under thirty minutes, something of a record for us – I felt like a pit-stop engineer as my driver passed under the chequered flag of the bathroom door with clean hair and scrubbed skin. Zahara arrived mid-afternoon, by which time I had managed to change the bedding in mine and Sam's room for freshly laundered and line-dried sheets – the height of luxury.

Sam and I left her with the children and Mum all sitting out in the garden, with strict instructions for Grace and Tom to help Zahara as much as possible. Even as I said this to them, the panic caused my throat to tighten and Grace had to rest her hand on my wrist and say, 'We'll be fine, Mum. Go and enjoy yourself,' which was touching, if a little unsettling.

We were staying in a small hotel on the other side of London from the party venue, having been too late to make the most of the group booking, so the logistics were a little fraught. I ended up with only twenty minutes to glam up before the taxi came to collect us, but we arrived at the party and, I'll admit, I was a bit giddy and excited. It was my first big night out in London town for years and the first opportunity to wear the dress. I was less excited about the heels (although still giddy because a three-inch stiletto will do that to you) and I managed to catch one of the buggers in my hem about fourteen times between the cab and our arrival at the divisional directors' table, where Brian immediately started talking to me about current fiscal policy. Veronica was sitting on the other side of me next to her partner, Glenda, who was a City analyst, and they were deep in conversation with Angus, another of Sam's colleagues, about retirement planning. So it was already a riotous affair.

Unfortunately, as is the way with these types of things, the meal (when it was eventually served) was delicious but minuscule. Combine this with free-flowing booze, a husband who was busy networking and a few months of poor sleep due to juggling an increasingly bonkers family life, and you have the recipe for a drunk and emotional Penny. Essentially, by ten o' clock I was an absolute mess. I decided in this state that the best option was to try my luck chatting with Veronica. I say chatting but she is quite a formidable woman and doesn't really *do* small talk. True to form, she settled in for a characteristically earnest discussion about the family.

'How *is* everything at home with your mother staying?' She launched straight in, no preamble. 'Sam has told us about a few of the challenges.'

'Oh, you know,' I said enigmatically, wafting my hands around. I always want to say *She's doing really well, thanks. In fact, she seems to be improving.* But I can't do that with any degree of honesty and the truth might put Veronica off her main course of partridge and quince ravioli, so I went for one of my stock answers. 'It's OK, thanks. We're managing.'

Veronica looked sceptical. 'Really?'

'Well, it's never going to be easy but you've just got to get on with it, haven't you?' (This was another phrase I kept in the jar by the door.)

She turned to me, abandoning her miniature pasta. 'Penny. My father had dementia. I know what it's like. You don't need to dress it up.'

This took me by surprise.

She continued. 'I know what it's like when people ask how things are and you try and make them feel more comfortable by pretending it's all fine and often it's not. It's a total bastard of a disease.'

'It is.' I'd put my knife and fork down and was giving her my full attention.

'I could never bring myself to say to friends, "Oh, you know, he's started parcelling up shit and putting it in his pocket, which is nice, so thanks for asking." The only person who knew the truth was Gee.' She gestured towards Glenda. 'And it nearly killed me, trying to put a brave face on the whole thing. It was a few years ago and he didn't live with me, thank goodness, because I'd never have managed to keep my sanity, let alone my job. So, fair play to you for taking it on.'

I was too relieved to speak for a few moments. As the youngsters say, I felt truly *seen* for the first time in ages. We ended up having a long conversation about the practical aspects of being a carer and I told her all about Singing for the Brain and how much I was enjoying the rehearsals for the upcoming concert.

'Sounds like a blast,' she said, topping my glass up with claret. 'Let me know the date, Gee and I would love to come.'

'Really? It's a bit out of your way,' I said. 'And the musical quality might not be quite what you're used to. It's hardly the ENO.'

'Oh, we saw them at Covent Garden only last week,' she said dismissively. 'Anyway, it does Gee and I a bit of good to get out to the provinces once in a while.' We both smiled and I looked around the table, noticing that Sam's seat had been vacant for some time.

'Hmmm. I appear to have lost my husband to the Bradford team again,' I said. 'I'd better just check everything's all right at home. I'll try and find some decent phone reception.'

I picked up my glass of claret and handbag and wobbled off to the cloakrooms, where I sent a quick text to Zahara. I didn't want to call and wake her up – it was now eleven o'clock and hopefully everyone would be tucked up in bed. I then got a little bit lost, ending up in the extravagantly titled Ladies Powder Room where a girl in a white jumpsuit was expertly reapplying her make-up. I took a second glance, thinking she looked familiar, and something twisted in my stomach as I realised she was Jenna; Jenna of the inappropriate Facebook photos and the 'my boss is such a great laugh' comments.

I suspected that she wouldn't have a clue who I was. Even if Sam had photos of me at work, I had my hair piled up, more make-up slapped on my face tonight than at any other time in my life, and the lighting was subdued enough to convey relative anonymity. I also had the misplaced confidence of being ever so slightly inebriated (absolutely hammered). I made a rash decision to try and do some digging.

(Note to self: in future, just don't. Don't ever do this again.)

'Love the jumpsuit,' I gushed, opening up my handbag and pulling out a lipstick to apply as I stood beside her.

She gave me a sideways glance. 'Thanks. It's Versace, actually.'

Versace – bloody hell. I must have looked surprised because she laughed. 'Oh, it's not *mine*. I'm renting it for the night. It's making me a bit paranoid actually. I'll lose the deposit if anything happens to it.'

It seemed the height of stupidity to rent a pure white outfit but it was clear that she never came into contact with anything remotely grubby like dogs or small children. 'Wow,' I said. 'Really pushing the boat out.'

She looked sheepish for a moment. 'Yeah, well, I wanted to make a big impression tonight.'

I tried to keep my voice casual as I applied a layer of gloss to my upper lip. 'Oh, yes. Trying to get someone's attention?'

She gave a self-deprecating little laugh that made me want to puke. 'Yeah, my boss actually.' She clocked my expression but mistook it for pity. 'I know, it's such a cliché.'

'No!' I was overzealous in my reassurance. 'It's only a cliché because it happens all the time. I mean, people spend a lot of time together at work, don't they? These things happen.' I spoke the next sentence through gritted teeth but she didn't notice. 'He's a lucky guy anyway. You look amazing.'

'Yeah, thanks.' She preened a little in the mirror and pouted her lips to check the outline. 'He's married though.'

Bang – there went any hope of the man she was referring to not being my Sam. My fingers were holding the wand from the lip gloss so tightly they went white.

Jenna had clearly decided I was interested in her predicament (well, I *was* interested but not for the reasons she thought). 'I know it's bad. I wouldn't normally do that. You know, I'm not, like, a bad person. But I don't think it's the happiest of marriages.' She turned to me and I could see her perfect profile in the mirror, the high cheekbones, the straight nose, the pert breasts. I felt immediately lumpier and saggier than I'd ever thought humanly possible.

She looked at me earnestly. 'He's always working late. I mean, it seems to me like the wife just doesn't want him at home.' She turned back to the mirror, unable to bear being parted from her beautiful reflection for too long. 'She certainly never comes along to work events. I don't even think she's bothered coming to this one and partners are definitely invited. I've seen him already this evening and he was on his own so, you know, what does she expect?'

'What indeed,' I said tightly, but she didn't notice my tone.

'She's probably one of these country wives, you know, the ones who've never had to work a day in their lives, expect the husband to keep them in the big house and pay for the kids to go to private school. Probably turns a blind eye to a bit on the side as long as hubby buys her a new Range Rover.' She thought for a moment. 'Or boob job more likely. She's over forty so I 'spect she needs one.' She glanced back at me smugly, 'No offense.'

'None taken,' I lied. God, I hated her.

'I think he's keen anyway.' She smacked her lips together, sealing the gloss. 'He's always friendly to everyone but he's *especially* nice to me, if you know what I mean.'

She clicked the catch on her make-up bag and gave herself one last appraising stare in the mirror. Evidently pleased with what she saw, she smiled in my direction. 'I like your dress too,' she said as she made her way over to the door. 'Where's it from?'

'Debenhams,' I said and she looked sympathetic. 'My husband doesn't make quite as much money as you seem to think,' I added quietly as she left the room.

I sat in one of the overstuffed powder-puff pink chairs in the corner and stared vacantly into space. Other women came and went. I barely noticed them. Eventually I realised that I couldn't stay there all night. I was going to have to make it through the last half hour and then maybe I could discuss this with Sam in the taxi on the way back to the hotel. Or maybe I was already too late. Maybe Jenna had cornered him in the corridor and was now batting her eyelashes at him sympathetically as he complained about his demanding yet emotionally unavailable wife. Or, just as easily, they could have skipped that bit and be rogering each other senseless in a cloakroom. Who knew? Wearily I got to my feet and collected my still-full glass of claret from the counter.

As soon as I re-entered the main hall I spotted the two of them. Sam had discarded his jacket and his bow tie was loosened around his neck. His head was thrown back in laughter at something hilarious that had just been uttered by the poisonous little witch in white, who was currently swishing her raven locks around like she'd walked off a shampoo advert. She was pressing her body in closer towards him and exuding pheromones like a bitch in heat. I had planned to meld discreetly into the background. To avoid a confrontation and discuss this particularly seductive fly in the ointment of our marriage later tonight, in private, like adults.

But…

Sod that.

I made it over to them in a few strides – suddenly my three-inch heels felt like weapons rather than liabilities and I crossed that floor like my brother would cross a battle-ground. I glared at my husband, who was looking slightly bemused by my expression. Jenna's back was turned to me.

'Whoops!' I said as I poured my full glass of red wine down her lovely Versace jumpsuit. 'How clumsy of me!'

Jenna screamed as she felt the liquid seeping through the fabric and running down her legs. It was like the scene in *Carrie*, where she's covered in pigs' blood.

'These heels,' I said. 'They've been a problem all night, haven't they, Sam? I can barely keep upright.' I smiled over-brightly at him, my husband and father of my children.

'You stupid bitch!' Jenna screeched, her face starting to turn a shade of puce. 'I've got to take this outfit back to the…' She peered more closely at me and then looked back at Sam with a question in her eyes.

'Jenna, this is my wife, Penny,' said Sam. 'And, erm, Penny, this is one of my colleagues, Jenna.'

There was a long drawn-out pause as realisation dawned on her face. 'You did this on purpose,' she hissed at me. 'You knew about the suit…' She shook her head. 'Jesus, are you fucking demented?'

I pulled myself up to my full height (which admittedly was not as tall as her but I had inches of anger on my side) and jabbed her hard in the chest. 'Don't you ever call me demented, you nasty little trollop. You have *no* idea.'

I turned to my husband, who was starting to realise that people around us had gone silent and were staring open-mouthed at the unfolding drama. 'Sam,' I said as imperiously as I could manage. 'We. Are. Leaving.'

–

Ten minutes later, we were sitting in the taxi crawling through London in stony silence. I hadn't told Sam the details of mine and Jenna's previous conversation – what happens in the powder room *stays* in the powder room and all that. But I had left him in no doubt that he was in the doghouse. He had also been barely able to disguise his horror at my performance, given that it was, from his point of view, completely unprovoked. Several senior colleagues and clients had witnessed the deliberate sabotage of Jenna's haute couture and it hadn't taken much to start tongues wagging. He was embarrassed. I knew he was. But I was furious and in the great ranking of emotional states, that put me higher up the scale. Neither of us wanted to have a massive row in earshot of the taxi driver, who was studiously ignoring our folded arms and livid faces as he blathered on about the fact that he'd had Rick Astley in the back of his cab last week.

'We will discuss this back at the hotel,' I muttered as I fished around in my bag for my phone. 'Shit.'

'What is it?' Sam peered over at my phone. 'Five missed calls. Jesus. Is it the kids?'

'I don't *know*, Sam.' My voice was icy as I returned the last of the missed calls from home.

Zahara picked up after two rings. 'Penny!' She sounded exhausted. 'I'm so sorry to interrupt your evening. I hope you're having a lovely time?'

'Not really mate, but crack on, what is it? Why are you even up? It's just gone midnight.'

She sighed. 'I didn't want to bother you – and I thought we'd find her – but it's your mum. She's gone missing.'

Chapter Forty-Eight

Sunday, 6 July

It seems that around eleven o'clock, Zahara had gone into the kitchen to let Colin out so he could bark at the neighbour's cat, as per his standard bedtime ritual. Once he was back indoors with his Bonio biscuit, she had returned to the sitting room to discover that Mum was no longer there. Nor was she in any of the other rooms, the airing cupboard or the shed. With an increasing sense of panic, Zahara had recruited Grace to stay at home and keep an eye on her siblings while she went out to trawl the village for a woman shuffling along in her slippers and a daffodil cardigan. Except the trawl had not so far been successful.

'Do you want me to phone the police?' Zahara's voice was small. It was clear she felt terrible about the whole thing.

I looked at my watch. Mum had been missing for less than an hour, it was a warm July night and I had a feeling she wouldn't have managed to get far. 'Let's give it another hour. I'll be home by then and if she hasn't returned we'll call them, OK?'

Sam was sitting across from me. There was real concern etched across his face but I was just too pissed off with him to put his mind at rest. I suddenly didn't want him anywhere near me. Everybody else seemed to bring me nothing but problems and I was clearly better off sorting this situation out myself, just like all the other occasions. The taxi had stopped outside our hotel and I gestured for Sam to get out, then I leaned across to the driver and asked if he would be OK to take a minor detour out of London altogether. I had to get home I explained to him, my mother had gone missing.

'Don't be ridiculous, Penny,' Sam said, standing help-lessly on the pavement. Light spilt out from the hotel and reflected off his face, which was shiny with perspiration. 'We'll both go. Sod the hotel. We'll…'

'Sorry, Sam.' I slammed the door shut and wound down the window. 'I think it's best if you stay here for the night. Give me a bit of space. I'll let you know what happens with Mum.' I tapped on the glass partition and the taxi driver eased off the clutch, the engine juddering back into action as we pulled away into the sprawl of city lights.

'I'll call you,' I shouted out of the window and then wound it back up again, tears prickling behind my eyes.

–

We pulled up outside our house an hour later, the roads had been quiet and the taxi driver had thankfully shut up somewhere around Brent Cross, sensing I was in a situation that even anecdotes about Rick Astley couldn't resolve. Sam had tried calling me repeatedly until I sent him a text asking him to stop and saying that I needed to keep the line free in case there was news about Mum. However, it became clear as the journey progressed that there was no news and by the time I got back, she was still missing.

'Penny, I'm so sorry.' Zahara's face was pale with worry. She was wringing her hands and pacing up and down the kitchen floor accompanied by Colin, trotting alongside her hopeful of a treat at this odd hour of the morning. Grace was sitting at the table. 'I think we should phone the police, Mum,' she said and a tear rolled down her cheek. 'We don't know where Granny is.'

'OK.' I was fired up with the adrenaline of recent combat. 'Zahara, this is absolutely not your fault. Mum does this. She'd do it with anyone. If anything, it's my fault for not having anticipated the problem. But before we call the police I'm going to head out for one last look, OK? Grace, you come with me. Zahara, could you put the kettle on?'

I slipped off my crazy heels and slid into a pair of wellies with relief. 'Wrap up,' I instructed Grace. 'And let's take a blanket for when we find her.'

–

We set off into the summer night; the air was chillier now, the sky bright with stars. We wandered up and down our street, poking our heads over fences and hedges, tiptoeing into back gardens and creaking open shed doors. The dog at number 14 nearly gave me a heart attack when I peered into their conservatory to be greeted by ferocious barking and a colossal set of paws inches from my nose. The owner of the dog thundered downstairs and I had to explain the situation. He then very kindly offered to give us a hand and called his wife and sons to assist in the search. Between us, we combed the streets of the village like a police patrol, moving slowly up towards the school. Suddenly, the man from number 14 stopped. 'Look,' he said, pointing over the road to the bus stop. 'Is that…? Is there someone there?'

I followed his gaze. There was a huddle of fabric tucked into the corner of the bus shelter and from a distance it looked more like a pale bin bag left out for collection, but I could see a faint pattern of daffodils…

'Mum,' I called out. There was no movement from the bundle and I started to run, barely looking as I crossed the road, narrowly missing a milk float doing its rounds. I reached the shelter a few moments before the others who were gathered on the other side.

'Mum?' It was her.

I sat down on the floor next to her and she turned to look at me.

'Hello, dear. Are you waiting too? I think it's been delayed.' She sighed. 'I've got to get back home before Mother catches me out of bed,' she said. 'She'll have my guts for garters!'

'Mum, it's me. Penny,' I said. 'Would you like to come back with me, warm up a bit?' I picked up one of her hands. It was stone cold, like a little dead bird. Grace had arrived and we put the blanket around her shoulders.

'Thank you, dear, but I really must catch this train,' she said, looking anxiously up and down the road.

'I think the train might be calling at our house,' said Grace and she extended her hand to her grandmother. 'Shall we go and see?'

Mum looked worried but she thought this over. 'Is it the nine thirty to Lydgate, do you know?'

Grace nodded. 'I think it is.'

'I'm sure that's what he said, the driver. Lydgate, nine thirty,' I said. 'If we hurry, we'll get there just in time.'

Mum pushed herself away from the floor and fell back down again with a little 'oh' of surprise. The man from number 14 crossed the road to help her up. 'Are you the driver?' Mum asked as she leant on his arm.

'Just go with it,' I muttered in his ear.

'I am indeed,' he said.

'The nine thirty? To Lydgate?'

'The very same. I'll escort you there myself, madam.'

'Well, that is very honourable of you.' She turned to one of his sons, who was watching this drama unfold in silent confusion. 'And it's lovely to see you again, Lionel, after all this time.'

By the time I had thanked the neighbours and we'd walked back to our respective houses, Mum had forgotten all about the train. She looked at our wheelie-bins with a frown. 'Gordon won't have put ours out yet,' she said, tutting. 'We'll miss the collection.'

'Never mind, Granny,' said Grace. 'Let's go inside, shall we?' She led her grandmother into the kitchen where Zahara nearly dropped her mug of coffee with joy. 'Oh, Mary! Oh, my goodness. Oh, thank GOD. Good grief. I… Would you like a drink, do you need anything?' She turned back to the kettle and Mum raised her eyebrows at me.

'What a ninny,' she said.

I sank into one of the chairs and put my head in my hands. 'Could you lock the doors, Grace,' I said, my voice muffled between my fingers. 'And text Dad, let him know we found Granny.' She nodded and scurried off. Out of everybody, Grace seemed to be least affected by the time of day. But I suppose she is semi-nocturnal, like a grumpy badger.

It made sense for Zahara to drive home and sleep in her own bed and her own unoccupied house, free from children, dogs and wandering women. She suggested that she return to help out later in the day, 'Just until Sam gets back. Where is he anyway?'

I told her I'd explain later and gave her a hug. 'Thank you,' I said, my voice brimming with tears as the tiredness hit me. 'I don't know what I'd have done without you.'

I said the same to Grace, who tolerated the hug with forbearance. 'I'm off to bed,' she said. 'Tell Tom and Maisie if they wake me up, they're dead.'

I could have slept in my own freshly laundered bed of loveliness but it felt a bit lonely without Sam in the room. I wondered whether Jenna had made any further overtures in his direction during the past few hours, or whether he had taken it upon himself to contact her since his wife had abandoned him to an empty hotel room. But instead of dwelling on those thoughts, I headed upstairs and got into bed with my mother, just as I had the first night she'd arrived. This was ostensibly to make sure she didn't wander off again but, given the fact that I had secured every door and window in the house, I had to concede that my real motivation was entirely selfish. I just wanted to cuddle up to her and reassure myself of her presence. She was my mum and I needed her.

Chapter Forty-Nine

Sunday, 6 July

Afternoon

I woke at seven, tucked up against Mum's solid warmth. She was snoring contentedly, almost drowning out the sound of my younger children as they watched international boxing on the television and pelted each other with Penguin bars. *Plus ça change.* I reached for my phone and read through the multitude of voicemails and texts from Sam. They varied from confused (*I don't understand what I'm supposed to have done? Is this about me working so much?*), to the cross (*Penny, this is ridiculous, why aren't you answering your phone? Whatever you think has been going on, you've got it wrong*), to the downright despairing (*Penny, where are you? Is your Mum safe? I don't know what to do, I don't understand how I've managed to upset you so badly but we need to talk about it and...* breaking off into tears). It wasn't an easy listen and I had to galvanise myself to call him back. He'd already checked out of the hotel but I asked him to stay away for the time being. I was just too exhausted to deal with anything else at the moment and suggested that he found somewhere else to sleep tonight. He was, as you would imagine, completely devastated, but I honestly found myself shutting off from it all, as if my mind simply couldn't cope with someone else's emotional burden in addition to my own.

Maisie and Tom didn't start to ask questions about their father until late in the afternoon. The day had been such an odd one; Granny and Grace were both still in bed long after lunchtime and maybe they assumed he was at work or simply busy doing Dad stuff. Zahara was the first to ask me what had happened outright and I explained the whole evening in a hushed whisper.

'I just can't face speaking to him at the moment,' I said eventually. 'I don't want to see him. Don't want him here. I told him not to come home until I've sorted things out in my head.'

Zahara nodded slowly. 'Oka-ay. I'm not sure that—'

I interrupted her. 'I just feel like I can't think straight at the moment. He wasn't happy about it but I think he realised how bloody furious I am and eventually he chose the path of least resistance. I told him if he cared about my feelings he'd give me some space. He couldn't really argue with that.'

Zahara shook her head. 'It doesn't sound as though he's actually done anything though?' she said. 'Don't get me wrong, I hear you if you think he's been playing away. But do you really think that? It sounds more like this girl's been trying it on and—'

'What, and he hasn't been encouraging her?' I said bitterly. 'You should see her, Zahara. You should have *heard* her. He's been telling her how unhappily married we are, how difficult I am—'

'Has he, though? You've only got her word for that. I just wonder if maybe you need to speak to him.'

'I will,' I said. 'Obviously I will, but it was just so hard hearing her talk about him, and me, like that and then to

339

come out and see them together, laughing, and her just *pouring* her body all over him…'

I raked my fingers through my ratty hair, un-brushed since the night before. 'It's hard to explain exactly what I'm up against here, Zahara. If you'd seen her in that outfit, honestly… Wait! You *can* see her.'

I pulled the laptop across the table and logged into Sam's Facebook page, 'See.' I scrolled up to Jenna's fashion query / porn shots from last week, gratified to see that Sam still hadn't commented on them. Zahara took a deep intake of breath. 'Yes, she's…'

'A hard act to follow? A massive challenge? A predatory threat to my marriage? All of the above?'

'Yes, but your Sam—'

'My Sam is good and honourable, yes, but he's just as susceptible to this,' I gestured towards the photo of Jenna in the bandage dress, 'as the next man. And probably more so given what's been going on at home. I wouldn't blame him for fancying her.'

'But there's fancying her and then there's…' She trailed off.

'I know, if he hasn't acted on it maybe it doesn't count,' I said. 'But maybe it does? Maybe it's a symptom of a bigger problem.'

I clicked onto Jenna's own page and scrolled up to her most recent post, which included twenty-three photos from last night, two of which included my husband in the same shot as her, cheeks pressed together to get into the selfie.

'See,' I said with empty triumph. 'They look like a couple. Look at the comments. It's all, *He's pretty hot, Jen. Is that your boss, Jen? Looks like you had a crazy night with*

Sam the Man, Jen.' My voice cracked on the final word and I closed the laptop.

She nodded slowly. 'I can see what you mean,' she said. 'I do see what you mean. But you've got to speak to him. Take it from one who knows, you don't want to be making assumptions in this scenario.'

I nodded. 'I know. I'm trying to be rational but that's exactly why I need a bit of distance. I feel like I'm hanging onto this family by my fingernails as it is. I just can't cope with a relationship crisis at the moment on top of everything else.'

I saw her look of concern and tried to reassure her. 'But, I know you're right and I *will* make sure we get a chance to talk properly. Just, when I'm ready. On my terms. Do you see? It feels like the only element of control I have left.'

Zahara looked doubtful. 'I understand,' she said, leaning over to give me a hug. 'But don't leave it too long. And give me a shout if you need me, any time, day or night.'

I hugged her back fiercely. 'Thank you.' My voice was muffled in her immaculate hair. 'You are such a great friend and you've got all your own stuff to deal with…'

I walked with her to the door and we stood, the summery breeze wafting round our ankles as Colin hurtled past, chasing Mr Tibbs into the kitchen.

'It's shit, isn't it?' she said. 'Really, bloody exhausting.'

'What?' I said. 'Life?'

She shook her head. 'No. I just meant being a grown-up. It's such hard work. How come nobody ever told us?'

341

Chapter Fifty

Monday, 7 July

Sam stayed at Brian's last night. At least that's what he told me. We talked briefly, our sentences so heavy with subtext, and pauses so loaded with emotion, that it was a relief to hand the phone over to the kids. They filled him in on Granny's adventures in the way that only small children who haven't been present for an event, but have magicked an idea of it into their heads, can. I had told him via text that Grace had been wonderful in helping me persuade Mum home and when she picked up the phone I could hear him singing 'Amazing Grace', which she pretends to hate.

'Shut uuuup, Dad,' she said. 'It was mainly Mum, anyway.' But two pink spots of pride had appeared on her cheeks.

I told him that we needed to talk but that I wasn't ready for a big emotional scene and that it might be best if he could stay at Brian's for a few nights while I sorted myself out. His voice cracked. 'But, what about the kids, Penny?'

'I'm sure they'll barely notice,' I said, my voice harsher than I'd intended. 'The younger ones never see you during the week. They'll just think you're at work.'

He sounded horribly flat. 'Penny, I just… I don't think this is the way to resolve this. We need to talk. And you need to listen when I say that I've—'

'*I* need to listen? It's *my* fault is it?'

'No, that's not what I—'

'I'll tell you what I need, shall I, Sam?' I tried to keep my voice calm but I was furious. The cheek of him. 'I need to *not* have this shit to deal with on top of everything else in my life. I need a husband who understands that if he can't be helpful he should stay the fuck away because he's just another problem for me to contend with.'

There was silence for a moment until he replied. His voice so quiet it was barely audible. 'Well, if that's what you want...'

'It is,' I said, my voice was shaking with emotion. 'Goodbye, Sam.'

I placed the phone down on the kitchen table and stared at it for a few moments, my head in my hands. And then I got up from the chair, wiped my eyes and set my shoulders back, reminding myself of Joy and Zahara's drunken words from our last night out, I am a coper, I am resilient, I can do this on my own.

Chapter Fifty-One

Tuesday, 8 July

Morning

Choir practice and another bombshell, this time delivered by Fizz's partner Doreen, who had come to see how we were getting on with our preparation for the imminent performance. I think we acquitted ourselves well and Doreen appeared to be impressed, although she doesn't do as much scarf-wafting or maraca-shaking as Fizz so it's not as easy to tell. Still, she was smiling broadly when she came up to me at the end of the session.

'Thank you so much, Penny,' she said, 'for everything you've done to keep this show on the road. Fizz will be delighted by your progress.'

'Oh, thanks, Doreen!' It was nice to feel appreciated, especially at the moment, and I actually found myself blushing as I packed away the instruments.

'Can I just ask how ticket sales are going?' She shifted her vibrantly patterned orange handbag onto her shoulder. 'Only it would be nice to let Fizz know that the deposit on the town hall has been covered at least.'

'I'm sorry?' The tambourine I was holding slipped from my grasp and hit the floor with a clatter.

'Tickets,' she repeated patiently. 'Just wondered how many you'd sold. Don't worry, I don't think she was expecting you to fill the hall, it's quite big… What? What is it?'

'Fizz was expecting me to sort out the ticket sales?' I said faintly. 'I thought it was just the performance, you know – rehearsals, musical arrangements, harmony groups…'

'Ye-es,' said Doreen, slowly. 'I thought – she did say – didn't she? When we saw you. When she asked you to take over? I mean obviously she hasn't been able to do any promotional work herself, or organise sales, or print tickets out, or anything really. We've been spending most of our time going back and forwards to the hospital, to be honest.'

'I know the feeling.' My voice was feeble as a squashed mouse. 'No, of course. I just didn't think that…'

I saw Doreen's look of alarm and managed to rescue the situation just in time. I didn't want her worrying Fizz, not in her current fragile state. 'It's absolutely fine, Doreen,' I said gamely, heart hammering as I picked up the tambourine and stuffed it into the holdall. 'Tell Fizz it's all under control. Majority of tickets sold and a new print-run underway.' I don't know why I felt the need to add this embellishment. It certainly wasn't going to help matters.

Doreen looked relived. 'Oh, thank goodness,' she said, beaming. 'I thought for one moment that you hadn't sold any!'

'Aha-ha-ha-hahahahaha!' I probably sounded a little unhinged. In fact, I think I might have thrown a jovial wink in there too. 'Just messing with you, Doreen,' I said. 'It's all fine. Complete sell-out. Tell Fizz it'll be standing room only.' *Shut up, Penny, for fuck's sake. You're making this so much worse.*

Her forehead creased a little, likely out of concern for my mental state. 'Are you OK, Penny?' she said. 'You seem...'

'Absolutely fine,' I boomed as I ushered her out of the hall. 'Couldn't be better!' *Other than my disintegrating marriage, my mother's dementia, my father's stroke, my friend's divorce, my neglected children, my weight gain and additional wrinkles, and the sudden hideous realisation that we have an enormous venue booked and not a single ticket sold, or even printed, or even designed! It's all absolutely bloody marvellous!*

By the time I'd gone around the room casually enquiring who was coming to support and watch each of the singers, I'd estimated total sales of thirty-four tickets and that was including all of my children and Marie's carer's friend from the nursing home, who might be on-call. Once I got home I searched up the town hall and established that it could comfortably hold two hundred people in its grand auditorium. I suddenly had visions of vast acres of space, tumbleweed rolling across it, George's light-show picking out a solitary person here and there, dotted amidst the endless empty chairs. The feeble voices of the choir echoing out across the cavernous void...

Just then my phone pinged. It was Rory, reminding me that he would be back in the UK at the weekend and would it be OK if he stayed at Mum and Dad's and used their car again, did I think? I punched the air. Rory. One more ticket sold – he couldn't refuse attendance at his own mother's performance, could he? No, not even Rory would do that. Especially if I put the screws on. I texted back to say I was sure he could have the car and let him know that I'd reserved a ticket for the concert. I then emailed Zahara, Joy and Caz with a message subject of *HEEEELLLLLLP* and a brief outline of the current

346

clusterfuck situation. And then I really didn't know what to do with myself, so Mum and I practiced some tunes on the keyboard in order to stave off my inevitable nervous breakdown. At least we'd be pitch perfect, even if nobody was there to hear us.

Chapter Fifty-Two

Afternoon

Sometimes friends really are just ruddy marvellous, aren't they?

At afternoon preschool pick-up, Joy handed me a box containing two hundred of the most beautifully designed tickets I'd ever seen. The font for the banner was eye-catching while still being legible, the colours were bold and the event information looked like it was being sung by a group of funky cartoon pensioners.

'Zahara designed them, obviously,' she said. 'And I asked one of the lads in the office to put them through the printer we use for all our marketing merchandise. He didn't dare argue. In fact, he was quite interested. Said his gran's got dementia and she likes singing. Asked if he could come along?'

'Oh. My. God.' I stared at the box of wonders and gave Joy a one-armed hug. 'These are amazing. Just amazing. You pair of freakin' superstars.'

'And I've printed out a whole load of posters too, look,' she said opening up another box on the doorstep of preschool. 'Caz is going to distribute them this evening and wants a pile of tickets to take to the leisure centre for when she's on reception. She says there's an over-sixties aqua-aerobics class, Tuesdays and Thursdays, and she's going to strong-arm at least half of them into coming along. Says they'll pitch up for anything if there's a free drink involved.'

'But there isn't a free...' I looked back at the ticket which clearly said *Complimentary drink on arrival.*

Joy looked sheepish. 'We thought it might help with marketing so I called the town hall. We don't need a license if it's included in the ticket price and they're happy as long as people use their bar for everything else, so me and Caz are going to pick up some bottles of prosecco from the cash-and-carry where her husband works on Friday and we'll sort out the trays and the nibbles and waitressing and all that.'

'Trays and nibbles...' I said faintly.

'Well, we'll need snacks to go with the drinks.' She closed the box of posters. 'Anyway. Key thing is, don't you worry your pretty little head about it. It's going to be a blast. It'll blow Tiggy's PTA events out of the water for a start. She'll be begging me to take over as entertainment secretary or whatever title it is she gives herself.'

'Joy, you are an absolute legend,' I said.

She shrugged, but I could tell she was pleased with her handiwork. 'Well, we were pretty happy considering the turnaround time,' she conceded.

–

I collected Maisie and Tom and we walked home via the play park – Maisie availed herself of the swings and climbing frame while Tom managed to persuade a group of older boys to let him join in their game of football. I sat on the bench in the mid-afternoon sun and stared and stared at the tickets, touching them occasionally to check they were real. There was a tiny ray of hope, a warm glow in my chest, and honestly it's been so long since I felt that, I had to remind myself it wasn't indigestion.

Later, when Grace came home complaining about her Spanish test, I told her about my minor oversight as regards securing actual punters to attend the concert.

'I don't suppose there's any chance some of your friends might want to come?' I said. 'Maybe Clark's parents or Rani or Millie? I know it's short notice.'

Grace looked doubtful but she could see the hope in my face and for once chose not to dash it instantly. 'I'll have a think,' she said. 'They are pretty cool-looking tickets but...'

'I know,' I said. 'Cool-looking tickets but not the coolest event in town. It'll be a hard sell. But if there's anyone...'

'I'll ask the school office if I can put a poster up,' she said. 'And I'll...' I could see she was pained by the decision, 'I'll put it on my Instagram if you like?'

'Oh, Gracie. Bless you.' I put my arm around her shoulders. 'You are a sweetheart sometimes.'

She shrugged me off. 'Yeah, yeah.'

She headed into the kitchen to make a start on her homework but turned in the doorway. 'Where's Dad?' she said.

'At work.'

'No but, where's he been? Your story about him needing to stay with a friend because of this big client needing entertaining, I don't buy it. What's going on?'

I followed her into the kitchen. 'Sit down, love.'

She opened up her rucksack and pulled a book out. 'I don't need, like, a big heart to heart, Mum. I've got to revise for this history thing tomorrow. I just want to know, are you, like, getting divorced or...?'

'Oh, Grace.' I pulled up a chair opposite her. 'Your dad and I, it's been difficult the past few months. Things at home have been more stressful.'

'Because of Granny?'

'Yes, a bit because of Granny. But there's other stuff too. I guess Granny being here has put a squeeze on my time, and maybe highlighted the fact that I didn't have that much time on my hands anyway. And that's made me pretty cranky. You know, the little things stack up, so having to clean and feed and clothe everyone but also needing to be here for you all emotionally, it's hard to do on my own. And sometimes, with Dad being at the office so much, it does feel like I'm on my own.'

'So, it's like, our fault, for creating all this work for you?' She put her fingers together in a bridge and stared at them.

'No, Grace.' I reached across and put my hands over hers. 'It's not about you, or Tom, or Maisie. Or even Granny. It's about me and your father. We need to work this out and it might take a bit of time, but I love him and...' my voice caught in my throat and Grace puffed out her breath. 'S'all right, Mum, I don't want to, like, get you all upset or whatever.'

I regained control. 'No, all I wanted to say was that we love each other and we will sort this out in a way that is best for us all. But at the moment, I'm feeling a bit wrung out and your dad and I need a bit of space to sort our heads out. Yes?'

Chapter Fifty-Three

Sunday, 13 July

Rory brought lunch with him today. His flight had got into Heathrow in the early hours of yesterday morning and he spent most of the day sleeping. Even so, he's a little disorientated with the jet lag and drove to the hospital instead of Rookwood to see Dad this morning. I'd given him a warning that Sam wouldn't be here for lunch. I could have left it at that but in a spirit of honesty and candour, I thought it best to give him the facts. After all, Rory, more than anyone, understands troubled relationships.

It's fair to say he was pretty surprised, both by the Jenna situation and the level of grievance on my part, taking a similar line to Zahara that he didn't really see what Sam had done wrong. Zahara is losing patience with me and told me in no uncertain terms when we met up for coffee yesterday that I would be making a mistake letting Sam go. She'd just come back from the solicitors reeling from the news that Nadia is apparently pregnant and Hugh wants to push the sale of the house through as soon as possible to get his new family installed on the property ladder.

'He doesn't give a shit about his current children and what the disruption is doing to them,' she'd said bitterly.

'It's all about him and Nadia and the imminent pitter-patter of tiny adulterous feet.'

I had commiserated but she lost her temper when I compared my situation to hers, telling me that Sam is worth twenty of Hugh and I should wake up and realise how lucky I am. She does have a point. Not helping around the house, forgetting to put the bins out and chatting to a pretty colleague at a party pales into insignificance compared to a full-blown affair. Sam has repeated his claims that nothing at all has happened with Jenna but even saying her name out loud fills me with the same nausea I felt in the powder room of that hotel. He's unfriended her on Facebook, which has to be a good thing although it could be an elaborate ploy. I just don't have the energy to try and unpick it all. Zahara told me that I was in danger of throwing the baby out with the bathwater and missing the wood for the trees and other such metaphors, but I stand by my decision to take a step back and re-evaluate our relationship. I simply feel that he hasn't been as supportive as he should have been over the past few months. Zahara says that's because I haven't let him.

Anyway, Rory, it seems, is full of the joys of a serious relationship. The irony being that having spent time in our domestic idyll, he and Candice decided that they wanted to start a family. I disabused him of this notion fairly quickly, although I am happy for him. This is the closest he's ever got to actual commitment.

In the spirit of our new caring, sharing sibling dynamic, I also told Rory that we'd be going to see the doctor next week to discuss the blood results. Unfortunately, this is another bone of contention between my husband and me. Sam came home to collect some clothes and bits yesterday.

He spent the afternoon with the children while I took Mum over to Caz's house to discuss ticket sales. When I returned he was standing in the corridor with the GP letter in his hand.

'I can't believe you didn't tell me about this?' He flicked the sheet of paper. 'Penny, I'm your husband. Did you not think it might be an important thing to mention, that your mum was having genetic testing?'

I was caught and immediately became defensive. 'Well, I don't think you're in a position to criticise me about keeping secrets,' I said. 'This business with Jenna—'

'What business? For God's sake, Pen. There is no *business* with Jenna. Why won't you talk about it? Who gains from all this guesswork? It's bloody exhausting.' He'd raised his voice and Tom stuck his head around the door of the sitting room. 'Dad?' he said, sounding concerned.

'It's nothing, Tom, don't worry,' Sam said. 'You get back to your programme. I'm just having a chat with Mum.'

'Her answering your mobile at work,' I hissed as he turned back to face me. 'Sending you photos of herself in completely inappropriate outfits, you making her feel *"special"*…' I put my fingers into aggressive quote marks to accompany the sneer. 'She told me, she said, "he's nice to everyone but *he's especially nice* to me", and that was evident in those bloody selfies on the night of the works do, wasn't it? Those hours I spent listening to Brian drone on or feeling awkward and shy with your colleagues while you were swigging champagne with that little tramp.'

He paled. 'Penny, you seemed happy chatting with Veronica? And I wasn't *with* Jenna during the evening. I was speaking to the Bradford team. *Like I said I was.* What you saw — before you threw your drink over her — that

355

was probably the only time we'd talked all evening. And she was taking selfies with everyone...' I saw a flicker of doubt cross his face. 'I think she was, anyway. It really wasn't like whatever you're imagining. She's just another person at work. I mean, yes, I can see how it might look, but—'

'Well, if you can see how it might look you should have nipped it in the bud.'

'There was nothing to—'

I interrupted him. 'It's no good you repeating "Oh, it was nothing, don't worry your pretty little head about it, doll." You're not stupid, Sam. You must have known how I'd react and you must have had some idea of what she was after. I honestly just can't believe you'd be so dense as to think that she was happy with being *just another person at work* or that I'd see her as such. She's gorgeous. And young. And, I dare say, *highly* attentive.'

'And that would make a bit of a change, wouldn't it?'

I released my hands from across my chest and curled them into fists by my sides. 'What?'

He looked sullen, like Tom when he's being told off. 'Well, it's not like I was getting much attention at home, is it?' I could see from his face that he was regretting those words before they were even out of his mouth.

'You have got to be fucking kidding me!' I hissed. 'Jesus. You sound like a kid.' I put on a baby voice. '*Poor lickle Sam wasn't the centre of the universe anymore and then the pretty lady was kind to him and he just couldn't help himself...*'

'NO! Penny it wasn't like that. Look.' He took a deep breath. 'Yes, I probably realised that she fancied me, OK? And yes, I was feeling a bit lonely and left out and like I was just another burden at home. And I'm not proud of that. It's selfish and clichéd; the whole "my wife doesn't understand me" routine. Because you *do* understand me. But you had so much else on your plate. There wasn't time for me anymore. And it's not your fault. But you said it yourself, I was suddenly just another problem for you to deal with. And that hurts.'

'But you're a grown-up, Sam. You have to hang on in there. You have to—'

'I have!' he bellowed and then lowered his voice. 'Sorry, I *have*. I've been *hanging on in there* for months. Trying to be supportive but feeling useless. You managing perfectly well without me, probably better in fact.'

'Look.' I'd had enough. 'I'm sorry, Sam. I just can't do this now. Get your things, say goodbye to the children and go.'

'But, Penny.' He put the letter from the doctors down on the hall table. 'This,' he said gesturing to it. His voice had calmed and he sounded almost gentle. 'You should have said. I could have…'

'What, Sam? You could have what? Taken me to the appointment? Fitted it into your busy schedule when you were getting *so little attention* yourself? While nobody was attending *to your precious needs*.'

'Yes, I mean, any of those things. That's my whole point. You should have included me. I could have supported you through it.'

'So you'd have suddenly been a tower of strength, would you, helping me face up to the possibility that I'm going to end up exactly like Mum?'

He faltered slightly. 'Well, yes. Of course I would… I'd have been there.'

'But you physically *being there* wouldn't have helped, Sam, do you see? One look at your face as they read out the results, watching your expression as you contemplated the prospect of having to look after me in the way that my father looks after Mum, that was never going to help me, because *I know*, and deep down, so do you. You don't love me enough to do it. You wouldn't cope with caring for me through this shitty disease; it would appear that you can barely cope without being the centre of attention for a few weeks let alone having to devote yourself to the needs of someone else for the remaining years of your life. Maybe it's better to face up to the realities sooner rather than later. Better to walk away now.'

He looked stunned, his face crumpling in on itself. 'You really think that?' He spoke slowly. 'You really think so little of me? My God, Penny. How have things come to this?'

He bent to pick up his bag. 'I'm going to go and say goodbye to the kids, OK? And I'm going to leave. Don't worry, I don't need to hear any more of your opinions regarding my lack of moral fibre or my disregard for our marriage vows.' He took a step towards the door but stopped, thinking better of it.

'I love you,' he said. 'And I'd do anything for you. If you can't see that, you're a fool. You've built up this wall, been so determined to prove yourself to everyone – your dad, Rory, even some of those daft cows up at school – that you've turned yourself into a martyr. It didn't need to be like this.' His voice cracked again. 'You've forgotten what *being married* means. We share. Good and bad. But you can't share any more. You've actually become possessive about your mum's dementia, like it's your special thing.' He shook his head in a mixture of sadness and disbelief.

'You've done this, Pen,' he said. 'And you've broken my heart.'

Chapter Fifty-Four

Saturday, 19 July

Showtime

Astonishingly, we seem to have sold out for tonight's concert. Joy and Caz have paid me for the tickets they took off my hands, I sold forty to friends and family of the choir and another fifty via school and preschool (I was quite the playground salesman – those business skills from my degree kicking in, along with some strong-arm tactics I've copied directly from Tiggy), and Grace and Tom have managed to offload the rest. For the life of me, I can't believe that a multitude of tweens are about to descend on the town hall for a dementia-choir performance but my children have both been very secretive about their distribution list, saying only that they had 'outside help'. While this fills me with dread, imagining some kind of County Lines scenario (is my ten-year-old son acting as a drugs mule in order to boost sales for a pensioner's concert?) they assure me that all is well and the money keeps rolling in. In fact, Zahara let it slip the other day that there had been a further emergency print-run and that Joy had to check with the town hall that standing room would be available for surplus guests if required. I can't begin to describe how touched I am by their hard work and generosity. I don't know how on earth I would have managed without their support.

As far as the choir itself is concerned, we are as ready as we'll ever be. One of the advantages about the disinhibiting side of Alzheimer's is that pre-performance nerves are kept to a minimum. Nobody has any real concept of time so the event could be next year or this evening and there would be little change in the sense of urgency. Likewise, the only people feeling anxious about singing off-key or forgetting the lyrics are the carers. Even so, I made sure that we had a rehearsal in the town hall itself and that George positioned the lights so as to blind us all to the actual size of the audience. There is the possibility that despite everyone's preparations and best intentions, the scale of the venue and crowd will freak everyone out and we may be faced with a mute display of terrified geriatrics. But there is little I can do about that now.

I, at least, am saved from direct audience contact by having the piano positioned at an angle where I will be looking at the singers rather than the rows and rows of seats. I have practised the pieces relentlessly and can adapt to changes in tempo, harmony or scale if everyone decides to go off-piste, as they sometimes do. I've even mastered the art of segueing between different melodies at various points in any given song, should this be required. Herbert has a habit of drifting into 'Bridge Over Troubled Water' halfway through 'Sweet Home Alabama' and sometimes the rest of the choir follow him instead of me, so I need to be alert at all times.

My biggest worry is what I'm going to do after tonight, when there is no more distraction. No more time to procrastinate about my marriage. No longer any need to rehearse, or work through the harmonies; no reason to spend entire days over at Tina and Bob's playing their beautiful piano, surrounded by these people who have become so dear to me. It's hard to quantify the benefits of being involved with a choir who not only put up with, but actively embrace, the range of behaviour and emotion that comes with dementia. The freedom that comes from not having to worry about what anyone else thinks; not caring that Mum has odd socks on or that she just stole someone else's snack or said something rude. Our tolerance as a choir knows no bounds. If you come to sing and make music then frankly you can be as offensive as you like – as evidenced by Ernest. As the Nirvana song-title says, come as you are.

And this sense of liberation filters out to everyone else. I find myself unconcerned about what people think of me; whether I made a mistake in a particular keyboard arrangement or a poor choice in terms of outfit on any given day; what kind of car I drive or house I live in; whether I should have eaten that second slice of pizza (or second pizza). Set that freedom alongside the joy of being able to sing and play music on a regular basis, add in the feeling of achievement at pulling together a musical event and you start to see the impact of this little enterprise on my life. This singing group has filled a void for those who had no social outlet, those who had no voice, and those who, like me, had all sorts of other shit going on but were blindly searching for a release; something more meaningful. As someone who felt that they had no space in their schedule, no single nanosecond to allocate to themselves, this choir has freed me up to sing, make music and be more like the person I want to be. There is never a time that I feel more at one with myself (to use a Tiggy phrase) than when I sing alongside others, and although tonight will be the culmination of months of hard work it has also been a form of therapy, not just for the people with dementia but for their carers too. I see the same transformation in people like Clive and Tina as I have in myself; sons and daughters, husband and wives who previously spent no time or thought on themselves now have a chance to vent all that frustration and pain through singing.

–

I am evangelical about our choir, unashamedly so, and I hope that this came across when I eventually made it out onto the stage and introduced our singers to the audience. I had spent most of the early part of the evening putting out chairs, assisting Joy, Caz and Zahara with the drinks and snacks and helping George gain access to the gantry area for the lighting. The speakers were synchronised, the stage and piano microphones restored to good working order after one of them blew during the sound check, and Herbert's nephew Dave had turned up to accompany our grand finale of 'With a Little Help from My Friends' on his trumpet. Finally, I had everyone in position on the stage with Tina and Clive peering excitedly through the curtains to see the audience arriving and taking their seats.

'There are hundreds of them,' Tina whispered loudly to me, her face flushed and shiny with excitement. Clive was dabbing his bald patch with a handkerchief – whether out of nerves or over-heating I couldn't tell. I had asked the girl on the bar if we could leave the main doors and windows open, which at least allowed a breeze to enter, although when I'd popped out to the car park during the sound check I had realised that the increased ventilation to the hall also allowed the noise to travel halfway down the high street. No matter. We can deal with complaints after the event.

I tiptoed over from the piano and looked through the chink in the curtains above Tina's head, seeing rows and rows of seats filling up with people. Fizz had made it, in spite of having just had the pins removed from her shoulder a few days earlier. She shuffled slowly down to her seat supported by Doreen, both awash with scarves and Batik print. Maisie was sitting in the very front with Evangeline, Darcy, Rex, Alex and Caz's older son, James. Rory was wedged at the end of their row and was ostensibly on child-care duty. I'd told him that if he and Candice were serious about starting a family he needed to get some practice in. He didn't look especially convinced as Evangeline tipped her bottle of J2O over herself and burst into tears, but she ran off to find Joy and saved him any real decision-making. Tom and Grace were up on stage with me. Grace was sitting with Mum to keep her company and stop her becoming distracted while I was at the piano. Tom was sitting between Ernest and Bob's wheelchairs as both had taken a bit of a shine to him and his presence freed Tina and Clive up to conduct and manage their respective harmony groups. Marie's carer was standing next to her with another woman from the nursing home, positioned on a stool in the wings just in case she made a run for it. We had designated a small area for Marie to 'freestyle' in, if the mood took her to air guitar or body pop. Tom had taught her the robot a few sessions ago but I'd already suggested that break-dancing should be kept to an absolute minimum. I didn't want anybody fracturing their hip while attempting the caterpillar.

Speaking of broken hips, who should I see emerging through the rear doors, pushing a Zimmer frame with military determination, but my very own father. 'Oh my God,' I whispered to Tina, my voice catching in my throat. 'It's my dad.'

'Where?' she whispered back.

I pointed to the far corner of the hall where Dad was making excruciatingly slow progress down the aisle.

'Who's that behind him, carrying his stuff?' she asked.

I was struggling to focus; the sight of my father had caused my eyes to fill with tears. I could imagine how hard he must have worked to be mobile enough to come here today. The hours of painful physio to build up enough muscle strength and the physical stamina to do this after major surgery and a stroke. Every time I'd visited over the past few weeks he'd been increasing his mobility and I'd seen him take a couple of steps with the frame, but nothing like this distance. It crossed my mind that Ben would be just as proud of how much had been achieved and I wondered briefly whether it was him who had brought Dad here. I felt a little rush of warm gratitude. Surely it was above and beyond the call of duty to help a patient attend a family function over a weekend, but that was the kind of guy Ben was. He'd go the extra mile.

'I think it's his physio, Ben,' I said to Tina and she raised her eyebrows in surprise as I looked back to audience. The figure, deep in shadow and still partially obscured behind Dad, pulled a chair out from one of the rows and positioned it against the back of my father's knees so he could sink gratefully down and relinquish the frame. As he turned to move the frame against the wall, he emerged into an orange shaft of evening sunlight and I realised with a sharp intake of breath that the mystery helper was not, in fact, Ben. It was Sam. My Sam. And suddenly everything fell into place.

He must have gone to collect Dad from Rookwood this afternoon. He would have known how desperate my father would be to attend and offer spousal support, just as he would have been desperate to support his own wife. Me. My mouth formed a little 'o' of surprise as I recognised a few faces now filing in behind him. There was Derek, head honcho from the office, with the current missus; Brian from accounts and another couple. Angus was there with his partner Rohan and Veronica seemed to have brought half of Hampstead with her, filling up two entire rows with an array of well-heeled women in Burberry check and Liberty prints. Tom and Grace's 'outside help' with ticket sales had clearly been their father who, judging by the number of people from his office, had sold about fifty tickets himself.

I quickly checked my watch. There wasn't enough time to run down and say hello. It would have to wait, but I opened the curtains a tiny chink further and, as if some intuitive sense had kicked in, Sam turned to look towards me at exactly the same moment. Our eyes met across the crowded auditorium and he offered a tentative wave and thumbs up. I beamed back at him as far as my teary eyes would allow and let the heavy fabric close again just as the lights dimmed. I heard the thunk of the spotlights and felt the heat of them bounce up from the floor as I walked to the central microphone. Clive, nodding at me from the wings, pulled the cord to draw back the curtains. The light was white hot in my eyes as I blinked out at the crowd and welcomed everyone to this, the world premiere performance of their local Singing for the Brain choir.

I was met by a dense wall of applause, whoops and cheers and could just about make out the figures of Caz, Joy and Zahara standing in the aisles raising a glass of

Derek, had presented me with a cheque to match the total and double it; from Tiggy's begrudging but heartfelt congratulations ('Although, if you need any help in future in terms of improving the branding and production, do just let me know, Penny.') to Veronica and Gee's insistence that the musical quality had been on a par with their last trip to Glyndebourne ('and in fact, you had much better snacks'); from Grace shyly informing me that she and George were planning on meeting up during the holidays to Tom, apoplectic with excitement about the crowds of people who, enticed by the music emanating from the town hall, had congregated around the open doors to listen from the pavement; from Ernest shouting 'Shit a Brick!' when he dropped his tambourine to Mum roaring with laughter apropos absolutely nothing halfway through 'Bridge Over Troubled Water'; from the children dancing in the aisles when we did 'Sweet Home Alabama' to the whole audience joining in the chorus to 'Hey Jude'. These were moments I would replay over and over again.

And for me, discovering that Sam and Dad had been hatching a plan, not only to get him to the concert but to move him much closer to us when he eventually leaves rehab, was one of the biggest revelations of the night. It seems that many of Sam's evening phone calls had involved sorting out the logistics of relocating my parents. Veronica told me about the additional hours he'd put in at work in order to help pay for the move and any adaptations that Mum and Dad might need in their new home. He hadn't wanted to tell me why he was working so hard because he didn't want me to feel guilty (obviously now I do feel hideously guilty when I think of the times I silently, or not so silently, cursed him for his absence). It seems he's also been putting aside some money to buy me a piano and, astonishingly, an upright Boston Steinway is being delivered next week. I cried for a solid twenty minutes when he told me last night, mainly because I felt dreadful for being such an ungrateful cow, but also because the idea of having a piano in the house again is just so overwhelmingly brilliant I couldn't really get my head around it. As if this wasn't enough in the world's best husband stakes, Veronica also mentioned that Sam has been in negotiations with Derek about spending more time working from home in future so that he could be around to help out with the children and with his in-laws.

'He's a good man, your Sam,' she said. 'Always talks about you with such pride. How you manage everything; keep the show on the road. You'll need him, you know, as things get worse with your mum, just like I needed Gee. But it makes all the difference, believe me, having someone like that in your corner.' She pressed her hands to mine. 'Oh, and you might be interested to know that one of our colleagues has moved across to marketing strategy. Jennifer Carmichael? Jenna? Yes, she requested a transfer last week.' She smiled and added, in an undertone, 'We paid for the dry-cleaning of that ridiculous jumpsuit on expenses. She seemed happy enough. Said she'd found the investment side of things a little dull anyway.'

–

When Mum had successfully navigated the stairs to make it off stage (it did take us a while), I led her over to where Dad was seated. She pulled up a chair beside him. 'Hello,' she said. 'Are you new here?'

Dad, completely unperturbed, picked up her hand in his and placed it on his lap. 'Yes,' he said. 'It's my first time at this venue. I came for the concert. Thought it was marvellous.'

Mum rested her head onto his shoulder. 'Really?' she said. 'I thought there were going to be more firemen than that. And no sequins?'

'Yes, that was disappointing,' said Dad.

'I think my mother might be under the impression that she's here to watch some male strippers,' I whispered to Sam.

'Is that the sort of entertainment you've been getting used to in my absence?' he said.

'Oh, yeah. The kids and I take Granny down to Rainbow Punters for a *Magic Mike* reprisal most evenings,' I said. 'Unless *Coronation Street*'s on.'

He nodded. He was smiling but looked a little unsure of himself.

'I've missed you,' he said. 'And I know you seem perfectly able to manage just fine without me, but I can't seem to manage very well without you.'

'I've missed you too,' I said. 'And I'm sorry. I think maybe I've been a bit of an idiot, pushing you away like I have.'

He brushed a tear off my cheek with his fingertips. 'How did the doctor's appointment go? I was thinking of you.'

'Oh, it was fine,' I said. 'Mum hasn't got any of the gene mutations for hereditary Alzheimer's.'

'That must be a relief.'

'Yes, but I'm still at higher risk than someone who didn't have it in the family. It could still happen. I could easily end up like that in twenty-odd years.' I pointed to Mum, who was giggling at something Dad had whispered in her ear. She rested her head back against him and he put his arm around her, his face creased with love.

'And would that be the worst thing in the world?' said Sam. 'I mean, look at them. I know it would be hard but none of us knows what's around the corner and as long as we're together, we'll be all right.' He turned my face to his and I was reminded of the words of the student nurse when we'd been watching my parents on the ward back in April.

You find someone who looks at you like that – hold onto them and never let them go.

371

Chapter Fifty-Six

Two years later

Tuesday 12 January

I'm halfway through downward dog when the noise starts. It's a high-pitched warbling sound coming from the mat just behind me. I peer upside down through the gap between my knees and can just make out Marie, who has rolled onto her side and is pressing her fingers into the sponge of her mat as if it were a piano keyboard, singing contentedly to herself.

'All right, Marie,' I call through my legs and she waves back.

'And relaxing out of the stretch...' Bendy Lydia realigns her spine and tiptoes over to Marie, handing her a foam block. Marie sits back on her heels and starts tapping out a rhythm as if her block were a small blue drum. I've always wondered what you were supposed to do with those rigid bits of foam; treating them as percussion instruments seems as good an option as any.

Out of the corner of my eye I can see Mum lying flat on her back and gazing up at the ceiling. There isn't much actual yoga going on as far as I can tell but she likes the tranquil music and the play of light on the architrave. She's also humming softly to herself but nobody minds because this is one of Lydia's weekly Yoga for The Brain sessions. When she was approached about doing these classes she was a little sceptical, but now admits that they are one of her favourites. ('God spare me from more Yummy Mummies,' she says. 'No offence.') The beauty of being here of course is that everything is dementia friendly – we're in what was Tina and Bob's drawing room, except now, it's a studio.

When Bob died eighteen months ago, Tina was bereft. She didn't know what to do with herself and sank into a deep depression. But with the help of the choir and, more specifically, Clive, she started to realise that there was a project crying out for her attention. Bob had left a considerable part of his vast amassed fortune in a legacy fund. Once he had ensured that his wife would be well-supported for the rest of her days and that his children from the first marriage would receive a substantial windfall (although they continue to complain bitterly about the 'paltry' sum they received to this day), he had explained to Tina in his more lucid moments that he wanted the remainder to be used to make the lives of people and families living with dementia more pleasant. 'You'll know what to do,' he'd said to her. And so Bob's Place was born.

Tina admitted that the idea had first come to her when we had been rehearsing for that first choir performance. Apparently, I'd said something about 'the perfect dementia hotel' and the more she thought about it, the more it seemed like exactly the legacy Bob was hoping for. 'We never had our own children,' she said to me. 'And Bob obviously made sure that his kids would be financially secure, that the grandchildren had trust funds and private-school fees paid and what have you. But he had earnt a lot of money over the years and his dementia was the one thing that cash just couldn't fix. It took him by surprise, I think, the fact that it didn't matter who you knew, what contacts you might have in whichever industry or how much those shares and investments increased, there was nothing at all he could do to protect himself or anyone else from this disease. It became a bit of an obsession for him.'

So she spoke to Bob's children. They weren't thrilled with the idea, to be honest, but when the publicity started rolling in they soon came around. There are many shots of Bob's son Darren cutting the ribbon on the front door, opening the curtains to reveal the commemorative plaque, attending high-profile events to publicise and humbly acknowledge the enormous contribution Bob's Place has made to dementia care. And I don't begrudge him that. I don't think Tina does either. Dementia's enough of a bitch to deal with without worrying about holding on to family vendettas. And the thing is, Bob's Place is an astonishing achievement. The house and grounds have undergone significant renovation. Luckily the rooms were already vast, with wide doorways and corridors in between, but everywhere is now equipped with rails, tracks for hoists and other mobility aids. The central staircase now runs around a lift shaft, wide enough for a wheelchair and carer to comfortably ascend to the higher floors. The fourteen bedrooms have been decorated according to Bob and Tina's travelling history and each room is themed around a particular destination; Tina's favourite is the Kathmandu suite, although it does prove more difficult for guests to pronounce. Every room has large pictures labelling all the appliances and amenities; there is a picture of a light on the relevant switch, a picture of a toilet on the en suite door and a white board in every room with individual information. So, when Mum comes to stay her board might say:

- My name is Mary. (Picture of Mum.)
- Today is Tuesday.
- It is winter. It is cold. (Picture of a jumper and snow.)
- Breakfast (picture of bacon and eggs) is downstairs (picture of stairs).
- Cathy (picture of Cathy) is here to help me.

There is a continuous itinerary of activities ranging from spa treatments to hydrotherapy in the newly refurbished pool. There are two elderly horses in the stable who welcome being petted and fussed over, four cats roaming freely and people are welcome to bring their own pets as long as they're not aggressive (the pets, not the people, although ideally both). A local gardener from the village runs daily sessions for those who want to prune and pot and mulch (not really my field of expertise as you can tell). Zahara comes in to help with craft sessions, specifically sewing, but also basic upholstery for one of our regular guests, Delia, who used to curate furniture exhibits at a local stately home. They love each other's company, those two; Delia knows all about Hugh's infidelity and sometimes has to be restrained from sticking pins into chair covers a little harder than strictly necessary when hearing of his exploits (he's moved on from Nadia and is currently dating a twenty-one-year-old Swedish waitress called Astrid). Zahara meanwhile is very happy with Rajesh, a computer programmer from Essex who she met through the *Guardian* dating website. Rajesh is quiet, introverted and unassuming, but apparently he's hung like a shire horse and is into tantric sex. Zahara wanders around with a permanent smile on her face.

And what of me, I hear you cry? What of Penny Baker: daughter, mother, wife and homemaker? Well, I am now head of arts and entertainment at Bob's Place as well as being on the board of trustees for the charity. Sam was very helpful in guiding Tina through the charitable status application and Veronica from his office was so excited by the whole project that she joined me on the board as a non-executive director shortly after we set up. On a day-to-day basis, I am responsible for overseeing the music and arts classes and events in the hotel – the downstairs rooms are opened up for community sessions Monday to Friday and our programme is packed. Fizz still runs her Singing for the Brain classes twice weekly, accompanied by me on the piano and Doreen on percussion. Anjali, a local clay and ceramics artist, has a pot-throwing class, which some of our visitors take a little too literally – there is now a considerable amount of plaster of Paris clinging to the cast-iron radiators in the studio, but I think it makes them more tactile and interesting, if a little abrasive to run your hand across. We also have painting, sculpture and ukulele classes and I've even managed to persuade one of the girls from the community centre's macramé group to attend on a fortnightly basis. Twice last year we ran a fundraising musical event. In the summer, a garden party with a marquee extending from the large orangery at the back of the house and tables dotted among the mature fruit trees where visitors ate picnics and drank Pimm's as they listen to the choir and musicians. Three weeks ago we had our first Christmas concert with the choir standing around the large tree in the studio, me on the grand piano and all our guests treated to trays of homemade mince pies and stollen courtesy of Tina's extraordinary baking skills. Our repertoire comprised an eclectic mix of old and new with 'Good King Wenceslas' merging seamlessly into 'Don't Let the Bells End' by The Darkness, with Ernest putting his own uniquely profane spin on the latter. Ernest is a regular visitor since his first weekend stay last year, when Clive finally managed to persuade Tina to go to Glastonbury with him. Separate tents, she said, but I've seen the way they look at each other.

The Christmas concert raised 5,000 pounds, which isn't a vast sum in the grand scheme of things, less than two month's salary for one of our carers, but Veronica is looking into other income streams and I am helping out with the marketing (which is lucky, seeing as Tina's first foray into publicity was to suggest the tagline, *Bob's Place: You don't have to be mad to visit here, but it helps!* I gently prompted a rethink). Irrespective of the finances, Tina is sanguine about the future. She doesn't expect to make a profit on this business, it's a bonus if we break even. But the ethos and the spirit of the place, that's what's important. At our first annual trustees meeting last August we toasted our success with a bottle of champagne and a bag of pork scratchings. Not for having reached the FTSE 100 but for having created something that meant the world to us three women: a haven for people with dementia and their carers – a place where nobody needed to feel embarrassed or frightened and where we could all be our best disinhibited selves. On a personal level, I was also raising a little toast to myself – for getting through the shit of the previous few years and emerging stronger, more fulfilled and ultimately happier in my own skin (don't worry – I'm not going to go all *Live Laugh Love* on you).

I cross the floor to where my mother is lying on her back, still looking up at the ceiling. I crouch down by her side and wave my hand in front of her face. 'Mum.'

She startles out of her reverie. Looks at me, unsure as to who I am.

'It's me, Penny. Class has finished now, Mum.' I hold her hand and help her to her feet. She's much less mobile now and the carers who come in to visit their bungalow spend much more of their time with her than they do with Dad, who can manage perfectly well with a walking stick thank you very much. It helps that they bought a place just down the road from us, particularly as it's right next to the bus stop when the kids come back from school. Tom has moved up to secondary with Grace now and they often stop in at Mum and Dad's for a biscuit and a glass of what Tom calls 'hilarious, old-person's cordial'.

I'm usually back at our house by the time they arrive and if not, Sam will often be there. He works from home a lot more now and has even been known to load the dishwasher or hang Tom's sports kit out if he has a moment. When it became clear that Tina needed me to put in some more regular hours for the charity, Sam and I sat down and devised a bit of a rota. Until that point, I don't think he'd ever realised quite how much effort and time goes into running a household and although I can't pretend that I don't instantly rearrange every item of clothing he's folded, or tut quietly to myself when I see where he's put the shopping (who puts cheese in the cupboard, for crying out loud?), the effort, and more importantly, the acknowledgement of how much I do, makes a big difference.

Some days, by the time the older two get home, I've already collected Maisie from the clutches of Mrs North (I don't know what the poor woman has done to deserve all three of my kids at various points in their primary school career – she still harks back to the time that Tom was *the only child not in mufti*, which is clearly tantamount to neglect in her book). Sometimes, I take her over to Bob's place where she lords it over the smaller children in the crèche while Tina and I go over the books. Sometimes Grace comes with me too – she's doing dance for one of her A-levels and a key component of her coursework is looking at 'expressive movement for the cognitively impaired', a project title she came up with herself and a subject she takes very seriously. 'How do you *feel*, Granny?' she asks Mum when they are swaying along to the music.

'Purple,' Mum replies and Grace dutifully notes this down in her book – purple equals good, we think.

Sometimes Rory and Candice come to visit, along with little Maddison. When Candice starts her new post in the paediatric department of QEH next April I expect I'll be called upon for a bit of Aunty Penny babysitting, but in all honesty, I can't wait. It's so much easier when you can hand them back – particularly if the person you're handing them back to is your brother, who for the first time in his life is struggling to navigate the entirely unpredictable terrain that is parenthood.

'Do they ever stop crying?' he asked me in the early months. 'I mean, seriously, Penny, do they? I feel like I'm losing my bloody mind. No offense, Mum,' he said as a quick aside, seeing our mother shuffling through the doorway carrying a large frying pan and a football, as if she were preparing for a game of tennis with Salvador Dali.

I roll up her mat with mine and we move through to the kitchen cafe, where Tina has baked a batch of almond macaroons. 'Cup of tea, ladies?' she asks and hands me a normal mug while offering Mum a more robust one with a spouted edge. Mum looks at it intently before picking it up. She needs a bit of help guiding it in the general direction of her mouth but we've got plenty of time, it doesn't matter if it spills, nobody's perfect. 'Here, let me help,' I say, tilting it towards her mouth.

She takes a sip and smiles as I wipe her chin. And then she looks at me. *Really* looks at me. 'Thank you, darling,' she says. 'For everything.'

A Letter from Nancy

Firstly, thank you so much for reading this book. Whether you bought it, borrowed it or illegally downloaded it (actually, I'd rather you *hadn't* done that to be honest), it means the world to a writer to know that someone out there has taken the time to indulge their ramblings. And it's hard to find the time to read an entire novel in this crazily fast-paced world we live in, so please know that your efforts are much appreciated.

The frenetic, hectic nature of modern life is a key feature of this story, how we make time for ourselves and our loved ones when there are so many demands that society makes of us. Being a good parent, a dutiful child, a loving spouse, a supportive friend and an active member of the local community is rewarding but exhausting. And yet, it is something we routinely expect, of women in particular, often in addition to their having a productive career, staying slim and attractive and not ageing (don't even get me started). This doesn't really seem a reasonable expectation and often leads to feelings of failure on multiple counts. It also leads to a loss of identity as we become defined exclusively by our roles in relation to other people. As Penny says at one point, 'I'm being stretched so thin I am in danger of disappearing entirely.'

I think it's important that we celebrate all those who are quietly going about their business of caring, holding families and communities together while everyone else charges on with their own lives and caters to their own needs. If this is you – if you are in danger of disappearing entirely, drowning under the weight of multiple demands and duties – then know that you are not alone. You are an absolute legend, and don't you forget it.

And now, having banged on for the past three-hundred pages about how difficult it is to find a moment for yourself, I'm going to ask you to give me a couple of additional minutes of your time and consider leaving a teeny-weeny review or rating for *The Mother of all Problems* on the bookshop website or social-media platform of your choice. It makes a huge difference in terms of raising the profile of the book, and if you have enjoyed Penny's story and want to show your appreciation by making an author extremely happy then this is by far the easiest route (other options include an all-expenses-paid Caribbean holiday or a lorry-load of dark chocolate).

If you *haven't* enjoyed the book but have nonetheless made it far enough to reach the author notes at the back then I commend your determination, while questioning your slightly masochistic streak. You are also more than welcome to leave a review – I'm keen you should be allowed to exercise your right to freedom of speech, and I've got broad shoulders, both figuratively and literally.

Either way – look after yourselves, lovely readers (not least because it's terribly important that you're all still around for the sequel next year) and give yourself a pat on the back for being a wonderful human being.

Love, Nancy x

Acknowledgements

The Mother of all Problems was always intended to reflect real life and people often say 'write what you know' – so I did. When I began writing this book, I was living the life of a woman in the Sandwich Generation (indeed, *Sandwich* was the original title), squeezed between caring for both the younger and older members of my family. I got there a little earlier than most of my friends due to my mum being diagnosed with young-onset dementia when my kids were still quite small, and there were times when the middle of a sandwich felt like a lonely place to be. But I realised over the years that this is a time of life that comes to us all. Anyone who has looked after children or has a parent needing care will already understand many of the themes in this book – and for those who have both, at the same time, I hope this story resonated and perhaps made you feel less alone. While laughing uproariously – obviously.

There were people in the publishing industry who felt that a story of a woman in her mid-forties wouldn't sell – people who told me that nobody would be interested in hearing about the bizarre and often farcical scenarios faced by a mother of small children who also cares for an ailing parent. But I always felt that Penny's story needed to be told, partly because it is my story – grounded in my experience. And because this experience is, in fact, a fairly universal one. The other people who realised this (thankfully) were the amazing publishing team at Hera.

Keshini Naidoo and Jennie Ayres picked *The Mother of all Problems* and instantly understood what I was trying to say. From the moment they first contacted me, I knew Penny's story was in safe hands, and their professionalism, attention to editorial detail and commitment to publishing real stories about real women has always shone through. Thank you both from the bottom of my heart for championing this book – I feel sure that Hera herself is smiling down on you both. She is the goddess of women, marriage and family – and a thoroughly good egg, after all.

Other organisations who deserve a massive shout-out in terms of amplifying the voices of women include the fabulous team at the Comedy Women in Print prize, led by Helen Lederer. *The Mother of all Problems* was longlisted for the CWIP prize way back in 2020, when I was but a tiny fledgling author as opposed to the international bestseller and publishing juggernaut you now see before you. Since that moment CWIP has been a constant presence and support in my writing life, and the friends I've made through the prize are a cherished bunch of hilarious babes. Equally instrumental in providing me with a rich seam of writerly chums is the Romantic Novelist Association – and our spin-off faction who meet regularly in a chocolate cafe to discuss writing and load up on carbs.

Penny's story is based in a village, which might lead you (not unreasonably) to conclude that I too live in such a place and have experienced some of the same highs and lows of village life. My local friends have kept me sane over the many years of raising my family and coping with my mum's illness. Ladies, you are all wonderful Zaharas and I couldn't have done it without you. Same goes for the friends who live further afield, some of whom I've known for gazillions of years – having you on the end of the phone has been a lifesaver, as well as a rich source of anecdotes.

I couldn't write an acknowledgements page without mentioning the wider community who provide care and support to those living with dementia and their families. Charities, volunteer groups, local choirs, befrienders, online supporters, NHS workers and professional care organisations – it is enough to fully restore your faith in humanity to see some of these people in action. Dementia can be hard to live with and while fabulous support is out there, much more is needed. When my debut *Love Life* (a romantic comedy set in a hospice) was published, I donated ten per cent of my first year's profit to charities working with people at the end of life. In a similar way, I will be donating ten per cent of the first year's profit for *The Mother of all Problems* to dementia charities.

And finally, for an author writing a book about family life, it helps enormously to have a warm supportive family, and a chaotic home full of love and hilarity to base it on. My three little peaches (now not so little), you are my proudest achievement, my hopes and dreams bundled up in reality. You are magical and funny, inspiring and wonderful – I love you all so very much. My husband, Mr Peach: your love and unwavering support through both the joys and tribulations of the past few years has stopped me unravelling – you're like an extremely handsome fabric adhesive, and I challenge you to find a better compliment than that. My dad and my sister who have been on the same journey through Mum's dementia – we were always the tight family unit but this rollercoaster has made us even closer. I can't honestly imagine how I'd have got through it without you both – your humour, pragmatism and resilience has made all the difference.

And of course, the beginning and the end is Mum. My lovely Mum. This book is for you. You are the one who taught me how to be a mother and showed me that a child raised with love can go on to do anything. Thank you for being the best of mummies. Thank you for everything. I miss you.